To Share

Beaver
2012

Muffy Morrigan

THE SAIL WEAVER

three
ravens

First Edition 2012

three
ravens

www.threeravensbooks.com
www.muffymorrigan.com

Cover design by Georgina Gibson

Library of Congress Cataloging-In-Publication Data
is available upon request

ISBN 13: 978-0-9844356-7-8
ISBN 10: 0-9844356-7-0

Dedication

*The Sail Weaver is lovingly dedicated to
all those people who have believed in the work
from its very beginning and who never let me lose faith.
Without them Tristan, Thom and Fenfyr would
not exist and the* Winged Victory *would never fly.*

I

There was increased activity in the skies over the massive compound of the Weavers' Guild. Shuttles were coming and going, buzzing around the buildings like flies gathering over a carcass. In the distance, far more graceful than the squat ungainly shuttles, dragons wheeled in an out of the mountain they claimed as their own. Every once in a while a dragon would come close to a shuttle bearing Naval insignia and the small craft would have to veer off. Under the Edicts, dragons, like sailing ships, always had the right of way over powered craft of any kind, and they knew it.

Tristan Weaver, Master Sail Weaver of the Guild, sat watching the activity through the huge bay windows in his office. He spotted one dragon, black, silvery gray and pearly white, dive directly towards a shuttle with an admiral's seal on the nose. The shuttle banked hard to avoid the creature, but the dragon followed it, making the pilot work hard to dodge the buildings around the port area of the Weavers' Guild compound. The dragon followed the shuttle down until, at the very last moment, the dragon pulled away, lifting into the air in a graceful upwards sweep.

The dragons didn't tolerate most humans, and when they chose to interact with humans they tended to deal primarily with the magicians of the Weavers' Guild or the elite Dragon Corps. The dragons had watched humanity for a long time before they had finally stepped forward and made contact. "The enemy of my enemy is my friend" was their attitude, and while they distrusted most humans—and the sentiment was more than returned in kind—the uneasy alliance had been made. The dragons had provided the first spell to Weave together the sails that allowed humanity to reach into the depths of space.

Tristan snorted. For all their reliance on science, it was magic that had proved to be the answer in the end. The first ships launched off world during the early decades of the Third World War had been a desperate act to rid the planet of some of the drain on the already over-extended resources. Most of the occupants of those first ships had been forced volunteers; criminals, the homeless—and then anyone else the governments could talk into walking onboard a ship that might take centuries to reach someplace habitable. A hundred years later, the first faster-than-light ships had been attempted, only to be destroyed by what would come to be called the Winds— powerful and massive cosmic forces that resisted any attempt to push against them.

The idea of using sails to propel ships through space wasn't new, solar sails had been used for centuries, but even with engines to boost their power they were slow and only used between closely connected space stations. In order to reach outside of the confines of the solar system, humanity needed something faster, and their first attempt to create sails to ride the Winds had proven disastrous. The crew and the ship had been crushed the instant it had moved into the Winds.

During the moments before the ship had been destroyed, its cameras had beamed back images of something riding the Winds. Science set out to study this phenomenon, naming them willowisps, and trying to recreate their unique properties in hopes of using them as a way to travel through space. It didn't work, and the willowisps they tried to bring into the labs tended to explode in human-normal gravity, leaving the studies stuck in the theoretical phase for decades.

One member of the research team suggested they go to the Spellworkers' Confederation, a group of loosely connected workers of various kinds of magic. The Craft, as it had become known, had been rediscovered in the early days of the Third World War, first healers, then others started showing abilities with different kinds of magic, and governments were quick to try to use them to their own advantage. The magicians decided to band together instead, and formed the Confederation. The scientific community had soundly rejected the idea of any connection with magic or anything "reeking" of the supernatural.

The buzz of Tristan's intercom interrupted his musings. "Yes?"

"Sorry to bother you, Master Tristan, but there are some, uh, gentlemen, from the Navy here to see you," his assistant, Scott, replied.

"Did you inform them they need an appointment?"

"Yes, sir, they... Wait!" There was a muffled grunt. "No! Stop!"

The door to Tristan's office banged open and several Naval officers walked in, a man in an admiral's uniform behind them.

"Security report to Master Tristan's office," Scott's voice sounded over the compound-wide comm system.

Tristan watched the men as they walked towards his desk. "Making an appointment is easier," he said with distaste. The tension between the Weavers' Guild and the Navy bordered on overt hostility. The only thing that kept the Navy in check was the fact that the Guild was the only entity in the galaxy that could train the Weavers to use the magic needed to create the sails for their warships. "As well you know, Davis."

"Admiral Davis," one of the other officers growled.

"We have a problem. I don't have time to do a song and dance with your secretary," the admiral snapped, walking up to Tristan's desk. "The Vermin are planning an attack and we have to stop it!"

"That's the Navy's job," Tristan answered calmly, counting off the seconds. The admiral had about fifteen seconds before security arrived.

"Yes, but you and your kind are suffered to exist..."

"Excuse me, what was that?" Tristan asked, leaning back in his chair.

"Sir," one of the others, a man in a captain's uniform, said under his breath.

"We need a set of sails," the admiral went on. Tristan just stared at him. Five seconds. "A special set," Davis growled.

"Oh?" Tristan smiled as security burst into the room.

"Master Tristan?" David Earle, Head of Guild Security, asked as he came into the room, weapon out at the ready.

"The Naval gentlemen were asking for a set of sails," Tristan said.

"They need to make an appointment," Earle snapped. "Show them out."

"No!" Davis shouted. "This is vital!"

The tension in the room had grown, Tristan could tell the other Naval officers didn't know what to do—if they should draw their own weapons or drag the admiral out of the room. It was a stand-off at the moment and Tristan was almost enjoying himself. He and Davis had something of a history, and watching the man squirm was amusing.

"What's going on?" a deep voice asked from the doorway. Brian Rhoads, Guild Master of the Weavers, strode into the room and up to Tristan's desk as if they were the only two in the room. He smiled his sly smile at Tristan before turning to face the admiral. "Ah, Davis, I thought you understood we had protocol here, or have you forgotten that at Naval headquarters?"

"I came to see the Weaver," Davis spat out.

"We have many Weavers, it is in fact our Guild, in case you hadn't noticed," Rhoads said in his bass voice. He loved the sound of it, Tristan knew, and the man was taking full advantage of the acoustics of the office.

"Sir, I said…" the man in the captain's uniform said. He looked young to be a full captain. Tristan guessed they were about the same age.

"What's that?" Rhoads picked up on it immediately.

"Nothing, Barrett is speaking out of turn." Davis turned to Tristan. "We need a set of sails."

"So? Go through channels," Rhoads interrupted.

"We don't have time! We received intelligence that the Vermin are planning an incursion into our home space. We need something big out there to stop them, and since we lost the *Constellation* we have nothing in that class."

"And that is our problem how?" Tristan asked, seemingly calm, but wondering why the Navy hadn't approached them sooner.

"We have a ship, we've been working on it, but we need the

sails for her, we need them quickly and…"

"You need the best," Rhoads finished for him. "Which is why you decided to storm into Master Tristan's office without bothering to ask or go through channels?"

"We don't have time!" Davis shouted. "We need these sails started immediately, we don't have time to play games with the Guild with assignments of a Weaver who won't be good enough; we don't have time to play games with you about who will be the Warrior you choose to assign to the sails."

"Oh, really?" Tristan spoke up for the first time since Rhoads' arrival. "What is so special about these sails?"

"I told you," the admiral growled.

"You said you needed them quickly, any one of my masters could Weave sails quickly. There is something more going on here." Tristan looked from the admiral to the other man, the one Davis called Barrett.

"It's the largest ship ever built," the man muttered, he glanced at the admiral, but went on. "The sails will need to be…" He made a gesture with his hands that was something between a shrug and something else, then slowly approached Tristan's desk. He carefully unrolled a set of plans on the wooden surface. Secret documents were all still rendered on paper. It made them harder to steal and reproduce.

Tristan stood to get a look at the design of the ship, running his hand along the graceful sweep of her decks. There was something *different* about the ship, he couldn't tell what it was, but there was something that spoke to him as he looked at the lines on the page. "*Winged Victory?*" he said, reading the name on the corner of the page.

"Yes," the man answered.

"Her masts must be," Tristan paused to calculate, "seven-hundred feet."

"Can't be done!" Rhoads said, peering at the plans.

"I…" Tristan looked at the plans for a long time, then out the window, thinking of what it would take to create those sails. "How soon would they need to be ready?"

"Yesterday," the admiral replied.

"Too bad, you should have thought of that the day before

yesterday, then," Rhoads said. "Get out."

"Wait," Tristan said softly, looking at the plans again. He let his hand rest over the drawing of the mainmast. Rhoads was glaring at him through narrowed eyes, and Tristan understood why, it looked like an impossible task, especially in a hurry; not only to build the sails, but then to attune the Warrior Weaver, the members of the Guild that served on the ships, to them. "It will take at least four weeks."

"Impossible! We need them sooner. I don't need to listen to Weaver rhetoric about…"

"Four weeks." Tristan's voice was barely above a whisper, but it had the effect of a shout. The admiral cut off his tirade in mid-sentence and stared at him with wide eyes. "Now get out of my office. Leave the plans."

Davis was opening and closing his mouth like a fish out of water, gasping for air. He blinked, started turning red, blinked again and one of the junior officers with him grabbed his arm and tugged him through the door, followed by Earle and the Weaver security detachment. The captain lingered behind, watching the admiral go.

"Thank you," he said quietly, and snapped off a formal salute.

"I haven't done anything yet," Tristan answered.

"You agreed to it, you didn't have to. She's such a beauty and her sails…" He trailed off dreamily. "I doubt we'll meet again, sir, in fact, I will probably be scouring the decks on a garbage scow within a week. So, thank you again," the captain said. He smiled hesitantly, then held out his hand.

"Barrett!" the admiral roared from the corridor.

"You're welcome, Captain Barrett," Tristan said, taking the man's hand in a firm handshake.

The officer nodded to Tristan, saluted Rhoads and left the room, carefully closing the doors behind him on the way out. The admiral's angry shouts were loud enough to carry through the heavy wood and Tristan was sure Barrett was already being assigned to a garbage scow or worse.

"Did you want to get it out of your system all at once, Brian?" Tristan asked, smiling at Rhoads.

"I was thinking of parceling it out bit by bit over the next few days, because if I let it all out right now, I'm pretty sure I'll set off the seismic warning systems."

"I can Weave them." Tristan looked down at the plans again, his eyes running along the lines of the masts. It was as if the ship were speaking to him. There was something about it.

"Weaving those sails could be suicide, Tristan, the spell to create them and hold them will be more than any of us has ever attempted."

"I know, and the Elemental Interface will need to be something special, unique. I'll have to start my search tomorrow. That's why I told them four weeks. It will take time to find the right Elements. There was a place I remember from when I was first in the Guild. The stones…" Tristan smiled. "What I am looking for might be there."

"No, I won't allow it," Rhoads said sternly. "You are the Master Weaver of the Guild. You cannot do this. Any Weaver will do, you know that as well as I do."

"I can't explain it, I just… I have to, Brian." Tristan took a deep breath, ready to go on when an alarm started blaring.

"Oh boy," Rhoads whispered.

Tristan turned. He knew what the alarm meant, but he was still surprised when he saw the massive gunmetal gray and deep sapphire blue dragon dropping down towards the Guild compound. The huge Dragons' Portal on the administration building swung open and a moment later Darius, Elder of the Dragons and Chief of the Guild Dragons, filled Tristan's office, most of his body and tail still trailing into the hallway.

"Guild Master, Master Weaver," Darius said in his grating voice.

"Welcome," Tristan said, recovering an instant faster than Rhoads. He kept his smile hidden, for all the years the Guild Master had been dealing with dragons, he was still usually struck speechless by their presence.

"I heard the Naval creatures were just here." The dragon moved to Tristan's desk, remarkably graceful for all his size. His tail was still trailing in the hallway when he reached the desk and looked down at the plans. "Ah, they were."

"Yes," Rhoads squeaked.

"They asked me to Weave the sails," Tristan offered.

"I told him he couldn't."

"Oh?" Darius rested his chin on the floor so he could look from Tristan to Rhoads without towering over them. "Why?"

"It's suicide. They're too big! Look at those things!" Rhoads waved his hand at the plans.

"Yes, we have been aware of this ship for some time," the dragon said. "We were going to come to you, but the Naval creatures beat us by a day."

"What's going on?" Tristan asked.

"There is something about this ship. We're not sure what it is. Only rumor. Puffs in a vacuum. Nothing solid."

"Why were you coming here, then?"

"For you, of course, Master Weaver."

"Me?"

"Him?" Rhoads looked from Tristan to the dragon.

"Yes. We, the Guild Dragons, have a request."

"Of me?" Tristan really hoped his voice hadn't just squeaked.

"Yes." Darius looked at him, his head tufts moving forward to gently touch Tristan on the shoulder. "We ask that you Weave the sails for this ship."

"What?" Tristan asked, wondering if he'd heard right.

"We want you, Tristan Weaver, and no one else, to Weave these sails. You and I, Guild Master, will find a Warrior to suit, but there is something about this ship, we need to have our claws, spells and hands as deeply into it as we possibly can."

Tristan walked to the window and looked out. It was a huge undertaking, and it could very well be fatal. The magic to create the sails was one thing, but then to hold them static long enough to get them into space, not to mention attuning of the Warrior and the finding of the Elements for the Interface...There was something else, far, far back in his mind that was there, like music so distant he could not make out the melody, merely acknowledge its presence.

"What say you, Master Weaver?"

Tristan turned back to the Guild Master and the dragon. "Yes."

II

The sun was still low in the sky when Tristan picked up his bag and walked out of his spacious quarters. He'd spent a long sleepless night thinking about the project he had committed himself to, the massive undertaking of the sails themselves was more than enough to be worrisome, but there was something else going on, he could sense it in his bones. He'd suspected it when Davis had stormed his office, and it had been confirmed when Darius had suddenly appeared.

The dragons had asked Tristan to Weave the sails. As far as he knew, it was the first time the Guild Dragons had ever made a request of that kind. Even though the dragons had given humanity the spell to create the sails from the willowisps, they had never involved themselves beyond that until the ships were in space. Though the dragons claimed there was no official assignment, every Naval ship had a dragon that was associated with it, flying as scout, occasionally defending the ship in battle. The Navy didn't like it, the dragons didn't care.

The corridors were nearly empty as he headed towards the parking area. One or two former students nodded as he passed. Since he'd become Master Weaver of the Guild, and a member of the council, he had less day-to-day contact with the students, although he did try to attend at least one class of each level a week. It also meant he spent less time working on the Weaving, and more time overseeing those he'd trained. The more important projects did fall to him, but there hadn't been a flagship launched since the *Constellation*. That ship had been destroyed in the *Jupiter* Incursion. The frigate *Jupiter* had been attacked in the space between the Rim stations and the inner system. The battle had left the Navy crippled even though the Vermin had been beaten back. In fact, since then the Navy had seemed to withdraw into itself, and had only been requesting smaller ships and light cruisers—fast ships designed as escorts for a larger ship.

Tristan paused for a moment, wondering when they'd gotten stupid. Every sail was for something small, every Warrior Weaver assigned to a frigate or smaller. Why hadn't they seen it? The Navy had been planning something all along and the *Winged Victory* was obviously at least part of that something. She was huge, the largest ship ever attempted, and in her graceful lines and massive masts, Tristan sensed something more. He still couldn't put his finger on it; neither could Darius even after long and careful questioning. Dragons lied to humans all the time, but Tristan knew Darius wasn't lying to him. This was too important to the dragons for a lie to stand between the two Guilds. Whatever was going on would affect them both.

"Good morning, Master Tristan," Erica, the security guard on duty at the parking docks, said as he approached.

"Good morning, am I set to go?" he asked. He'd requested his shuttlecar be ready for an early departure.

"Yes, sir! I even made sure there was a cup of hot coffee waiting for you."

"Thank you." Tristan walked through the building to his parking stall and stepped into the vehicle, flicking on the engines and waiting as the portal over his spot opened and he was given the okay for take-off.

Once he cleared the compound, he turned south, carefully setting a course, then leaning back to sip his coffee. He planned to head deep into the desert, an area that had remained miraculously untouched through centuries of warfare. In order to Weave the sails and then contain and control them, he would need Elements. Each set of sails required a unique set, and choosing them was one of the most important steps in their creation. If the Elements were wrong, the sails would never fly, in fact the willowisps might "die" before they ever had a chance to become sails at all.

When humanity had first started working with the willowisps, there had been some concern about the fact that they might be sentient life forms, and the ethical question of slavery had loomed for several years. The dragons had explained, repeatedly, that the willowisps were the by-product of something else. They had their own energy, and they definitely had a feeling of "life", but Tristan, in all his years of Weaving, had never felt that the willowisps were unhappy with where they were or disliked what they were doing. It was almost impossible to explain, even to another Weaver. There was a spark of something in them that reacted to the spells of the Weaver. If the spell was wrong, if the Elements were wrong, sometimes even if the Warrior Weaver was wrong, the ship would not fly. The Weaving was a delicate task, mixing the magic with the willowisps to create the spells, moving the particles in such a way that they fit. It took years before a Weaver attempted their first sails—the magic also drained the Weaver, sometimes dangerously.

The console beeped, Tristan's destination was coming up fast. The area was now designated as Wilderness, and a Dragon Sanctuary. It was off limits to humans except members of the Weavers' Guild or those who had been given a permit by the Guild. Even Weavers were required to walk in to the canyons so as to not disturb the wildlife or the inherent magic of the area. The entire area had a proximity alarm, if anyone tried to fly too low—or land—the alarms would go off. Violating a Sanctuary was a very serious offense.

The Guild and dragons had carefully protected the remaining places. Many had been destroyed during centuries of war, but some had survived because the land wasn't deemed strategic, or it had been so inhospitable that it just wasn't worth fighting for, and in a very few cases monuments had been saved because they were monuments and it was recognized that they had value. That hadn't stopped various governments from holding those places hostage, but at least they had survived. Things changed when the Guild came into being, and now all those places deemed "special or sacred" were under the protection of either the Weavers or the Dragons.

Tristan grabbed his pack out of the back and secured the

shuttlecar. Taking a deep breath he listened to the world around him, letting the sounds flow into him for a moment, before one tugged at him. He turned in that direction and started along a path that led towards a deeply cut canyon, the walls rising up over his head, dark red and black against the bright blue sky. A bird circled above him, its call echoing through the air.

Tristan stopped.

He sometimes forgot what it was like, being out in the wild and silent places. When he'd first joined the Guild and been sent out on his first search for an Element, he'd left the safety of the compound hesitantly. The wild places of the Earth were generally avoided by humans. His second night away from civilization he'd sat beside his small fire and listened to the sound the world made, the soft whispers of the magic that had always been there, but had been lost in the noise of technology. It was that night he realized that this had been a test, to see if he could sense what was there and if he was willing to find it—and come back alive. Some students walked into the wilds and never returned.

Taking another deep breath, he moved on, stepping carefully along the path, all his senses open for the touch of an Element. He didn't expect to find one on his first day, in fact he was hoping he wouldn't, but they came when they wanted to, and he had to be ready. The sun was beginning to warm the rocks and some of them were humming a little in the light. He stopped to pick up a piece of quartz, but it wasn't right so he set it back down, carefully positioning it exactly as it had been. It was tricky business, finding the totality of the Element. A cross between a computer interface and a wizard's staff, it functioned to link the computers and technology of the ship with the magic of the Weaver and the sails. It was all a very delicate business.

The place he was sure he needed to go to was still several miles further in the canyon and it would take time to get there, walking over the uneven stones. What looked like a short distance on the map was a long day's travel in reality. Something told him at least part of what he needed was there: the spot was ancient, a stopping place, a sacred place. It was a spring at the base of an enormous cliff, and when he was there he could feel the magic that buzzed through it. Tristan had been there before looking for Elements, but never had found the right one for the sails he was Weaving at the time. He knew that it would be there this time.

A dark shadow momentarily blocked the sun, then was gone before Tristan could look up.

When he looked down, something caught his eye—a gnarled piece of wood, so long exposed to wind and weather it was a soft silver-gray and glinting in the sun. He picked it up and felt the soft thrum of magic in it. Gently closing both hands over it, he spoke quietly and felt the magic build. This was it, the first part of the Element. He opened his eyes and really looked at it. The wood was beautiful, shining in the sunlight like quicksilver. It was perfect.

The dark shadow flickered over the sun again. Tristan looked up, shielding his eyes with his hand. If a buzzard had decided to follow him, it wouldn't be big enough to cast a shadow. Rolling his shoulders, he tried to settle a feeling of unease.

Opening his pack, he carefully wrapped the wood in a piece of linen and silk and tucked it away before slinging the bag back over his shoulder and walking on. The heat was beginning to shimmer over the land, intensified by the close walls of the canyon. It was going to be warmer than he expected, and Tristan decided that he would stop at the small spring about halfway to his destination. Even though it was dry most of the year, a huge cottonwood tree shaded the area, and there was a deep cave that was always cool, even on the hottest days.

Edging a little to the south, he headed towards the spring. A rock rattled down the ridge behind him, tumbling down to land with a loud *thump* where he had been standing moments before. Tristan walked back and looked at it, one side of the stone showed a fresh break. He glanced up the canyon wall, nothing was there now, but that didn't mean some desert creature hadn't passed through, dislodging the stone. The last time he was out here there was a small landslide in almost the exact same spot. That one had been caused by an earthquake on a fault north of the area. Shrugging, he turned away and headed on towards the spring.

The shadow flitted between him and the sun again. This time he thought he heard something as well. He paused and looked up, scanning the sky. As he did, he realized he was getting jumpy. There was cover at the spring, so if it happened again, maybe he could finally get a look at what was creating that shadow.

There were several Big Horned sheep at the spring when he got there. He walked as quietly as possible, so as not to disturb them, then sat down in the shade of the tree, closing his eyes and resting his back against its ancient trunk. The tangy scent of cottonwood filled the air around him, he sighed and let it fill him. This place was full of magic and it was good to feel it there in the earth, whispering around him with the soft breeze.

A ripple in the wind alerted him to something else moving there. It was a distinctive movement, the brush of immense energy and control like a lightning storm contained in a small glass whirling through the air. The creatures that were resting in the shade around him let out a collective squeak of terror and ran. Tristan even heard the hooves of the Big Horned sheep clattering away.

A huge puff of air blasted over him. "Suicide!" The anger in the booming voice made the leaves on the tree tremble. "Suicide!"

Tristan didn't even open his eyes. "What?"

"I will not allow it!"

"You won't?" Tristan did look now, the dragon nearly filled the canyon with his bulk.

"Did you think I wouldn't find out?"

"I wasn't trying to hide it from you."

"You left without telling me," the dragon continued, offended, his head tufts trembling. Most humans would turn the other way and run in the face of a dragon that was obviously that angry, but this wasn't just any dragon. Tristan and Lokey Fenfyr of the Guild Dragons knew each other, more than that, they had formed a friendship beyond the formality of their Guilds, perhaps the only one between their two species.

"Fenfyr? What is it?" Tristan asked, sitting up.

"Now you ask!" Fenfyr huffed out a breath of frustration, then the dragon settled down. "There is something wrong with this, the sails are too big, the Naval creatures are evil, this thing smells of rotting flesh and…"

"And?"

"I don't like it."

"You don't like it?" Tristan asked, amused.

"No, I don't. There is wrongness."

"Wrongness?"

"Yes."

"Would you care to be more specific or are you just going to sit there huffing at me?"

The dragon lowered his head and let his chin rest on the ground beside Tristan. "I'm worried."

"That still doesn't tell me much."

"Something was following you."

"Yes, a large dragon." Tristan laughed.

"No! There was a vehicle. They followed you from the compound," Fenfyr said with a low growl.

"What are you talking about?"

"They followed you almost all the way here, they turned off right before you reached the canyon, but they were there."

"Who was it?" Tristan looked over at the dragon.

"I don't know, there were no markings on the shuttlecar. If it had been Guild, there would have been no reason to hide," he said. "I tell you, this stinks of rotting flesh. Darius is worried. There is something about this ship that is concerning. We are not sure what's going on, but the Naval creatures have been far too secretive in building it. We saw the dome at the docks, but they denied entrance to everyone. In fact, they have been claiming there was nothing there but two small ships."

"No one's checked?" Tristan suddenly felt like he hadn't been paying attention to current events, even though he had. "Wait, we did check, there was a small runner in the dome, nothing else."

"That was several months ago. No one has been in since. We've been watching. There is something wrong. I was just out there, it smells wrong."

"You keep saying smells. Do you mean that literally?"

"Yes. No. I'm not sure." The dragon sighed. "It's hard to get a feeling for something when I am in space. I function differently there, so things smell different."

Tristan nodded. Dragons were almost like amphibians. They could function in the vacuum of space as easily as in the atmosphere of a planet, even on worlds that would be toxic to humans. What looked like scales were actually small "feathers" that the dragons could extend to allow them to ride the Winds. Sometimes when he saw dragons drifting in space, the dragons reminded Tristan of a leafy sea-dragon with wings.

"Do you think it's the *Winged Victory* in the dome?"

"Yes, we believe so." Fenfyr sighed. "Why did you agree to Weave the sails?"

"Darius asked me." Tristan shrugged.

"Not because no one has ever made sails like that before?"

"No."

"Of course not." The dragon nudged him. "You are lying to me, Tristan Weaver."

"What? No, I'm not."

"So the lure of creating sails like that has no attraction?"

"Of course it does, but I am Weaving them because Darius asked me," Tristan insisted, but heard the uncertainty in his voice.

"Hmph."

"The dragons have never asked us to Weave for them."

"True."

"And these sails are unprecedented."

"Also true."

"The Weaving is dangerous."

"Yes."

Tristan cocked his head at the dragon. "You know me too well, Fen."

"Your motives are different than you stated?" Fenfyr asked.

"No…"

"But?"

"It's…" Tristan paused, trying for the right words, trying to express what he'd felt the first time he'd seen the plans of the *Winged Victory.* It was almost impossible to explain the attraction for the ship and the desire to be the one to Weave the sails for her.

"Ah," Fenfyr said with a soft noise. "I understand." He shifted his head, peering around the canyon. "You have come here seeking the Elements?"

"Yes, as soon as I saw the plans for the ship, I knew this was where I would find them."

The dragon made a humming noise, encouraging him to go on.

"I've been here before, but never felt a pull like this. I already found a piece." Tristan grabbed his pack and pulled out the wood he'd found earlier, carefully unwrapping it and showing it to the dragon.

"I see." Fenfyr bent closer, his head dwarfing Tristan as he examined the piece. "Yes, very good, very old, very beautiful. The willowisps will love it."

"You think so?" Tristan asked hopefully.

"Yes. When have they ever rejected your Elements? You are the Master Weaver for a reason, Tris," he said gently.

"Thank you."

"You are worried about this Weaving as well."

Tristan cast a smile at the dragon. "Yes, I am. The Navy and Darius asked me to do it. The sails are huge, and you are very right, there is something off in the whole thing. There is more here than we know and that bothers me."

"If it makes you feel better, we have sent someone out to investigate," Fenfyr offered.

"You have?"

"Darius and Rhoads and the Guilds. We are united in this and we are suspicious of the Naval creatures. You do not know, for we have not spoken of it, but there was some... trouble a year ago."

"Trouble?" Tristan leaned forward, the dragon was agitated.

"Yes."

"Fenfyr? What aren't you telling me?"

"We cannot confirm the information, but there is a possibility that the Naval creatures managed to capture a Vermin ship."

"They didn't kill it?" Tristan asked horrified.

"That's the problem, we aren't sure."

"But..."

"Yes, it violates the Treaty, it violates everything," the dragon said softly.

"No, they couldn't, they wouldn't! It's one of the Founding Principles of the Treaty. Fenfyr, if it's true..."

"If it is true, our two people could be at war within a year."

III

The small canyon was bathed in long shadows as Tristan reached the spring. He'd left the comforting shade of the cottonwood several hours before, knowing that the cool was almost more illusion than reality. This time of year the rock walls heated up to furnace levels by mid-day. The massive cliff that marked the end of his journey soared over his head. He was skirting the edges as he walked towards the spring that had been sacred since before humans had discovered how to forge metal. It had remained a stopping point for millennia, the graffiti that scarred its bright red walls showed this in intimate detail.

Tristan paused by one that he remembered from the first time he'd come here. He felt a connection to this man who had lived centuries before him, and it wasn't merely because of the obvious. "Sgt. Tristan Means passed by here in the co. of Gen. Knox, 1853, lost all but four men, heading west." He gently traced the deeply etched name and message with his finger, imagining what it must have been like, being alone out here, facing miles and miles of unrelenting wilderness. A dark shadow flickered over him, he glanced up, expecting to see Fenfyr.

Only it wasn't the dragon.

A squat shuttlecar, about as graceful as an overweight beetle, hovered over the canyon. Tristan clamped down his first reaction—

anger that someone had violated the sanctuary—and pressed into a small crevasse in the rock. If someone was risking violation of the area, it could mean danger. He held perfectly still, in the cover of shadow of the rock, and hoped he wouldn't be noticed. The vehicle dropped closer to the ground, still being careful to stay above the "red zone" that would trigger alarms. It turned slowly, for the first time ever Tristan was glad the cliffs were hot, the temperature would cover any attempt to locate him by body heat. He held his breath, not daring to move. Sweat trickled off his face and ran over his scalp, feeling like the feet of tiny insects.

The nose of the car swung slowly towards him, and Tristan knew they had a lock on him. He closed his eyes, waiting for what was to come. Suddenly, he heard the claxon as the shuttlecar brushed the top of the "red zone." Opening his eyes, he saw it shoot off towards the north at high speed. Tristan let out the breath he was holding and slid down the rock, listening to the hammering of his heart, wondering what had happened.

"They can spot tiny you down there, but they miss me right here," Fenfyr huffed from above his head. Tristan looked up, the dragon was peering over the cliff at him. "Are you okay?"

"Yes." Tristan stood. "What did you do?"

"I just fanned my wings a little, just enough to push them into the alarms. This is a secluded sanctuary for dragons, how dare they invade it!" the dragon said, sounding aggrieved.

"Which is why you did it?" Tristan asked with a snort.

"Of course."

"Thanks."

There was a soft *whoosh* of air as Fenfyr dropped to the ground, by the time Tristan rounded the corner where the spring trickled out of the rock and into a deep pool, the dragon was stretched out, basking in the rays of the setting sun. Tristan set his pack down in the mouth of the cave at the back of the pool and unrolled his bed roll. He grabbed his cook-kit and carried it back out to sit beside Fenfyr. After heating some soup, with the comforting flame of the small camp stove lighting the walls and glistening on the dragon's feathers, Tristan sighed and leaned back against Fenfyr.

"Remember?" the dragon asked softly.

"How could I forget?" Tristan smiled gently at the dragon.

They had met in this spot when he was first in the Guild. Before Weaving his first set of sails, he was sent out to find the Elements for the Interface. It was his second day out when he realized that part of the test was surviving in the desert. He had been watching a huge electrical storm building in the west for hours as he headed towards a massive red cliff, hoping to find shelter there. The imbalance in the world caused by massive plasma and other weapons used during the last part of the Great Second War made for deadly storms if you were caught out in them. He guessed he had less than an hour before it struck, and he was hurrying towards shelter when he realized he wasn't alone. There was nothing to confirm that notion, he just knew. When he reached the cliff and the spring, the rain was starting and he dove into the cave. A deep growl greeted him as the first strike of lightning slammed into the ground.

"I considered eating you," Fenfyr joked, nudging him out of the memory.

"I expected you to," Tristan replied.

"You were too scrawny, not enough meat. Besides, I like flavored protein soup, and I didn't want to have to cook it myself."

"You *are* lazy."

"And diabolical," the dragon added.

Tristan laughed softly. "Right, that's what it is. I knew it was something like that." Had he known that long-ago storm would bring this friendship, he would have walked into the desert more sure of himself. Their friendship was not well known, Darius knew, and for reasons only known to him, encouraged it. Brian Rhoads knew and was a little less sure, but it was generally not known that Fenfyr was more attached to the Weavers' Guild than just "security"—that is, when he chose to perform his duties and not chase Naval shuttles.

"Why were they trying to kill you?" Fenfyr asked suddenly.

"I have no idea who 'they' even were, do you?"

"No, there were no markings on the shuttle, but they were so intent on getting to you, they didn't notice me. And really," he snorted out a burst of laughter, "you should watch out for dragons."

"Very true." Tristan laughed with him, feeling a niggle of unease at the base of his spine. "What were you saying earlier about the Navy?"

"It's nothing we can confirm, but there is something going on, and we think this ship you are foolishly killing yourself for is the reason."

"Obviously, someone thinks I am not killing myself, Fen."

"I don't either." A huge sigh buffeted Tristan. "But it is a massive undertaking, you know it is; and it irks me that it might be for naught."

"What do you mean?"

"I don't think they want the sails at all."

"They can't fly without them," Tristan protested. "There is no way!"

"But there is," Fenfyr insisted.

"No! There's..." Tristan broke off and looked in horror at the dragon. "No."

"It's what we fear."

"They wouldn't!" He turned to look at Fenfyr. The dragon was regarding him, his eyes dark. "But..."

"I told you, it could mean war."

Tristan realized he was shaking his head in denial. What Fenfyr was proposing was beyond horrific. It broke the Treaty with the dragons, it tossed the Edicts aside. But that wasn't the worst part of it. "You mean they..."

"I told you, they took a ship, and we believe it was not killed."

Tristan swallowed the bile that rose in his throat as he considered what Fenfyr was implying. During humanity's first stumbling steps off-world they had sent generational ships. The ships, though traveling at less than light speed, had penetrated out into the galaxy. Most of them were lost, four survived, and it was one of these that started the battle in what would become the Great Galactic War, though most people called it The War. The hapless settlers had stumbled into "Vermin" space.

The Vermin were creatures that destroyed without thought or pity. No matter how hard the settlers had tried to make peace, that was not an option. They were killed and eaten. The last image to reach Earth was of the side of a ship bearing symbols that looked like VRM, since then humans had called them Vermin. The more they learned about them, the worse it was. The final blow came when the dragons broke their long silence and stepped forward, offering humans the spell to Weave the willowisps into sails for faster-than-light ships. Humankind and dragonkind had a common enemy. Vermin found human flesh satisfying in many ways, and dragons—what happened to dragons that fell to Vermin was enough to make the toughest Naval Officer blanch. The aliens used captured dragons that they had essentially lobotomized and "slaved" to fly their ships in the Winds, it was a complex process, but the end was the same. The "slaved" dragons were still aware enough to know what was happening, and while there was no way to save them once they had been taken, they could at least be freed by death.

"Humans would never do that!" Tristan said, hearing the quiver in his own voice.

"They might already be doing that, maybe not taking dragons, but capturing a Vermin ship and planning to use the technology somehow on this ship you are Weaving."

"Then why come to us?"

The dragon snorted. "A ship that big would be noticed; they have to have the Guild Weave sails for it even if they never intend to use them."

"I don't believe it," Tristan said, leaning back against the dragon.

"I don't want to either," the dragon said softly. "You will seek the rest of the Elements tomorrow?"

"Yes, there is a planetary conjunction, it will increase the magic and I will need all the help I can get."

"Sleep, Tris. I will watch."

The soft light of dawn bathed the cliff in pink when Tristan woke. He had sat with Fenfyr until the moon began to rise, then settled down in the cave, lighting a small fire in the approved ring, more for comfort than warmth. As he looked out of the cave, he noticed the dragon was gone—he briefly wondered why, but knew if there had been something serious Fenfyr would have made sure he was awake before he left. There were enough clouds in the sky to give it an odd blood-red color. It wasn't a good omen. He laughed to himself, the rest of the world might dismiss omens, but then again, the rest of the world was not entrusted with the magic to make sails.

Although fewer people dismissed magic now than they once had. Tristan remembered reading history books of the time before the

Third World War when magic had remained untapped. It wasn't until a freak incident on the battlefield that someone finally put two and two together and realized many of the "miraculous" things that happened were actually not good luck, but in fact magic. The first workers had mostly been healers, and there were still healers among the magic workers, although they all fell under the auspices of the Weavers' Guild.

Those gifted with healing proved to be adept at another kind of Weaving. It was the second hurdle they had to jump before launching the first ship more than a century before. In order for the ship to fly, the sails had to come into contact with the Winds—but the crew still needed access to the masts and the decks of the ships. After several failed attempts at creating a ship with plating to protect the crew, they had discovered the spell that would create the other major wing of the Weavers' craft. The Air Weavers could use their magic not to mend flesh and bone, but to Weave together the particles of space and make a bubble of atmosphere and gravity, creating an artificial environment that allowed activity on the deck and the masts while still leaving the sails free to catch the Winds. It was an eerie feeling, even Tristan admitted, to watch the great plates that protected the ship until the Air Weavers' spell took over drop down, leaving the ship open to the stars. Some people never adapted, and when the Navy had resurrected the practice of "pressing" crews—forcing them to serve on ships whether they wanted to or not—more than one crew member died when the plates dropped. Knowing that there was nothing more than a spell between you and the vacuum of space was unsettling.

Tristan rolled up his things and tucked them in the pack. This morning he could hear the soft call of one of the Elements for the Interface. It might be all he needed with the piece he'd found the day before, he wouldn't know until he found it, but now he had a definite direction to go. Pausing long enough to whisper a thank you to the spring for keeping him safe through the night, he set out to the west. The canyon turned and narrowed again. A small ground squirrel wandered under a scrub oak tree gathering acorns, and a lizard was lying on a rock doing the funny push-ups they always did in the morning sun.

The walls of the canyon were humming quietly as the sun rose,

Tristan could feel the tug of the far-off alignment of planets as he walked and he hurried his steps. The Element's call was getting stronger and the piece he had found the day before was vibrating in his backpack, letting him know that the other half of it was getting close. He rounded a corner, the cliffs soared over his head but were so close together it was almost like a cave, only a tiny slit of the red sun filtering through, and there it was. Tristan knew it the moment he saw it. A stone, egg-shaped and close to the size of an emu's egg was lying partially buried. He realized he was almost running as he reached the rock and knelt beside it. Laying his hand on it, he felt the jolt of connection explode between his eyes.

He pulled the wood out of his pack and placed it on the ground before gently freeing the stone from the earth that had held it safe for him to find. The stone was black, a few bright flecks caught the light on the surface, deep lines ran along the length of it. He caressed it gently before putting it beside the branch and got out the rest of the items he would need to bond the pieces together to make the Element. Lighting a candle, he focused his mind, feeling the planets lining up. Sensing the sun rising in the sky, he began to speak the spell that would join the Elements. The ground trembled and sand slid down the canyon walls as he recited the spell, his hand tracing patterns in the air as the Latin words fell from his tongue. Reaching down, he picked up the wood and the stone and held them aloft, letting the magic grow until he felt it hum in his bones. He pressed the two Elements together and held them, speaking the final words of the spell. The blast that joined them slammed through his body and pulled his legs out from under him.

He heard a *crack* and everything went black.

IV

After the silence of the desert, the Weavers' Guild Compound was almost overwhelming. The shuttlecars buzzing in and out of the parking garage, the larger shuttles from Terra Secundus dropping to the port area and the dragons drifting lazily out of their mountain all fought for Tristan's attention as he sat behind his desk. The Elemental Interface sat there, the wood wound around the rock as if it had grown around the stone, the soft silver and dark black blending harmoniously. It was proving to be a distraction. Of all the Elemental Interfaces he had made over the years, this one was special—he could feel its soft hum through the desk. The Weaving would begin the next day, Tristan had just returned from gathering the willowisps, coaxing them out of the Winds and into a spell that let them be safely transported to Earth. Now they were waiting patiently to become sails. He wished he could cast aside the doubt that fluttered to life every time he thought of the massive undertaking, but he couldn't. The sails were more than twice as large as any ever attempted.

Also there at the back of his mind was the information that Fenfyr had passed along. Tristan still refused to believe that humans were capable of using anything that resembled Vermin technology, but it was worrying. The dragon had asked him not to mention it to anyone. The Guild Master knew and the dragons, but that was all.

They all believed that letting the information out could prove disastrous, but it weighed heavily on his heart as he contemplated the Weaving to come.

"Master Tristan?" The voice pulled him back from his musings.

"Yes?"

"Master Rhoads is here."

"Thank you, let him in." He sat up and focused on the door.

"Tristan!" Brian's voice boomed as he entered the room, and Tristan smiled. "Back four days and not a word, I've been worried."

"Has it been four days? I was helping gather the willowisps."

"So I heard, are you sure that's wise?" Brian dropped into the chair in front of Tristan's desk and put his feet up.

""Why wouldn't it be? I always help gather..."

"I know about the attempt on your life." The man cut him off. "Lokey Fenfyr informed Darius and Darius informed me. I've let you stew about it long enough. We are concerned, as you know."

"About more than me, I hope."

"The attempts are part of a larger scheme, yes. We just aren't sure what it is."

Tristan sighed. "If it even is, I'm not convinced."

"We know the ship is there, so that much is confirmed." Brian met his eyes. "As to the rest, it is yet to be seen."

"Yes."

"I have assigned Alden Soldat to *Winged Victory*."

"I guessed as much when I saw him in the hall the other day." Tristan tried to hide his distaste. Alden had risen to the top of the ranks of Warrior Weavers—the Guild member assigned to a ship to control her sails—but he didn't like Alden. The man was vain, egotistical...

"And a pain in the ass," Brian said, finishing his thought. "I know what you think about him, but he is the best we have and we need the best for this ship. These sails are massive, and I don't even know if he can handle it. There are twelve Air Weavers assigned to the project, they've been there since the Navy requested Air Weavers for two ships."

"You're as worried about this as I am."

"No, Tristan." Brian dropped his feet to the floor. "I'm more worried. The closer it gets, the more I hear, and that makes me uncomfortable. Frankly, I've considered pulling out more than once. If Darius hadn't asked us specifically to be involved, I would."

"Why do you think the dragons are so interested?" Tristan asked.

"Besides the rumors?" The Guild Master shrugged. "I'm not sure. I don't trust them to tell us everything, and there is far more going on than we know. I did hear from Sandlin on the corvette *Fury*. They're patrolling the Outer Reaches. There have been several Vermin attacks in the last few weeks, like they are probing for a weakness in our defenses."

"Even if they broke through there, it's a long way into our space."

"Not that far, not for Vermin. It's why the Navy wants the *Victory* to fly so soon."

The intercom buzzed. "Sorry, Master Tristan, but Master Alden is here to see you."

"That didn't take him long," Rhoads said. "I sent him his papers this morning."

"Let him in, Scott," Tristan said, sitting up straight in his chair. He ranked the warrior by several levels, but Alden tended to behave as if he were the ranking officer no matter what company he was in.

The door opened and Alden strode in, his dark uniform impeccable and his hair worn clubbed at the back of his neck, the formal bow tied so precisely Tristan suspected that it was glued on after the fact by one of his underlings. Stopping in front of the desk, he glanced at Tristan and snapped off a crisp salute to the Guild Master. "Sirs!"

"At ease," Rhoads said.

"Sir!" Alden made a point of staying at military correct "at ease", and he looked at the Elemental Interface lying on the desk. "Reporting for duty."

"A little premature, Alden," Tristan said, trying to keep the annoyance out of his voice.

"I wanted to be in at the beginning, sir. This project is so important I assumed you would want me present from day one, sir."

Tristan ground his teeth together. He really despised the man. "It's not customary to report until the sails are complete."

"Ah, yes, but this is far from a customary assignment, sir."

"You're right, Alden," Rhoads said, standing and slapping the Warrior on the back hard enough to knock him off balance for a second. "I think having a Warrior at your back is not a bad idea this time, Master Tristan."

"Perhaps," Tristan agreed, trying to decide whether he liked the idea of Alden lurking around while he was Weaving.

"Thank you, sirs!" Alden grinned slyly at Tristan.

Rhoads moved between them. "I mean watching his back, Alden. No matter what else is going on in the Guild, we are all Guild. You understand me? We watch out for our own. You have had to have heard the rumors. If anything happens on your watch I will personally take you to Darius to have you explain why these sails are not completed by the Master Weaver."

Alden took a half-step back as if he had been punched, his face flushing. "No, sir! I mean yes, sir! I mean..." He cleared his throat, his shoulders slumping for a moment. "Yes, Guild Master, the Guild comes first always."

"Remember that," Rhoads snapped. "Master Tristan, excuse me, I have a meeting with the Worlds Council and Navy."

"Good luck, sir," Alden said.

"You'll need it," Tristan added under his breath.

The massive building that housed the Weaving area was at the far side of the compound from the port. The Guild had discovered that any energy affected the way the willowisps bound themselves together, and the energy output of shuttles seemed to affect them more than anything. The fact that they survived at all at normal Earth gravity was a part of the spell the dragons had given them. For particles that existed in interstellar space, Earth-norm was a crushing weight.

Tristan walked through the front of the building towards his office there. It was quiet, the pristine walls glistened softly in the gentle lighting. It seemed a whole world away from the rest of Earth. He laughed, in a way it was, it was different from any place else, anywhere. It was the only Weaving area in the galaxy. Early on, they had discovered that the balance of Weaver to willowisps seemed only to function on Earth—even if the Weaver had been raised entirely off world—which was generally the norm. Most humans had fled their decimated planet and lived on the hundreds of stations that dotted the solar system and reached attentively beyond.

There was a large medical area at the front of the building, specially shielded from magic and other energies. Weavers were vulnerable after creating a set of sails—usually they just needed a day or two of isolation, but the larger the sails, the more immense the risk. There was already a med team on the alert and a shielded room in the most protected area ready for Tristan. He had no illusions about it, this Weaving was serious—if it didn't kill him, he would be lucky.

"Sir!" Alden's voice brought his attention to the doors of his office.

"You are here bright and early, Alden," Tristan said.

"I am excited to see the beginning of the sails for my ship," Alden said slyly.

Tristan fixed the man with a cold look and opened the door to his office, well aware that the Warrior had broken protocol and just followed him in. The subtle reminder that Alden would be flying the ship was a calculated insult. Many of the Warrior wing of the Guild felt that they should outrank the other members of the Guild. The Weavers' Guild and the dragons did not agree, believing that the creators of the sails should be in charge. It had been decided when the Guild was first formed that the Guild Master would be a human with no ability with magic at all. Brian Rhoads, the Guild Master, knew the basics behind all the spells, understood the magic at the most basic levels, was a brilliant particle physicist but—as he was fond of saying—"couldn't bend a spoon without a set of pliers if I tried"—and so was completely removed from all the emotional aspects of the magic.

Making a point of ignoring the man in his office, Tristan sat down at his desk and opened his computer, taking his time before looking up at Alden, who was still standing at Parade Rest in front of his desk. "You seem overly anxious about these sails."

"*Winged Victory* is the most important ship to ever sail, of course I am concerned! I am the one representing the Guild."

"Representing them with sails I have created and attuned for you," Tristan chided, none-too-gently.

"Of course, sir!"

Tristan kept himself from sighing or rolling his eyes. He was used to Alden, however: they were almost the same age and had started in the Guild together. Alden had wanted to be a Sail Weaver—everyone who entered the Guild did—but lacked the skill. He was fortunate enough to have the ability to be "tuned" to the sails. It was hard to explain to others, but the sails, once created, would only react to the Weaver who created them and someone that their creator had essentially introduced to them. The Warrior was trained to use the Elemental Interface to interact with the sails. It was a delicate process and took a great deal of skill. Tristan often wondered why some of the Warriors felt inferior. What they did was highly skilled and very important. The Guild was symbiotic, and all parts had to function for it to work effectively.

"Um. Sir?" Alden asked, his voice less sure.

"Yes?" Tristan looked up.

"I've heard a rumor."

"What?" Tristan waved him to sit in the chair in front of the desk. "What kind of rumor?"

Alden sat, glanced at the door to make sure it was closed and looked back at Tristan. "I was invited to the Naval Mess the other night. There was a dinner and ball in honor of the First Rim War."

"Yes?" Tristan nodded.

"One of the officers I know—I hate the man, he's a flogging captain—but I served with him once when I was young, anyway, I heard him talking." Alden leaned a little closer. "There is something going on with *Winged Victory.*"

"What do you mean?"

"I'm pretty sure I wasn't supposed to hear the conversation. They had all kinds of... entertainment to distract me, but I heard them talking about the sails and testing them."

"What?"

"It was strange, the way they were talking about it, like they weren't sure the sails would fly. I know that there is always a worry that the sails won't bond with a ship, but no set of sails you have ever created has failed to bond. I assumed that's why they wanted you to do it. There was something in the *way* they were talking that made the alarms ring, you know?"

"We've heard rumors too, Alden," Tristan said, realizing that he hadn't been paying attention. "I am not sure what it means, but I know the dragons have asked for me personally to do these sails."

"So that rumor is true!" Alden said, his eyes getting wide. "I'd heard that, but it is unprecedented."

"I know, and it makes me nervous."

"And I understand there was an attempt on your life, the Guild Master briefed me about that. While you were out gathering the Elements."

"I am not sure what it was, I know someone risked following me into the Wilderness Area that is part of the Sanctuary."

"You can't take that as anything less than a threat," Alden said, all business. "If they are willing to risk that, then they were there to stop you. Getting caught there is death without trial, so whatever they wished to accomplish had to be worth that risk."

Tristan opened his mouth, then stopped. He hadn't thought about it that way, but it was true. "You're right," he agreed reluctantly.

"It's a good thing I am here, if they will risk that, who knows what else they will risk. We have our differences, sir, you know it, I know it, but I know my duty as well."

Tristan regarded him steadily. Alden was telling the truth and no matter how egotistical he was, he was loyal first and foremost to the Guild. The watch bell chimed the beginning of the forenoon watch. The Weavers' Guild had reinstated the Navel practice of watches governed by bells and the entire Guild and Navy was set to "Guild Mean Time" so that no matter where they were, they would be on the same time as the rest of the Guild. The Navy didn't like it, but the Guild called the shots. When Tristan had first joined the Guild, learning the series of watches broken up into "Bells" was one of his first memories of his days at the Guild Compound.

"Thank you." Tristan stared at his computer for a moment, wondering if he was ready. "Let's do this."

The Elemental Interface was already waiting for him on its pedestal under the huge dome of the Weaving room. The willowisps sparkled in the perpetual dusk-dark of the room, drifting through the dome like tiny golden stars. Tristan paused long enough for his eyes to adjust before walking into the center of the room where a Circle was carved into the floor. Created from a combination of ancient human and dragon symbols, it glowed faintly with its own power. As he stepped in, Tristan felt the gentle push of resistance that was part of the Circle's security. Only Weavers could enter: the spell that had created the Circle made sure of that. He could see Alden standing just outside the Circle, and the medical team waiting by the door with a stretcher and a variety of life-saving devices. He hoped they wouldn't be needed.

Tristan looked up, letting his mind clear and the Latin of the spell start to work its way through his mind. The spell the dragons had given them wasn't originally in Latin, but even before the dragons' appearance, the Magic Confederation had used Latin for their spells, believing that using a thoroughly dead language reduced the risk of the inexperienced attempting to work spells. Once the Guild was formed, they made it illegal for non-Guild members to even learn the basics of Latin with the exception of those few who were destined to become Guild Masters, and high ranking members of the Dragon Corps. Though the space stations stretching across the galaxy were designated by Latin numbers, the population at large had long forgotten that those names were indeed Latin.

Once he felt ready, he began to speak, the Circle glowing brightly as the words fell from him, filling the air. The willowisps began to move, he could feel them tugging and pulling in the air as he began to bring them together. One hand reached unconsciously towards the Elemental Interface and the Weaving truly began. The willowisps were dancing, shimmering in and out, up and down as the massive sails began to take shape. Tristan stared up at them, mesmerized, the tiny lights of the individual willowisps becoming larger and larger until the giant sails billowed over his head., hanging from the special hardware they used in the Weaving dome to protect the sails from harm during their creation. He built each mast's sails carefully, starting with the mainsail of the mainmast and finishing with the top gallants. He lost track of time, of everything, as he focused on the sails. He was only vaguely aware when, sometime later, he was gently guided onto the stretcher. He caught a last view of the golden sails as he was wheeled out, fluttering in the soft breezes in the chamber.

He sighed, it was finished and they were perfect. He could rest.

V

The soft strains of music surrounded Tristan as he slowly became aware again. He opened his eyes and gazed up at the ceiling of the room he was in, the star-covered tiles marking it as one of the Weaving medical bays. He could hear the sounds of the machines that were monitoring him as well, but they were muted so that they were only the gentlest backdrop to the music. His preferences were clear: the Ancient Music of Eighteenth Century on the old calendar. As he cast through his mind, he realized he had no sense of time—how long he'd been there or how long it had been since he'd created the massive sails. Smiling, he remembered the sparkling sails fluttering over his head as they rolled him to the medical facility.

He wished he could just lie there a little longer enjoying the quiet, but the job of attuning Alden to the sails had to begin as soon as possible. With a sigh, he punched the call button, an instant later one of the staff appeared at the door.

"Master Tristan!" he said, smiling.

"Doctor Soronson? Why are you here?" Tristan asked. Ron Soronson was Head of Medical for the Guild.

"It was a close call," the doctor said frankly. "We were sure we were going to lose you."

"What?" Tristan punched the button that lifted the head of the bed. "No."

"Yes. We've had Darius in here twice." Soronson pulled a pad out of his pocket and began poking at it. "Do you know what it does to my staff to have *Darius* in here? Half of them refused to come to work for fear you would die on their watch, and Darius was very clear in the fact that if you died he would be *very displeased.*"

"Sorry. How long has it been?"

"Five days."

"Five?!?" Tristan exclaimed. No wonder Darius had been worried. Fenfyr must be frantic. "What do you mean, five?"

"As I said, we were sure we were going to lose you. Medical science can only do so much when you drain your body like that, you know, sir." The doctor made a *tsking* noise. "I am shocked they allowed it in the first place." He brushed a gray hair back from his face and met Tristan's eyes. "We had to place you in a coma."

Tristan relaxed and let the man mumble as he checked the monitors and made notes on his pad. Five days was unprecedented, and he knew he was lucky to be alive. The fact that he had no memory of anything since that last glimpse of the sails was proof enough. They must have induced a coma to block him from any stray energies that were in the air, but to force a coma was extreme. After several more *hmphs* and *tsks,* the doctor smiled at Tristan and left the room.

As soon as he was gone, Tristan reached for the communicator on the wall and called the dragon compound. Most humans found it difficult to understand that the dragons used electronic communications, believing they would prefer to use magical methods. Tristan laughed, dragons were nothing if not practical, and the electronic system was practical and not taxing.

"Guild Dragons," Ceriwyn, the operator answered, she was human but had lived at the dragon compound for her entire life.

"Ceriwyn, it's Tristan Weaver, can you connect me with…"

"Of course!" she practically shouted before he could finish.

A moment later Fenfyr's voice rumbled over the line. "Tris?"

"Fine thing, I wake up and I'm all alone," he said in a teasing voice.

"I was there!" Fenfyr boomed. "They wouldn't let me stay! I tried everything, even hiding in the corner! They said the staff couldn't function with me there, but your room is big enough! I finally had Darius come."

"I know, Fen, I was teasing," Tristan said.

"I know," the dragon replied, and Tristan could picture him, his fore feathers drooping in relief. "I didn't know what to do when they said they were going to put you into a coma. What if..."

"No need to worry about that, there wasn't a what if, so all is well," he said lightly, then realized the dragon had paused. He could hear the soft intake of Fenfyr's breath. "Okay, so things aren't good. What, Fenfyr?"

"We will speak with you when you are well enough to come back to the compound."

"We?" Tristan asked, sitting up.

"The Guild Master, Darius and myself. There was an incident."

"What happened?"

"No, rest, my friend, an hour or two or a day will not make a difference. We have much to discuss. Wait until medical clears you and we will see you at your office."

"Fen?"

"Things are worse than we ever dreamed, I think," the dragon said softly. "But that you are alive is all that matters to me right now."

"I'm okay."

"You just better be, or I will be down to eat everyone there. I am bored with protein soup."

Tristan laughed, a little louder than usual, more to reassure Fenfyr than anything. "See you soon."

"Yes," the dragon replied and broke the connection.

Six hours later, Tristan walked down the corridor to his office in the main compound. His assistant, Scott, stood at attention as he approached, a broad smile on his face, and with a "welcome back, sir!" handed Tristan a cup of the hot spiced tea he preferred in the afternoon. Mornings were for coffee, afternoons for spiced tea. Little eccentricities were not only tolerated but encouraged, and spiced tea seemed innocent enough. Some of the other masters took it too far in Tristan's opinion, although he never brought it up unless it became disruptive.

He set the tea down, and before he could step around the desk the alarms announcing the arrival of the dragons began to blare. "Let him in," Tristan said into the intercom before Scott could buzz him, and an instant later Brian Rhoads strode into the room.

"Tristan! By the First Spell!" The man quickly crossed the room and crushed Tristan in a tight hug, pounding him soundly on the back before letting him go. "I thought we'd lost you."

"So everyone says."

"Because it is true, Tristan Weaver," Darius said as he came through the door. Just behind him was Fenfyr, his feathers fluffed out in agitation. He waited until Darius stepped aside, then walked to Tristan, tapping him with his head tufts and wrapping one enormous claw around him. Tristan leaned into the embrace.

"I have to admit I'm a little surprised to see you all," he said mildly. Fenfyr growled, the tone low enough that it wasn't a sound, only a rumble against Tristan's back.

"There was an incident," Darius said.

"Yes, Fenfyr mentioned it, but didn't say what it was. And where is Alden, shouldn't he be here?" Tristan stopped as he looked at their faces. "Ah, so the incident is Alden?"

"I'm afraid so," Brian said with none of his usual volume.

"What?" Tristan asked.

"His shuttlecar exploded," Darius said.

"Exploded? There's no way it could unless..." Tristan stopped.

"Right. Someone tried to kill him," Brian finished for him.

"Tried? Is he alive, then?"

"He is," Darius said. "We have taken him under our wings and have him at our mountain. You must come and speak with him."

"I will, of course," Tristan said immediately. "We will need a new Warrior." The silence that greeted that remark made him nervous. "Won't we?"

"The Naval creatures have suggested a Warrior of their own," Fenfyr said.

"They did what!" Tristan exclaimed. It was beyond unheard of, it was a breach of protocol that had been in place for two centuries.

"Yes." Brian's voice lowered to a growl that mimicked the dragons. "A Rogue Weaver, left Guild formally two years ago."

"And they think we will allow that?" Tristan was shocked by the suggestion.

"They do." Brian and Darius shared a look and Fenfyr growled again. That's when Tristan realized there was considerable tension between the three. "We have a plan to trump them."

"How?"

Fenfyr's growl became audible.

"With you, Tristan Weaver. With the exception of the Guild Master you are the highest ranking member of the Guild. You created the sails, you do not need to be attuned to them, they are your sails. The Navy cannot refuse you as Warrior."

Tristan was staring. He knew he was. When he'd entered the Guild, he'd actually thought about qualifying as a Warrior. The chance to fly one of the great warships was very tempting, but he had proved too gifted to be "just" a Warrior. He was fully trained in the Warrior's art, of course, but had never served as such. Generally when he flew on a ship he occupied a position rather like an admiral—a ranking officer, but not part of the day-to-day functioning of the ship itself. This was something entirely new.

"Me?" Tristan asked, aghast.

"Yes, you, Tristan Weaver," Darius said. "We need this ship launched because we must know what is going on, what better way than have you there? You will reside with us until you leave for Terra Secundus."

"I will?"

"Yes, and the dragons will escort you there. We aren't taking any chances with your life," Brian said. "This is too important."

Fenfyr growled again, and Tristan found himself in agreement with the dragon. "This is insane, I am no Warrior."

"You are the only one they absolutely cannot refuse, Tristan," Brian said, raising his voice. "The only one."

Tristan knew it was true, and he knew they had to find out what was going on with the *Winged Victory,* but still there were so many reservations. He was not a Warrior, he could Weave and Bond the sails, but could he make the ship fly? And what if they engaged in combat? "Just until we find out what's going on," he said firmly, coming up with a solution he thought was a reasonable balance between his hammering heart and their insistence.

"Of course, that is all we ask, Tristan Weaver. Just the maiden voyage, and we will find a Warrior or perhaps Alden will have gotten used to working with one arm by then."

"One...?" Tristan shook his head. "I'll get my things."

"Don't worry, we've already got your apartment ready for you," Brian said. "You leave now."

"Why the hurry? I just got here!" Tristan protested.

"Because the shuttlecar that brought you back from the Weaving area has caught fire. Your life is in danger and you are better off with the dragons than here. No one is getting up there."

"Only dinner," Fenfyr said, still growling but with a note of humor in his voice. "I will take you myself. Get a coat. It is cold."

"What?" He looked up at the dragon.

"I'm flying you," Fenfyr said. "I am in charge of security, and from here on out you are under my personal protection."

"Until I reach the *Victory*."

"No, I'm going with you. All ships have dragons, you are closer to the dragon than most," Fenfyr growled. "Now, get your coat and let's fly."

Tristan stepped carefully over the dragon's claw and headed to the closet to get his coat, hiding his smile. From what Darius and the Guild Master had said things were grim, but the prospect of flying on Fenfyr *with* permission for a change made his heart sing. He remembered the night he was declared Master Weaver of the Guild. The warm buzz of happiness that filled him every time he remembered that moment tingled along his spine, a laugh bubbling up as he recalled Fenfyr's antics at the news. The dragon had launched himself over the ocean, silver, black and pearly gray feathers puffed out, his wings fully extended, skimming the waves, trumpeting at the top of his lungs, returning to grab Tristan in gentle claws before carrying them far from the land, soaring on the wind as the sun set and the stars flickered to life over their heads. They had returned long after the Weavers' Guild compound was closed, the watchtower firing warning shots before they identified themselves. Fenfyr, as usual, thought it was a game and chased the missile before swatting it out of the sky with one sweep of his tail.

Tristan turned back from the closet, coat in hand, and caught the sparkle in the dragon's eye. Fenfyr was remembering one of their adventures as well. That night they had managed to get away with more than usual, since Tristan had just been raised in rank and Fenfyr was on the Council of the Dragons. Even so, since then they had gotten a stern talking to from Darius more than once.

"We will continue this at the mountain," Darius said, turning and leaving. "Guild Master?" he called from the hall.

"I am summoned," Rhoads laughed and left.

"How bad is Alden?" Tristan asked as the others left.

"He is badly wounded. He lost his right arm and eye. They saved his leg, but he will walk with a limp for the rest of his life. He is awake, but on many pain medications. The Healers have been in as well," Fenfyr said.

"Not good." Tristan pulled on his coat and walked out of the office. The fact they were calling in Healers did not speak well for Alden's chances of survival. Medical science had advanced to the point that magical healing was very rarely needed, and Alden needing it was worrying. The *Winged Victory* project was beginning to seem sinister.

They reached the Dragon's Portal and Fenfyr hopped out, then reached down and clasped Tristan in his claws. The dragon waited until he was settled and secure, some of the dragon's feathers holding him gently, yet firmly in place. After a moment, Fenfyr leaped skyward and Tristan laughed with happiness. No matter what was coming, flying with Fenfyr was always an amazing experience, and as they twisted through the port traffic, he noticed how the dragon buzzed too close to some of the Naval vessels, making them swerve, and he took the "long" way, flying out to sea before swinging in and back towards the mountain that housed the Guild Dragons. By the time they landed, Tristan felt lighter. He squared his shoulders and headed into the giant cave and towards the living quarters.

VI

The soft chiming of bells filled the apartment. Tristan lay in bed and absently counted them, three bells in the morning watch. He still had time before he needed to get up and go out for the meeting with Darius, Brian and Fenfyr. After the meeting he planned to go see Alden. He hadn't had a chance the day before. Once he set foot in the Dragon's Compound, he was whisked away by the human staff. They checked him over and the chief of medical ordered him to eat then straight to bed, threatening him with a sedative if he refused. Tristan hadn't even considered refusing; he had a lot to think about.

The idea of becoming the designated Warrior for the *Winged Victory* was beginning to sink in, and as it did, it was becoming more and more terrifying. He knew the basics, but that was not what he did—he created sails. Understanding how the ships worked was one thing—and as Master Weaver, and a member of the Council, he had to qualify at a master's level in all aspects of the Guild, but it was still mostly theory. He *had* flown a ship once, briefly, on a calm day, between Terra Sextus and Terra Septimus. This was entirely different, because even a milk run in this ship would take them out of the solar system to the edge of the Rim Satellites. Deep space.

Four bells chimed and Tristan pushed himself out of bed. After showering he opened his closet and stopped—alongside the usual uniforms he wore as Master Weaver were five new coats in the deep sapphire blue of the Warrior Weavers. He stared at them for a long time before reaching for his usual clothing and dressing. With one last glance at the other jackets, he closed the door and headed towards the humans' mess.

There was a brief hush when he walked in, every head turned his way, then back again as if they didn't want him to know they had looked. He smiled to the room at large and nodded at two people he recognized. Grabbing a tray, he wandered along the buffet, aware that he was being watched again. It was hard not to react, but he focused on the fruit, got himself a cup of coffee and wandered towards an empty table in the far corner of the room. Once he sat down with his back to the wall, he felt better. After the first sip of coffee he improved even more. He sighed and took the chance to look at the other humans filling the room.

Most of them were wearing the black of the Dragon Corps. It was an elite group that served out their lives in the Compound here or on the stations in space that specifically cared for and acted as representatives for the dragons. The dragons kept themselves aloof from dealings with humanity as much as possible and the Corps served as their buffer. Very few humans were chosen and even fewer made it all the way through the training. Some died, some left, some were killed by those opposed to the dragons' existence.

"Master Tristan?" a baritone voice asked. "Might I join you?"

"Please do." Tristan laughed and waved the man to sit. "I hope Fenfyr hasn't destroyed anything important?"

"No," the man, Chris Muher, said, laughing. The night they had met was the night Tristan had become the Master Weaver and Fenfyr had wreaked a little havoc. Muher, a man in his early forties, had risen quickly up through the Corps to become General and second-in-command of the Corps. Though a few years older than Tristan, Muher often sought him out at functions, they weren't close enough to be friends, but Tristan enjoyed his company. "Are you okay, sir? We heard about the Weaving. I saw the sails as they were being rolled into their containers. They were perfect!" He grinned enthusiastically.

"I remember them, they were lovely," Tristan said cautiously. "I'm okay, sails that large take a lot."

"I bet! I heard the *Victory* sails with four full Aether level Air Weavers! I wish I could be there to see her sail."

"I suspect everyone who can is going to find a way to get out to Terra Secundus to see her launch."

Muher frowned. "Yes, I suspect the same thing. The Corps intends to be there in force, as well as Weaver security. Since the three attempts have been made, we are taking no chances."

"Three?" Tristan asked, feeling a little stupid.

"Yes, the violation of the Sanctuary Lokey Fenfyr informed us of, the one on Alden, and then your shuttlecar deciding it wanted to catch fire." He shook his head. "It's too coincidental, so it has to be intentional. Someone nearly killed Alden and less than twenty minutes after the Guild informed the Navy you were to be the warrior for *Victory* your vehicle blows? Nope, no way is that chance."

"You think it's the Navy?"

"I don't have a clue who it is. Some splinter group claimed responsibility for Alden, I'm not sure if they are behind it, if they did it on someone else's request or just want their name in the news." Muher slammed his cup down on the table. "Sorry, sir."

"It's okay. I expect I'll get a full briefing later, I like to hear what people are saying, though." He smiled. "What are they saying?"

"Here or out there?"

"Both?"

Muher took another drink of coffee and sighed, looking at Tristan over the rim of his cup. "Here, the dragons and the Corps think it's the Navy up to something, but what that is they don't know. In the Corps, once we found out about the *Victory,* they think the Navy has gotten their hands on a Rogue Weaver who is willing to try to fly the ship for them to get their flagship completely out of the hands of the Weavers." He paused. "Out on the streets, people think the Navy has come up with the answer to everything. They don't know what it is, but they think it will stop the Vermin incursions and drive them back to where they're from once and for all. An awful lot of them don't care how it's accomplished—and that's a problem. Because the dragons think the Navy is withholding Vermin technology and the majority of the humans just want the war over, and if this would help them win…"

"Not good."

The other man frowned. "Not good is an understatement, as you well know. If they are using that filth on a Navy vessel, the dragons will put an end to humanity!"

"At least the Navy," Tristan said with a smile.

"No, sir, you don't understand. I've heard rumors from my people who are out in the cities. The general population is terrified of the Vermin since the attack on Terra Undecimus, people want the Vermin stopped. They don't care how. There are several groups openly agitating against the Weavers, saying the Navy needs to be in control. There are civilians who don't care how the end of the war is achieved, they just want it over. And then there are the few whack-jobs who think we should try to make peace with the Vermin."

"Didn't the only attempt at that end up with the humans being eaten alive?" Tristan asked, digesting the information he'd just been given.

"It did, they were dressed out like a butchered steer, the films were sent back to the Worlds Council."

"They were more hopeful in those days?"

"After a hundred and fifty years of world war?" Muher snorted. "No, I think they were looking for a way to stop our own wars."

"Well, that worked, Earth is united."

"Sort of." The man's communicator beeped. "If you'll excuse me."

"Of course. I will see you again, I'm sure."

For some reason Muher laughed at him and held his hand out, shaking it then walking away. Tristan stared after him, a sinking feeling beginning to overwhelm him.

"Ah, there you are, Tristan Weaver," Darius said as he was ushered into the cave that served as the dragon's office later that morning. The cavern was enormous and it was the only place Tristan had ever been that made the dragon look almost normal-sized. Fenfyr was leaning against the wall, his tail curled neatly around his feet. By comparison Brian and General Cairn, the ranking officer of the Dragon Corps, looked tiny in the vast space.

"How are you?" Brian asked, looking him up and down.

"Fine. I was fine yesterday too. You really didn't need to set the medical hyenas on me."

At this Cairn burst out laughing. He'd been the first to coin the term for the medical staff and it amused him every time he heard it used. "They were out in force, hunting everyone yesterday," Cairn said when he finished laughing. "Someone decided to try to drop a bomb in."

"Bomb?" Tristan asked in alarm.

"Nothing to worry about, it was just those idiots in the 'Equality for Vermin' group. We should feed them to the filth and have it done."

"We're better than that," Brian scolded him.

"Only on Tuesdays," Cairn replied.

"To business?" Darius interrupted.

Tristan sat down, aware that Fenfyr had moved to stand protectively behind him. "What's going on?"

"It is our…" Darius began.

"Your," Brian corrected him.

"*Our* opinion that the Naval creatures are trying to prevent a Weaver who is loyal to Guild and Dragon from controlling the sails of the *Winged Victory*. We sent a patrol out to see what they could find at the docks and the patrol found only a locked docking sphere. When they demanded to be shown in, it was refused." The dragon paused while Cairn swore. "Finished? Since then we have not been able to get any information at all."

Tristan smiled, remembering the beautiful lines of the ship. "We have a set of the plans."

"We do," Rhoads said.

"Then what?"

"They do not want a Weaver onboard."

"They need one to fly that ship. Those sails are massive. You need a fully-trained Warrior Weaver, not just someone with a back-station knowledge of Weaving and magic," Tristan said.

"They might have one. Remember Taylor McKay? He's been seen on Terra Secundus recently."

Fenfyr's low growl mirrored Tristan's feeling. "That… That… Son of a bitch is on Terra Secundus? He actually has the gall to show his face this close to Earth?"

"Yes, and we think he is going to try and fly that ship."

"Unless this is all for show and they have other sails," Darius said grimly. "It is quite conceivable that they asked you to Weave those sails in hopes it would kill you, and they could convince the incoming Master they needed to fly sooner rather than later and it was just all part of something else. Something hideous."

"I'm a little confused," Tristan said, frowning at the dragons.

"Think about it, Master Tristan, if you were killed and the sails completed, they could be shipped and they could attempt to attune them to a Rogue."

"Yes," Tristan said "But a Rogue could never control those sails. We know they can only control the sails created by the Master that taught them, and even then it's chancy."

"Very true," Darius said. "Or maybe they have another way altogether."

"What?"

"We think they have slaved Vermin Tech on the ship."

"No." Tristan was shaking his head. The thought of the filth of any kind of Vermin technology touching the beauty of the ship made him sick. "So we have a plan to beat them at their own game," Cairn said smugly.

"Yes, we do," Darius agreed.

Fenfyr growled.

"What?"

"The sails are shipping right now, you will be on Terra Secundus tomorrow, the ship will sail in three days."

"Um…" Tristan looked at them all, feeling stupid again. "What was that?"

Fenfyr growled again.

"We're beating them at their own game. We are going to move the sailing of *Winged Victory* up by a full three weeks. Whatever they were planning will have to be stopped and something new started. It will give us time to figure out what is going on here, and you can get the ship out to the Rim, there was a Vermin attack last night. Terra Duodecimus was nearly destroyed. Luckily the frigate *Surprise* was there, they managed to stop the attack, but they can't keep them away for long."

"So I leave when?" Tristan asked.

"As soon as you talk to Alden. We will have your things

packed, but wear the Warrior Weaver uniform when you ship out."

"Okay." Tristan stood, feeling a little stunned. "I'll go see Alden."

"Tris?" Fenfyr asked softly. "I'll be right behind you, I promise."

"Thanks," he whispered back and walked out of the room.

By contrast to the rest of the Dragon's Compound, the small medical area reserved for humans was small, and sized for people. The cavern itself was even lower in height than the rest of the area. Dragons could come into the area, and occasionally did, but generally they left the care of humans to humans. Tristan stopped as he entered, the familiar smells triggering the memory of his own time there. After the bombing of the Guild Council the few who survived were brought to the dragons for protection. From a council of eighteen, there had only been three left. A group calling the act the Stars Plot claimed responsibility. The Guild and dragons had gone after them and discovered at least some of the guilty parties had been active-duty Naval officers. Tristan vaguely remembered when they first mentioned it to him. He had been gravely injured, the only thing that saved him was the fact that the huge granite council table had blocked him from part of the blast. Absently rubbing his leg, he swallowed back an upwelling of grief. With the exception of Brian Rhoads, he'd lost his closest friends and more. Miri, the Master Warrior, and his lover, had been killed, blown apart beyond recognition. Tristan cleared his throat and shoved the memory away. At least those responsible had paid for their crime.

He enquired about Alden at security and was shown to a room at the back, deep in the recesses of the medical cave. After a quick rap on the door he walked in, only to stop momentarily in shock. The man he had known for years was gone and in his place was a broken human being. A patch covered one eye and the right arm was gone below the elbow.

"Alden?" he asked softly as he walked towards the bed.

The Warrior's eye opened. "Sir."

Tristan grasped his hand. "No rank here, Alden."

"Thank you, si… Tristan." He sighed. "I'm sorry I won't get to fly your sails."

"Me too," Tristan answered with a rueful grin.

"Who did they pick to replace me?" Alden blinked, a tear leaking down his face.

"Not replace, just fill your spot until you're able to fly."

"The sails have to be attuned, you don't have to feed me a line, I know the deal," he said bitterly.

"Not really, you don't. I'm flying her maiden voyage."

"You?" The comical look on Alden's face was a hint of the man Tristan had known before—haughty, sure of himself and a little disrespectful of authority.

"Yes." Tristan sighed. "It was Darius and the Guild's choice. They want to catch the Navy off-guard."

Alden nodded, glancing around the room. "There is something going on, we all know it. I… I was thinking of a plan."

"Plan?"

"I wanted to run it past you before I proposed it to Darius and Rhoads, sir." The man was suddenly looking him in the eye, like he was gaging his response.

"What is it?"

"We need to know what's going on, and we know there is a group of Rogue Weavers serving the Navy and others."

"The pirates." Tristan couldn't keep the disgust out of his voice.

"Right, so I was thinking, when they release me from here—no one knows I've been here—I will 'leave' the Guild publically and join the Rogues."

Tristan considered the proposition. They had tried to infiltrate the Rogues many times, but their spies had always been discovered. "Why would they take you?"

"You bastards let this happen to me. I can still fly and you dry dock me because of injuries sustained in the line of duty? Can you believe it?" Alden's voice dripped with derision. Tristan stared at him in surprise, then relaxed when the man grinned at him. "I've been working on it."

"You would be a catch for them. They will want something—proof—to let you in though."

"I've been thinking about that, too, and I thought we could arranged a little faked intelligence I could take with me. Something that is 'top secret' that I took before I left."

"It could work." Tristan mulled it over, considering the question from every angle. If Alden pulled it off, they would finally have a foot into the Rogues and a way to maybe break the group up. The fact that men and women he had trained were working for pirates deeply distressed Tristan and he took the Rogues' offenses personally. "Talk to them about it. Tell them I am behind you one hundred percent."

The grin that lit Alden's face traveled up to his eye. "I won't let the Guild down. I support Guild and Dragon."

"Thank you." Tristan squeezed the man's hand. "Have someone let me know what's going on."

"I will, sir, and thank you."

"No, thank you, Alden. You know what this means." He saluted the Warrior with a smile and turned to leave.

Chris Muher met him at the door. "Your shuttle is waiting, you should change."

Tristan swallowed against the sudden dryness in his mouth. He was really doing this. He squared his shoulders and walked to the small room Muher had pointed towards. The uniform hung there, rank clearly indicated. He grinned, they would have had to custom make this one, he was the highest ranking Weaver to ever wear a Warrior Weaver's uniform. He ran a hand over the sleeve. It was time.

VII

The trip from Earth to Terra Secundus took five hours. Tristan spent the time reading, trying to ignore the stares of the other passengers. There had been a public shuttle leaving at six bells in the forenoon, and he was on it, his ticket purchased at the gate so there was no forewarning to anyone who might want to make an attempt on his life. The trip itself was uneventful for the most part; a young woman behind him had a child with her who kept kicking the back of Tristan's seat. By hour four, he was tempted to say something, but just let it pass. The less noticeable he was the better. When he walked up the gangway to the station, he still had a phantom rhythm beating in his lower back. Even with that he stepped out and into the station with a smile on his face.

Small puffs of white clouds drifted overhead as Tristan made his way through the busy corridor leading to the Naval docks. The artificial sunlight touched his face even though there was a slight chill in the air. It was autumn in the Northern Hemisphere on Earth and Terra Secundus reflected the season. The digital photos on the wall were full of golden yellow, deep red and soft brown leaves fluttering down from the branches overhead.

He could see his reflection in the shop windows as he passed, the dark uniform standing in contrast to the brighter clothing of the civilians moving around him. A smile ghosted over his lips, he'd never really expected to see that particular reflection. Turning his head, he caught the dark ponytail, clubbed with a formal bow over his collar. It still had a feeling of unreality to it. He shifted the satchel he was carrying and moved on.

Tristan was surprised when someone slammed into him, the man in a Naval uniform growling as he walked past. He stared at the man in shock. He knew the friction between the Guild and the Navy was more open on some of the stations, but this came close to being a disciplinary offense, particularly since the man was only wearing the uniform of a boatswain's mate.

"Ass," a young girl said. Tristan looked over, she was wearing a shirt that had a figure of a dragon in front of massive sails, in bright pink letters it said "I support Guild and Dragon." She smiled shyly at him. Tristan smiled back, feeling a blush creep up his cheeks, and walked on.

"Sir?"

Tristan looked up. A man wearing a Naval uniform and the stripes of a First Officer stood in front of him. He looked vaguely familiar for some reason. "Yes?" Tristan replied, putting on his official face, his eyes cold as he appraised the man.

"Are you for *Winged Victory*, sir?"

"Yes?"

"Sir! It's a pleasure, sir! I am Thom Barrett, First of the *Victory*," he said, his hazel eyes shining as a lock of brown hair tumbled over his forehead.

"Barrett? We've met? In my office?"

"Yes, sir!"

"You were a captain."

"Technically, I still am, I am functioning as First because I wanted the *Victory*." He grinned. "There was no way Davis was getting me off her."

"Why not?"

Barrett smiled. "It's hard to demote one of her designers to a garbage scow for long."

"Designer?" Tristan looked at him again, reassessing his initial impression.

"Yes, sir! I was on the team that designed the *Constellation*, too. I missed the chance to serve on her. Captain Jackson was a good man, though, his loss is sorely felt." There was something in Barrett's eyes that warned Tristan this was a point of grief for the man. "I was given a small frigate escort for her, but after the loss of the *Constellation,* I was recalled and asked to help with *Winged Victory*... Oh, sorry, sir, I tend to run on at times."

"Of course, Mr. Barrett," Tristan said, wondering if the overly talkative, almost too talkative, officer was something of an act. If Barrett was capable of designing a ship like the *Victory,* he was no fool.

"We weren't expecting you until later, sir."

"There was an early transport from the Guild."

Barrett nodded, still smiling as he glanced around the crowd. "Can I offer you an escort, sir?"

Tristan weighed the offer, shifting the satchel on his shoulder as he considered it. As they got closer to the Naval docks, the chance of an incident would grow; if he was with Barrett, it was less likely. Deciding that a confrontation before he even reached the ship was a bad idea, he smiled his official smile at Barrett and gestured with his hand for the man to lead the way. "Thank you, Mr. Barrett."

"I am just back from leave, I haven't been on her since they finished the officers' quarters. I was slinging my hammock below decks before I left." He chuckled. "I haven't had to do that since I was a mid, I don't fit as well as I once did."

Tristan hid a smile at the man's chatter, Barrett reminded him of a midshipman far more than the officer he was, a child-like enthusiasm eddying around him. Despite the man's seeming youth, the Naval officers and enlisted men moved away with a quiet acknowledgment of his authority.

"Oh! Oh, look!" Barrett had stopped and was looking out a tiny porthole. "A dragon! A big one!" He turned to Tristan with a sheepish smile. "Sorry, sir, you see dragons all the time, don't you?"

"I do," Tristan said.

"I've seen them around the station and when I was out on the *Endeavor* we had a scout, of course, but she didn't mingle with us at all, just perched on her roost now and then." His eyes were fixed on the porthole, tracking the movement of the creature beyond them. "And I've been working on *Winged Victory*, the plating's been up and... Oh!" Barrett turned to him with wide eyes. "Oh, sir, is that...?"

Tristan moved so he could peek around the man, smiling as Fenfyr wheeled around a cargo ship lumbering out into space, his silver scales glinting in the dull light from the station. "That's Lokey Fenfyr."

"*The* Lokey Fenfyr? Why is he here?"

"Yes." Tristan hoped that the look of awe on Barrett's face wouldn't be replaced by something else once he got to know Fenfyr. The dragon didn't really take the dignity of his position seriously. "Didn't they tell you? He will be serving as scout for the maiden flight."

"Oh, sir, really!?!" Barrett took one last look out the porthole and turned back into the crowd. "Fitting for *Winged Victory,* though. She's the most beautiful thing the Navy has ever produced." A gentle smile lit his face. "I've worked on her since day one, I even served some time on a construction gang, just to keep my hands on her and the men focused. You will love her the instant you see her, sir, she has a grace despite her size."

"Grace?"

"Oh, I know I haven't seen her with her sails. I know there are those who say she never will sail, but she is so beautiful and I know, deep down in my bones, the sails will take to her and she will be able to fly," the man went on enthusiastically. Tristan hoped that if there was something amiss with the ship, this open and friendly man had nothing to do with it.

"Her sails will love her," Tristan said softly. From the moment he had gathered the willowisps together he had felt an affinity for the ship and knew the first delicate task—the sails bonding to the ship— would be accomplished easily. The Guild informed him before he left Earth that the sails were on the ship and waiting for the maiden flight.

Barrett led the way across the crowded dock towards the airlock at the far side of the bay. Tristan followed, keeping his face carefully neutral even though each step caused an increase in his heart rate as it started to really sink in that he was here. A huge *thump* boomed through the deck, causing everyone to freeze, and look up towards the ceiling and the massive Dragon's Portal slowly spinning open.

The door clanked open and Fenfyr dropped down to the deck plating, his wings and feathers tucked against his body. The dragon let out a huge *whooshing* sound, his body adapting to the atmosphere after being in space. Tristan resisted teasing him about his tendency to make an entrance, and Fenfyr knew it. The dragon's sly chuckle rumbled through the deck plating before he looked at Barrett with his head tufts forward.

"Lokey Fenfyr of the Guild Dragons," Tristan said, waving his hand in the dragon's direction.

Barrett bowed. "First Officer Thom Barrett of *Winged Victory,*" he said, straightening and eyeing the dragon with awe.

Fenfyr inclined his head in a short bob, grumbling softly before glancing around the docks with a snort.

"Mr. Barrett?" Tristan snapped, the man was staring at Fenfyr as if he'd never seen a dragon up close.

"Sir?" Barrett blinked at Fenfyr then turned to Tristan. "Sorry, sir! This way."

As they approached the portal to the gangway for *Winged Victory* Tristan felt his mouth go dry. He had no idea what he was walking into, and he knew that even though he was comfortable as a Weaver, this was the first time he had served, truly served, as Warrior. It was a daunting feeling, that flutter of nervousness in his gut as he considered the enormity of what he'd agreed to—or been railroaded into at least.

"Mr. Barrett, sir!" a man in a petty officer's uniform said, snapping to attention.

"Shearer," Barrett said with a nod.

"It's good to see you back, sir."

"It's good to be back. These are *Winged Victory's* Warrior Weaver and Lokey Fenfyr who will serve as scout."

"Sirs!" Shearer straightened even more. "Boatswain James Shearer, sirs."

"Shearer, good to meet you." Tristan nodded at the man.

"Sir! Thank you, sir." Shearer saluted, opened the portal and strode up the gangplank. He stopped and turned back, boatswain's whistle in his hand. Its shrill blast echoed around them and Tristan looked up as the crew stood to attention when Barrett walked up the gangplank. Tristan followed, Fenfyr right behind him, the metal bending under the dragon's weight.

"Barrett! What the devil do you mean by..." A short man stormed across the deck, his uniform impeccable as he stomped towards them. He stopped as Tristan stepped onto the deck beside Barrett. His face went from a frown of irritation to outright hostility. "Captain Gary Stemmer," he growled. "Are you the Weaver?"

Tristan eyed him coldly. "Yes. This is Lokey Fenfyr of the Guild Dragons," he said as Fenfyr stuck his head over the edge of the airlock then slipped onto the deck with a silent, fluid grace.

"We weren't expecting you yet," Stemmer snarled, every line of his body indicating disapproval.

Tristan glanced around the deck, lifting his eyebrow as he looked back at the captain. "Obviously. We sail in three days and this is what greets me?" He was aware that Barrett had stiffened in anger beside him. "You aren't even ready to drop the sails."

"They only just arrived," Stemmer snapped, a sneer on his face, his tone bordering on outright insubordination.

"The point is they *have* arrived."

"I am captain here."

"And *I* am Weaver." Tristan felt Fenfyr's growl of agreement tremble through the deck beneath them.

Stemmer's eyes were fixed on the dragon towering over them, his feathers and tufts puffed out, making him seem even larger. The captain swallowed nervously, his face turning from white to red. "We haven't had time to inspect them!"

"Inspect?" Tristan asked mildly, Fenfyr rumbled beside him. "My sails? We will drop them as soon as I see my cabin." He turned to walk away.

"Are you giving me an order, Weaver?"

Tristan turned back. "Yes," he said firmly, waiting to the count of three before he walked across the deck and down to the doors of the Weaver's Quarters, the largest in the ship, a deck above the captain's and complete with a stern gallery. He dropped his bag on the table and wandered through the large cabin, taking his time and letting Stemmer stew for several minutes. After checking to make sure his trunks were still locked, he headed back up to deck.

Barrett was directing the men as they carefully cut away the packing on the sails. Though referred to as "dropping the sails", it more closely resembled a bonding. The sails had to fit to the ship and vice versa or they would not respond to the Winds, instead leaving the ship to flounder and be torn apart in the forces whipping through space. Tristan was sure his sails would take to the ship. They had to, he only hoped that something hadn't happened to prevent that. He closed his eyes and spoke a small spell, feeling the Weaving hum under his feet. He had to make sure the sails caught.

"Are we ready, Mr. Barrett?" he asked, turning his back to the captain as he addressed the first officer in an obvious snub.

"Sir! Everything is set!" Barrett said.

Without sparing Stemmer even the smallest glance, he nodded. "Proceed."

"Drop the sails!" Barrett called.

"Drop the sails!" Shearer repeated and the men started to sing, a soft rhythmic chanting, and moved the sails into position. "Open the panels!"

Tristan held his breath as the panels that covered the masts and crosstrees while the masts were retracted in the hull opened. He softly repeated the spell that had created the sails, hoping the extra encouragement would help them bond with the ship. Of course, there was no knowing for sure until the moment they moved into the Winds. Life or death was decided in that instant and most people were expecting their deaths, the loss of the ship and an end to the dream. Fenfyr crooned from behind him, one giant claw curling protectively around Tristan's feet as they waited.

The first sail was dropped off the deck, falling hundreds of feet down towards the bottom of the mainmast. The sound of its passage whistled through the below decks, filtering up in an eerie echo. The boatswain moved to watch its fall. Long seconds passed. "It caught!" he shouted. Cheers broke out as the second sail followed the first, the volume increasing as each fell into place, the crosstrees soon full, the massive sails waiting for their maiden flight.

"Will she fly?" Barrett asked breathlessly.

"I won't know until you do," Tristan said as he and Fenfyr walked to the mainmast panel. He peered down into the depths of the ship, seeing the soft sparkle of the willowisps waiting for their first chance to catch the Winds. The dragon nudged him gently, Tristan leaned a shoulder against him, trying to sound casual. "Looks good, we will sail on schedule."

"Very good, sir," Barrett replied quickly.

"Soon," Tristan whispered—to the sails, the ship, he wasn't sure who, but Fenfyr heard him and answered with a soft huff of breath, before resting his chin on the deck and looking down at the sails as well.

"Your sails passed the first test, Weaver," Stemmer said from beside him.

"You were expecting something else?" Tristan turned to face the man.

"On this ship? We had no reason to believe you were capable of making them."

"Odd, then why build it?" Tristan asked mildly. The captain's face turned red. "Darius asked me personally to see to it, so of course they would catch."

"We'll see what happens."

"Yes," the Weaver said softly, a warning in his voice. "We will." Stemmer looked from him down to the sails, grunted and walked away without another word. "We might have problems with him," Tristan commented.

Fenfyr hummed an affirmative before moving closer, stretching his neck so his head disappeared. A terrified shout wafted up, followed by a warm chuckle from the dragon.

"Some of the men haven't seen a dragon before," Barrett said. "The latest group just arrived."

"Pressed?"

"Not many, mostly volunteers, and only then just the lowest ranks. Almost the entire crew is Skilled at least." Barrett smiled. "She deserves no less."

Fenfyr pulled his head out and snorted.

"Did they meet with your approval?" Tristan asked, amused.

"Hmm," the dragon muttered. "The Dragon's Roost is too small."

"You can talk!" Barrett's eyes were huge.

"Of course I can," Fenfyr laughed.

"I..." Barrett swallowed nervously. "I'm sorry, sir, I didn't mean it like that, I just meant—the dragons I've served with, they never spoke, I thought they... I mean I know dragons talk to Weavers but…"

"We're particular, and don't speak to just anyone." He nudged Tristan gently. "I am going to inspect things."

"Don't scare anyone to death," Tristan chided.

"Not all the way," Fenfyr rumbled softly before he disappeared over the edge of the opening, shortly after muffled screams drifted up from below decks. The Weaver smiled as he watched the soft glow reflecting off Fenfyr's wings move deeper into the darkness along the masts.

"Would you like to see the ship, sir?"

Tristan pulled his attention from the dragon and focused on Barrett. "I would, thank you, Mr. Barrett."

A bright smile lit the officer's face as he led the way across the deck. "The plating is the latest design," he said, gesturing at the dome that soared over their heads. "*Winged Victory's* masts are the largest ever constructed, when fully extended the mainmast is more than seven hundred feet. The sails…" He stopped and coughed. "Of course, you know about the sails, sir! We have eighteen decks, nine of which are gun decks with a full sweep. We have a crew of twelve hundred." Barrett opened a hatch and held it while Tristan stepped through into an elevator. "We have four main engines and thirty thrusters. The crew is housed primarily on the decks twelve through fifteen, the officers on deck sixteen, with the captain's quarters directly below yours."

The elevator slid to a stop and Barrett stepped out, waiting for Tristan before he started down a corridor. He stopped in front of a large hatch and swung it open to reveal a huge greenhouse. "This is our farm, most of our foodstuffs are raised here. Very little is brought in, and once we are deep space sailing, everything will come from here. It also contributes eighty percent of our oxygen below decks, letting the Air Weavers focus on the open areas of the ship."

Tristan stepped into the vast compartment. Trees soared over his head, the scent of blossoms filled the air. Hydroponic tanks dangled from the ceiling, giving the place the feel of a jungle, vines and flowers intertwining to hide the walls in a mass of greenery. "The fruit is on a rotation?" he asked, spying a tree heavy with pears.

"Yes, at least a third of the trees are always bearing." Barrett trailed behind him. "We also have a collection of flowers and ornamental plants so there is some place green for the crew to visit." The officer made a face. "Some people didn't think that was a good idea."

"It's sound thinking, humankind needs green sometimes."

"Thank you!" Barrett said, beaming.

"I should warn you that dragons occasionally like greenery." Tristan smiled. "And grapefruit."

"We have several grapefruit trees."

"I will make sure he leaves a few."

"They are the captain's favorite." The officer was looking at him with a glint in his eye, as if he were testing the waters.

"I'll tell Fenfyr to take as many as he wants."

"Very good, sir," Barrett said, nodding smartly before turning to lead the way out.

"Mr. Barrett?"

"Sir?"

A hail suddenly broke the quiet. "First Officer Barrett report to the quarterdeck."

Barrett pulled a small phone out of his pocket. "I am escorting the Weaver on a tour of the ship."

"The... The captain says you must come, sir," a voice stammered.

"I am with the Weaver, Riggan."

"I don't care who you are with," Stemmer's shout blasted out. "Get up here now."

"Sir..." Barrett glanced at Tristan.

"You are dismissed, Mr. Barrett," Tristan said with a smile.

The officer nodded his thanks and walked quickly out of the compartment, leaving the hatch ajar as he exited. Tristan watched him thoughtfully.

"There will be trouble with the captain," Fenfyr rumbled, coming up behind him.

"I think so."

"We'll handle it, Tris," the dragon assured him.

"It's not going to be easy."

"It never is." Fenfyr laughed, a gust of grapefruit-scented breath washing over Tristan. "It never is."

VIII

The crew was busy on deck, some of them high up on the plating that covered the ship until the sails were raised. Tristan tried to imagine how it would look with the ugly plates gone and the massive sweep of sails and stars over his head. It was still hard to believe that there would be nothing but a spell between the crew and death in deep space. Even Tristan had been unnerved the first time he'd sailed and the massive plates gave way to the vastness of space.

"We had a jumper on my last ship, sir," Barrett said, coming up silently beside him.

"A jumper?" Tristan turned to him with a frown.

"He actually climbed the plates as they were coming down, there was no way the Air Weavers could save him in time." Barrett stared up at the massive dome over their heads. "It's hard for the pressed crew to understand. It was hard for me the first time. I know in theory how it works, the ships are in the dome until we need the sails, and the Air Weavers make the atmosphere so we can function on deck and still take advantage of the sails. But the fact that it is all..."

"Magic?" Tristan supplied helpfully.

"Yes, that makes it hard to understand. The plating I know. The decks I know like that back of my hand, the fact that it will all be open to space soon is still a little disturbing." He grinned. "Exciting too, sir, don't get me wrong."

"Barrett! You have better things to be doing than standing around on deck!" the captain snarled, walking towards them, a small man following behind him.

"He was discussing the sails with me," Tristan said simply. It should have been enough.

"He needs to be at his duties," Stemmer snapped.

"He is," Tristan dropped his voice to a growl. "When I dismiss him, he may return to his other duties."

The small man was tugging desperately at the captain's sleeve, trying to get him away from the Weaver. "Get off me, Riggan!" the captain snapped. Without a thought Stemmer hit the man hard enough to knock him down. Tristan ground his teeth together, he knew that kind of treatment happened on some ships, especially the bigger ones, but he had no intention of allowing it on *his* ship.

"Stop," Tristan said softly when Stemmer raised his hand again.

"What did you say to me?"

"I said *stop!*" He stepped forward.

"Captain! We need you on the lower deck!" Shearer called from the hatchway nearest to them. Stemmer turned and stalked away from them, slamming the hatch hard enough for the sound to buzz through the deck under their feet.

"Do I have a servant assigned to me yet?" Tristan didn't wait for an answer. "Assign him." He pointed at Riggan, still crouched on the ground.

"But, sir," Barrett said softly, then stopped. "Yes, sir."

"Thank you." He waited until the man scuttled away before turning to the First Officer. "How much of that is there on this ship?"

"Sir?"

"I know you are a new crew, but you would know something about it already. Is he a flogging captain?"

Barrett looked at him, his jaw clenching, bright spots on his cheeks. "He follows Naval procedure for discipline, sir."

"Of course. You don't agree?" Tristan needed to know where the officers stood on the regulations. If things got out of control he needed to know who he could go to for help.

"Sir, I..." Barrett stood straighter. "I believe the men respond well to orders without the need for the whip. I believe that there are those that require more, but it is certainly not needed regularly."

"Very good, Mr. Barrett, thank you. Please have Riggan escorted to my servant's quarters."

"Yes, sir." Barrett turned to go, pausing to look over his shoulder. "You know he was assigned to the captain?"

"I guessed as much."

"Sir, you need to know, I've heard rumors that…"

A loud crash came from the panel to the mainmast and shook the ship. Barrett was running and Tristan right behind him before the sound died away. The crew was gathered around the open panel. Tristan didn't even pause to think about the fact that it should have been closed as he moved through the crowd to where the panel opened to the lower parts of the ships. There were muted screams from somewhere below, the grinding of metal and over it all the shouts of officers trying to get control over the crew below.

"What's happened?" he heard Barrett demand.

"Part of the mast collapsed under the sails," a voice crackled through the comm. "We have several men… What's going on?"

"Shearer!" Barrett nearly shouted.

"Let me help," Fenfyr's deep growl rumbled through the ship.

Tristan bent closer to the edge, he could see the soft glow of the dragon. "Fenfyr?" he shouted, his voice echoing through the emptiness.

"They are trapped, bleeding, I can free them faster. Tell them," the dragon replied.

"Mr. Barrett?" Tristan looked at the first officer.

"Let the dragon help! What are you thinking!" Barrett snapped.

The screech of metal being dragged over metal trembled through the ship, then a huge crack shook the deck. Tristan tried to see what was happening, all he could see was shifting shadows and the confused sparkling of the willowisps on the sails. Fenfyr's growls punctuated the calls of the crew and suddenly an alarm started blaring, followed shortly by a hail, "Medical emergency Deck Thirteen, Med team respond. Medical emergency Deck Thirteen, Med team respond."

Several long moments later Fenfyr appeared over the edge of the panels, his great claws bloody and his eyes sad. "One of them was… I couldn't get to him in time." He hung his head, his chin resting on the deck plating. Tristan walked over and laid his hand on the dragon's neck as Fenfyr let out a soft sigh, the dragon equivalent of silent tears. "One of the others injured is an Air Weaver."

"What?" Tristan asked.

"I know they were working on the lower plating, we always have an Air Weaver there in case of emergency," Barrett replied.

"They weren't going to let me help," the dragon lamented. "If they had, I could have saved them all."

"I am sorry about that, sir," Shearer said, approaching them. "It will never happen again. I want to thank you for myself and on behalf of the crew for what you did. Without you, all of them would have died."

"What happened?" Barrett said, looking at the boatswain.

"I don't know, sir. If I didn't know better, I'd say it was a rigged explosion."

"Why?" Tristan glanced at the man as Fenfyr lifted his head off the deck.

"The way things fell, the way it happened. I will be in there checking as soon as the metal cools enough to touch," Shearer assured them.

"Let me know as soon as you do, Shearer, so we can deal with the problem," Barrett said softly, a threat in his voice.

"Yes, sir!" Shearer agreed with a growl. Before leaving he stopped in front of the dragon and looked up at him. "Thank you again, sir, and welcome aboard, we are glad, very glad to have you."

Fenfyr bobbed his head in acknowledgment and watched the man go before he said, "Something smelled wrong down there."

"Wrong?" Tristan asked.

"I'm not sure, but wrong," the dragon said, before standing. "I need to fly." With that he headed towards the gangplank so he could use the station's portal into space.

There was an uncomfortable silence after the dragon left. Barrett was focused on the hatchway to the lower deck and Tristan was staring up at the huge dome over their heads, imagining Fenfyr wheeling through the stars. He sighed, Fenfyr was deeply affected by what had happened, he could tell from the droop of the dragon's feathers as he walked away.

"If someone sabotaged my ship," Barrett growled, "I will keel haul them."

"Keel haul?"

"Yes." Barrett shook himself.

"Can someone show me to sickbay? I would like to check on the injured Air Weaver. They should have introduced themselves when they heard I was onboard." Tristan frowned, annoyed by the breach in protocol, but then, he had only recently arrived and they had purposefully not announced his arrival time.

Barrett pulled out his phone. "Riggan? Report to the quarterdeck, the Weaver needs to be shown to sickbay."

"Thank you." Tristan tried not to look too embarrassed, he'd forgotten about his servant already. Of course, he wasn't accustomed to having one. There had been students assigned to him at the Guild, but that was an entirely different thing.

"Sir?" Barrett suddenly sounded young and unsure.

"Yes?"

"Would you dine at my table this evening?"

Tristan paused. To not dine at the captain's table the first night would be considered a huge insult, but the captain had made no move to invite him. He weighed his options. If he did this, it would send a definite message. Even though Tristan had his own "table" it was traditional that on the first night the Weaver was invited to dine with the captain and his officers. "Thank you, Mr. Barrett. When do we dine?"

"Eight bells in the last dog, sir. Thank you, sir!" He snapped off a salute, then grinned sheepishly.

"Sir," someone said, tugging at Tristan's coattail.

"Yes?" He looked down, Riggan was hunched over beside him. "Riggan, right?"

"Yes, sir," the man mumbled.

"Look up when you speak to me, Riggan," Tristan said firmly. "I need to go to sickbay."

"Yes, sir, this way, sir," Riggan said to the decking. "After I show you, would you like me to unpack your things, sir?"

"My formal uniform needs pressing, if you can see to that for me?"

"Of course, sir. Are you dining with the captain, then?" he asked, then stopped, turning pale and ducking his head as if he expected a blow.

"No, Mr. Barrett invited me to the gunroom."

"Oh!" Riggan scuttled ahead to open a hatchway. "He is a good officer, sir."

"Are you frightened of dragons?"

"Dragons?" Riggan stopped and looked back at him with wide eyes.

"I should have asked before I had you assigned to me, but Fenfyr said he plans on sleeping on the stern gallery as much as he can get away with, which means he will have his head in the cabin a lot of the time."

"Really?"

"Really." Tristan smiled at the man's happy look.

"Here we are, sir, sickbay."

"Thank you, Riggan, I will see you later," he dismissed him and stepped into the room.

Several beds were occupied, each screened from the others by curtains that shimmered almost like sails. In the far corner of the room a group was clustered around a bed. He recognized the uniform of an Air Weaver among them, so he headed towards them. A tall woman, her silver-shot black hair cropped close to her head, turned to him as he approached. She stepped to the end of the bed, eyeing him with the almost purple eyes that marked her as a front-line veteran of the Rim War. The exposure to the toxins on one of the worlds had caused a number of abnormalities in humans, purple eyes being one of the less common.

"Dr. Rose Webber, sir," she said, extending her hand. The medical services fell under a different jurisdiction than the Navy and most medical officers were less resentful of the Guild than the military.

"Tristan Weaver," he answered, accepting her hand.

"I heard the dragon saved the crew."

"Yes, he was sorry that one of them was lost."

"The ones that survived are damn lucky he was there. They would have been burned alive. Between his efforts and those of the Air Weavers, they were saved." She turned back to the bed. "Damn crew ought to think about that sometimes," she muttered to herself.

"What was that?"

"Nothing," she replied. "Theresa Aether." She nodded at the woman lying on the bed, burns marring one side of her face.

"Sir!" the man in the Air Weaver's uniform said, snapping to attention. "Sir! I didn't see you! I didn't know you were on board until Fenfyr appeared below or we would have been there to welcome you, sir!"

"It's okay."

"No, sir, it's not, Master Tristan! We were so honored to hear it would be you serving on *Victory,* and then…"

"Calm down." Tristan raised a hand, the man was turning red. "You are?"

"Sullivan Aether, sir! Theresa is my partner and we are the senior Air Weavers. Seconds are West and Sheea Aether, they are below, helping with the damage." He glanced down at Theresa, then back up at Tristan. "You have four full Air Weavers, all Aether level, and then we have eight journeymen as well."

"How is she?" Tristan asked gently, he could tell that for all his information, Sullivan's attention was focused on Theresa.

"They say she won't die."

"She won't," the doctor said tersely. "I think I said she would be fine with a night's rest."

"She will?" Tristan inquired.

"She will. No lasting damage, a little scarring is all, and that's not much considering what could have happened." The doctor turned away. "I have other patients, if you will excuse me."

"Thank you," Tristan said, waiting until she left before focusing his attention back onto Sullivan. "Do you know what happened? Fenfyr said he smelled something wrong?" Air Weavers had heightened senses of smell, no one knew why, but it was one of the marks of their trade.

"I'm not sure, there was so much happening. We were trying to keep a small hole blocked so they could work on the plating." He cocked his head to the side. "Now that you mention it, I thought I smelled something right before the explosion."

"What?"

"I don't know for sure, but it was out of place. The kind of thing your brain registers, but you aren't sure why?"

"I understand. If you think of something, let me know

immediately." Tristan smiled at the Air Weaver. "Let me know when she is awake, I would like to pay my respects. I will expect you all to report to my office at two bells in the forenoon watch tomorrow."

"Yes, sir!"

"Dismissed, Sullivan."

"Thank you, Master Tristan."

Tristan walked out of sickbay, glancing at the other occupied beds on the way out, the men were burned and unconscious. He silently cursed the prejudice that kept them from allowing Fenfyr to help until it was too late to save the crew member who had died.

The Naval prejudice, even hatred, of the Guild was beginning to become a serious problem. It had been there since the Weavers spun the first sail. The problem was getting worse, after the Edicts that set the Guild apart, and in many ways above the Navy, the one-time dislike had grown into full-blown hatred in many parts of the service. The Navy was even dividing itself between "sympathizers"—those that supported the Guild—and the old line. The hatred had over-flowed in the Stars Plot when an attack had been made on the Weavers' Guild Council, and the first council hall was destroyed in an act of terrorism. Most of the Masters had been killed, the few who escaped barely survived. No one could trace the attack to the Navy, the perpetrators had been incinerated in the blast, but there was enough intelligence to arrest two ranking Naval officers.

Tristan absently scratched the scar on his back as he followed the shimmering stripe marked "quarterdeck" towards his quarters. When he opened the door, Riggan stopped what he was doing and snapped to attention. Glancing around the room, Tristan stepped in and closed the door. "I need to know something about you, Riggan."

"Sir?" the man said timidly.

"Where do you stand on the Guild?" the Weaver asked quietly, in case there were listening devices in his quarters.

Riggan smiled. "Oh, talk freely, sir, I checked around and I removed all the monitors in the place, sir, and out the airlock they went first thing when I walked in. Ask Mr. Barrett, sir. We would have no ships without our sails and no sails without our Weavers, sir. And, well, the dragons, they serve as our eyes, they defend us, and I was there sir, when Darius came out to defend the supply line! I saw it, sir!" Riggan's eyes sparkled with life and his face glowed with light. "I was serving on the *Constellation* then. She was a beautiful ship, her loss…" He hung his head. "Did you know Master Griffith, sir?"

"I did, we trained together." Tristan said softly, remembering the huge man, full of laughter and life. The *Constellation* had been destroyed during the *Jupiter* Incursion. The Guild suspected that the attack by the Vermin played right into the hands of the Stars Plot and the destruction of the *Constellation* and her very pro-Weaver captain were a little too coincidental for comfort.

"He was my friend." Riggan looked up, his eyes sad. "Your uniform is ready for dinner, sir, though the gunroom isn't as formal as the captain's table."

"I know," Tristan said, with a smile.

"I know you know, sir." Riggan answered his smile with a knowing grin. It was as close to an open insult as Tristan dared on his first day on board.

"We're going to get along fine, Riggan."

"Yes, sir."

IX

Several hours later, Tristan was sitting at the desk on the portside of his cabin when there was a soft scratching at the Stern gallery door. Riggan glanced at him for permission before opening the portal. Fenfyr stuck his nose in and the small man stumbled back a step.

"Riggan, this is Lokey Fenfyr of the Guild Dragons. This is Riggan, my assistant," Tristan said.

"I'm his servant, sir," Riggan said, speaking to Fenfyr.

The dragon let out a puff of laughter that was enough to blow the man into the side of the desk. "Sorry," Fenfyr said, a smile in his voice. Tristan was glad to hear it, Fen must have "flown" himself free of the earlier incident.

"Assistant," Tristan corrected for the fourth time in an hour. They had been arguing about it since one of the crew had brought a message from the captain.

"Servant. I'll just nip off and see about that information on Theresa Aether you wanted. I'll be back. It is a pleasure to serve with you," Riggan said, bowing to Fenfyr. "Sir." He sketched a salute and scuttled out the door.

"Servant?" Fenfyr chuckled, easing further into the room.

"He was the captain's."

"Oh." The dragon's head tufts quivered. Fenfyr was laughing at him. "I went to speak with Darius after I flew." Fenfyr moved a little further so the entire starboard side of the room was filled with dragon.

"Darius?"

"Yes, he is concerned. We are keeping word of the explosion quiet, but we are also taking measures to protect you and this ship more than we had originally planned."

Tristan didn't like the sound of that. "Oh?"

"Yes, and you will accept with good grace. When do you leave to dine with the captain?"

"I was not invited to his table."

Fenfyr fluffed up like an angry kitten "What?" he demanded, the question coming out in a hiss of shock.

"The captain has not invited me." Tristan straightened the papers on his desk, most of his notes were in Latin, it prevented people from reading them, even if they got a hold of them. He also enjoyed the process of writing in the ancient language. He felt that using it for notes and things other than spells kept the language "alive" somehow. "I informed the Guild of his oversight." Tristan smiled, remembering Rhoads' reaction to the news. It was an outright snub of both his rank and position and the Guild. Brian was making a formal protest to the Navy, so Tristan was half-expecting an invitation to arrive at any moment.

"I am shocked, Tris, that is a breach of protocol that is almost unforgivable."

"For you or me?"

"Well, I sure as the Winds move won't leave him one single grapefruit within easy reach."

A soft tap, and the door opened. "Theresa Aether is recovering very well, sir. She will not need a Healer at all. Dr. Webber assured me of that. You should get ready for dinner, sir. Seven bells just went."

"Thank you, Riggan." Tristan stood and walked around the desk. "What?" He could tell Fenfyr was amused.

"Just remember to use the right fork," the dragon said with a snort. "I'm staying here, you won't get me in one of those death-trap uniforms."

"Death traps?" Riggan asked.

"He thinks it looks like the uniforms are strangling the wearer," the dragon said.

"They are, I have heard you say it more than once."

Tristan sighed. "I said it *feels* that way."

"Same thing." Fenfyr put his head on the deck and watched as Tristan got ready.

At five minutes before eight bells in the second dog watch, he stepped over the threshold and into the Gunroom. When humanity had embarked into the stars in sailing ships, they had reclaimed the old names from the Great Age of Sail and the Gunroom was now, as then, the dining area for the officers. The first officer presided over the group, and it included the sailing master and the boatswain—the only deviation from the old days of sail.

Tristan smiled at Shearer as he entered, and waited for Barrett to introduce him to the rest of the officers. There were two men and a woman in Naval uniforms, a Marine colonel in bright red and, to Tristan's surprise, the formal black uniform of the Dragon Corps— worn in this case by a grinning Chris Muher. That must be part of the extra security Darius had been talking about.

"Sir, welcome to the Gunroom!" Barrett said, approaching him with a smile. "I'd like you to meet the officers of *Winged Victory.* The Air Weavers often dine with us, but they have opted to stay with Theresa Aether."

"Of course," Tristan said with a smile.

"This is Second Officer, Commander Patrick Aubrey; Navigator Elizabeth Avila; Third Officer and Gunner Richard Fuhrman. You know Shearer, and our Ship's Master is Geoffrey Kinser. Colonel Steven Hall leads the Marines, and I believe you know General Muher?"

"Yes." Tristan nodded to each as he was introduced, smiling at Muher. "Thank you for inviting me for dinner."

"Our pleasure," Aubrey said. "Believe me!"

Barrett indicated that Tristan should take the seat of honor at the foot of the table and then they were all seated. The first course was served, the wine glasses filled with a rich dark red wine. Tristan took a sip, but no more. He knew that there was more food—and alcohol—yet to come. By the third course, several of the officers were speaking more freely, and from what Tristan could tell, they seemed to be generally loyal to the Guild, although Fuhrman was keeping quiet.

Interestingly, Aubrey had served on the *Constellation,* but had been transferred before the ship's final battle. He was a man in his early fifties, comfortable in his rank and his place in the ship's day-to-day operation. He didn't seem to be one of the overly ambitious men that ended up never reaching their desired commands, although there was something—Tristan couldn't put his finger on what—that *was* upsetting the man about his position on the *Victory.* It wasn't anything he said directly, only an offhand comment or two that got him a growl from Avila once and a kick under the table from Colonel Hall.

The colonel had served in the Rim Wars and was in the middle of a particularly gory story when dessert was served—unfortunately for the diners, it was a cake drizzled with raspberry syrup that almost perfectly matched Hall's description of the blood-smeared severed limbs he'd encountered on the ground. Most of the officers looked a little white and turned away, but Tristan ate. He knew they were watching him, gauging his reaction, and he suspected this had been, in part, staged.

When the meal was over, Hall and Kinser left together, staggering towards a hatchway that was on the far side of the room from Tristan. Shortly after they left, Fuhrman stalked off alone, then Shearer, Avila and Aubrey, leaving only Tristan, Muher and Barrett.

"A glass of wine before you turn in, sir?" Barrett asked, turning away from the table. "I have some stock in my room…"

"Of course," Tristan agreed, he half-expected Muher to leave, but the man merely stretched his legs under the table and leaned back in the chair.

"It's quite an honor, having the Dragon Corps serving with us," Barrett said, returning with three glasses and a bottle of wine. "My family owns a vineyard." He poured them each a glass and Tristan could tell the difference in the quality of the wine even before he picked it up. The wine served with dinner had been good, but this— this was in the "great" wine category and more what he would expect from the Captain's Table. He frowned at Barrett for a moment. He needed to find out more about him.

"It's a pleasure to be in space again," Muher said, pulling Tristan from his musings. "I was out to the Rim but was recalled to Earth when the Stars Plot raised its ugly head. I've been following the threads of that for some time."

"It sickens me to think there were Naval officers involved," Barrett said, sitting down again. He glanced casually around, and Tristan got the message. The room was monitored. They could speak a little, but not much.

"Yes, but many more were loyal," Tristan said, then stopped. Muher had been in charge of the Stars Plot investigation—and as far as he knew the case was still unsolved. They had caught some of the conspirators but not all of them. If the general was on the *Victory,* did that mean that they suspected... "What was that?" He looked up when he realized they were speaking to him.

"How do you like the wine?" Barrett asked.

"It's magnificent! I'm not just saying that because I prefer Zinfandel, this is magnificent!"

"Don't get him started on wine. He can get boring about it," Muher said to Barrett with a laugh.

"Just the one time," Tristan replied. "And that doesn't count."

Barrett grinned at them. "Why not?"

"It was a wine tasting. I was supposed to talk about the wine."

"Not for four hours," Muher grumbled.

"It wasn't four hours," Tristan corrected him. "Closer to three." He smiled at Barrett. "There was a lot of wine."

"I can be boring about it, I will admit it," Barrett said, smiling. "My elder brother inherited the vineyard, it's been in the family since the Second World War in the Twentieth Century. There is even a rumor that one of the vines is from a planting made by the very first Barrett to till the earth. I'm not sure I believe it, but I loved the story as a child." He sighed. "We were very lucky, the family's land actually abuts one of the Sanctuaries, and so was protected during attacks and never destroyed by developers."

"I am sure I have consumed many a bottle of your family's wine then." Tristan took another sip, watching the man. "Are you looking forward to sailing?"

"I am!" Barrett said enthusiastically. "I am not even sure why the Navy was delaying the launch. The only reasonable delay I could see was for the sails, but once they were finished and the Warrior attuned, there was no reason to just sit in dry dock! How is the original Warrior?"

"He lost an eye and an arm," Tristan said quietly. "He's a good man."

"I'm sure, or he wouldn't have been chosen, although having *the* Master Weaver here is such an honor! And not only you, but we're also assigned a ranking member of the Dragon Corps and Lokey Fenfyr himself!"

"Don't talk like that around him," Muher said under his breath. "We'll never get him to shut up."

"What was that?" Barrett asked.

"Never mind," Muher said, standing. "It's getting late. Master Tristan, can I escort you to your cabin?"

Tristan stood, and bowed his head to Barrett. "Thank you for the warm welcome, Mr. Barrett. Perhaps you can join me in my office tomorrow at two bells in the afternoon watch? If it's convenient?"

"Of course!" Barrett stood, too, and walked with them to the door. "See you then, sir."

"We need to talk," Muher said quietly.

Tristan frowned at him. "No."

"Oh." Muher laughed, leaned a little closer and spoke in Latin. *"I know you are surprised they sent me, but there are sound reasons. Things are looking grim."*

Glancing around before he answered, Tristan said, *"We'll discuss it tomorrow, off ship where we can't be overheard. There is an Adjunct Guild Office on the station. Tomorrow at six bells in the afternoon?"*

Muher nodded. "Here you are, sir." He opened the door. "Lokey Fenfyr, it's good to see you, sir."

Tristan smiled and headed in, carefully closing the door. He had the feeling he was going to have a headache tomorrow that had nothing to do with the wine.

"So they sent Muher?" Fenfyr asked as Riggan took Tristan's coat and carefully hung it in the closet.

"Don't play innocent with me."

"I'm not, I didn't know. Darius said they were going to add to the security, but I was not expecting Muher. I was expecting Earle from the Weavers' Guild, actually."

"Well, they sent Muher, and he wants to meet with me. I said we would meet at the Guild offices on the station tomorrow."

"Good idea, no one can overhear. Take someone with you. You need to have someone watching your back."

Tristan sighed. The dragon was right, he could sense the tension in the ship. The officers were jovial at dinner, but there was an underlying current that was disturbing. He was becoming convinced that the explosion earlier had been an act of sabotage and not an accident, judging by the many snippets he'd heard throughout the afternoon.

"Sir?" Riggan asked.

"Dismissed, Riggan, thank you." Tristan waited until the man left before giving Fenfyr a gentle pat and heading towards the small room that served as his bed chamber.

He had no sooner put his head down, than he was fast asleep.

X

Tristan was awake before four bells in the morning watch. It was his usual time, and that was one of the nice things about the entire Navy being on Guild Mean Time—his schedule didn't have to change. He stretched and rolled his neck before doing several rounds of yoga. He knew the ship had a gym, and he would take advantage of that at some point, but right now exercise in the safety of his cabin seemed wiser. When he was finished, he showered and put on his uniform, still surprised by the reflection of the dark blue in the mirror. Making sure his hair was clubbed correctly and his ribbons were on straight, he stepped into the main cabin. Fenfyr was gone. Tristan wondered where the dragon was off to; Fenfyr was security as well as a "scout", and Tristan suspected the dragon was exploring the darker parts of the massive ship. His kind had a hyper-acute sense of smell—if they chose—when in an atmosphere, and Fenfyr might be "sniffing out trouble", as he liked to say.

Tristan hadn't been in the room for more than five minutes when there was a scratching on the door and Riggan entered with a tray with a coffee service on it. He set it on Tristan's desk in the office area and smiled. "How do you take your coffee, sir?"

"Milk and cream, Riggan, thank you." Tristan strode across the room to his desk. "And how are you today?"

"Fine, sir! I was down in the crews' quarters earlier, giving a listen." Riggan grinned—as the Weaver's servant he had a cabin next to Tristan's and didn't bunk with the rest of the crew.

"Oh?" Tristan sipped his coffee.

"Yes, sir. There's a lot of speculation about what happened yesterday. Some of the crew want off the ship. There is a rumor that she's haunted by those that have already died."

"How many is that?"

"Well, not counting the one yesterday, about seventeen since they began working on her." Riggan paused. "There's some that say there is a weird smell that comes from the lowest deck—no one is allowed in and the only portal is soldered shut. They told the crew it's because there is no air down there and there is no need to be there yet, but there's talk, sir, you know?"

"I do. What do you think, Riggan?"

"Me? Well, sir, I don't believe in ghosts, but there is something odd about the *Victory,* I wish I could tell you what it was, but I can't, it's just a feeling in my bones and I've served the Navy since I was fifteen, thirty years now, sir." The man refilled Tristan's cup. "The crew like Mr. Barrett and Mr. Aubrey, Captain Stemmer is a different story. He's a flogging captain and Navy-loyal, and not much liked. Most of the crew support Guild and Dragon, there are a few pressed men who don't, although that always amazes me, it wasn't the Guild that pressed them into service, it was the Navy."

"It's true, in fact, we've put several motions before the Worlds Council to end the practice." Tristan sighed, he'd been called to witness against the practice. When he'd been in his teens he'd actually seen the Navy pressgang come in town and take men right off the street, one or two had been shot before his eyes. It was something he would never forget. He'd known that the war was serious, and they needed crews for the ships he would be Weaving sails for, but even then he saw no reason for the brutality.

"I know, sir, I was there for the testimony! I saw you! I never thought I'd get to meet you!" Riggan said enthusiastically.

"I wish we could have done more," Tristan said sadly. Despite their weeks of testimony, the Council had decided that there were not enough volunteers to fill the Navy and the forced draft was needed. The Weavers had argued that the other branches of service didn't rely on pressed men, but the Navy's rebuttal that they didn't see the same amount of service was, unfortunately, true.

"You tried, and the men know. It's why we are loyal to Guild and Dragon." Riggan refilled his cup again. "So, how much coffee do you require in the morning, sir?"

Tristan laughed. "No more than two pots, if I am to function at all. I prefer spiced tea in the afternoon. I think it's uploaded in my personal information?" Riggan nodded. "Good," Tristan continued. "Don't let me have too much coffee, it makes me jittery. I also prefer a light breakfast in my office."

"Will you dine alone regularly, sir? Or invite the officers?"

"I think we will play that one by ear. I will be having the officers and Air Weavers to dinner some evening, but for the most part, I think I will dine alone and wait for invitations."

"A very good plan, sir," Riggan said, smiling at him. "I have laid in a few extra grapefruits for Lokey Fenfyr."

"He'll appreciate that," Tristan replied. "I have several appointments today. Sullivan Aether and the other Air Weavers will be here at two bells in the forenoon. This afternoon I will be going to the Guild office on the station."

"Ah, yes, very good, sir." Riggan saluted. "I'll have your second pot of coffee ready for the meeting with the Air Weavers, then?"

"Thank you, Riggan, that will be fine."

The Air Weavers were prompt, Riggan ushered them into the office as the second bell chimed. Tristan smiled at them. "Sit down, Riggan is getting coffee."

"Thank you, Master Tristan," Sullivan said. "May I present Sheea and West Aether."

"It's nice to meet you," Tristan said, looking at them. Sheea was a tiny woman, barely five feet tall with white hair and blue eyes so light they looked like glacial ice. West was her opposite in almost every way, tall and dark, he had a comforting presence about him that exuded a sense of security. Tristan had experienced it before, it was a function, at least partially, of the healing magic the Air Weavers drew on to create an atmosphere.

Riggan brought the tray in and served them. He already knew the Air Weavers' preferences and set the cups before them, then walked out of the room. Tristan watched him. There was a definite change in the man already. He was actually walking upright, not creeping as before. His head was still down a little, but he was no longer hunched as if waiting for a blow.

"How is Theresa?" Tristan asked.

"Much better," Sullivan answered. "Dr. Webber said she can be moved to our cabin tonight. We're partners." He added the last a little hesitantly, some members of the Guild Council frowned on couples serving together. Tristan saw no reason to keep them apart, particularly on the larger, deep-space sailing vessels.

"Very good, and I am glad she's doing better." He leaned back in his chair. "Tell me about the *Winged Victory*."

"Where do you want us to start, Master Tristan?" West asked with a laugh. "The hauntings? The deaths? The gossip?"

"West, please," Sheea hissed. "He's sorry, Master Tristan. This is a trying ship for us to serve on. It is so huge and we are required whenever they are working on the lower decks, even though with the dome, the ship should never be exposed to space."

"Right, except it was," Sullivan said quietly.

"What?" Tristan sat up.

"It was shortly after we arrived. Theresa and Sheea were serving on Deck Three and something went wrong, we're still not sure what, but not only did the deck blow the dome did as well. If they hadn't been down there more than five people would have died."

"We were caught off-guard, no one should have died," Sheea said angrily. "We just never expected it to happen. Our presence is usually more of a formality, as you know, Master Tristan. I have never had to actually Weave the Air before launch in any ship I've served on, and *Victory* is the tenth ship."

"Since then, we make sure there are always two Masters and two journeymen at every major repair," Sullivan said. "And we have started serving regular watches early. We might as well get used to them before launch, but we have started them now, in dock, just in case someone decides to blow the dome."

"Good idea. Make sure I have a schedule of the watches," Tristan said. "What else?"

"The rest? It's mostly the mutterings of the crew. There aren't as many pressed hands as usual on this ship, so they aren't as terrified of us as usual, but there is a lot of muttering. The ship is haunted, the ship is doomed and then there is that hatch."

"The one that's closed?" Tristan asked. "Riggan told me."

"Yes," West said. "There is something there, I am not sure what. It smells wrong. I think Lokey Fenfyr was down there sniffing this morning. I have the morning watch, and he asked about the door."

"The officers ever say anything about it?" Tristan watched as they all shook their heads.

"The only ones we've ever seen down there are Stemmer and Fuhrman. They might know. Don't expect them to talk. Stemmer is a bastard and Fuhrman is his weasel," Sullivan said.

"We'll learn more. Did the Guild tell you we sail in two days?" Tristan said.

"Two... No! But that's good, the sooner we are out of the dome the better. I don't like being in an atmo I can't control," West said earnestly.

"Most people tend to feel the other way, West," Sheea said.

"They're idiots," he retorted with a laugh.

"Please keep me up to date on Theresa's condition and anything you hear from the crew. I am always available. And please, plan on dinner tomorrow night at my table."

"Thank you!" the three chorused, understanding the dismissal. They stood and with a final salute left the room.

"Riggan?"

"Sir?" Riggan appeared, seemingly from nowhere.

"Can you see if it's convenient for Mr. Barrett to speak with me? I made an appointment for this afternoon, but I might want to head over to the Guild office a little early."

"Of course, sir," he said and walked quickly out of the cabin.

Tristan jotted down some notes based on what the Air Weavers had told him, and compared it to the information Riggan had given him earlier. He didn't think Riggan had been lying, but everything he'd said had been confirmed by the Air Weavers. The fact that Fenfyr was out sniffing around was both comforting and a little worrying. All ships had problems before launch, and all had a death or two. Tristan cringed, no matter how many safety precautions were in place, there were always deaths. In the early days, before ships were built in domes, they lost many more.

There was a tap on the door and Riggan stuck his head in. "Mr. Barrett, sir."

"Thank you, Riggan." Tristan stood. "Good morning," he said as the officer walked into the room. "I appreciate you coming on such short notice."

Barrett smiled. "No problem, sir, I have the morning watch, so I was taking a quick break."

"The morning watch?" Tristan couldn't stop the surprise in his voice, that watch was generally reserved for midshipmen and junior officers.

"Yes, sir."

"Riggan swept the cabin."

"I guessed he might," Barrett said with an easy smile, almost boyish in glee.

"Tell me about the ship."

Barrett's demeanor changed, the aura of authority that sat on his shoulders like a comfortable cape settled on him. He was used to command, and it showed in the way he sat and the confident way he met Tristan's gaze. "Where do you want me to begin?"

"I've spoken with Riggan and the Air Weavers, so I know a little about the feelings of the crew and the usual gossip."

"Very good, sir." Barrett met his eyes and held them for a long time. "What do you want from me?"

"Your insight?"

"I know there are rumors of the ship being haunted, and cursed." The man laughed bitterly. "Sometimes I wonder, we've had more accidents than most large ships do during building."

"Can I ask why she is so close to complete? The Guild knew nothing of her until the day you and Davis walked into my office."

"What?!? That's a breach of every protocol…" Barrett took a deep breath. "I didn't know, sir. I've been working on her for a long time. It never occurred to me that the Guild didn't know… Why wouldn't you know? We need sails, so you would have to know." He was talking more to himself than Tristan. "Then what was…"

"Mr. Barrett?"

"Sorry, sir, I never realized you didn't know. I assumed that day we came to the office that it had been arranged, I honestly thought we had an appointment, so you can imagine my surprise when security was called!"

Tristan nodded to indicate he was listening, but didn't want to interrupt.

"We started building her more than a year ago, the Air Weavers must have informed the Guild?"

"We were told there were two frigates being built. We haven't had a communication from them, and none of us have spoken to them until my conference with them this morning."

"Isn't that odd?" Barrett asked.

"No, usually Air Weavers are assigned and generally work independently until the ship is due to launch." Tristan frowned. He should have looked into that, they should have seen this coming, but not even the dragons had been suspicious until recently.

"I didn't know. This is really the first ship I have served on from the very beginning, I mean with the building and all. Usually I've joined when they are set to launch, or when I was promoted."

"So, tell me about this ship from your perspective, nothing leaves this room."

"She has a good crew for the most part, as I told you, we do have some pressed men, but they are a minority on this ship. Crew morale is generally good, although yesterday's incident has started tongues wagging again. Some of the crew believe it was caused by the first five killed, trying to keep the ship from launching. They believe the bottom deck is full of bodies of convicts and others that have committed crimes against Naval code and are to be jettisoned in deep space."

"What is the bottom deck?" Tristan asked.

"I don't know. Captain's discretion only. It was added onto the plans by Davis and some of the others at Headquarters, it was not part of the ship I designed. It adds a cumbersome heaviness to her lines that I would never allow. I've asked what it was, and that plus the incident in your office turned me into a first officer."

"Turned you into a first officer? What do you mean?"

Barrett smiled at him, the smile wistful and bitter at the same time. "*Winged Victory…*"

"Yes?"

"I was to be her Captain."

XI

Terra Secundus was bustling in noontime traffic when Tristan left the ship. People were busily dashing in and out of the shops lining the main corridor of the major section of the station. Like a large city, the station had a "downtown" and then smaller outlying areas that functioned as suburbs. As he walked through the shopping district, he noticed people were watching him. They were used to seeing Warrior Weavers, but very few had probably seen a Sail Weaver and so the badge of rank he wore as Master Weaver was getting a lot of curious looks.

The large building housing the Guild's offices on the station was at the far end of the district, and Tristan was taking his time, enjoying the walk. He knew that long walks were out once they were in deep space, although he was sure he could devise a tour through the decks that would keep his brain in shape. Walking always let him stay focused and he regularly walked on Earth to relax after a rough day or get ready for a Council meeting. When he reached the building, he was surprised, it didn't feel like he had gone very far, but as he looked back down the street he guessed it was close to a mile.

Tristan pushed open the door, the receptionist looked up and then jumped to his feet as soon as he recognized him. Tristan hid a smile, the poor man looked like he was ready to faint. "Master Tristan!" the receptionist said, looking nervous. "Can I help you, sir?"

"I need space to have a meeting with General Muher of the Dragon Corps, he should be here shortly. I'd also like a secure line to the Guild Master." As with his meeting with Muher, Tristan felt safer using the Guild office on the station for his secure communication with Brian Rhoads, saving his onboard line for emergencies.

"Yes, sir!" The receptionist sat down and punched the button on an intercom. "Karen, please come to the front desk."

Within moments a young woman wearing a senior Warrior Weaver apprentice badge appeared. "Master Tristan! A pleasure, sir!"

"Can you escort Master Tristan to the office on level five?"

Karen smiled. "Yes, sir. This way." She punched a code into a security panel on the back wall and part of the wall slid open. "Blast proof," she said casually. "When we heard you were assigned to *Winged Victory* we were hoping you would stop by the offices before you shipped out." They stepped onto a lift. "I'm so sorry about Alden. I trained with him when I was on Earth. He was a good man."

"He was."

They stepped out of the elevator onto a floor decorated in soothing greens and browns, giving it the feeling of a park or forest. Karen led him down the hall and through another security door, this one opened onto a large office. There was a large desk and chair, an impressive array of computer monitors and a sideboard sparkling with bottles.

"Can I get you anything, sir?"

"I'd like some spiced tea, and bring coffee for General Muher, he will be here within the hour."

"General Muher?" Karen gasped. "*The* General Muher?"

"As far as I know there is only one," Tristan replied as he sat down at the desk. "Will you escort him up when he arrives?"

"Yes, sir, and I will get that tea right now, sir!"

Tristan nodded and waited for her to leave before powering up the computer and punching in the secure codes to contact Brian Rhoads. While he waited for the Guild Master to answer, he watched the people in the street below, mostly civilians, but there were some Naval and Weaver uniforms as well.

"Tristan!" Brian boomed over the connection. "What's going on up there? I've already gotten one report from Darius."

"I don't know, Brian, I was hoping you might have heard something."

"There are rumors of rumors, a lot of finger pointing and a few dragons so angry they look like a puffball factory exploded." Rhoads laughed, but Tristan could hear the worry in the laugh. "There's a group calling itself Galactic Freedom that took responsibility for the bombing of a cargo ship destined for *Victory* yesterday. "

"And the others?"

"Different groups."

"That's not helpful," Tristan grumbled. "Things aren't rosy onboard either." He proceeded to bring the Guild Master up-to-date on what was happening on the *Victory* and what Riggan, the Air Weavers and Barrett had told him.

"Sir, General Muher is here," Karen said as Tristan was closing the connection with Rhoads.

"Send him in, please."

Muher strode into the office and sat in the chair across from him, waiting while Karen placed a cup of coffee in front of him. He watched her go, then turned to Tristan with a wink. "She likes me."

"Hero worship is different than 'likes you', you know."

"I know, more's the pity," Muher said with a sigh. Taking a drink of his coffee, he looked up at Tristan. "We are neck deep in a pit of vipers, aren't we?"

"What do you mean?"

"I've been doing a little poking and prodding around and there is a lot of unrest on the ship. The lower decks are close to revolution for some reason—and not against the Navy that pressed them, but against the Guild and Dragon. They are the ones who prevented Fenfyr from helping yesterday when the plating blew." He leaned back. "And Shearer and I had a good, long look at that and, I am sure you won't be surprised, that it was no accident. It was a small shaped charge. Really good work too. Maximum damage with minimum explosive used."

"Why?" Tristan asked.

"Shearer thinks it's one of those 'Save the Vermin' groups. I think they were trying to take out the sails." He frowned. "They were a little sloppy and that's why it didn't work. Whoever set them expected the sail to catch about ten feet lower than it did. If it had been the mainmast we would have been without sails, because as you know, once the willowisps catch they blast apart like fluff in a string wind. Lucky for us, they—whoever they are—screwed up."

"Are you sure? Why would they be after the sails?"

"Well if it's the STV idiots, they just want to stop us from making war on the poor, poor Vermin. I think we should introduce them to a survivor someday. If it's someone else, I don't know. I've heard rumors. You know the dragons suspect that the Navy has Vermin tech and plans to use it."

"How would destroying the sails…?"

"Don't ask me. There is something wrong on that ship. Fenfyr was down at that lower hatch, sniffing away. He said it smells wrong and then took off to talk to Darius. I asked for entry and was told there was no atmo. I pointed out there were plenty of Air Weavers and was told it was storage for a new weapon, poison to humans."

"So which is it?" Tristan asked.

"I have no idea." Muher set the cup down. "I heard you took Stemmer's servant."

"Yes."

"He hates you, you know, maybe not specifically, but at least in general."

"Riggan?" Tristan was confused.

"No, Stemmer. He was acquitted because the witnesses against him disappeared, but he was originally a suspect in the Stars Plot."

"That's why you're here," Tristan said.

"Yes. We need to keep you alive, and they damned near killed you last time."

"They tried to take out the whole Guild Council," Tristan said defensively.

"Right, they did, but that didn't work, and as near as we can tell, they have one target now."

"Who?"

"You."

Tristan laughed. "Why would they kill the only person that can fly their ship?"

"Because they don't need you? Remember they made the run at

Alden first. You're next. They have someone lined up to step in—or at least that's our best guess. One of my men who spends time in the less savory parts of our worlds reported that some Navy-types were looking for Rogue Weavers. Thinking about that, I heard that Alden left the Dragon Compound and disappeared. Do you think he would go Rogue?"

Tristan opened his mouth to tell Muher about his conversation with the Warrior Weaver, then stopped. The fewer people who knew what was going on, the better, in fact, he didn't see anything wrong with fanning the flames a little. "He might. He was angry when I saw him, he wouldn't be assigned to another ship for a long time."

"But he was second…"

Shrugging, Tristan straightened some papers and sighed. "He is a proud man, and his craft was everything. I can't see him trapped, unable to fly, so he might find a way to achieve that." That much was true.

"It's a pity to lose a man like that to the Rogues."

"It is, hopefully he will come to his senses and come back to the fold," Tristan said earnestly, wondering just what Alden was up to. If he was missing, he might already be working his way onto a ship. "What does Darius say about it?"

"Darius? He said 'you humans are usually annoying.' That was all I got."

"The dragons aren't always helpful."

"No. We should get back to the ship before it gets late. They plan on sending out a pressgang tonight. It would be a good excuse to make a run at you."

"Fine, give me a few minutes to finish this report and we can head back to the ship."

"Okay by me," Muher said, picking up his coffee and putting his feet on the desk.

When they left the Guild offices, Tristan could sense a different atmosphere in the crowds. Instead of the easy bustle of shoppers, now the area seemed to be full of people moving out of the area as quickly as possible. He could tell Muher was on edge, the man's hand was hovering near his sidearm as they walked through the crowds. Most of the civilians smiled and moved out of their way. A few actually stopped and thanked them for their service—a new experience for Tristan—but most seemed intent on leaving and getting out of the district.

They were halfway down the long wide boulevard when Tristan heard screams. Instinctively he turned towards them, meaning to go help, only to find himself stopped by Muher. "Don't be a fool," the general said.

Tristan nodded and kept going, trying to ignore the screams that were becoming more common the closer they got to the Naval docks. The *Winged Victory* did not need that many more crew members, so the pressgangs must be looking for crew for any of the ships that were currently in dock. A young woman was kneeling on the pavement, blood spilling over her shirt. Tristan clenched his fists in frustration. He wanted to help, but he knew that it could be a trap. He'd seen it when he was young, a member of the pressgang would be injured and then wait for a potential victim to come, by the time the victim realized it was a trap, it was too late.

"Where are you going?" a deep voice growled from the dark to their left.

"Back to our ship, back off," Muher snapped.

"Now, maybe we don't think we believe you."

"I don't care," the general said, his hand still over his as yet holstered sidearm.

"We're thinking maybe you should come along with us."

"No." Muher drew his gun, but a chain snapped out of the dark and wrapped around his wrist. Tristan heard the crunch as bones broke.

"Now," the man said, stepping from the shadows with three other men. "Let's discuss this like gentlemen."

"No," Tristan said.

"And you're going to stop us, Warrior? We aren't frightened of your kind, we've pressed a few of you, too."

"I doubt that." Tristan forced a cold smile. He would have to get that bit of information back to the Guild as soon as possible.

"It's true. We've taken them and sold them to the highest bidder more than once."

"You're slavers?" Muher said in surprise.

"Who'd you expect, that namby-pamby pressgang working the

shopping mall? No, we came after something we could sell, something of value and him…" He pointed at Tristan. "Him would bring a good price. Warriors always do."

"You made a mistake with this one," another voice said softly.

"And why is that," the slaver said, still focused on Tristan and Muher.

"Because this Warrior is my friend," the voice continued.

"I'd listen to him," Tristan said, grinning.

"Why?"

"Because," Fenfyr said, stepping into their line of sight, "I am a lot bigger than you and you look very tasty?" The slavers started backing away. "I alerted the Corps patrol, they should be… Here they are now."

Five men in Dragon Corps uniforms pulled up next to them in one of the electric cars they used for transportation on the station. Four of them go out with guns levels on the slavers. One of them headed towards Tristan and Muher with a first aid kit in his hand. He checked Muher and made sure Tristan hadn't been hurt then turned towards the slavers. "You will be coming with us."

"No." The slavers were trying to get away.

"I'll bring them," Fenfyr said happily.

"No tasting on route," Tristan said, smiling at the dragon.

"Yeah, yeah, no tasting makes it hard to torture." The dragon sighed, a huge *whuff* of grapefruit-scented air whipped around them. "I will be back on the ship as soon as I dispose of these men." The dragon's eyes were glinting. "Less than an hour."

"I'll see you then."

"We'll escort you, sirs. Just to make sure you get on the ship okay, and the general gets to sickbay safely," one of the men, wearing Master Sergeant's stripes, said. "Sorry, we heard the slavers were out, we never guessed they would come after you!"

Tristan got into the back of the transport. So, the Dragon Corps knew about the slave trade? Or was it only on this station? He needed to get a hold of the Guild and Darius again, everywhere he turned, things seemed to take a new twist. He was still deep in thought when they reached the gangway for the ship. Tristan headed up, and managed to get onboard without being piped on. He went to his cabin and Muher was taken to sickbay.

Riggan was waiting with a pot of tea. "I heard what happened, sir."

"How?"

"The only thing faster than light, sir, is gossip. Are you injured?"

"No," Tristan said, stripping off his jacket. Riggan took it and hung it in the closet. "General Muher was, they broke his wrist."

Pouring the tea, Riggan made a *tsking* noise. "They're getting bolder. They always go out on nights when the pressgangs are out, that way no one's the wiser."

"How common are they?" Tristan asked, sinking into the comfortable chair by the stern gallery door.

"More common than they once were. They 'recruit' for all kinds of people, the mines, the cargo-haulers, the pirates, sometimes even the Navy will buy one or two, depending on what they've got."

"The Navy? Surely they don't need to purchase crew with the pressgangs?"

"No, but they purchase, um, entertainment, sir."

"Oh," Tristan said. He sipped his tea. "So most people know about the practice?"

"No, I didn't say that, sir. There are officers on ships with slaves who never know that there are slaves amongst them. The slave quarters are in the parts of the ship where the officers don't go, or they are moved during inspection. The slaves are kept off the fighting decks, so when they sweep for the guns the slaves won't be discovered."

"Riggan?"

"Sir?"

"Does this ship have slaves?"

"Not yet, sir, no."

"Well, that's something." Tristan put his feet up and waited until he heard the rumble of Fenfyr on the stern gallery.

When the dragon put his head through the door Tristan sighed in relief, feeling safe for the first time all day.

XII

The decks were alive with activity when Tristan walked out onto the quarterdeck from his cabin the next morning. As Weaver, his cabin both opened to the corridor below the deck and had a set of steps that led directly to the quarterdeck. It allowed him quick access to the Elemental Interface when needed. It also allowed him to come and go quietly if he wanted to. Watching the men clean the decks, he tried to relax, they were raising the masts in less than an hour, and it was an activity that was perilous, even on tiny sailing vessels.

"Good morning, sir," Barrett said.

"Good morning, Mr. Barrett. How goes it?"

"We are on schedule for the masts, sir, and should be set to sail when you are ready this afternoon."

"Very good, Mr. Barrett." Tristan paused, considering the wisdom of what he was about to do. "I am having the Air Weavers and General Muher to dine in my cabin this evening, will you join us?"

Barrett beamed at him. "Yes, sir!"

Tristan smiled and leaned against the Interface housing. It was merely a pedestal with a number of computer inputs on it for the time being. He would connect the Elemental Interface right before the ship sailed. He could see Shearer calmly directing the men, even though he could sense a level of tension around him. The crew was worried, and judging but Riggan's morning report, even more convinced the ship was haunted than ever. After the near loss of their Weaver to slavers and a member of the crew found dead by the soldered hatch, their mutterings were becoming outright complaints. The general consensus was that the masts were going to fall through the bottom of the hull and expose them all to space so quickly that the Air Weavers couldn't save them.

"Barrett!" Stemmer stormed onto the quarterdeck, ignoring Tristan. "You need to check that mess on the mainmast crosstrees. The sails are a disaster."

The first officer cast a glance at Tristan. "Sir?"

"The sails, they are in such a state I doubt we can raise the masts at all," Stemmer said.

"What is wrong with the sails?" Tristan said, stepping forward.

The captain turned on him with a growl, and Tristan realized the man hadn't noticed him, rather than purposefully ignored him. "Your sails are a mess, Weaver."

"I'll be the judge of that," he said, walking towards the steps that led to the main deck. Some of the men paused to watch as he headed towards the main hatch to below deck. He could hear the captain berating Barrett, and everyone was pointedly ignoring them. When he reached the hatch, Shearer was there, waiting for him.

"Sir?" the boatswain asked as he walked up.

"The captain said there is an issue with the sails on the mainmast. I was going to see what was wrong."

The other man frowned. "I hadn't heard. I'll come with you." He swung open the hatch and led the way to the lift. "I heard about the attack last night, sir. We never expected that slavers would come after you and the general."

"You know about them?"

"If you are around the stations long enough, you hear about them. I've been sailing for years. It was five years before I heard about them. They do fly under cover a lot of the time." The lift doors opened. "Have you been in the lower decks before?"

"No." Tristan opened his mouth to elaborate, but changed his mind.

The corridor was lit with bright industrial lights, quite different from the decks that housed the crew. Tristan could hear the sounds of work going on all around them, the clank of metal on metal, voices raised in song and others shouting orders. Unlike the upper decks, these decks had the massive masts, crosstrees and sails barring their way. Shearer led Tristan on a walkway over the crosstrees for the mizenmast, as they crossed Tristan looked down towards the bottom of the ship. He could see the soft sparkles of the willowisps reflecting on something—then realized he was seeing the shine of a dragon. Stopping for a minute, he bent to get a better look. Two dragons. He recognized Fenfyr, with him was a dragon that shone a soft red in the light of the sails.

They stepped back on the deck and made their way further down the corridor, finally stopping at the massive mainmast. Even though they were nearer the topgallants than the mainsail, the mast towered above them. Tristan immediately looked over the exposed sails, still tied to the masts like giant glowing worms. He let his eyes travel over them, checking them. He could hear Shearer speaking to someone to his left. Without thinking, he stepped forward and looked down into the depths of the ship, trying to see if there was something wrong with the sails further down. As he bent over the edge he felt a hand grab his ankle, yanking his foot out from under him. It was only his surprised shout and Shearer's speed that saved him from a fatal fall.

"Are you okay, sir?" the boatswain asked, concerned.

"Yes."

"What happened?"

"Someone grabbed my ankle."

Shearer growled. "Not on my ship they won't." He headed towards the edge where Tristan had been and swung down over the opening with the ease of a circus performer. Tristan walked back over and, staying back from the edge, tried to see what was happening. He could just make out the boatswain on the rigging of the mainsail. There was another figure ahead of him, but as Shearer got closer the man let go of the ropes and dropped, bouncing off rigging and masts as he fell. The *thud* when he hit bottom was barely audible.

Tristan took a moment to look over the sails, all the while aware of Shearer swinging back up through the rigging. There was nothing wrong with the sails, they were sparkling gently with their golden glow, waiting for their release. It was then that it hit Tristan— there had never been anything wrong with the sails. It had been a set up. But who and why? Stemmer had ordered Barrett below, and Tristan had gone instead. Traditionally, the captain would have checked the sails first. So—who was meant to be standing there?

Without a word, he and Shearer headed back to the lift. "I couldn't see who it was. Not that I know all the men by sight. Especially if he was one of the new crew."

"This is not your fault, Shearer."

"This is my ship, my men and I am more than a little annoyed that one of them tried to kill our Weaver," the man growled. "You know how long I have worked to serve on a ship like this? This is unacceptable. I am just going to settle this now." He got off the lift at deck ten. "I will see you for the raising."

Tristan nodded and leaned against the wall of the lift as it traveled up to the top deck. It had been close, and he didn't like that feeling. The question of why kept bouncing around in his mind, but since the "who" was an unanswered question, the "why" wouldn't be answered anytime soon. The lift slowed and he stood, straightening his jacket and stepping out of the lift when the doors opened. The corridor was empty, the soft lights of the crew decks a contrast to the lights below. He decided to stop by his cabin and return to the quarterdeck via his private staircase.

He closed the door to his cabin and walked to his desk, turning on the secure line to the Guild Master. Rhoads was in his office when he called and Tristan related the latest incident. Brian muttered something about security, then signed off without another word. Tristan hoped he wasn't going to be saddled with more security traipsing around behind him.

Once that was done, he headed back up on deck. It was time to raise the masts. As much of the crew as possible was crowded on the decks. The quarterdeck was crammed with all the officers. Tristan stood by the Interface, watching as the last of the crew jockeyed for positions to watch the raising. Fenfyr had appeared and was sitting on the stern gallery with his head over the taffrail.

"Prepare to raise the masts!" Stemmer called.

"Prepare to raise the masts!" Shearer repeated.

"Masts at the ready!" a call came from in the decks.

"Masts at the ready!" Shearer said.

"Raise the masts!" the captain ordered.

"Raise the masts!" Shearer said.

The massive plates rolled slowly open again, and the first tip of the main topgallant mast came into view. Tristan had the impression that the entire crew drew in a breath. The fore topgallant mast eased up, and as the main topmast came up the mizzenmast began to rise from the depths of the ship. They continued slowly up, like massive trees rising around them, towering over their heads until finally with a huge *boom* that rocked the entire ship, the great masts locked into place.

It was silent for a long moment, then the crew let out the breath they had been holding in a collective cheer.

The bells were chiming the change of the watch when Tristan stepped off the gangway into the shipyards where Fenfyr was waiting for him. He smiled up at the dragon, then stopped in shock when he noticed Brian Rhoads and Darius standing there as well. "What's going on?"

"We decided the ship needed a proper send off, since they were trying to sneak it out of port on us," Rhoads said.

"Yes, Tristan Weaver, it is true. We have gathered loyal vessels and all the dragons in the area to give you a proper launching. There will even be fireworks," Darius added.

Tristan's stomach lurched. "Oh?"

"It is a wise thing, Tristan, the more people who know, the better," Rhoads said. "The more public this event, the better."

Tristan couldn't disagree with the logic, he only wished they'd warned him. He was nervous enough about this as it was. "Sounds fun."

"It will be," Brian said, looking a little disappointed that the docks didn't have good enough acoustics to give his voice the boost he liked. "About the attacks…"

"We are concerned," Darius finished.

"I'm not even sure who was supposed to be the victim. Stemmer should have been down there, he told Barrett to go, and I volunteered. If the man hadn't committed suicide I wouldn't even have thought it was an attack, more a mistake."

"But he did, and when he hit the deck, he smelled odd," Fenfyr said. "Taminick could smell it as well."

"That was Taminick?" Tristan asked. He'd only met the other dragon twice before, she generally served in deep space, hunting Rogue ships or Vermin. She had lost her siblings to a Vermin attack and was right on the edge of being a renegade.

"Yes, she came to smell. She said there is something wrong, too, she can tell. They have done something so we can't tell what it is, but there is a wrong smell there."

"Wrong how?" Rhoads asked.

"Wrong, I can't explain it to a numb nose," Fenfyr grumbled. Tristan hid a smile.

"But it is wrong?" Darius looked at Fenfyr.

"Very. We want to know why it is sealed down there. Taminick almost tore the door off, then we realized—it is booby-trapped."

"What?" General Muher said from behind Tristan. "Booby-trapped?"

"Damn, Chris, you walk like a cat, scare a man to death," Brian said.

"Yes, booby-trapped, if we had tried to open it, we would have been hurt if not killed, there are anti-personnel and anti-dragon traps on it."

"Which means we need to get in there," Muher said, frowning. "Once we are in space, we will get on that."

"We who?" Tristan asked.

"Some Dragon Corps members were accidently pressed the other day," Muher laughed.

"Accidently?"

"Okay, planted," the general said, grinning. "But we have Corps on board as well as the Marines. Hall is a bit of an ass, but loyal."

Tristan leaned against Fenfyr, feeling overwhelmed. It felt like it was all getting out of control. Fen made a soft thrumming noise— the dragon equivalent of a purr—and Tristan relaxed a little. "Okay, how many ships and dragons are going to be here?"

"Just don't hit anyone and you will be fine," Rhoads said.

"Oh." Tristan sighed. "I am going to get a few things at the shops before we sail."

"Oddly enough, so am I," Muher said.

"We'll be waiting," Fenfyr said, stretching out on the docks.

"I don't need a babysitter," Tristan said to Muher as they walked into the shopping district.

"No, I don't think you do out here during the day, I actually want a few things to take with me. When I got shipped out to join *Victory,* I didn't really have much time to get luxuries for a long deep-space cruise, and I would like a few things to keep me from going insane." As he spoke, he was absently rubbing his arm. Even though the break was easily healed by the tissue-binders, Tristan knew it would ache for a few days after. His left leg had been broken in the blast that leveled the Council Chambers in the Stars Plot attack and even now ached, along with the scar on his back.

As they made their way through the shops, it became clear that Muher had been telling the truth. Even if he was also keeping an eye on Tristan, his main objective seemed to be getting things to take with him on the ship. In two hours the man had collected enough stuff to require a porter to take it back to the ship. He tipped the man and grinned at Tristan. "Told you."

"I'm impressed," Tristan said wryly. "I don't feel bad at all."

"I am used to a certain lifestyle, I know I can't always maintain it, I do have to go out in the field now and then, but that doesn't mean if I have the chance to take luxury with me I'll pass it up."

"You don't have to defend yourself to me." Tristan laughed.

When they reached the docks, Fenfyr was still stretched out, his eyes turned towards the corridor that led into the shopping district. He raised his head when Tristan and Muher walked out. The dragon stood and stretched, then fluffed his feathers before heading to the Dragon's Portal. "I'll see you for the sailing." He gently touched Tristan with his head tufts, then hopped up through the portal.

"Almost time," Muher said.

"Yeah," Tristan said, swallowing nervously.

The ship was set to sail at eight bells in the afternoon watch. The crew was assembled on the ship, ready to lower the sails. Tristan stepped out on the quarterdeck and slipped the Elemental Interface into its pedestal. The lights hummed to life and when he laid his hand on it, he could feel the power of the sails connecting to the Interface.

The hiss of the atmospherics was all around him as the dome's massive metal shields dropped and the *Winged Victory* was free to her first gentle touch of the stars. Tristan stood on the quarterdeck as the call went out to the ships gathered around them and the escort moved away from Terra Secundus, smaller ships and dragons winging ahead and around them. With a soft sound the engines began to hum and the ship came to life. *Winged Victory* edged away from the dock, the propulsion system pushing it slowly forward, moving them towards the vast expanse in front of them. Fireworks exploded overhead, their bright sparks blending with the stars around them, the lights slowly dying as the ship slipped further away.

Tristan was aware of the activity around him, the crew moving up into the spider webs of rigging over his head as they prepared to drop the sails for the first time, the officers watching them nervously, wondering if the magic was right and the massive sails would fly—If the dream of *Winged Victory* would become a graceful reality. Tristan held his breath, not wanting to show the uneasiness that was thrumming though his body. If the sails refused to catch the Winds—then what?

A soft rustle of sound shimmered down from high up in the masts. Glancing up, he saw Fenfyr settle onto his place in the tops of the mainmast, his great silver, ebony and pearl wings canted to catch the first whisper of the Winds. His head was up, tasting the air as he, too, waited for the moment.

"Loose the sails!" the captain ordered.

First the royals, then the topgallants dropped into place, the first small puff of the Winds fluttering through them, making the willowisps sparkle. Tristan stood transfixed for a moment as the sails glittered with soft waves of light, the glow reflecting on the faces of the crew hundreds of feet above him. Knowing the moment was quickly approaching, he concentrated and focused, placing both hands on the Elemental Interface, the black stone warm in the center of the silver wood. He softly recited the first of the spell and felt the answering hush in the sails as they readied themselves for their first flight.

"Loose the mainsail," the captain called and the sail rolled into place, slack, the tiny movements lost in the vast expanse of the mainsail.

"Ship to the Weaver!" the captain snapped.

"Ship to the Weaver!" The order echoed down the decks and slithered up the masts to whisper there for a moment before Fenfyr's confident "Ship to the Weaver!" dropped back down to settle on the quarterdeck.

"The ship is yours, sir," Barrett said.

"Thank you, Mr. Barrett," Tristan said crisply.

"Weaver has the ship!"

Tristan closed his eyes and began the final part of the spell, the words building around him. The Interface began to tremble under his hand as it focused the magic and guided it outwards. He felt the whisper of the Winds now, their breath pressing against him as he reached out and let the magic go. He knew the instant the sails caught, the great boom of the massive mainsail snapping into place resonating through him. The rigging was beginning to sing as the Winds found them, the pitch changing as the Winds increased until the sails filled with them and the huge ship began to pick up speed, the mainsail taut as the ship wheeled and slid into the center of the channel leaving Terra Secundus far behind them in seconds.

XIII

There was a soft hum in the rigging as the ship wheeled through space, the tone like a baritone singing softly in the distance. The sails were sparkling as the willowisps moved through the Weaving, a continual movement to catch each tiny whisper of the Winds to use them to their best advantage. After the exit from space dock, most of the sails had been furled, the Winds were heavy between Saturn and the outer planets and only the large sails were in use. Further out they would need the topgallants and perhaps even the royals, but for now Tristan could retire to his quarters and take a break. He would be required on deck to check the sails again at the changing of the watch, but all was well at this point and he was ready to sit down.

The ship had pulled away from Terra Secundus a full watch—four hours—before, and Tristan had stayed on deck as they had adjusted the sails to suit the ship. He made sure as each set of smaller sails were furled they were tucked in correctly, so they could wait patiently until they were needed. That was his excuse at least. He was caught up in the excitement of the sailing of *Winged Victory.* The escorting ships had peeled away about an hour after launch, but even now a few of the dragons circled the *Victory,* swinging around her in playful arcs. Tristan could see Fenfyr and Taminick, as well as a few dragons he didn't know by name. The group with Fenfyr, though playful, seemed to have more purpose than the other dragons, and they swept closer to the hull on their passes than the others. He meant to ask Fenfyr about it later, but for now, he needed to get ready for dinner. He'd invited the Air Weavers and several of the officers and wanted to make sure everything was ready.

"Riggan?" he said as he entered the cabin—then stopped dead, the table was set in the center of the room, silver and crystal shining in the soft lighting.

"Sir?" Riggan appeared from behind him.

"I was about to tell you that we needed to get ready for dinner."

"Way ahead of you, sir," the man said with a grin. "It was the Air Weavers, Mr. Barrett, General Muher, Colonel Hall and Mr. Aubrey, yes?"

"Yes." Tristan grinned. "I shouldn't have worried." He sighed and dropped into one of the comfortable chairs by the stern gallery windows.

"The ship is sailing well, sir," Riggan said, bringing him a cup of tea. "They're saying below decks, you've lifted the curse that was following us. Some say at least, others aren't as sure, but they said they would be willing to wait and give it a chance before deciding."

"Kind of them," Tristan replied with a wry smile.

"They've noticed the dragons and wonder what's going on."

"What do you mean?"

"Well, sir, usually dragons don't fly with a ship this long, they head back to their own ships or business as soon as they can. No one is sure why they are with us so long."

Tristan eyed the man seriously. "*Winged Victory* is a special ship, maybe that's why? The biggest yet?"

"That could be it, no one was expecting Darius to come to the launching, and there he was, flying alongside us! I can tell you, that set a few tongues wagging."

"He was flying with us?" Tristan asked, he was surprised, he knew the dragon had been there for the launch, but he hadn't expected him to fly with the ship. "I didn't see him once we were moving."

"You were a little preoccupied, sir, it was to be expected," Riggan laughed. "I saw him, though. I remember him from the *Jupiter* Incursion. A fierce fighter. They are such wonderful creatures, then when you see them fight—I just can't describe it! It's amazing. When I was a lad, on one of my first voyages, we ran across some pirates which were using a Vermin ship—horrible, I have no idea how humans could do that, but they did—and the dragon swept in, killed the ship humanely, then tore it apart with her claws, including the humans that were stupid enough to still be on board. I think they all should have died, for a crime like that, but those that got off the ship were sentenced to hard labor in the Mines." Riggan shook his head. "Horrible things, those Vermin ships, sir. The dragon, she found the Rogue Weaver and, well, he met an unfortunate end as her dinner, I believe, and more power to her is all I have to say." He refilled Tristan's cup. "Ever since then, I wait for them to come, to watch them end those poor ships' anguish and then destroy those that fly them. I think the humans that use Vermin ships are worse than the Vermin themselves, humans doing that. And that's all I have to say about it."

Tristan grinned. "Oh?"

"Yes, sir, I do. I won't say more, but the Weavers that fly for the pirates are no better than pirates and Vermin themselves." He refreshed Tristan's cup again, then smiled. "Dinner is in fifteen minutes if you wish to change, sir."

Pushing himself out of the chair, Tristan went into his bedchamber and changed into his formal uniform, carefully tying the cravat then running a finger under it to relieve the sense of being choked. After a quick check in the mirror, he went back into the main room. Riggan was waiting by the door, in his formal uniform as well. Tristan noticed that he had the bar and dragons that indicated he was in service to the Guild pinned proudly to his uniform.

At the soft tap on the door, Riggan opened it. "Mr. Barrett, First Officer, sir," he announced formally.

"Thank you, Riggan," Tristan said, hiding a smile as he stepped forward and shook the officer's hand. "Everything set topside?"

"When I left it was, the captain is still pacing, but he usually does until he turns in," Barrett replied, grinning. The fact the captain had not been invited had spread through the ship like wildfire.

"The Air Weavers, Theresa, Sullivan, Sheea and West Aether," Riggan said.

Tristan ushered them into the room and over to the sideboard where a bottle of wine was waiting. It was from his private reserve, and until he'd discovered that Barrett's family were vintners he'd been rather proud of his selections. Now he waited anxiously as the first officer went through the ritual of tasting the wine. Tristan let out the breath he was holding when Barrett smiled. Muher, Aubrey and Hall arrived together soon after and they all sat down as Riggan and the other servants served the first course.

As Tristan watched the servants, he marveled at Riggan. The man had arranged the entire thing with no more than a word from him—just the information he was having the Air Weavers and several officers to dinner, and the man had produced this. No discussion of menu, or even of other servants to keep the glasses full and the food coming and going from the galley. He was beginning to realize that Riggan was worth far more than he'd assumed.

"Guild and Dragon," Tristan raised his glass in the traditional toast; even though there were Naval officers present, it was his table.

"Guild and Dragon," the others replied.

"How are you?" he asked Theresa as they set the cups down.

"I'm doing much better, Master Tristan, thank you. I was on deck for the launch." She laughed, a bright and happy sound like tiny bells. "Of course, I would have dragged myself up there if I had been on my death bed."

"It was something to see!" Hall agreed. "I've been on many ships, but there is something about that mainmast, it's so massive it takes my breath away every time I see it."

"We try and prevent that!" West said with a laugh.

"Touché, Aether," Hall said, laughing. "Still, it was a magnificent launch. Do you know why the dragons are still with us?" This was directed to Muher.

"No, they haven't informed me. I expected most of them to turn back hours ago. Of course, Fenfyr is flying with us, but the others, I am surprised about myself," the general said.

Tristan looked at the man, wondering if he was lying. The Dragon Corps was there for many reasons, and he suspected at least one of them had to do with why Taminick was still flying with them.

"No shop talk," Aubrey said, taking another drink. "Once we clear the system, we won't have nearly enough time for long dinners, we should relax and enjoy."

"You're right," Barrett agreed readily.

The talk turned from the ship to events on Earth. With the exception of Barrett, the officers and Air Weavers had been isolated for several months, and Muher spent fifteen minutes bringing them up-to-date on the latest sports scores. Barrett was an avid lacrosse and curling fan, and Tristan listened in growing amazement as Muher and Barrett discussed the curling championships. He'd watched the game several times and had no idea it was so intricate or required quite as much skill as it seemed to. Aubrey and Hall shared Barrett's love of lacrosse, and so for half an hour the table was filled with sports talk. After that it turned to the latest movement to expand the Dragon Sanctuaries. There was a brief lull as the main dish was served, then they started chatting again.

It was while dessert was being served that Fenfyr decided to make his grand entrance. A tiny tap on the stern gallery door, Riggan paused as the air pressure was balanced by the Air Weavers on deck and answered the door. "Lokey Fenfyr of the Guild Dragons." Fenfyr stuck his head in and grinned at them all. There was a soft *whoosh* as he adjusted to the atmosphere. "Can I get you a grapefruit, sir? I put some by this afternoon."

Fenfyr huffed happily as Riggan brought him the fruit. Tristan sighed, he would have to talk to the dragon about dramatic entrances. Poor Aubrey looked like he was ready to faint, and Hall was pale as well. Without a word Fenfyr munched on a grapefruit, looking at the table expectantly.

"Did you have a good launching, sir?" Barrett ventured after a moment of silence increasingly filled with the scent of grapefruit.

Fenfyr made a happy sound and nodded. "We enjoyed it," he said.

"Good gad!" Aubrey exclaimed and went another shade paler, then blushed. "Sorry, sirs, I've never been to dinner with a dragon, sir."

"You'll have to excuse his table manners," Tristan said with a laugh.

"Tables," Fenfyr huffed in derision.

There was another moment of silence, then Riggan brought out the dessert wine and Barrett started chatting about his family's vineyard. Tristan knew Fenfyr was looking over the officers and Air Weavers, and he had a feeling the dragon was looking forward to giving him a full report of the launch, knowing that Tristan had been caught up in the spell and unaware of a lot of the action. After they had finished dessert, the others lingered for another glass of wine, but then Hall and Aubrey left, followed by Muher and the Air Weavers. Tristan found himself alone at the table with Barrett.

"Another glass?" he asked the officer.

"Thank you, Master Tristan." Barrett held his glass out.

Tristan poured. "Tristan," he said, offering the informality.

"Thom," Barrett replied with a smile.

"Fenfyr," the dragon said with a chuckle, his head tufts quivering happily. "We've been busy."

"What?" Tristan asked.

"Taminick and I, we've been checking things, and there is something wrong. We just can't be sure what. The other dragons could sense it. She said she will be coming in close to look again, and expects to be let onboard when she asks. Apparently, she was refused," the dragon said, the horror in his voice only partially feigned.

"What's going on?" Thom asked.

"We don't know, that's the thing," Fenfyr answered.

"The dragons and Guild have received unsettling intelligence about the ship."

"What?!? *My ship?!?* What have they done?" the first officer demanded, his face turning red.

"We're not sure. We are still checking," Fenfyr said. "But there is something up, and it stinks like day-old fish."

"Whatever help you need, let me know. How dare they touch my ship!"

"Your ship?" the dragon asked.

"Thom designed her," Tristan said.

"Ah, do you know what the bottom deck is? And why the hatch is soldered shut?" Fenfyr asked.

"No, I had nothing to do with it. I was told it was designed for cargo and extra supplies. I have no idea why it's soldered closed. I asked Stemmer and he said it wasn't in use for this flight and they were just cutting off the need for atmo on that level. It's a good excuse, I just don't buy it."

"Neither do we. Taminick is quite anxious to get in there."

"Who is Taminick?" Thom asked, looking from Fenfyr to Tristan.

"She's the red dragon that's been flying with Fenfyr. She's with… with the dragon equivalent of the intelligence service."

"Black ops," Fenfyr said. "You never even saw her." He burst out laughing, blasting them both with grapefruit-scented breath. "Seriously, though, she is one of our top intelligence agents, and a bit of a wild one, she specializes in finding and killing Vermin technology."

"You think they…?" Thom broke off in horror.

"We're not sure of anything at this point," the dragon said. "In fact, we hope it's not true."

"You really know how to ruin dinner," Tristan said with a sigh.

"Not ruined, pour me another glass of wine," Thom said with a laugh, glancing around the cabin. "You play backgammon?"

"What?" Tristan turned, his backgammon board was sitting on a small table between two chairs. When Riggan said he was going to unpack, he must have set it up. "Yes, although it's hard to find people who want to play. It's not as exciting as most games."

"Well, consider yourself challenged!" Barrett picked up his glass and walked over to the table. "Shall we wager?"

"Of course," Tristan said innocently. Fenfyr snorted.

At the change of the watch, Tristan and Thom walked onto deck. Tristan immediately checked the trim of the sails, watching the willowisps. He walked over and laid his hand on the Elemental Interface and whispered a soft spell, checking that the sails were functioning correctly. For an instant he thought he caught an undercurrent of something else, like the sludge of willowisps past their prime—*No,* he said to himself, *it felt different.* Chocking up the feeling to the remnants of the conversation at dinner, Tristan shrugged the feeling off. Even so, he checked the Interface again. "All's well with the sails, Mr. Barrett."

"Thank you, Master Weaver," Barrett replied formally. "Master of the Watch, report."

While the officer made his report, Tristan took a moment to wander onto the deck. Most of the crew smiled at him as he walked past, but there were a few that turned away, and one or two fixed him with a hostile glance. Ignoring them, he proceeded to the bow and stepped up on the bowsprit. There was a feeling of freedom here. He stayed near the deck, close enough so he was still safely onboard ship, not out at the end hanging in open space, but it was still exhilarating. Out of the corner of his eye, he caught stealthy movement against the hull. Without turning his head, he tried to see what was there, and spotted the very tip of a red dragon tail.

After several minutes he stepped back down on deck. The long day was finally starting to catch up with him. He would need to be back on deck at eight bells in the morning watch and it was already well into the night watch. As he turned, he thought he saw someone move quickly away, as if he had startled them. Shaking off the feeling, and blaming it on lack of sleep and the various conversations he'd had lately, he walked across the deck.

"I think it best I turn in, Mr. Barrett, call me if anything is needed."

"Of course, sir, I have this watch and will keep you informed."

Tristan stepped down the stairs to his cabin, the table was gone, the silver and crystal stored away. Fenfyr was still in the middle of the room, his head through one of the stern gallery doors and his tail through another. "Do you like your cabin?" Tristan asked with a laugh.

"It could be bigger," the dragon complained.

"There is a dragon's roost."

"Ah, yes, but I can't keep my eye on you from there. My presence will discourage people from disturbing your sleep." Fenfyr looked at him. "And I think they might try."

"Thank you." On that unsettling thought, Tristan turned to his bedchamber and closed the door, listening to the hum of the Winds in the rigging until he fell asleep.

XIV

Four bells chimed, the sound running through the ship. Tristan rolled over and looked at the ceiling of his bedchamber. They'd left the outer system two days before, the ship was sailing towards Terra Triovingensimus. They were planning on docking for a day before pushing out further towards the Rim. He was still having trouble getting used to deep-space sailing. There were no planets hanging over their heads as the ship sailed on. He'd been on deck in the graveyard watch to help set the topgallants when the Winds had inexplicably dropped. Tristan had asked Thom about it, and the first officer was stumped, they should still be sailing in heavy Winds. The Doldrums were further out towards the Rim.

He could hear Riggan moving around in the cabin. The man was proving invaluable and kept Tristan up-to-date on the ship's gossip. Some of it he passed along to Barrett, some he kept to himself—it was still Guild business. There seemed to be a growing movement among the recently pressed men against the Guild. Riggan had circumspectly set enquiries in motion, but so far he had come back with nothing. Since it seemed confined primarily to the last group of pressed men, Tristan and Muher were becoming convinced it had been a purposeful move on someone's part. The problem was they had no idea who it could be.

The Dragon Corps general had stopped by Tristan's office—a room off the main cabin—and told him about a few small accidents that looked like they could have been sabotage. Nothing big, little things here and there—enough to keep the superstitious members of the crew on edge, but not enough to do real damage. Taminick continued to fly with them, although most of the crew was unaware of her presence now. Tristan knew she was still with them because Fenfyr told him—the two dragons were trying to figure out a way into the blocked-off bottom deck. All-in-all they agreed there was something not quite right, and Muher and Hall had decided to leave some of the more questionable pressed men behind at the station.

Rolling out of bed, Tristan did his yoga, put on his uniform and walked into the main cabin. Fenfyr was gone on his morning patrols—whatever that entailed. Riggan had the coffee service sitting next to one of the chairs in the main room. "Morning, Riggan."

"Good morning, sir, I thought you might want coffee in the main room this morning since you have no meetings until later."

"Thank you," Tristan said, dropping into the chair.

"There's talk, sir."

"Oh?" Tristan waited while Riggan poured coffee.

"Someone said they saw someone sneaking into that hatchway, then soldering it up again. They said they saw them breaking the seal themselves. Of course, they couldn't tell who it was because they were set up in a suit, there's no air on that deck, but they said they saw it all the same. It could be true, I'm not sure. They're saying it's where they keep the bodies of the dead men by order of the Guild. I told them that was crazy talk, sir, like the Guild would have anything to do with that."

"No, we would never do something like that."

"I know, that's what I said, and some got agitated, like, and kept on about it. I didn't want to say too much, so as they'd keep talking in front of me, but there's some crazy talk in the lower decks. I'm not saying there are those that are encouraging it, but the whispers are all coming from the same direction, that's all I'm saying."

"The new pressed men?"

"Aye, they seem to be the source, and I'm not saying they hate the Guild or Dragon, but the things they say, sir, would make Master Fenfyr's feathers stand on end!" A soft tap on the door stopped

Riggan. "That'd be Mr. Barrett." He walked to the door to let the first officer in.

Since the dinner in his cabin, Tristan and Barrett had begun to play backgammon on a regular basis, and as the officer was on watch when Tristan was getting up, he usually came down for a cup of coffee. "Good morning, Riggan," Thom said as he walked in.

"Morning, sir, coffee is waiting."

"Thank you, Riggan," Thom said and walked over, sitting down across from Tristan. "Something's off."

"What?"

"I'm not sure, I've checked and rechecked, but if I didn't know better—or at least if the nav computers weren't telling me—I would be sure we were off course."

"What do you mean?" Tristan asked curiously, aware Riggan was listening in the background.

"The Winds aren't right for this part of space, but I've run diagnostics twice. The thing is, I can't shake the feeling something is wrong."

"Chris Muher thinks so too, although he hasn't mentioned our course, that's not his domain. I can ask Fenfyr to fly further out and check?"

"That might help, have you ever had that feeling that something is just wrong?"

"Once."

"When?" Thom asked curiously.

"The day I walked into the council chambers when the Stars Plot came to light with a bang. I'd had a bad feeling all day, just couldn't shake it. I guess that's why I was on guard more than the others. Not many survived."

"You were there, Tristan?" The officer looked sheepish. "Of course you were. You are the Master Weaver of the Guild. I do tend to forget out here, but back home you outrank me by more than a little."

"I forget it out here, too, Thom, if that helps. I'm only the Warrior Weaver for *Winged Victory* for the most part. I would only ever use my rank if I had to, and even as Warrior I outrank the captain, so it shouldn't be a problem."

Thom nodded and took a sip of coffee. "I saw Taminick earlier.

Well, more to the point I saw the tip of a red tail earlier. She's still with us."

"Yes, and with everything that's going on, I think she will be with us for the duration of this cruise, at least until they figure out what's going on."

"I'd like to know as..." Thom broke off when a huge *boom* rocked the ship. He and Tristan were on their feet as the call to quarters rang through the ship. They ran onto the quarterdeck. "Report, Mr. Aubrey!" Thom demanded.

"Pirates, sir, four ships."

"I'm at the sails," Tristan said, laying his hand on the Elemental Interface, getting ready to move the ship into her first battle.

"We're at battle ready, sir!" Sullivan Aether said, running onto the quarterdeck. The Air Weavers maintained the shields around the upper, open deck while the ship was in flight, deflecting space debris and other physical hazards. They maintained it as long as possible during a fight. Although they could only do so much against the shot from the cannons of the four ships lining up to fire at them, they could at least maintain the atmosphere. Once the ships began firing, the "shielding" would drop as the Air Weavers focused to keep the atmosphere on the open deck and masts.

"Make sure you have guards on the Air Weavers." Barrett said to the Marine stationed on the quarterdeck, then turned to Aubrey. "Where did they come from?"

"Out of nowhere it seems, sir. They got in close before we spotted them, the proximity alarms were off," Aubrey replied.

"Damn! Bring her around." Barrett was the calm officer now. "Where's the captain?"

"I don't know, sir, surely he heard the call."

"Guns are at the ready!" Third Officer Fuhrman's voice called over the ship-wide system. "Ready to return fire!"

"Bring us around," Barrett snapped.

Men scrambled up the masts and Tristan focused on the sails, swinging them with the ship, keeping the willowisps in tight battle formation. Even though he was concentrating on the sails, Tristan caught a glimpse of the four ships. Three were hijacked Naval vessels, but one bore the blackened sails of a former Vermin vessel.

"Target the Vermin ship!" Barrett called.

The *Victory's* guns fired, sending projectiles across the void and rocking the ship with the blast. Tristan fought to keep the sails in line as the pirates retuned fire. Another round from the *Victory* took out one of the smaller vessels but the former Vermin ship was still there, its filthy sails mocking them as it swung slowly around to hit them with a full broadside.

"Target that ship!" Thom shouted. "What's going on down there?" he demanded.

"We're having an issue with some of the guns, sir," Shearer's voice came up over the intercom. "They aren't firing."

"Get them firing!"

"Working on it, sir."

"Incoming!" someone on deck shouted. "It's going to breach the shields!"

Tristan heard the call but was focused on keeping the sails in fighting trim. He didn't register the words until he was knocked to the ground by Barrett an instant before the rattle of shot rolled over their heads, whipping through the air with a whistling sound. The hard projectiles tore up the deck around them and blasted apart like small bombs on impact. The pirates were using a combination load—utilizing both energy rounds and hard shot to do the most damage. What the metal didn't destroy, the blast of energy often did. The rounds had been outlawed during the last years of the Third World War and the Navy stuck to that prohibition even against the Vermin.

"Are you okay?" Thom demanded, standing up and looking across the deck. "Med teams topside!" he called into the intership system. "Tristan?"

"Yeah, I'm okay, sorry," Tristan said. He stood and swallowed hard as he saw the damage on deck to both the ship and the men that had been there. Medical teams appeared a moment later and he was back at the Elemental Interface, bringing the willowisps back into line and beginning the spell to fix a massive hole in the mainsail. He had to turn all his concentration to the spell. The willowisps had been injured and needed to be Healed before he could Weave them into place again.

The battle raged on, he could hear the shouts of the men and Barrett's calm orders. After what seemed a lifetime, a harsh voice took over. Some part of Tristan identified it as the captain. Another broadside shook the ship, the former Vermin vessel was bringing her guns to bear when suddenly some of the crew started cheering. Tristan broke his concentration enough to look up and see Fenfyr and Taminick enter the battle, focusing their attack on the Vermin ship. The smaller pirate ships turned and headed away, putting as much distance as they could between themselves and the *Winged Victory.*

"Concentrate all guns on that ship!"

The *Victory's* guns fired, then Fenfyr and Taminick descended on the former Vermin ship. Tristan uttered a soft spell of release as Fenfyr swept in to release the ship. They killed it as the enslaved dragon was released. Fenfyr and Taminick didn't give the pirates on the ship the chance to escape. They tore it to shreds, yanking it apart as the *Victory* continued to fire into it.

"That's done it!" Barrett said, and a cheer went up.

Tristan was still focused on fixing the damage to the sails. He looked up and noticed blood on the first officer's face, right before the man collapsed. Aubrey was shouting for a medical team. Tristan turned his attention away, he had to fix the sails before anything else, and Weaving battle-damaged sails was a chore he hadn't expected to ever do. He knew how, of course, but theory and practice in the calm didn't really compare to a ship with wounded screaming and the air hissing around him as the Air Weavers struggled to keep the ship's atmosphere in place until the hull could be repaired.

As Tristan finally finished the Weaving and stepped back, he knew, without a doubt, that Thom had been right. They *had* been off course—and headed right into a trap.

Sometime later Riggan appeared and grabbed Tristan's arm. "Sir! The sails are okay, you need care!"

"What?" Tristan asked, blinking.

"Your face is covered with blood, I'm taking you down to sickbay right now, sir."

"Blood?" Tristan reached up and felt the sticky stuff near his hairline, wondering when it had happened.

"Yes, sir, blood, sir."

"Riggan! Get over here!" Stemmer shouted.

"Sorry, sir, I have to take care of the Weaver, sir," Riggan said with a smile. "Now come along, Master Tristan." He tugged Tristan away from the Elemental Interface towards a lift. Stemmer shouted at Riggan again as the lift doors closed. "He's still not used to my being your servant." Riggan laughed under his breath. "Not that I'm saying anything about it, you know."

"Of course," Tristan answered, suddenly feeling weary. "I just need to rest, Riggan, Weaving is hard work."

"You need to get that wound seen to, then you can rest, and if anyone wishes to disturb you, well, they can discuss that with Master Fenfyr. I think he is in a rather bad mood."

"He's okay?" Tristan realized that he hadn't seen the dragon since he and Taminick killed the Vermin ship—but his concentration had been elsewhere.

"Yes, sir, he is patrolling while Mr. Aubrey gets us back on our proper course."

"And Thom?"

"He's still in sickbay, so you can visit him while they patch you up, sir."

Tristan nodded and let himself be pulled out of the lift and along the corridor towards sickbay. There was more activity than there had been the first time he'd been in sickbay. As soon as they walked in, he realized the beds were all filled with injured men and women. The medical staff moved between the beds efficiently, somewhere someone was screaming.

"The Weaver is injured," Riggan said to the ward at large.

A moment later Rose Webber appeared. "How badly?" she asked, taking Tristan's arm and gently guiding him to a bed at the back of the ward. "When did this happen?"

"I'm not sure, I was focused on the sails."

"This won't take long to fix, I just need to make sure your skull is intact." She stepped away, returning a moment later with a scanner in her hand. She carefully scanned him, then smiled. "It's only a flesh wound, sir, I'll fix that and you can go to your cabin *to get some rest.* Do you understand me?"

"Yes, Dr. Webber," Tristan said with a smile. "How is Mr. Barrett?"

"You can check on him on the way out. I'm keeping him here for another couple of hours, and he is to be on light duty for the next three days," she said as she used a dermo-repair kit to fix the tear in

Tristan's scalp. There was a slight tingling sensation as the skin was mended. "There you go. Now, go rest."

"Thank you." He smiled. There was something very solid and comforting in the matter-of-fact way the doctor ran the sickbay. He also knew that for Thom to still be there, he must have been seriously injured, but her calm demeanor helped ease his worry. Getting up, he walked to the curtained bed she pointed at, and opened the curtain. "How do you feel?"

"Like half the deck hit me," Barrett said with a soft laugh. "Which I guess it did." He looked terrible, deep bruising that not even the medical staff could completely treat marred his face and upper body. "I got to keep my leg, which is a plus."

"Always a plus," Tristan replied, trying not to let worry creep into his voice.

"We were off course?" Barrett asked.

"Yes, Aubrey has been working on it for the last..." Tristan had no idea how long it had been since the battle.

"Two hours, sir," Riggan supplied. "I'm not saying anything, but I heard that he said the nav computer had been fed completely new data. He has no idea how it happened—or why the proximity alarms weren't working. Mr. Shearer and Mr. Fuhrman are equally disturbed by the non-functioning guns, sirs."

Thom met Tristan's eyes. "So now we know."

"Yeah, but who?"

"And more to the point, Tristan, why?" Thom asked softly.

Tristan shook his head. They couldn't talk in sickbay, there were too many ears. "Come to my cabin for a game of backgammon as soon as you can."

"I'll be there at the usual time," Thom said. They both knew it was the only place they could talk freely.

"There's a red tail down the corridor," Riggan said under his breath. "Watching sickbay."

"You're in good hands, then, Thom. We'll talk later. Rest."

"You too."

Tristan smiled and stood. "I'll see you in the morning." Thom nodded and Tristan left. As he stepped out of the main sickbay he noticed the tip of a red dragon's tail lurking around the bend in the corridor. "Good night, Taminick," he said softly, knowing the dragon would hear him. A soft huff let him know she was on guard.

XV

The rest Tristan had been counting on didn't last as long as he expected. The Officer of the Watch called him back on deck to Weave one of the topgallants that had been destroyed in the battle about three hours after he had finally managed to get to his cabin. Once the big sails were done, the crew had set to fixing the damage to the ship, relying on the slower engines rather than the sails. However, once they cycled on the main engines, they discovered that two of them were not running at even half power and so they had to get the sails functioning sooner than expected. Running with the sails unfurled in the Winds meant they would reach Terra Octodecimus and the Naval dockyards there—where they were now headed to do repairs—much sooner. Tristan could also use the Guild offices and the secure line back to the Weavers' Compound.

The door to his cabin opened before he reached for the knob, Riggan *tsking* worriedly. "You've been on deck for hours, sir, without a break." He gently eased Tristan's uniform coat from his shoulders. "I was about to send Master Fenfyr up to get you."

"He was, too," Thom said from where he was sitting in the chair by the stern gallery doors. They were closed so the Air Weavers could focus on helping the crew work on the battle-damaged hull. "I just got here, Riggan was going to make coffee and then send Fenfyr for you."

"He did settle on deck more than once," Tristan said, dropping into a chair with a sigh. "I think he was reminding some of the crew there was a dragon around. He huffed over to a group that was working out on the forecastle, I'm not sure why—but whatever it was they scattered when he showed up."

"I'm hoping we can replace some of the crew at the station," Thom said as Riggan brought in the coffee service.

"Not that I'm saying anything, sir, mind you, but I heard that the captain was set on keeping the crew as it is," Riggan said, pouring them coffee. "Word has it he is keeping everyone that's still alive. I'm not saying as I heard Colonel Hall saying he wanted to deep space a few before we got there to thin the ranks, mind you, but I think he and General Muher have something up their sleeves."

"Thank you, Riggan."

"Yes, sir, if you need me sir, just buzz. I'll go get some food while you rest." He fixed Tristan with a look that reminded him so much of his first teacher at the Guild he almost burst out laughing. "I will be right back," Riggan added, then headed out the door.

"He's a gossip," Tristan remarked, looking over at Thom. Some of the dark bruising was beginning to fade.

"A useful one, too." The officer grinned. "He always has been, even when he was the captain's servant he would drop a word in my ear now and then."

"Did he come with Stemmer or the ship?"

"The ship," Thom said, making a face. "He was to be the captain's servant."

"No wonder he reports to you, because he would know."

"Yes, he knows." Thom laughed. "Not that he's saying anything, mind you." Tristan laughed too, the man's imitation of Riggan was almost perfect. "Stemmer got him, and, of course, as First Officer, I rate a Gunroom servant, not a personal servant."

"Stemmer is one of Davis's gang?"

"Oh, yes, and then some. I was shocked when they chose him as captain, frankly. Even though he was acquitted, there is still the question of his involvement in the Stars Plot and the anti-Weaver movement. He's never been caught at anything, but he is part of the group at Naval headquarters that want to see the Guild gone once and for all."

"You can't have ships without sails, and you can't have sails without the Guild," Tristan said.

"I know, and that's got me worried. I think they are up to something, I'm not sure what." Thom said. "On my first command the Weaver was anti-social, but made sure I understood that without him there would be no ship to command." He laughed. "It was an emergency command too—I was promoted because the ship's captain literally dropped dead at the helm, I was First and command defaulted me. It was an interesting trip."

"What kind of ship?"

"She was a frigate, we were part of an escort for a while, then went hunting a group of pirates that were plaguing one of the Rim stations."

"Have you been on the Rim for a long time?" Tristan asked. Thom didn't show a lot of the usual tell-tale marks of service on the Rim.

"Off and on. I'm not overly popular with Headquarters, so they give me ships, but send me deep-space sailing. We were the ones who first got a whiff of the possible incursion that led to the creation of the *Victory*. I'd helped design a lot of ships and Admiral O'Brian called me in for the project, trusting my knowledge of battle. Unlike a lot of captains, I've seen a fair amount of battle. He figured I could help make the *Victory* less vulnerable to attack from the Vermin. They tend to use the same style of attack over and over, it gives us an advantage. I was promised command." He sighed. "Of course, that didn't work so well."

"Nothing about this ship is as it was planned, Thom."

"Thinking about that, whatever happened to Alden?"

"The last we heard he'd left Terra Secundus bound towards the Rim," Tristan answered. He'd received a message from Rhoads about the former Warrior saying "heading out, keep your eyes open", but he had no idea what that meant.

"I spoke with Aubrey, he said we should make station-fall in less than five hours. He and Navigator Avila are still trying to figure out what went wrong with the computer." He stopped as Riggan entered pushing a cart of food.

"Master Fenfyr is resting in the gardens, sir, under the

grapefruit trees," Riggan said, setting plates on the small table. "I went in to get some for him and there he was, sound asleep. The captain is a little distressed." The man chuckled. "But there was no waking him, sir, so I left him to sleep. He's been out patrolling since the battle."

"I hope he's not disturbing anyone," Tristan said.

"None of the crew would even know he's there, he's curled up and quiet. The only ones who know are the captain and his new servant, on account of where Master Fenfyr chose to bed down. If I might be so bold, sirs, you both should eat and do as he is, I heard them say we'd be at Terra Octodecimus at six bells in the afternoon watch."

"Thank you, Riggan," Barrett said with a smile. "We'll do that."

They made station fall shortly after seven bells, having had to wait as a slow cruiser was cleared out of the only dock big enough for the *Winged Victory*. Tristan was sure he heard a collective sigh of relief from the crew as the masts were lowered into the ship far enough for the massive dome to close around them. Even he had to admit to a feeling of relief, more because it meant he could use the secure line back to the Guild than anything else. He was putting on his uniform when Muher knocked on the door.

"I understand you are heading towards the Guild annex?" the general said, stepping into Tristan's cabin.

"Yes, I take your appearance to mean I am being escorted?" Tristan asked with a laugh.

"Not so much escorted as accompanied. It's rougher out here, and I thought it might be wise to have a little firepower at your back, just in case." Muher smiled. "These outer stations are a bit different than Terra Secundus and the inner system network. It's just better to have a little extra help at times."

"That's fine, I don't want to run into slavers again." Tristan grabbed his bag. "Ready?"

As they stepped off the gangplank and onto the station's plating, Tristan was sure he saw something red disappear further down the docks. He didn't mention it to Muher, if the general saw Taminick, he saw her, if not, it was better to keep her presence a secret.

Once they left the docks, Tristan could see what Muher had meant. The station was very different from the order of Terra Secundus. Instead of the artificial trees and climate, it was clearly just what it was—a space station, with heavy plating and pipes exposed. There were colored lines on the floor, at every junction the lines were labeled to lead to the shopping area, the residential area or the docks. There were some that had no lettering, Tristan wondered where they went. One of them, a dark gray, headed off in the direction of the docks, but branched off. "What's that for?"

"The secondary docks."

"Secondary docks?" Tristan asked in confusion.

"The ones we don't go to and avoid at all costs. Terra Octodecimus services pirates now and then, and the secondary docks are where their ships would be if they're here."

"If you know the pirates are here, why not just arrest them?"

"And put them where?" Muher asked. "Half this station sympathizes with them. The pirates bring in goods they don't often see, big cruisers from the inner system don't stop here as often as they should—then tend to push on to Terra Vingensumus."

"That's criminal!"

"Yes, sir, but there's more profit the further out you get. Once you reach these parts, a lot of the people in the inner system and the pirates are regarded in the same light for the most part on the smaller stations—well, except for those that fly Vermin ships. The Vermin have raided in this close before and it was a massacre."

"So the ships that came after us probably weren't docked here?"

"I doubt it," Muher said, "but I am going to check it out as soon as you are safe at the Guild offices."

Tristan was quiet, digesting the information. The cruisers had Navy escorts, so they were purposefully flying past these stations, leaving them to the pirates. It wasn't a good situation. As they rounded the corner, he noticed a huge banner declaring "Loyal to Guild and Dragon" on one rusted wall of a large open area. Across from them he could see the Guild insignia on a door. Looking down, he noted that the blue line led towards the Guild offices. He opened the door and a journeyman Weaver looked up at him with a bored sigh. His eyes widened, then he stood, snapping to attention.

"Master Tristan! Sir! I didn't know you were coming!" he

nearly shouted.

Tristan hid a smile, after being onboard he'd nearly forgotten that he was recognizable to every member of the Guild. "It's okay, I just came in with the *Winged Victory* and I need to use the secure line to speak with the Guild Master." Since the incident with the ship's nav systems, Tristan didn't trust the line in his cabin to be secure.

"Of course! This way!" The poor man was nearly falling over his feet as he led Tristan down the corridor towards an office. "Will this do?"

"Yes, thank you."

"I'll be around, don't leave without me," Muher said, snapped off a salute and left.

Tristan waited until they left then closed the door, locking it automatically and then walked to the desk. He sat down and powered up the communications system, typing in his secure code and dialing straight through to the Guild Master's office.

"Tristan! What the hell are you doing on Terra Octodecimus?" Rhoads demanded as he answered the call.

"We got caught out by pirates, the ship was off course and they did enough damage to require a stopover." Tristan sighed.

"Okay, give me the full report."

Tristan started talking, waiting between the moments when the Guild Master would break his narration with a string of expletives. By the time he had brought Rhoads completely up-to-date, it was chiming two bells in the first dog watch. "And so, last I heard, Muher and Hall were going to try and remove some of the suspect pressed men at the station, but they were expecting a fight from the captain, so I don't know what's going to happen with that."

"We knew there was something wrong with the ship, we just didn't know how wrong." Rhoads sighed. "The Navy has made a move in the Worlds Council to downgrade the Guild again, it was overturned as soon as it was suggested, but there were murmurs afterwards that the Navy would soon have a way to circumvent us entirely."

"There's no way they can, Brian, unless the rumors are true."

"And if they are, then we are in trouble," the Guild Master said, his voice worried. "We have to find out about the sealed deck. Muher reported to Darius about it, and the Guild Dragons are insisting someone get in there. They fear the worst."

"I'm beginning to. Riggan, my servant, said someone saw someone going in there, then re-soldering it."

"Sounds like gossip."

"True, but his gossip is very reliable." Tristan laughed. "In fact, he should work in intelligence. He's very good at it."

"We'll see what we can do. You need to be careful, Tristan, there is an ugly mood brewing."

"I know, it is onboard too."

"We also just received a report that the Vermin have been sighted heading in, a major invasion force. The Navy has started massing ships. If we get hit by a full Vermin assault while the *Victory* is in dry dock, even with the rest of the ships, we don't stand a chance."

"Yeah, and the attack by the pirates was designed to cripple the ship. They were using combination loads and a particle cutter on the lower decks. The first officer said they knew exactly where to hit to do the most damage. He thinks they wanted to put the ship out of action, not take it."

"Not good," Rhoads said.

"No, not good at all." Tristan broke the connection and leaned back in the chair.

Someone knocked on the door, Tristan got up and unlocked it. The journeyman stuck his head in. "Excuse me sir, but there is a message for you."

"A message?"

"Yes, it was dropped off for you three days ago by one of the delivery services." The man held out a paper envelope. It was sealed with a wax seal.

"Thank you," Tristan said, taking it.

He looked at it carefully, it had his name on it. Running his hand over it, he made sure there was no electronic device in it—although the scan on the door should have picked that up. Once he was fairly confident it wasn't booby-trapped he carefully broke the seal and pulled out the single sheet of paper.

Master Tristan, there is active recruiting among the pirates by an unknown group. They are particularly seeking out those ships that are former Vermin vessels. No word as to why, but there is to be a rendezvous in the space between Terra Octodecimus and Terra Vingensumus within the week. Beware.

The letter was unsigned, but the handwriting was oddly familiar. Tristan tried to remember where he had seen it before. They used paper at the Guild for most of their important information, and handwritten at that, but he couldn't place it.

He did wonder how the writer knew he would be on Terra Octodecimus in time to receive the message.

XVI

The office was quiet and Tristan took the opportunity to make a few more calls on the secure line. He brought Darius up-to-date as well. The Elder dragon was deeply concerned about the news he was receiving, and passed along the information that a dragon had run across a Vermin ship on the outer Rim less than a day before. The dragons were sure it was a scout for the incoming invasion fleet. It had been alone, and there had been no other ships within three days' flight, but the dragons were still convinced that it was the first of many. The Navy, in this case, was agreeing with the dragons, and had called in most of the inner system fleet and sent them out towards the Rim; since they were still not sure where the Vermin might try and break through, they were patrolling a huge arcing ring that left them spread out and easy targets, unless they got enough warning to pull the fleet in for action.

While he was waiting for Muher to return, Tristan put together a list of things he wanted to purchase in the shops. It was really more an excuse to get out and get a feeling of the mood of the station. Was the pro-Guild banner there by choice or by force? He really didn't like to think of the idea of the Guild forcing itself on the population, but he honestly had no experience with the outer stations, much less the Rim, and so he wanted to experience it for himself. Once he was done with the list, he stared at the paper in the desk drawer. Pulling out a sheet, he wrote a note to the anonymous person who had sent him the message. After sealing it with his personal seal, he carried it down to the front desk.

"Sir!" The journeyman jumped up.

"Relax," Tristan said, smiling. "Can you get this to the messenger who brought you the note the other day?"

The man looked nervous for a moment. "Um…"

"No questions asked, I just want it delivered."

"I can do that, sir." He took the note from Tristan and set it carefully on the desk. "They should have it tonight."

"Thank you."

Tristan walked across the lobby, even the Guild offices had a more industrial feel than the ones on other stations he'd been to before. These were decorated, they'd taken the time to paint the exposed pipes and conduits, but they hadn't hidden them behind panels. That fact interested him. It was almost like it was a mark of pride that they hadn't covered anything, only colored what was there. It made him anxious to get out and see more of the station. He was actually considering setting out on his own when Muher showed up again.

"What happened to you?" Tristan asked. The man was sporting a black eye.

"I had a disagreement with someone," the general said with a grin. "I won the argument. I meant to be back sooner. Would you like to see some of the station before we go back?"

"Are you going to be having more discussions?" Tristan asked.

"You never know." Muher cracked his knuckles. "I never start them."

"I'm sure you don't." Tristan walked back to the office and grabbed his bag and list. "Ready."

"Then let's go—the shopping district first?"

"That sounds good."

They walked out of the building and followed a green line on the floor that led across the plaza in front of the Guild office and down a short corridor. On the other side was the busiest shopping area Tristan had ever been in. It was also the most foreign. Instead of shops, many sellers were hawking their wares from stalls backed up against the rusting walls. The wide area had a small park in the center, the trees and grass there were carefully tended, but even they looked a little... Tristan tried to think of a good word. *Wild* was the only one that really came to mind. He followed Muher into the throng of people.

A man was playing a violin, the case open in front of him. Tristan stopped and listened for a moment, then tossed a few coins into the case. The man smiled at him and kept playing. As they walked further into the shopping area, Tristan realized that people were beginning to notice his uniform and were glancing his way, some were outright staring at him. Muher had moved so he was half a step ahead of him, his weapon's arm free. Tristan didn't get a sense of danger from the crowd, however, it was more curiosity.

"Master Tristan!" a familiar voice called out, Tristan turned and smiled as Thom hurried through the crowd towards them. It took him half a second to register the fact that the first officer was not in uniform. "What brings you out shopping?"

"Just thought I'd get a few things while we were in dock," Tristan answered. "And you?"

"Oh, you know." Thom made a vague motion with his hand.

"Yeah," Muher said, narrowing his eyes.

A couple of well-dressed women walked past, slowing to look at the three of them. Tristan felt a blush creep up his cheeks. Muher took full advantage of it, however, and bowed formally to the women, grinning at them. "Can I offer you ladies escort?" the general asked.

"Thank you," one of them said, twittering. The general smiled at Tristan and Thom, took the women's arms and led them away.

"Is he on the prowl? Or just being kind?" Thom asked, falling in beside Tristan.

"I don't know. He's already had a disagreement that led to a black eye."

"There's an odd mood on the station, Tristan," Thom said, lowering his voice. "Let's get a drink."

Tristan trailed along as Thom led them across the plaza towards a small restaurant. As he went, he stopped to pick up a few of the items on his list, always aware of the way people reacted to his uniform. There didn't seem to be an anti-Weaver feeling in the shopping area, in fact everyone seemed open and friendly and many asked him for news from the inner system.

When they reached the restaurant, Thom was ushered to a quiet table in the back. "I've been here before," he said when Tristan looked at him in surprise. "I've been doing a little listening."

"Listening?"

"Yeah, wandering around, listening to what people are saying—about the pirates, about the Vermin—about the fact the *Winged Victory* is in dock."

"Yeah?" Tristan waited while Thom ordered for them both.

"Yeah, and the thing is, the cruiser was already packing up so that dock would be ready *if* we got here."

"If?" Tristan repeated.

"Yes, if. It's been made very clear that we were expected to be coming in—if we came in at all—in bad shape. The attack on us was a pretty open secret in certain areas of the station. No one knows who ordered it, but several crews turned down the offer, even though it was a heavy bounty. The fact that they had to fly with a former Vermin vessel bothered a few—believe it or not, they don't all think that captured Vermin ships should be used, and others were worried that even with the plans they were given, the *Victory* would shred them before they got a chance to hit her hard." Thom glanced around. "So the question is, were they plumbing for weaknesses or trying to cripple us? Either one is a possibility, and both bother me more than I like to say."

"How do you mean?"

"I've been out on a ship or two that were attacked on purpose."

Tristan knew he was staring. "What are you implying?"

"I'm not implying, Tristan. It's a fact. Sometimes pirates are hired to attack a new crew and vessel to give them a proper shakedown. Battle brings a crew together and tests the ship. It's not well known, or officially approved of—but it happens. The thing that disturbs me is the requirement that one of the vessels would be former Vermin—and someone had the plans to the ship. They knew right where to hit us. Alden was taller than you, wasn't he?"

"He was, quite a bit taller."

"Would you say a head taller?"

Tristan thought for a minute. Even though he was fairly tall, Alden had towered over him. "At least, maybe a little more. We called him the giant when he first got to the Guild and we were all in training together as children."

"That's what I was afraid of," Thom said worriedly.

"What are you talking about?"

"That round of combination-loaded grape-shot—if you had been a head taller it would have taken your head off instead of just grazing you before I knocked you down. The shot came from your side of the ship—it was meant to take out the Weaver."

"No," Tristan said, shaking his head. "You were there too, and the other officers."

"Yes, we were, but that round was specifically aimed at what would have been Alden's head. They had the height pre-programmed in their guns."

"That's why the Elemental Interface survived as well. The housing for it would have been set to be taller if Alden had been Warrior." Tristan met Thom's eyes. "Why would they be trying to get rid of the Warrior?"

"We're back at the 'why did they attack us' part of the equation. If they wanted to cripple the ship and take it, then they probably were hoping to use their own Rogue to pilot the *Victory*."

"And if it's something else?"

"Then I don't know. That's what I was doing down on the secondary docks. I was trying to figure out just what was up. I met up with a few people I've chatted with in the past. One knows who I am, the others think I am one of them."

"One of them? You mean a pirate?"

Thom shrugged. "The second ship I served on when I first shipped out was taken by pirates. Most of the crew was killed, but a few of us were left alive—mostly the officers that had a key role in the actual running of the ship. I was with the pirate ship for nearly a year before I managed to escape. I played along with them, trying to get as much information as I could. It comes in handy sometimes, even now."

"You speak their language?" Tristan asked.

"Something like that. They don't trust me, but they don't distrust me either." He shrugged again. "I was hoping to hear more. There was word of a ship out beyond the Rim that was taken by Vermin. A single Vermin ship, but from the last communication it was supposedly a big one."

"Darius said a dragon had spotted a ship, too."

"The Vermin are going to try again," Thom said with certainty. "And we need to know who is going to fight with us."

"You don't mean the pirates?"

"Yeah, some of them will. They're outlaws and would kill you or I without a thought. In fact they would kill half this station without a thought—but the Vermin ruin commerce. They leave nothing behind and how can you make money without people to sell your wares to?"

"I hadn't thought of it that way," Tristan admitted.

"Some will fight to get their hands on the Vermin ships, too, then as soon as the battle is over they will turn the guns on the Navy."

"It has to take a little time to get the sails under control, though."

"It does, and when we go into battle, we try hard to kill the ships and worry about the Vermin onboard after. Of course the dragons go straight for the ships."

"Of course."

"Tommy Boy, that you?" a man asked, coming up to the table.

"Harkins!" Thom said, standing and taking the man's hand. "This is Harkins, we've served together before. Harkins this is…"

"No need to introduce the Weaver. It's all over the market. The bleeding Master Weaver of the whole Guild is walking our corridors! It's quite a stir, let me tell you."

"I'm not sure if that's good or bad," Tristan said, holding out his hand and shaking the one the man extended.

"'Tis good, lad,'tis good. They're loyal to Guild and Dragon here, though there're a few lurking down deep might have a word or two against, most of us are chuffed up to see you here!" He dragged a chair over and sat down. "Chuffed up and proud, I tell you. We've seen a few dragons, of course, but never a Weaver of true Rank out here. I heard you were around, Tommy, and wanted to find you."

"You did?" Barrett asked with a smile.

"I did, I heard something the other day that made me think as how the Navy should know. I knew you were going to be coming in, so I was waiting to tell you. But hell, I thought you were meant to be captain of that ship. Those bastards!" Harkins growled.

"Harkins?"

"Oh right! I heard from someone who heard from someone who saw…"

"I get the idea," Thom said with a sigh.

"There were some suspicious types out here looking into the former Vermin ships. One or two of them disappeared and the crews were later, um, found."

"Found?"

"Well, the parts the rats didn't like, at least."

"What happened to the ships?" Thom leaned forward, watching the man's face intently.

"No one knows. They disappeared. Everyone connected with them is gone as well. For a while there were rumors Vermin were walking the stations, that they had somehow managed to make themselves look like us. Of course, I knew that was just talk to scare the stupid, but it doesn't change the fact things went missing." Harkins shook his head. "It's worrying, especially with the word about the dragons dying."

"What?" Tristan asked, focusing on the man.

"Yeah, I heard that there's some dragons that have gone missing, not heard from again."

"How many?"

"Numbers vary, you know how it is, Master Weaver. Some say one, others a hundred, the answer is in the middle somewhere, would be my guess."

"Harkins!" someone shouted from the streets.

"I hear my name," he laughed. "I'll be back here for the next few days with any news I can get, Tommy."

"Thank you, Harkins."

"Sir." The man walked out of the restaurant, Tristan noticed he had a pronounced limp. When he reached the outer corridor, he waved then turned and walked into the crowd.

"Tommy?" Tristan asked, raising his eyebrows.

"Harkins knew me when I was a mid, and later we served on a ship together." Thom glanced away. "The one I was telling you about. He was Ship's Master when it was taken. He helped me escape, but he didn't get away for another four years. When he did, the Navy ruled that he was too unpredictable to stay in the service and stripped him of his rank."

"So he stayed out here?"

"Yeah, he stuck with the sailors out here, there are groups of them that hire themselves out for various ships for a set amount of time. He's done rather well for himself really, but he's not all that fond of the Navy." Thom smiled. "He's the reason I survived that first attack, so he can call me Tommy to his dying day." Shaking himself, he looked over at Tristan. "Have you ever been this far out?"

"No."

"Then you need to see more of the station!" Thom said excitedly. "It's different from the ones in the inner system, but there is really no way to explain it, you just have to see it for yourself."

"That was my plan before you showed up and Muher got distracted."

"You're safe on this level, and most of the lower ones as well. The Guild is well liked here. I can't say it is on every station out here, but Terra Octodecimus is loyal to Guild and Dragon."

"That's comforting," Tristan said, standing. "Although I thought Terra Secundus was, and I almost got taken by slavers."

They headed back out into the shopping area. Tristan wandered past the stalls, getting a few more items, sharing news of the inner systems. On the other side of the shopping area, Thom turned and they started following a stripe of purple. "This heads to another shopping area, one with some more interesting items. It's the crafters' market."

The corridor was rusted, and somewhere something was dripping. An odd smell pervaded the area, but Tristan trusted Thom and followed him as he led the way to the next plaza. This was, if anything, even more foreign. There was an actual blacksmith working, his forge warming one corner of the plaza. A woman sat on a table weaving baskets. As they wandered through the market, Tristan bought a few odds and ends. And then they found an artisan who had a collection of various games. After marveling at the craftsmanship of several different ones, Tristan ended up buying an ornate backgammon board that was for sale. It had been made from a collection of spare parts, cogs and wheels carefully crafted. The board itself was inlaid with steel and black iron. He gladly paid for it and tucked it in his bag.

"It's getting late, Tristan, we should head back. The station is friendly, but we don't want to be caught out at night."

"We don't?"

"No, definitely not. We can head down to the lower docks tomorrow, if you want. I was down there earlier and everything is calm at the moment. I thought I saw a couple familiar dragon tails," Thom said with a laugh.

"What are they doing down there?"

"Maybe Fenfyr will tell you when we get back." Thom led the way back down the corridor. "But I'm not taking a chance with your life and staying out too late."

As they walked back, Tristan noticed that all the stalls were closing and the stores locking their doors. Apparently he and Thom weren't the only ones who weren't safe at night.

XVII

A soft tapping woke Tristan as three bells in the morning watch sounded. He frowned and rolled over, thinking it was someone making repairs nearby, but the tapping came again, this time more insistent. He pushed himself out of bed and walked through the cabin. Fenfyr hadn't returned to the ship and the room felt empty without his comforting presence. The third time the knock sounded, Tristan wrenched the door open, ready to let whoever was there know it wasn't a good idea to wake him up. He stopped when he realized it was Thom, once again not in uniform. The first officer smiled and slipped into the room.

"A little early, isn't it?" Tristan asked, closing the door.

"It is. I'm heading down to the lower levels, I heard something and I thought I should check it out, but I figured I should leave word with someone—just in case I don't come back."

"Right," Tristan said, heading to his bedchamber and grabbing civilian clothes.

"What are you doing?"

"Going with you, of course. You didn't really think you could drop by and say something like that and then expect me to let you leave?"

"It's too dangerous." Thom's voice was low and urgent. "Muher didn't come back last night, or report in this morning."

"Fenfyr's not back either," Tristan said, suddenly worried about the dragon's absence. "I'm going." He held his hand up when Thom opened his mouth to protest. "No one will recognize me without the uniform."

"I don't like it," Thom muttered.

"Riggan?" Tristan called.

"Sir?" the man answered immediately.

"If we're not back by eight bells in the afternoon watch, go into the Guild offices and tell them what's going on."

"Yes, sir. And I will just make sure everyone thinks you and Mr. Barrett are off on station again."

"Thank you, Riggan," Tristan said, then turned to Thom. "I'm ready."

Thom nodded and they slipped up the stairway to the quarterdeck. There was a small group of men working on the forecastle, but they didn't even turn as Tristan and Thom walked across the quarterdeck and onto the gangway. Once they were on the dock, Thom headed in the opposite direction from the one Tristan had taken the day before. As they turned into a corridor, he noticed that the lines of color that guided people through the station were mostly missing here. The purple one to the crafters' market was there, but very few others. Thom knew where he was going, however, and after a few turns they reached a lift. A few moments later they were twenty levels down.

"This is where the other docks are," Thom said, stepping out of the lift.

The first thing Tristan noticed was the smell—the scent of mildew, rust and rot that filled the corridor. Enough so that he wondered if it was purposeful to discourage visitors. Since Thom made no mention of it, he followed the officer along the passageway. It opened up into a shopping plaza, the shops and restaurants were opening as they arrived. Without stopping, they crossed the area and went into another corridor marked with a gray line.

It was darker here, only every third light was working and Tristan was beginning to feel vulnerable. Thom had been right, he should have stayed on the ship. This was no place for him. It was a little late for regret, though, and he ignored the feeling of a knife between his shoulders and plowed on. They had been in the passageway for several minutes when Thom stopped.

"Did you hear that?" he asked.

"What?" Tristan said.

"It sounded like…" He stopped as a low groan reached them.

"I heard that." Tristan turned in the direction of the sound. There was a door in a recess in the hallway, mostly closed.

Thom walked over and pushed it open. Tristan noticed the dark uniform of the Dragon Corps before he actually recognized Chris Muher. "General?" Thom was beside him an instant later.

"Wha…" Muher groaned again.

"Is he hurt?" Tristan asked.

"So far no bones broken," Thom reassured him.

"Master Tristan? What are you…?" Muher opened his eyes. "Help me up."

"Are you okay?" Tristan asked, concerned.

"Yeah, well, no, but not so bad. Someone was through a little while ago to check on me, and I wanted them to think I was still down for the count," he said, sitting up and looking at them. His face had several bruises on it.

"Disagree with someone again?" Tristan said, eying the man.

"You could say that. I think it was more they disagreed with me being down here at all. I was following a bit of information I heard and ended up in the middle of a brawl somehow."

"Just somehow?" Thom asked sarcastically. "You stumble into them often?"

"Sometimes," the general said.

"What did you hear?" Tristan looked out into the corridor to make sure they were still alone.

"There's a Vermin ship in one of the docking stations."

"What?" Tristan turned back to him in shock.

"I thought as much, from what I've been hearing." Thom said, nodding. "We need to get a look at it."

"More than that," Muher said, carefully easing himself onto his feet. "Dome Twelve."

"I was asking around earlier and found out they were looking for a crew for a ship docked there. I said I would come by," Thom said.

"How were you planning on getting off?" the general asked.

"Running," Thom said with a laugh.

"Have you seen Fenfyr or Taminick?" Tristan asked quietly as they headed back into the passages, then on towards the docks.

"No, I thought I saw Taminick for an instant yesterday, but I wouldn't swear to it."

"You can't come with us to check out the ship," Thom said firmly. "At least not in that coat."

"What?" Muher looked confused for an instant. "Oh." He shed his uniform coat and tore the ceremonial buttons of the Corps off his pants. "For the first time ever I am glad they aren't really buttons." He rolled them in his coat and tucked it in a dark corner.

When they stepped out onto the docks, Tristan didn't notice anything different—at least not at first. There were no complete Naval uniforms here, only pieces of them—a tattered coat or set of breeches, but only here and there. Tristan remembered what Thom had said about being trapped on a pirate vessel for a year and wondered if those tattered uniforms belonged to prisoners—or dead men. Shoving the morbid thought away, he followed Thom across the plating towards Dome Twelve.

When they reached the gangway, Tristan noticed a foul odor—the sick-sweet scent of rotting flesh. Squaring his shoulders, he walked up the gangway behind Thom, trying his best to look like he belonged. It was harder than he thought, especially as they reached the ship. A man stopped them at the end of the gangway.

"Where are you heading?" he sneered.

"Where do you think?" Thom snapped. "Or weren't you told to be expecting your new gunner and mates this morning?" He leaned in close to the man, threatening without being overly so.

"I was, just making sure. There was a Dragon Corps officer spotted earlier. Can't stand those men, get all teary-eyed over a pack of draft horses."

Thom laughed. "Good man, keep your eyes peeled." He stepped onboard and gestured for Tristan and Muher to follow him. As they walked on deck it took everything Tristan had in him to keep going.

It *was* a Vermin ship. Tristan had to swallow the bile that rose in his throat several times, trying to keep from getting sick. He doubted their cover story would work if he vomited all over the place. The dark deck was stained and the masts were stripped, the sails wound tight, held in check by massive chains to prevent their escape. The further he walked onto the ship, the stronger a voice in his head became. All it said was *"release me"* over and over. The last spark of what had been an immensely beautiful and intelligent creature, reduced to a life of slavery and servitude, begging for death. *"I will, I promise,"* he thought back. He was sure he felt the ship sigh. The true horror of the ship was ground into his memory forever when he noticed what had once been the graceful head tufts now mounted next to what must be the Elemental Interface. Tristan turned away from it.

Thom had disappeared below deck, reappearing a moment later with something in his hands. "We need to go, now."

"What?"

"We need to get off the ship. Now. I programmed the weapons systems to overload and blow. The ship knows and won't let anything stop it now."

Tristan nodded, his throat dry. The crew on deck looked at them oddly as they ran for the gangway, several stopped what they were working on to watch them. The man standing guard at the door tried to stop them, Thom knocked him over and they pounded down the gangway. Tristan heard a shout behind them, but ignored it as he whispered the spell of release, freeing the trapped dragon's soul and letting it die in peace. Muher slammed the portal between the gangway and the dock closed behind them right as the chain reaction started and the ship exploded.

Tristan felt her death, felt the loss of the dragon. He'd never been this close to a Vermin ship, but he sensed her as she died, happy in the instant of release from her life of slavery. He must have stumbled, because the next thing he was really aware of was Thom propping him up as they ran across the docks and up another gangway.

"Harkins!" Thom shouted as they stepped onto the ship.

"Tommy Boy, what brings you here?" the man said calmly, Tristan heard it all though a ringing in his head.

"I thought I'd come to see your new ship. Can we get a cup of tea?" Thom asked, sounding out of breath.

"Of course, come below."

Tristan let himself be led below deck and set in a chair. He was still dazed from what had happened. When a cup of tea was put in front of him, he looked up. "Where are we?"

"On the *Noble Lady*," Harkins answered with a laugh. "A bit run-down in her old age, but still dignified. I'm her Master these days, and 'tis a good crew she has, out for the bounty on them that prey on others."

"It's a privateer ship, Tristan," Thom said, sitting down. "They hunt pirates."

"Isn't it a little dangerous to be docked here?"

"We only hunt those that use them vile ships, so the others leave us be," Harkins said with a smile. "Was that your handiwork, Tommy lad?"

"It was, I remembered what you taught me." Thom grinned. "The ship was ready to go."

"What's wrong with this one?" Harkins pointed to Muher, who was paper-white.

"I knew, I've been told, I've seen them in space," Muher said, shaking his head. "I never really believed."

"What?" Harkins asked.

"About the Vermin ships."

"What did you think it was? Tales to scare children?" Harkins laughed bitterly.

"I thought it was..." Muher looked helplessly at Tristan.

"Not a dragon?" Tristan said sadly. "I know. I wanted to think so too. Fenfyr explained it to me, they slave the dragon to the technology, so all but a tiny bit of the dragon's intelligence is gone, but it is aware. It has to be to use the Winds so the ship can fly, to control the ship's systems. The dragons *are* the Vermins' ships. They can't kill themselves, the Vermin make sure of that, but if the chance arises, they will not fight death."

"No, they won't," Thom said. "In fact, they will even help overload the systems—at least of the captured pirate vessels."

"It wasn't your first time?" Tristan asked, looking at the man with new respect.

"No, me and Harkins have taken out a few along the way." Thom glanced up at the older man. "We even earned a bounty or two."

"Indeed we did," Harkins said.

"I still..." Muher was shaking his head. "I just..."

"You never got out to the Rim?" Thom asked the general.

"I have, I've even been in a battle with a Vermin ship, I just never realized. I thought it was only part—the sails, not the... By the Eldest, that was a *dragon.*"

"She's free now," Tristan said softly. "And grateful she was released." He looked over at Barrett. "We have to find Fenfyr and Taminick and let them know."

"Would that be the big black and silver dragon or the red one?" Harkins asked.

"Both of them."

"They were here earlier, I saw them over by Dome Twelve. They knew what was there, but there was no way for them to get on the ship right then. That's why I got word to you, Tommy."

"Thank you, Harkins."

"Harkins! What in all the damn worlds is going on?" a man said, storming into the room. He was about Muher's age and wearing a civilian coat that resembled a captain's uniform.

"Seems as if the Vermin ship went and got itself blown up," Harkins said amiably.

"Well, that's unfortunate," the man laughed. "Pity when a bit of filth like that gets blown to bits. If it had sat much longer, I probably would have arranged a similar accident. Ah, well, I'll find something else to do with myself."

"Gentlemen, I'd like you to meet my mate, and Ship's Commander, Cook. He's been with the *Noble Lady* since before I joined her, doing the good work that needs to be done."

"Pleasure's mine," Cook said. "Docks are clear if your friends need to get out of here while the getting's good."

"Thanks again, Harkins," Thom said. "I'll be at the restaurant tomorrow if you hear anything."

"I'll see you then, lad," the man smiled. "It was good work. Very good work."

Thom smiled and they left the ship

Following Barrett through the twisting and turning corridors, they stopped long enough for Muher to retrieve his uniform, then got on a lift, headed for the upper decks of the station. Tristan believed they should report the Vermin vessel to the Guild and Dragons, Thom and Muher agreed, so they were heading towards the Guild offices. By the time they reached the plaza where the huge pro-Guild banner was hanging, Tristan was exhausted. He felt like he'd been running for hours. Thom had hurried them through the station at a fast clip, and he couldn't shake the feeling of something aimed at his back the entire time.

They reached the Guild offices at eight bells in the forenoon watch. There was a different person sitting behind the desk, she looked up and smiled, then her eyes widened as she recognized him. "Master Tristan?"

"Yes. I need to use the secure line," he said, heading straight towards the office he had used the day before. He closed the door behind the three of them and noticed that Thom still had something in his hand. "What's that?" he asked, pointing to the bundle in his hand.

"I grabbed them from the ship—the gunroom table—it's plans for the *Winged Victory.*"

"They had the plans?" Muher asked.

"Yes." Thom laid them out on the desk. Parts of the ship were marked with red lines, dots and Xs. "I think they were planning another attack, and marking the weak spots. This one here," he pointed to a large dot, "is where that ship hit us with the damn cutter. If they hit us there again—even in dry dock—it would take us a month to make the ship space-worthy again."

"This is not good," Muher said, looking through the plans.

"No, it's not," Tristan agreed, dialing through on the secure line. When Brian answered, he asked the Guild Master to connect them with Darius as well. That way he would only have to tell the story once. When he was done, they both had questions for the three of them. Darius reported that he had heard from both Fenfyr and Taminick earlier, and the dragons were both safe. Tristan let out a breath he hadn't been aware he'd been holding. After several more questions and an ominous promise from Darius to do something, they broke the connection.

"You look like you're going to be sick," Tristan said to Muher.

"I am, I think."

"How did you get to be a General in the Corps and not know

that?"

"Hard-working denial is my best guess. I think I just couldn't believe anything was that vile, that they would—could—do that." He swallowed. "And the fact that humans are using those ships! I've hated the pirate trade most of my life—I lost a friend to slavers out on the Rim, but there are grades of evil, and…"

"And anyone who flies a Vermin ship should be exterminated?" Thom said, his voice deceptively mild.

"At least exterminated," the general growled. "There should be something worse."

"If the dragons get to them, there usually is," Thom said. "If that makes you feel any better."

"A little," Muher said. "Not much. The days of my denial are over." He looked at them with haunted eyes.

"I didn't believe until Fenfyr told me—one of his hatchmates was taken by the Vermin before I met him. He hunted the ship down and killed it. It's why Taminick does what she does, she's lost too many friends."

"With the reports of dragons disappearing, it means those Vermin are massing a new fleet."

"It could," Thom agreed. "It shows all the signs of an invasion. What is beginning to make me sick is it is starting to look like there are humans helping the Vermin. Why else try and take out the *Winged Victory*?"

"I'm not sure. It's something we need to find out," Tristan said.

There was a tap on the door. Muher answered it. "Message for you, Master Weaver."

It was the same paper, written in the same hand as the one from the day before.

Master Tristan, I am not sure where the orders are coming from, but you need to be careful. A price was placed on your head. Stay out of the lower station at all costs.

Tristan looked up at the other two and smiled. "I'm glad I didn't know this earlier." He laughed, hearing the slightly hysterical edge in his voice as he did so.

XVIII

Tristan was staring at the note in his hand and neither Thom nor Muher seemed willing to break the silence and ask what was in it. Taking a deep breath, Tristan forced another laugh and handed the paper to Thom. While the two read the message, he walked to the desk and sat down, wondering if he should alert the Guild.

"Call Rhoads right now," Muher said, answering Tristan's thought.

"Who sent this?" Thom asked.

"I don't know, there was a message waiting for me yesterday, too. Same handwriting. I have no idea who it is, although the style looks vaguely familiar."

"He's right, you need to let the Guild know. They need to get you back to the Guild Compound," Thom said, his voice firm.

Tristan was already dialing through to the Guild, waiting for Brian to answer. "I am not going back. You won't have a Warrior for the sails for one thing. There isn't time to attune someone before I leave, and if there is a Vermin fleet on the way in, you can't risk not having a Weaver to man the sails."

"Tristan? What do you need now?" Brian Rhoads sounded aggrieved. Darius had probably been lecturing him.

"I received a handwritten message informing me that there is a price on my head," Tristan said casually.

"You what?!?" Brain boomed, Tristan heard the echo in the Guild Master's vast office.

"I received a…"

"I got that. Who? When?"

"Who when what, Brian?"

"Who is behind it? When did it happen?"

"I don't know, it might even be leftover from the Stars Plot. You know they promised to destroy all of us who survived."

"True, I know there is a bounty on me, although they would have one hell of a time getting anywhere near me now. The Guild is going to take this seriously, Tristan. You know you have to stay with the ship?" the Guild Master said almost apologetically.

"I was just explaining that to First Officer Barrett and General Muher." Tristan couldn't help the triumphant grin.

"We need to get that ship headed back towards the inner system. I will speak with Darius, and then we will speak with the Navy. Until then, try not to get yourself killed."

"I will," Tristan said, knowing that the casual joke was Rhoads' way of dealing with something out of his control. "We shouldn't be in dock long, and once we're out of the station things should get better."

"Yeah," Brian said, sounding unconvinced for some reason. "Be careful."

Tristan broke the connection and looked at the other two. "He's worried."

"I think it's safe to say we are too," Muher said.

"Definitely," Thom agreed.

The watch was chiming six bells in the afternoon when Tristan reached the *Winged Victory*. Riggan was hovering in the cabin, waiting for him, looking concerned. When Tristan opened the door, for a moment he thought the other man was going to embrace him, but instead Riggan grinned and sighed in relief.

"You made it back, sir," he said, taking the package Tristan had in his hands.

"I did." Tristan walked over and dropped into a chair. Riggan must have known he was on his way, because the tea service appeared almost immediately. "Thank you," he said, as Riggan poured a cup of the spiced tea he preferred in the afternoon. "It's been a long day."

"Aye, word made it back that there was an explosion down on the other docks, not that I was listening to gossip, mind you, but they said three men, one of whom looked remarkably like our first officer, were seen on the dock just prior to the explosion."

"They say that, do they?"

"And more. That it was a Vermin ship," Riggan said, his face twisting in disgust.

"It was." Tristan sipped at the tea, trying to drive the morning out of his head.

"Was, sir?"

"Yes."

"Well, then, that's some good done today." The servant fussed around the cabin straightening things as Tristan drank his tea. "Master Fenfyr is down in the gardens again, if you want to go down. A nice walk in the green might make you feel better before dinner."

"Dinner?"

"Yes, sir, you and the officers are to dine with the captain tonight," Riggan said, watching Tristan.

"Oh, we are?"

"Yes, sir, the invitation came this morning after you'd left. Well, less invitation more like orders, but I'm not saying anything about that."

"Thank you, Riggan. I will go find Fenfyr, then be back in time to change. When is dinner?"

"Eight bells in the second dog, sir, as always."

Tristan poured himself a cup of tea in the larger cup he used to carry the beverage up on deck, and stood. Wandering through the corridors on the ship seemed so different from the station's busy corridors. He got to the officers' lift and punched the button that would take him to the massive 'gardens'. He hadn't been there since his first tour with Thom, even though Fenfyr enjoyed the space. Thinking about it, Tristan realized he tended to stay in his quarters or on deck. He didn't mix much with the crew—not through any prejudice, it was just that he had gotten used to being alone as Master Weaver of the Guild once Miri had been killed. He was generally so busy, he didn't have much of a chance to socialize, and when he did, it was with the other Masters, and their number had been greatly reduced with the terrorist attack of the Stars Plot. Since then, with the exception of well-guarded events under the watchful eyes of the dragons, the Masters rarely gathered in groups.

Opening the hatch to the gardens was like stepping into another world. His senses were assaulted with the sweet scent of citrus and other blossoms, the rich earthy smell of growing greenery and ripening fruit. He wandered in, marveling at the space. He hadn't had much of a chance to look that first time he'd been here, and now he took his time, walking past the vegetable patches, tiers of the plants slowly rotating in the artificial light. The path wound around past flowers, some of them edible, he knew, but others were there for enjoyment. He remembered that from his first time there. The "orchards" were at the back of the space, first the pears, cherries and apples, then peaches and apricots and at the very back pomegranates and citrus.

It was in the citrus trees he found the dragon. Fenfyr was stretched out along the back wall, his tail wrapped possessively around one of the trees. His eyes were closed, but Tristan knew the dragon had smelled him as soon as he'd stepped through the door. Without announcing himself, he walked over to Fenfyr and sat down on the ground, leaning his back against the crook in the dragon's foreleg.

"I was worried about you," he said after they had sat quietly together for several minutes.

"You were worried about me?" Fenfyr snorted. "I was a little worried about you, especially when I scented you all over the docks where the ship was killed."

"You were there?"

"Of course we were, we have been trying to figure a way into that dome since we arrived. Leave it to Thom to just walk onboard like he owns the place and blow it up. And after I spent hours scheming." The dragon sighed. "Hours and hours of quality scheming gone to waste."

"Sorry to ruin your scheming."

"No, Tris," Fenfyr said, gently touching him with a head tuft. "You released her, you did the best thing. It was brave."

"It wasn't, if I'd known that's what he was up to when we went onboard, I don't think I would have gone," Tristan said, turning so he could see Fenfyr.

"I sincerely doubt that. If you had known, you would have gone to free her as soon as you found out. Although, I trust you would have the good sense to call me first."

"Yes." Tristan laughed. "I met members of a crew that hunt pirates that use former Vermin vessels."

"Ah, yes, Taminick was speaking with one of them earlier, a man named Cook. He has been hunting them for a long time."

"I met him." Sipping his tea and leaning against the dragon, Tristan realized he was relaxing for the first time since they had docked. "The captain has invited me to dinner."

"He left it long enough to be a very clear insult, didn't he?" Fenfyr chuckled, the rumble more a vibration than a sound. "I think I might need to come to dessert."

Tristan laughed. "I'm not sure he'd enjoy that."

"He should have considered that before he ate *my* grapefruit."

Riggan had gone to extra pains with Tristan's uniform. It was brushed and clean, his dress shirt blindingly white, the cravat had enough starch to stand on its own, the buttons were polished to a mirror finish and even his boots looked bright and new. Tristan made sure his hair was clubbed perfectly, the bow the correct size and the ends hanging correctly over his collar. When he stepped out of his bedchamber, Riggan was waiting—and equally splendid. His dress uniform was brushed, polished and starched. The formal badge of service to the Guild was proudly displayed on his left breast, replacing the less formal bar he wore on a daily basis. The servant grinned at Tristan, then opened the door, waiting for him to step out before closing and securing it behind them.

They took the lift down to the deck that housed the captain's cabin. It was directly below Tristan's, although not quite as large. Several officers shared the other cabins on that deck, usually the captain's favorites. When Tristan stepped out of the lift, he noticed the door to the captain's cabin was open and Stemmer's new servant standing at the door. The man looked at Tristan and Riggan with open distaste then announced them.

Tristan walked into the cabin—and realized the captain was not as neat as most Naval officers he'd encountered. That or his servant was lazy—either way the cabin had a feeling of being not quite clean, and it was definitely cluttered. After glancing around the room, Tristan made his way towards the table, set back by the stern gallery windows. The Gunner Fuhrman was already sitting at the foot of the table, and there was a midshipman sitting to the immediate left and right of the captain. Thom was in the middle, Muher on his left and Rose Webber, the ship's doctor, on his right. Tristan noticed a place card with his name on it sitting on a plate directly across from Thom. The captain could not have made the insult more clear, unless of course he had asked Tristan to dine with the servants—indicating Tristan did not deserve the respect of the officers and crew. Smiling at the captain, Tristan took his chair, aware of Riggan standing behind him at parade rest.

"Now that the Weaver has decided to arrive, we can begin," the captain said. Their glasses were filled with wine. "To the Navy, Service and Victory," the captain proclaimed. Fuhrman and the midshipmen repeated the toast loudly enough to drown out the other voices.

The doctor looked at the captain for a long moment. "The Guild and Dragon." She raised her glass. Tristan repeated the toast as did Muher, Thom, Aubrey, Colonel Hall and the Navigator Elizabeth Avila. The others were silent. Not sure what to do with that information, Tristan filed it away for later.

The servants brought the first course. The diners ate in silence, except for the occasional request to pass the salt or a condiment. When the first course was finished, the plates were removed and the second course was brought in, still in silence. Judging from the others, Tristan assumed this was how most meals in the cabin went. Technically no one could speak until the captain did—well, no one except someone of a higher rank. He was playing with the idea of asking someone a question just to annoy the captain when Stemmer turned to Muher.

"I heard you were down on the secondary docks, General," the captain said.

"You did? There must have been a mistake," Muher replied, calmly taking a drink of wine.

"They said they recognized the uniform."

"What would I be doing down on the secondary docks?" Muher asked.

"That's what I want to know," Stemmer growled.

"It wasn't me." The general grinned. "Of course, there is always the very good chance I am not the only Corps member on the station. We get around a bit, you know."

"They said it was you."

"And how did they know it was me?" Muher said. "And who do you know on those docks that feels it necessary to report to you?"

"What are you implying?"

"Nothing, it was just an idle question, Captain."

"The general was with me most of the day," Rose Webber said. "We were shopping."

"Shopping?" Stemmer sputtered.

"Oh, yes," Muher said, his voice warm. "The doctor asked me to escort her to the crafters' market."

"We had lunch at that little shop that serves those lovely rolls—you know the ones, Mr. Aubrey—with the spiced meats in them?"

"If we stay here much longer that place will be responsible for me gaining a stone," Aubrey said with a sigh.

"They were pretty sure it was you," the captain persisted.

"Well, they were wrong," Webber said firmly. "How are you finding the station, Master Tristan?"

"It's very different than the inner system ones. I really enjoyed the crafters' market. I bought a backgammon board from an artisan there—his work was extraordinary."

"Backgammon? Isn't that a little old-fashioned?" Fuhrman spoke up for the first time.

"Not really, it's popular at the Guild. When Weavers go out to find Elements, sometimes they go in pairs, and a game that doesn't rely on power is handy. I started playing when I was first at the Guild."

"I know a lot of the Medical Corps out on the Rim play backgammon, chess or cribbage. During the wars, we never could be sure when we would have power for anything other than life support, so we found a lot of other ways to amuse ourselves," Webber said.

"I just bet you did," Muher said, winking at her.

"Enough!" Stemmer snapped. "Serve the main course!" The

servants took the plates away and brought in the main course. The conversation at the table fell silent again. "We will be sailing in two days," Stemmer said with a sly look at Tristan.

"Two days? Will the repairs be done then?" Aubrey asked.

"Shearer assures me we will be fit to leave dock then, assuming the Weaver is up to it."

"Why wouldn't I be?" Tristan looked at the captain.

"No reason."

The table was silent again. Tristan was happy he hadn't had to endure this before now. If the captain chose to insult him and never invite him again, it would be fine. He did take the time to observe his fellow diners. He knew all of them except the two midshipmen sitting with the captain. In fact, he'd never seen the two young men before, and he wondered if they were new recruits. It seemed odd that they would take on new officers at the station. He did know there had been a pressgang from the ship roaming the station to replace the men killed in the pirate attack.

He suddenly realized something that had been bothering him since the attack. It had been at the back of his mind, but it was clear now. The attack did far more damage than it should—because of the *Victory's* inability to return fire, because of the fact the pirates had the plans of the ship and knew exactly where to hit them, and the fact that the first shots from the former-Vermin vessel were anti-personnel rounds, not the larger shot designed to take apart the ship. He let the facts roll around in his head, and the more they pinged back and forth, the more he became convinced that someone on board had to be working with the pirates. Tristan glanced around the table again, trying to get an idea of who it might be—of course it didn't have to be an officer. But how had they gotten their hands on a copy of the plans?

A soft tap brushed against the stern gallery window. Tristan looked over, trying to hide a grin. Fenfyr wouldn't –would he? *Tap, tap, tap.* Stemmer's servant opened the window and Fenfyr's nose appeared.

"Sorry I'm late, my invitation seems to have gone astray," the dragon said. "Have I missed dessert?"

The look of shock and outright horror on the captain's face would keep Tristan laughing for many years.

XIX

Tristan was up before his usual time the next morning. He actually wasn't asleep when the call came down from the quarterdeck. Since dinner, he'd been mulling over the various interactions and reactions he'd witnessed at the captain's table. It was obvious that Stemmer, Fuhrman and the midshipmen were anti-Weaver. Rose Webber was definitely pro-Guild and—judging by the looks she was exchanging with Chris Muher—pro-Dragon Corps as well. There was tension between the officers, more than Tristan had realized before and the captain, unlike Thom Barrett, did not consider either the ship's master or the boatswain fit to dine at his table. The Air Weavers were also notable by their absence. Fenfyr's arrival had upped the tension, although for Tristan it had been hard to keep a straight face after that. The captain kept looking over his shoulder as if he expected the dragon to eat him.

Sighing, he pulled his focus back to the task at hand. He'd been called on deck to check the sails on the mizzenmast. Shearer had said they looked "sickly." After examining them, Tristan found himself agreeing with the boatswain and had spent an hour working on a spell to Weave the sails back to health. He had no idea what was causing the problem, but as soon as he was finished with the mizzen sails, he asked Shearer to inspect them all. He had a funny feeling that they would all need care before they left dock. Something was draining their energy and he needed to find the source.

It was just past six bells when he and Thom headed down to his cabin for coffee and breakfast. Riggan was waiting, the table already set. Tristan couldn't help smiling, the longer Riggan served him, the bolder the man was getting—up to the point of sending notes on deck for "the Weaver to eat his meal before it gets cold." He poured himself a cup of coffee, already tired, and wondered if he should go into the station one last time. They were due to sail the next day and there were a few things he still wanted to pick up.

"I'm going to the markets later," Thom said, picking up the coffee pot as Tristan set it down. "Do you want to go?"

"I thought you and Muher had decided I couldn't go?"

"The markets are very public places, and if we go early and you are in uniform, no one is going to make a run at you. The station is heavily pro-Guild. I'm actually surprised at just how pro-Guild and Dragon they are, for all that it acts as a pirate port as well." Thom waited while Riggan served them food. "Asking around, I discovered that very few of the pirates that use Vermin ships ever dock here, and most that do either don't stay long or, um, don't last long, if you get my meaning."

"Accidentally blow up?" Tristan asked with a laugh.

"Usually, since the raids last year the anti-Vermin feeling has grown, and that is automatically transferred to anyone flying their ships."

"That's good to know. I do want to go one more time. I should check in with Brian—um, Rhoads, the Guild Master—and the Guild too."

"We can leave after breakfast, if you want. I plan on wearing my uniform on today. I heard that Muher really is escorting the doctor in today. I think a lot of the crew will be off ship. It's the last chance before we get to Terra Vigensumus."

"Fenfyr and Taminick are off for one last cruise around the station as well."

"They won't find more Vermin ships. Not that I'm saying anything, mind you, but I heard that since the explosion yesterday, the ships that were inbound to the station turned around and headed towards Terra Septemdecimus," Riggan said, pouring more coffee. "Them that was Vermin ships at least."

"Huh, I wonder why?" Thom said with a grin. "Can I ask something personal?"

Tristan looked over at the officer. "What?"

"You don't have to answer, but you are Master Sail Weaver for the whole Guild, so I guess it makes sense that you can step into the Warrior's role, even though you are not Master Warrior, but what about the other facets of the Guild?"

"You mean like the Air Weavers or the Healers?"

"Yeah."

"All of the Masters of the Guild—in other words the chief Master of that portion of the Guild—have to be able to perform the spells for all the different areas of the Guild. Maybe not well—I know for a fact that Sullivan and Sheea are far better Air Weavers than I could every dream to be, but I do know how, I know the spells. I adapted to the Warrior role because I am usually responsible for attuning the Warrior to the sails, so I'm more familiar with that part of the craft than others. The former Master Warrior used to tease me about it." He swallowed back the lump of grief. "As you know, she was killed in the Stars Plot attack. We haven't found a permanent replacement yet." Tristan sighed.

"You were fond of her?"

"Very. She was…" Tristan broke off, surprised at the sudden upwelling of grief. He still missed her. It was quiet for a few moments. "I want to go back to the crafters' market and get that other backgammon board, and then go to a sweets shop. Fenfyr is fond of chocolates."

"Chocolate? I didn't know dragons ate chocolate." Thom shrugged. "Of course, I didn't know they liked grapefruit either. What kind of chocolate does he like?"

"The dark kind with stuff inside—that's a quote," Tristan said, laughing. "Which doesn't really narrow it down a lot."

"No, not really," Thom agreed.

The station was already busy when they walked into the plaza by the Guild offices. Tristan decided to wait to contact Brian until the end of the day in case something happened. They wandered through the market. Thom went in several places and then stopped at the sweets shop. Tristan was surprised by the variety the store offered.

Thom grabbed a tray and started filling it from various bins, but Tristan headed straight for the huge glass case at the front of the store filled with gourmet chocolates.

"Can I help you, Master Weaver?" the shop girl asked as he approached.

"I want some filled chocolates."

"What do you like?"

"I'm buying them for a friend, mostly. None filled with alcohol."

"No alcohol at all?" she asked.

"No, it's poison to dragons."

"Dragons! You're buying chocolates for a dragon?"

"Yes, Lokey Fenfyr of the Guild Dragons." Tristan was eyeing a collection of citrus-filled chocolate. "Maybe some orange nougat, and the dark chocolate…"

"Do you have any with grapefruit?" Thom asked with a laugh.

"We do, would you like some?" She smiled at Thom, blushing at the same time.

"Yes, definitely. What else, Tristan?" Thom set his tray on the counter.

"I'd like that one." Tristan pointed to a candy that was shaped like a tiny shot glass made of chocolate with three pieces of salt on top. "A dozen of those. And then seven dozen each of all the other ones as well."

"That dragon is going to get fat," Thom pointed out.

"It shouldn't be a problem unless he talks Riggan into giving them to him. The salted ones are for me."

They paid for their items and headed to the crafters' market. After buying the other backgammon board from the artist, they went across the plaza to a restaurant with a garish sign out front. Like the place they had dined in the day before, they were led to a back table. Thom ordered several items from the menu and they sat back to wait for their food.

"Tommy boy," Harkins said, walking up to the table. "I've been waiting for you."

"I thought you might."

"I heard the ship is sailing tomorrow."

"That's the captain's plan."

"Is she ready to fly? The gossip on the docks is it's not in any shape to head out to Terra Vigensumus. In fact, one worker said he was in the dome yesterday and there's a bloody gaping hole in the side of the ship still."

"I know there is," Thom said calmly.

"How can you leave dock? Your Air Weavers can't keep that hole patched if you get hit in space!"

"I know. Shearer is working on it right now. It's a priority. I ordered people off other jobs to get that done. I didn't bother to inform the captain, of course."

"Of course not." Harkins sat down and set his drink on the table. "We're shipping out soon, too. We've heard there's a collection of former Vermin ships heading out towards sector nineteen, and we thought we might do a little hunting. The captain is keen to get himself one or two of the bastards, and maybe a little extra along the way."

"Sector nineteen? There's nothing out there," Thom said, frowning.

"I know, it's making us a little curious." Harkins finished his drink. "I'll get word to you if I can. Usual channels."

"Thank you, Harkins. Take care of yourself."

"Always, Tommy, always, you too. I think you'll need it more than I will." The man clapped Thom on the back and offered his hand to Tristan, shaking it hard enough to make him wince. "Look after yourself, Weaver. There's a price on your head, big enough that if I weren't reformed I might go after it myself." He grinned.

"I will, thank you, Harkins."

The man saluted them and left.

"Hmm," Thom said thoughtfully, waiting while the waiter served their food. "That was an interesting bit of information."

"What?" Tristan asked, taking a bite—then pausing as the spice from the food seared its way across his tongue, down his throat and exploded in his brain. He was pleased he managed not to start coughing.

"That he knows where we stand as far as repairs, that there is a fleet massing and the bounty on you is common knowledge. Is the food okay?"

"It's great," Tristan said. "Why is it interesting?"

"It means someone from the ship is talking, for one." Thom narrowed his eyes. "I wonder who? It's hard to tell, the crew often go to the secondary docks—the red light district is down there as well. You just found out about the bounty yesterday, but Harkins knows today. He didn't mention it yesterday, which leads me to think it's new. And then that fleet of former Vermin vessels. Why are they meeting out there? That's empty space."

"Why would they be meeting at all? I thought the pirates tended to sail in small groups."

"They do," Thom agreed. "It's odd. I want to know more. Who ordered them out there? Why? Maybe the dragons have heard something."

"Maybe they've heard something at the Guild. I need to report all this anyway."

"After dessert."

"As long as it isn't this spicy."

"So the chili ice cream is out," Thom said, laughing at him. "Fine, spoilsport."

After reporting to the Guild, Tristan and Thom made their way back to the ship. The call to the Guild had been frustrating, Brian couldn't offer any answers and said that he would have to speak with Darius. The call left Tristan on edge. It was hard to shake the feeling of being followed as they headed through the docks. It kept getting worse as they walked through the last of the corridors before they reached the main docking area. Tristan stopped. This was more than the paranoia that had been haunting him since he'd received the note about the bounty on his life. No, this feeling was concrete. As a Weaver and spellworker he was mildly psychic, and whatever was ahead of them was casting off enough malevolence to make the hairs on the back of his neck stand on end.

Without asking what was going on, Thom had stepped in front of him. "Something's there," he said in a nearly silent whisper.

"Yes," Tristan agreed. Thom must have sensed it as well.

"Stay behind me." Thom eased his gun out of the holster, thumbing the safety off. "Show yourself!" he demanded.

"I have no quarrel with you, I want the Weaver."

"Oh, well then, we have a problem," Thom lowered the gun.

"I'm not giving up the Weaver."

"The bounty is mine, I don't mind killing you. I will have him, though, and take his hands and feet to prove he's dead."

"No," Thom said. "He's mine."

"No," the other said. "However, I would be willing to split the bounty, it is most generous."

"It will never be paid, you can't be that stupid. Everyone in the Worlds will be hunting the killer of the Master Weaver of the Guild."

"I will be paid. I guess you'll be a little extra bonus."

Tristan saw something shift ever so slightly in the shadows, and without hesitation Thom lifted his gun and fired three rounds. There was no noise, only the *pfft* of the firing gun, then the sound of a body falling. Thom stepped forward, his gun still out. "Whittington, figures."

"You know him?" Tristan asked, staring down at the body.

"He's been around for a long time, and will work for anyone who's willing to pay the price. You should appreciate it, really, it means that the bounty is very high."

"I think I would be more comforted if it was low."

"Why is that?" Thom asked as he inspected the body.

"Because if they can pay for the best, it means that people are going to keep coming after me until I'm dead."

"True," Thom said grimly as he stood, a piece of paper in his hand. "The bounty is new. Listen to this: 'Tristan Weaver, Master Weaver of the Guild, Bounty Five Million. Dead, with proof.' It's dated yesterday and handwritten, so they are being careful, whoever they are."

"I'm getting sick of them."

Thom laughed and clapped him on the shoulder. "If it helps, I am too."

"By the way, Thom? Thank you."

"What?"

"You saved my life."

"Well, if I hadn't, who would play backgammon with me? Everyone else is already in the hole by a thousand or so." Thom laughed again.

"What do we do with him?"

"Leave him for the scavengers. I have his papers, let someone else have use of everything else."

Tristan decided he didn't want to know exactly what Thom was talking about.

The docks were busy, crew members from a dozen ships mixing with the longshoremen for the station. Thom walked briskly across the plating towards the gangway to the *Victory*. Tristan noticed he hadn't holstered his gun. In fact, the tension in Thom's shoulders didn't relax until they were onboard the ship. As they stepped onto the deck, he slid the gun away.

"Master Weaver, the sails on the foremast are getting dim again," Shearer said within moments of their arrival.

"Again?" Tristan started to walk across the deck, then stopped. His hands were full of packages.

"I'll take those, sir," Riggan said, appearing at his elbow.

"Thank you, Riggan." Tristan handed them over and continued across the deck. There was definitely something wrong with the willowisps. They were sparkling sluggishly on the one sail that was unfurled. He walked closer to the sail, laying his hand on the mast and looking up. Even though they were in the dome and the masts were partially down, they still soared over the deck. He needed to get a better look. Toeing off his shoes and taking a deep breath, he began climbing up the rigging to reach the top set of crosstrees where the sails were. He leaned against the mast and stared at the sails. The willowisps weren't moving. Grabbing one of the ropes, he walked along the crosstree, trying to see if something there was causing it. Not finding anything on the port side, he turned and headed to starboard.

It was there, hidden behind the mast and almost invisible—a small black canister.

"Mr. Barrett?" he called.

"Sir!" Thom answered.

"Can you send someone up with a hazmat containment bag?"

"Yes, sir!"

Tristan turned to the sails. Someone had deliberately poisoned them. He reached out and placed his hand in amongst the willowisps, feeling them wrap around his hand and arm. "I'll get you fixed in a moment," he told them.

"Here it is," Thom said as he reached the crosstree. "What's it for?"

"That, whatever it is." Tristan pointed to the black canister. "We need to check all the masts and every single crosstree and set of rigging for more of those things. Whatever is in there is what is killing our sails."

Thom carefully picked up the canister and put it in the bag, sealing it and then turned to Tristan. "I'll have the labs try and figure out what it is, too."

"Thanks, Thom, as soon as they're all gone, I'll fix the sails, I can't really help until that poison is gone."

"I understand. Shearer!"

"Sir!" The boatswain answered immediately.

"We need to inspect all the masts, someone has been poisoning the willowisps. Check everything for small black canisters. Put them in hazmat containment and then get them to the labs for analysis and disposal."

"Yes, sir! On it now, sir!" Shearer said.

"I'll meet you on deck," Thom said, grabbed one of the massive backstays and jumped, sliding all the way down the rope to the deck. Tristan sighed and decided it would be better to go back down the more traditional—and safer—way.

XX

It took almost six hours to find all the sinister canisters. By the time the last one was removed, Shearer was in a fury and most of the crew was avoiding the man at all costs. Thom was in a similar state, and even the officers were creeping past him as quietly as possible. The ship had grown silent, the usual calls between the crew were now hushed whispers as the Marines, led by Colonel Hall and the Dragon Corps with Chris Muher, swept the ship in hopes of finding out who had placed the poison on the sails. The captain was pacing on the quarterdeck, snapping at anyone who was foolish enough to get close to him. At the sounding of every bell, he would ask how soon they could sail, and with each postponement he would become more intractable.

Fenfyr and Taminick had returned to the ship and were slipping silently through the decks trying to scent the source of the poison canisters. Whoever had placed them had waited until the dragons were gone to bring them onboard or Fenfyr and Taminick would have smelled them. The fact that the person who had done it was nowhere to be found worried Tristan. Their saboteur had known the routine of the ship and had also known most of the crew and officers would be on the station before the launch.

Tristan was leaning on the rail by the Elemental Interface when Thom walked onto the quarterdeck. The first officer looked exhausted. He glanced around to make sure there was no one nearby, then headed over to stand by Tristan.

"We have them all. The dragons confirmed it," Thom said, pitching his voice low so it wouldn't carry. "We still don't know who did it. Everyone is coming up clean. I'm beginning to think the person who actually placed those damned canisters was let onboard and is back on the station now."

"If Fenfyr can't find them, that seems likely," Tristan replied. "I'll start repairing the sails as soon as Shearer and Aubrey give me the all-clear."

"About ten minutes now. How long do you think it will take to make them space-worthy?"

"I'm not sure, I won't be until I know how badly damaged they are. I'll have to use a combination of Healing and Weaving to get them back to shipshape." Tristan met the first officer's eyes. "Thom, when I am Weaving, I am vulnerable…"

"Say no more. I'll be right here, and make sure General Muher is on the quarterdeck as well."

"Thank you."

"Well, Weaver," Stemmer said, walking towards them. "I have been informed that the last of the canisters is in containment. You can start working now."

Tristan stared at the man. "I'll start working, Captain, when I feel the moment is right. Weaving and Healing are delicate tasks to undertake. Usually we perform only one at a time."

The captain was staring back, undeterred by Tristan's tone. "You are supposedly the Master Weaver. One would assume you are better at this sort of thing than the average Warrior Weaver."

"One would," Tristan said mildly, smiling.

"Everything is clear and ready, Master Tristan!" Muher called from beside the mainmast.

"Thank you, General. Please raise the masts and loose the sails so I may begin," Tristan ordered, turning away from the captain and towards the Elemental Interface.

The masts rose slowly as far as they could in the dome. They couldn't extend to their full height, but it was enough for Tristan to work on the sails. As the mast rose, he noticed that Fenfyr appeared on deck and perched so that no one could get onto the quarterdeck without going past him. Feeling safe, Tristan laid his hands on the Interface and began to whisper the Healing spell. He could feel the sluggish willowisps, the poison had sapped them of energy. They began to respond and he slowly added the spell for Weaving into the one for Healing, carefully crafting them together, and as he felt where the vulnerability had come from, he built in a shield so that the poison could not affect them any longer, in a way inoculating them against that particular attack.

He had no idea how long he worked on the sails. The light on the deck changed as the willowisps began to glow once more. Tristan could feel the buzz of their energy in the Elemental Interface now, feel their connection with the ship sliding back into place. He followed that thought through the sails. The attack had been designed to make the sails reject the ship. He focused more healing into that spot, binding the sails firmly to the ship. As he finished, he spoke the final words of the Weaving, then lifted his hands off the Elemental Interface.

It felt like the ship tilted, it took a moment for Tristan to realize it wasn't the ship. His fall was stopped by a combination of human hands and dragon wing. He tried to focus on what was going on, but the magic had left him drained and the residue of the poison felt like it had worked into his bones. There was a flurry of activity around him, the shadows falling across his face made him sick to his stomach. He closed his eyes in hopes of easing the nausea.

"He's not been up, sir, no. I just checked on him," Riggan was saying when Tristan opened his eyes. He was lying in his bedchamber. "His color has improved, though, sir, so I have high hopes he will wake any time."

"The doctor wants him in sickbay," Thom said.

"Aye, and I would agree, but Master Fenfyr won't let me move him. You tell him you want to remove Master Tristan from the cabin and see how far you get."

Tristan sat up, he was still tired but it was no longer debilitating, although he could still feel some of the "sludge" from the sails in his system. He would need to speak to one of the ship's Healers about that. Getting up, he realized he was still in his uniform, only his jacket, cravat and boots had been removed. He walked to his chamber door and opened it. "Riggan? Can I have coffee, please?"

"Tristan!" Thom stepped into the cabin. "Thank all that's holy."

"I told you Weaving left me vulnerable," Tristan said.

"You didn't say it made you collapse," Thom said, looking at him worriedly.

"It was serious," Fenfyr agreed from the main room.

Tristan smiled. "I wasn't expecting it to take quite that much out of me. It was the poison that caused the trouble." He walked over to his chair in the cabin and sank down, gently laying his hand on Fenfyr's head. "It was still there in the willowisps and some of it seeped back down the spell towards me."

"We were worried," Fenfyr said softly, patting him with his head tuft.

"Something beyond that," Thom said, dropping into the other chair. "Webber wanted you in sickbay, but Fenfyr insisted you stay here."

"I can't protect you in sickbay," the dragon said.

"Are you okay?" Thom asked.

"I am, once I have coffee and maybe some food, I will be ready to sail."

Fenfyr huffed. "You sail when you are strong. Not before."

"I agree," Thom said softly.

"Here's your coffee, sir," Riggan said, coming back into the cabin. "The captain's servant asked me if I knew when you would be able to sail."

"The captain's servant can just wait," Thom snapped.

"That's what I told him, sir," Riggan said, setting down the coffee tray and serving them. "All the crew is onboard, although there is some talk that the new men brought on from the station are of a different type."

"Different?" Tristan asked.

"They aren't the type usually pressed, they seem to be more skilled than pressed men usually are."

"Are you saying they grabbed pirate crews?" Thom asked.

"I'm just passing on what I heard, sir, not gossiping mind you, but the crew is wary of the newcomers, and there is talk of one that is *very* different that no one has seen since he was first pressed."

"Why was he different?"

"Ah, well, that I don't know, they just said different, sir. I will try and hear more later. I will go get you some food ready and perhaps someone will say something."

"Thank you, Riggan," Tristan said. Once Riggan was gone, Tristan turned back to Thom. "What do you think is going on?"

"I don't know, I've been trying to find who put the poison on the sails, so I haven't had the chance to check the pressed crew as carefully as usual. Shearer hasn't either."

"So the poison was helpful for that as well," Fenfyr said thoughtfully.

"What?" Tristan looked at the dragon.

"Men came onto the ship without Thom or the boatswain seeing them. The poison was a distraction for many things. We were all so focused on the search for the canisters and the saboteur that we might have missed something important."

"It's a good point," Thom agreed. "But what?"

"I have a feeling we'll find out." Tristan took a drink of coffee, letting the hot liquid slide down his throat.

Thom got up and paced back and forth. "I don't like it. Although it did give us a chance to get the one large hole in the hull patched. So that part of their, whoever they are, plan is hopefully stopped. If there was even a plan."

"You know there was, Thom," Tristan said, watching the first officer. "You know what we found on the ship we killed."

"And there was the attempt on your life."

"What attempt?" Fenfyr growled.

"A man on the station tried to kill Tristan," Thom said, his eyes angry. "I stopped him."

"As long as he is food for the scavengers, I approve," the dragon said.

"He is, and we have his papers as well. He was a man called Whittington. He served as a hired killer, one of the best."

"One of the best no more," Tristan added, remembering Thom's easy handling of the situation. He was beginning to get the feeling there were things in Thom's past that were more interesting than the man had let on.

"Good," Fenfyr huffed happily. "Oh good, grapefruit!" he added, spying Riggan coming into the room with a cart of food.

"Let's eat."

The crew was on deck three hours later, watching as the dome over the ship was slowly opened and the masts rose to their full height. Tristan was at the Elemental Interface waiting as the *Winged Victory* was readied for launch. The great engines pushed her out into space and the crew climbed the masts.

"Loose the sails!" The sails began to drop, shimmering light sparkling over the deck, very different from the initial launch from Terra Secundus and the inner system stations.

Then the call went through the ship, it still gave Tristan a thrill to hear it. "Ship to the Weaver!"

"Ship to you, sir," Thom said.

"Thank you, Mr. Barrett," Tristan replied.

"Weaver has the ship!"

Tristan eased the sails into the Winds, feeling the first puff of air brush over them. He moved them, canting them as the crew eased the ropes, and the great mainsail snapped into the Winds with a huge boom that rattled everything onboard. Men scrambled to roll up the smaller sails, for some reason the usually calm Winds were blowing at a rate unknown this close to the station. Tristan whispered the spell to the willowisps, and the ship wheeled into the current, tipped over so that—if they had been on the water and not in space—their deck would have been awash with the speed and force of the Winds. It was thrilling. Tristan could feel the willowisps arranging themselves for the most efficient use of the Winds. Once he was satisfied with the hum in the rigging, He stepped back. He was beginning to learn the music of the ropes and sails and could tell by the pitch when things were running smoothly.

"Good launch," Thom said, standing beside him.

"Yes." Tristan grinned. "I wasn't nearly as nervous." He looked up at the sails, watching them shimmer. It was a sight he never tired of, the beauty of sails. Even though this was his first real experience as a Warrior, there were many ships flying with sails he had created, and they were all beautiful. When he finally tore his gaze from them, he noticed Thom was watching something on the forecastle. "What is it?"

"Nothing, I thought I saw…" He laughed. "It's nothing. Out in deep space you see things sometimes."

"You do?"

"Yeah, some people go completely insane. We still don't understand everything that's out here, and the unexpected comes up sometimes. Deciding what is real and what isn't is the trick."

"Like?"

Thom shrugged. "When I was on the pirate vessel, we went through this storm. It was the strangest thing. Out in the middle of deep space." He shivered. "I never want to experience something like that again."

"What happened?"

"We were four days out from a station and the Winds suddenly changed. We lowered the sails, but ended up being tossed around. The Rogue Weaver was at the Interface for two days, trying to keep us in one piece. Then, in the middle of the storm..." Thom swallowed. "Never mind. It was really something you don't want to see. Trust me."

Tristan wanted to ask him more, but stopped when he noticed Second Officer Aubrey coming their way.

"All's well so far," Aubrey said.

"So far?" Tristan repeated.

"Well, I'm not planning on anything bad happening, but I am making sure we're prepared," Thom said.

"So you think something bad is going to happen?" Tristan asked.

"Yes, sir," Aubrey said. "We're just trying to limit how bad it gets."

"How bad?"

"Very, Master Tristan," Thom said. "We're preparing for the worst."

"And then some," Aubrey added.

XXI

The *Winged Victory* was two days out from Terra Octodecimus and things were going smoothly. The last of the repairs had been finished and the crew had settled down for the long run to Terra Vingensumus. Tristan had spent most of the first day on deck, making sure the sails were functioning correctly. The Winds were still unexpectedly strong, something that was worrying the ship's officers. They had contacted Naval headquarters and had been informed that there were no storms or anomalies in the area. Stemmer had taken to stalking across the deck from bow to stern through the daytime watches, and Thom was beginning to show the edges of exhaustion from serving the morning watch in addition to being on deck all day.

Taminick had quietly left the ship partway through their first day away from the station. Fenfyr let Tristan know she was gone, but nothing else. He didn't press the dragon for answers, there was a very good chance that whatever errand she was on was one Fenfyr knew nothing about. The dragon was making his presence felt throughout the ship, turning up at odd moments on every deck, and in every public space. Once every other watch he would check the soldered hatchway to the lower deck. The dragon told Tristan he smelled fresh solder: the hatch had been opened and closed while they were on the station. There was a hint of something else, but the dragon couldn't explain what it was.

Tristan had invited Thom and Muher to his cabin for tea, and Riggan was happily preparing a fancy meal, despite Tristan's insistence that it wasn't necessary. The servant had *tsked* in mock-horror and gone on setting up the tea service and a selection of food on a table that sat between the three wing-back easy chairs in the main cabin. Now that things were settling down, Tristan wanted to talk to the others about the rumors that Riggan had been relating to him. Riggan still regularly checked for listening devices and Fenfyr gave the cabin "a thorough sniffing" every evening, giving them a safe place to talk.

The men arrived together. Riggan showed them in, poured tea into the cups and quietly absented himself. Tristan suspected he was standing outside the door to make sure no one got too close while the three were meeting.

"You said tea," Thom said, looking at the pile of food.

"Riggan has his own ideas," Tristan said with a laugh.

"I told you, Thom." Muher was laughing. "He didn't believe me."

"I forget that Riggan is the only one that gets to push Master Tristan around, Chris," Thom pointed out with a sly smile.

"He doesn't push me around; he just has very clear ideas of my dignity as Warrior Weaver."

"And Master Weaver of the whole Guild," Muher said, sounding remarkably like Riggan. "He makes sure the crew knows and never forgets that little tidbit. It's interesting, watching the reactions. Some of the crew is happy with it—others not so much, and the new crew is downright hostile."

"The new crew?" Tristan asked. "The men brought on board at the station?"

"Yes. They are a very different group. All skilled sailors and they have all been moved into positions of relative authority, which is unheard of for pressed men. It's making me a little nervous."

"It makes me more than a little nervous. When I asked the captain about it, he nearly took my head off. I was sure I was going to end up flogged in front of the crew." Thom looked at them, and Tristan could see the man was not joking about the punishment. "They are being positioned throughout the ship too, gunners, communications, on the sails, everywhere."

"Then we have the problem of the men Hall and I wanted to get rid of that are still here—the ones that survived the attack. They are all anti-Weaver and very vocal about it. The attitude is being openly encouraged," Muher added.

"Is that why I am not allowed out of my cabin alone anymore?" Tristan asked with a half-smile.

"Yes, and you are not to go anywhere on the ship without someone trustworthy with you. If you can arrange for Fenfyr to be with you, it's the best option," Muher said vehemently.

"We're being serious," Thom said, meeting Tristan's eyes. "There is something *wrong* onboard and removing you seems to be part of the plan. I only wish I knew what it was."

"Fenfyr told you that the hatch had been re-soldered?" Tristan sipped his tea.

"Yes, and I went down to check it personally. There is no way to tell what went in or came out," Muher said.

"Fenfyr said it smelled different, too."

"I wish I had a dragon's nose sometimes, but we still don't know what any of it means." Thom sighed. "And the Winds are behaving oddly, it's almost like there is a storm brewing somewhere, but headquarters said no."

"A storm? You're being literal?" Tristan asked.

"Yes. I told you a little about the one when I was onboard the pirate vessel. They happen in space; the thing is, usually there is more warning. The one that hit us back then was like a squall, it came up out of nowhere. The Winds had been off for a few days, then we were hit." Thom was quiet for a minute. "I am a fool."

"What?" Tristan and Muher said together.

"The Winds, the storm—it came up out of nowhere and right behind it was a Vermin scout ship riding in on the backend of the storm."

"So you think that might be happening now?" Tristan was watching the first officer, there was more to it than what Thom was telling them.

"I think it might."

"So how do we locate the squall?"

"I'm not sure, it was just suddenly there—at least from my

perspective. I wasn't on the nav boards or communications. We need to get word to Terra Vigensumus to watch out for a possible storm and Vermin incursion."

"You think that's where they will come through?" Muher asked, grabbing a sandwich.

"No, I think they will come through someplace where there is a hole in our defenses, then head straight for the inner system. I think when they come this time, they are going to come in full force, and I think no matter what the Navy thinks, we have never faced them in force before. They are going to cut through our defenses like a hot knife through butter unless the Navy gets the fleet—the whole fleet—in to meet them."

"You think it's come to that?" Tristan had never heard Thom talk this way.

"I do! I have since I first started work on this ship. We are supposed to be the ship that stops them, but how can we if we are out here in deep space and they invade on the other side somewhere?"

"Those pirates did a lot of damage to us, how can we stop the Vermin fleet?" Muher's voice had a hint of sarcasm in it.

"Those pirates, Chris," Thom growled, "had copies of the plans of this ship. They knew exactly what they were doing to cripple her. The captain was fighting them as if they were simple pirates. If he had taken the time to notice, he would have seen that all the shot raining on deck was a distraction for the real damage being done to our hull."

"The attack also killed off a lot of the non-pressed crew, didn't it, Thom?" The thought had just occurred to Tristan.

"It did, they were on deck or manning guns that didn't fire."

"I didn't know," Muher said. "Helps if you keep me in the loop, you know."

Thom looked away for a minute, then back, meeting Muher's eyes. "I wasn't sure who I could trust at that point, Chris. I know you are Dragon Corps, but…"

"Yeah, I get it. You were all suspect too, until I got to know you," the general agreed. "So far you, Aubrey, Webber and Avila seem okay. And Riggan, of course."

"Of course," Tristan said with a laugh, then realized something. "You didn't list the Air Weavers."

"No, I didn't." The words hung in the air between the three of them for a long time. "I still haven't decided. They are Guild members, but they tend to run closer to the Navy than Warriors and Weavers, and the Navy is far more tolerant of them. They don't rank senior officers, they can't give orders. So, no, I don't trust them completely yet."

"I'll remember that," Tristan said, remembering his first day onboard and how the Air Weavers hadn't made a point of welcoming him. "Anyone else?"

Muher laughed. "Everyone else."

They walked onto the quarterdeck after tea. Tristan checked the sails, listening to the hum in the rigging. There was a high-note to the sound, the Winds were still whipping the *Victory* through space at an incredible pace, even though almost all the sails were tightly furled. He noticed that Thom stared off into the empty space in the direction the Winds were blowing; the first officer shook his head and turned back to the ship.

"What?" Tristan asked.

"Nothing, I hope," Thom replied. "What's he doing?" He pointed towards the top of the mainmast.

Tristan looked up and caught the gleam of Fenfyr's scales at the top of the mast, in the Dragon's Roost. He was standing up, his wings canted to catch some of the Winds as if testing them. Tristan noticed the dragon turned his head, and he suddenly leaped free of the ship, swinging out into space. Surprised, Tristan watched until the dragon was out of sight.

"What was that about?" Thom was looking in the same direction.

"I don't know. Dragons are unpredictable at times."

"Very, excuse me for a moment," Thom said, heading down from the quarterdeck. He got to the main deck as a fight broke out amongst the crew. Shearer appeared on deck, the shrill sound of his whistle cutting through the air. Tristan started towards the stairs off the quarterdeck when Muher grabbed him.

"No, sir, sorry, but you are staying right here." The general moved to stand in front of him. "I am not letting you down on the deck in the middle of a brawl. Thom is capable of handling this, he has Shearer and Hall's Marines with him."

Tristan sighed. Muher was right, but it didn't make it easier watching his friend walk into the middle of the growing fight. More and more of the crew were getting involved, he saw the bright flash of a knife and someone shouted in pain. Suddenly three loud shots rang out and the deck fell silent. Colonel Hall stood to the side of the group, his gun out.

"Who started this?" Shearer demanded, his voice harsh in the quiet. The crew parted. A body lay on the deck, a knife protruding from its throat. "This is the man?"

"Aye, sir, 'twas him," the boatswain's mate said.

"Why?"

"He were speaking against the Navy, sir, and saying unkind things about the officers, sir. There's some of us that didn't agree with that."

"Who killed him?" Thom demanded.

The group stood still, none moving, none speaking.

"Well?" Shearer snapped.

Still no one spoke.

"Fine," Thom said, his voice clear. "Double duty for all on deck and no ration tonight." There was an angry muttering. "Does anyone wish to disagree?"

Tristan guessed that no one did when the group dispersed back to their duty stations. The med team arrived and took the body away, and after pacing out to the bowsprit and back, Thom came back onto the quarterdeck. "Damn all," he said as he walked over.

"What?" Muher asked.

"He was one of the pro-Guild crewmen. I doubt he was saying anything about the Navy. I think he was being removed."

"You think he was killed on purpose?" Tristan asked, aghast.

"Yes, like Anderson while we were still on station. They said he got drunk in the red light district and ran into a group of pirates. This death leads me to think he was killed. Horne and Anderson were close, they worked the same gun."

"Why?"

"I don't know, but I am going to find out. I am not letting murderers run lose on this ship," Thom growled.

"Barrett, report," Stemmer called from the other side of the quarterdeck. Thom stalked towards the captain, defiance in every line of his body.

"Things are getting ugly, Master Tristan," Muher said quietly. "I wish I knew why."

"I do, too, there has been something off about this ship since Darius first came to my office. I sometimes forget that. I've gotten caught up on life aboard her." Tristan looked up and saw Fenfyr sweeping back in, angling down towards the stern gallery on his cabin. "Excuse me, General."

"Of course," Muher said, then escorted Tristan to the staircase that led to the private entrance to his quarters.

Fenfyr was just poking his nose through the door when Tristan walked into the cabin. "Fenfyr? Where have you been?"

"Following a scent on the Winds. Taminick is flying further, but there is something happening. The Vermin are on the move, their stink is filling space, blowing on the Winds and fouling the stars with their passing."

"How many, Fen?"

"Many, Tris. I'm not sure. That's what Taminick is trying to find out, but there is a fleet coming, a big one. Bigger than the *Jupiter* Incursion. We have alerted our Guild, and Darius has spoken to the Weavers."

"We need to tell Thom."

"We do, we need to tell him to be ready," the dragon said, sounding sad.

"What is it?"

"Unless we find more ships to fight with us, Tristan, we are dead. That's how many are coming."

"Fen…"

"We will fight, I know we will, but if they come through here, there is nothing we can do."

XXII

The call for the crew to report rang through the ship several minutes after Fenfyr returned. The dragon slipped out of the cabin, heading up to perch on deck, and Tristan walked up to the quarterdeck to stand by the Elemental Interface. All the officers were gathered together by the taffrail and the captain was standing in front of them. He frowned when he noticed Tristan, his frown becoming a scowl as he watched Fenfyr settle on the main deck.

"Quiet!" the captain called, his voice amplified by the ship-wide com system. "I have news!" The mutterings fell silent. "I have been informed by Naval Headquarters that a Vermin Scout has been sighted!"

The crew growled angrily.

"Listen!" the captain continued. "They have assigned us the task of tracking this ship and killing it! They know that nothing will stand between this ship and victory!"

The crew let out a cheer.

"Mr. Aubrey, change our course to a heading of one fourteen mark seven. We are on our way. Prepare for battle!"

The cheer slowly built until it became a roar.

"Dismissed." The captain turned towards the officers. "I expect you to be every bit as ready as the crew."

"Yes, sir!" they said in unison.

"Very good," Stemmer said, then walked to Tristan. "I trust you are ready for battle as well, Weaver?" Tristan stared at the man. The quarterdeck grew quiet as the tension grew between them. The captain cleared his throat. "You will be ready for battle, Master Weaver, *sir,*" he said, grating over the last three words as if they caused him physical pain.

"Of course," Tristan answered, making a point of not using the man's rank. "As will Lokey Fenfyr, I am sure."

"Of course," the captain spat out and stalked away.

Tristan turned to look at the settings on the Interface, trying to hide his annoyance. The captain was openly insulting him in front of the crew and officers. It didn't bode well. When the time for battle came, who would they follow, the captain or the Weaver? It shouldn't be a question of either or, they should work together as a team, but Stemmer's hatred of the Guild was palpable.

"One fourteen mark seven, very interesting," Thom said, coming up beside Tristan.

"Why?"

"Remember what we heard from Harkins and Cook of the *Noble Lady*?"

"About the pirates meeting in sector nineteen?" Tristan said.

"Yes. Our new heading will take us right into the heart of that sector."

"That, of course, is followed by the question of where the captain got the information," Muher said, joining them. "As far as I know, nothing has come over the comm in the last six hours."

"The Vermin are heading in," Tristan said, telling them what Fenfyr had told him. "But he had no idea where they would break through. Taminick is still out, trying to find out where they are."

"So who is this mysterious scout ship?" Muher asked.

"And why does it happen to be entering our space in a sector where pirates manning Vermin vessels just happen to be gathering?" Thom frowned. "Something stinks here."

The ship suddenly rocked to the side. The blast of the Winds that hit them was strong enough to tear one corner of the sail on the mizzenmast away. Tristan grabbed onto the Elemental Interface as Thom and the officers began shouting orders. Fenfyr launched himself off the ship, flying to the mast and grabbing the sail in his massive foreclaws and holding on while the crew scrambled up the mast. Tristan tuned it all out and focused on keeping the sails in one piece as the Winds increased in force. He was aware as the crew got each sail furled and tightly secured so only the smallest bit of sail on the mainmast remained. There was enough to maneuver and keep them on an even keel, but nothing else. As he did that, he spoke the spell for Healing into the mizzensail that Fenfyr was holding, feeling it bond to the ship again. When that was accomplished, he took a step back from the Interface and looked around.

The Winds had caught them by surprise and the *Winged Victory* was showing the damage. A few ropes hung slack on deck and several large pieces of equipment had broken loose and rolled across the deck. One man was pinned under a large square box of some kind. He was screaming, his mates trying to keep him calm until the med teams could get to them. Looking across the quarterdeck, he noticed that Aubrey was holding his right arm very carefully and the Navigator Avila had blood on her face. A medical team arrived and took them both away. Tristan glanced around, looking for Thom and Muher, but they were nowhere to be found.

On a hunch he went below and called Riggan. "Did you see Mr. Barrett and the general?"

"I certainly didn't see them get into the private elevator and head for the lower decks, Master Tristan, if that's what you are asking."

"Perhaps we shouldn't do that either," Tristan said with a smile. He walked to the lift and punched the button. Considering the time it took for the car to get back to him, Thom and Muher must have taken the opportunity to go to the bottom deck. "Go tell Fenfyr what's happening," he said to Riggan then got into the lift and hit the button for the bottom deck.

By the time the doors opened, he was beginning to wonder if this was a good idea. Stepping out into the semi-darkness of the lower decks, he could hear his heart slamming against his ribs and hoped that nothing else could hear that deafening noise. He walked silently along the corridor. He'd never been there, but Riggan and Fenfyr had both described it to him, so he knew where he was and where he was going. The hatch that had been soldered closed was at the fourth turning on the left on the passage.

There was no one there, no crew wandering on errands, nothing, only the creaking of the ship and the soft sound of the atmospherics—the lower decks used forced air to reduce the strain on the Air Weavers. As he moved, he became aware of a soft break in the silence, it was not really loud enough to make out, the barest whisper of sound. Looking ahead, he guessed it was coming from the hall to the sealed hatch.

When he reached the corner, he stopped and turned so he could look where he was going without exposing too much of himself. Peering around the wall, he could make out two uniforms, Thom's Naval blue and the black of the Dragon Corps. Breathing a sigh of relief, he stepped into the hallway, still silent, wondering how to let the other's know he was there without breaking the quiet—without letting anyone know they were there.

That was when it hit him. It felt like he'd been punched. A wave of nausea engulfed him and he hit the deck, his cheek slamming into the cold plating. Trying to fight the nausea, part of his mind was telling him to keep quiet and not give into the urge to vomit while the rest of him was fighting to rid itself of whatever was filling him. As he fought it, he realized what it was—there was magic there, something vile and filthy in every inch of the hallway. Someone yanked him over, and he looked up at Thom's white face, the magic was affecting him as well, although he probably didn't realize what it was. Tristan shook his head and tried to stand. When he couldn't manage that, he rolled back over onto his hands and knees and crawled out of the passage and into the wider corridor as far as he could go before he collapsed again.

A sound came from the opposite direction and Tristan braced himself for the worst, only to be carefully picked up by Fenfyr. He heard the dragon hiss angrily, and a moment later he was being carried and then dropped into the lift. Muher and Thom stepped in and with a growling *"Go!"* from the dragon, the lift was in motion.

"Help me up," Tristan said, holding out his hand.

"What happened?" Thom asked, hauling him to his feet.

"There was something in the hall," Tristan explained.

"I felt it too, I think we both did. I was sick from the minute I turned the corner." Muher waited as the doors opened and they walked into Tristan's cabin. "What exactly were you doing down there?"

"I could ask you the same thing," Tristan replied.

"We had a reason to be there," Thom said. "You have no reason to be on those levels. You could have been killed. How many times have we told you…"

"I'm okay, so stop yelling, I have a headache." Tristan rubbed his head.

"Here you go, sir, this will help." Riggan appeared with the tea service. He set it down on the table, gave Thom and Muher a stern look and left.

"You can't go wandering all over the ship!" Muher snapped.

"I was not wandering all over. I knew right where I was going, I was following you two." Tristan poured himself a cup of tea, trying not to let his hands shake too much. "How are you feeling?"

"A little sick," Thom admitted, dropping into one of the chairs. He reached for the tea pot. "Chris?"

"Me too. There was something in that hallway. Poison?"

"No, it was dirty magic," Tristan said.

"Dirty?" Thom looked confused.

"A long time ago, a very, very long time ago, they used to divide magic into two kinds—white and black, good and bad, but it's not that simple. Over the centuries, magic and spellworkers have evolved and things changed. Magic is not black and white, but there are shades of intent or use. Dirty magic is magic designed to poison, to stop, to harm someone. It's Healing turned backwards. I've only met a few practitioners of that aspect of the craft, and oddly they were all Rogues."

"Rogues?" Muher stared at him. "You think there is a Rogue Weaver on this ship?"

"I don't know, it hit me too hard to do any kind of diagnostic. I know there was one on the ship at some point, because they cast a net over that hallway. If you had spent more time there, it would have eventually killed you. I'm more sensitive so it hit me harder and faster. I wonder if that's what Fenfyr has been smelling? Magic does have a scent, according to dragons."

"We have to get back down there," Thom said.

"If you go back, the magic will kill you, Thom." Tristan leaned forward. "We need to find a way into that area that doesn't involve going through that hatch."

"It's the only one into the bottom hold."

"There has to be another way."

Muher laughed bitterly. "If the weather were better we could go out and cut a hole in the hull. What did I say? Why are you staring at me?"

"The hole, could it have reached that deck?" Tristan asked.

"It not only could, but it did. Damn! Why didn't I realize that?"

"Realize what?" Muher asked.

"The pirate attack, they cut a damn precise hole in our hull. I thought they were probing for weaknesses, but they weren't."

"What then?" The general looked from Tristan to Thom.

"They were making a way to get something or someone onboard ship. But what and when? It must have been in the graveyard watch when the work crews were done and the area closed off so the Air Weavers could take a break." Thom huffed angrily. "I need to get into that hold!"

"We have to be careful, whoever performed the magic might have left a marker in the spell so it will hit you harder when you go down there again," Tristan explained. "We have to find another way in."

"We do," Muher agreed. "Until then, we play it low and slow and keep our ears open."

"I'll let Riggan know to be extra careful."

"All of us, Master Tristan," Muher said. "I think we all need to be careful."

They finished tea and then headed up to the quarterdeck. Tristan wanted to check the sails before he went to sleep, and Thom wanted to make sure everything was running smoothly. Muher tagged along "just to look threatening". The deck was quiet as the ship settled down for the night, a small crew was on deck, but most were below at dinner or already in their bunks. Tristan glanced at the Elemental Interface, then stopped. His heart started hammering again. Someone had been at the intricate device, he could see a deep scratch in the surface of the deck by the bottom of the piece. Bending over, he checked it carefully. Nothing had been unseated yet, but that's what it looked like they had been trying to do.

He quietly left the quarterdeck and walked into his cabin. "Riggan, can you come up on deck in about three minutes? Bring a bag of some kind."

"Of course," Riggan said.

Tristan went back on deck and looked around, Thom and Aubrey were talking quietly on the other side of the quarterdeck and Muher was gazing over the taffrail. Moving slowly so no one would notice, Tristan bent over the Interface again and spoke softly, the Latin comforting in the situation. The clips that held the device to the deck slid away and Tristan stood; keeping his hand on the Interface, he turned so he was blocking it from the view from the deck. A moment later Riggan appeared. Without a word, Tristan lifted the Elemental Interface up and slid it into the bag. Riggan met his eyes for a moment, Tristan mouthed *"hide it well"* and the servant disappeared.

"Weaver!" Stemmer said from behind him.

"Yes, Captain?" he asked mildly. He noticed that Fuhrman was walking towards Thom and Aubrey.

"We need to have a talk," Stemmer said with a laugh. "Then you are taking a walk."

"Are you threatening me?" Tristan smiled.

"It's not a threat." The captain pulled a gun. "And don't count on that damned draft horse to help you, he's already drifting." The captain waved his hand and Tristan could make out the tumbling form of Fenfyr in the Winds, a limp body buffeted by the gale around him. "Greedy bastard likes grapefruit and you can get a lot of poison in one of those."

"Fenfyr!" Tristan cried, his heart breaking. "No." He dove at the captain, there was a sharp pain in his head and everything went black.

XXIII

There was a cold sticky feeling on Tristan's cheek as he regained consciousness. His wrists ached and with a tiny motion, he discovered he was shackled, the metal digging into his wrists as the fog cleared from his mind. The weight on his ankles he guessed came from similar shackles. He opened his eyes to total darkness, sighing he tried to figure out where he was.

"Tristan? Are you awake?" Thom's voice was anxious, an undercurrent of pain filling it.

"Yes. Where are we?"

"Brig," Muher replied. "Deck five, second cell."

"Aubrey?" Tristan asked, easing himself into a sitting position.

"He was taken prisoner, and Avila. Fuhrman was brutal handling Aubrey, I think they ended up dumping him back in sickbay."

"Do we know why?" Tristan reached back, hoping to find a wall to lean on.

"No," Thom answered. "Tristan, about Fenfyr…"

"He…" Tristan shook his head, willing the tears away. "He can't be dead." The grief threatened to tear him apart.

"They'll pay for it, Master Tristan," Muher said.

"Since we're stuck in the same brig, I think it's safe to drop the formality, Chris," Tristan said with a bitter laugh.

There was a beeping at the door and it slid open. When their eyes adjusted to the bright light from the corridor they saw Fuhrman and one of the crew were standing outside the cell with guns trained on them. Tristan glanced over at Thom and noticed the bruises on the man's face, similar wounds marked the general.

"Up," Fuhrman snapped. "We need you on deck."

"Doing Stemmer's bidding?" Thom asked, but didn't move.

Fuhrman started laughing. "You fools, spending all your energies worrying about Stemmer. Did you really think we would leave this in the hands of that clumsy idiot? Now get up."

"Um, no," Muher said.

"General Muher, this makes me so happy. You see his defiance, men?" This comment was directed to someone in the passageway outside. "Let's show the crew what defiance gets you." Two men came into the cell and dragged Muher to his feet. "You two, come with us or I'll shoot him."

Tristan stood, swaying as a wave of dizziness washed over him. Thom was beside him and leaned over to steady him. "You aren't going to get away with this," Tristan said.

"Get away? The Navy *planned* this." Fuhrman waited as they shuffled out behind the men dragging Muher. "This was in the works all along, you only just slowed our plans a little."

They trudged down the hall and to the lift. Muher fought the men holding him the whole way until one of them hit him hard enough to stun him. After that, the general's struggles were more token protests than anything. When they got on deck, Tristan realized that it must be at least six bells in the morning watch. A large number of the crew was gathered and there was a grating erected in the center of the deck.

"He wouldn't," Thom muttered.

"Shut up," Fuhrman snapped. "Tie the good general up." He walked over to the grating as the men secured Muher to it. "You and I have been at odds for a long time, although I am not sure you realized it was me. There were ten involved in the Stars Plot, and it's not over, it's just beginning, general, and you have only arrested five of the ten." He laughed. "And now, I am going to enjoy something that I have been looking forward to since you stepped onboard." He held out his hand and one of the crew handed him a cat o'nine tails.

"I think twenty will be enough to subdue you into behaving as *my servant should.*"

"Drop dead," Muher spat back as they tore his shirt off.

"Thom, are they going to…" Tristan broke off in horror as Fuhrman lashed the whip over Muher's back. He opened his mouth to protest, but Muher caught his look and shook his head. Tristan clenched his fists in helpless frustration.

"And that is one," Fuhrman said happily. "Two, three, four…" When he reached twelve, the general's knees buckled and at fifteen Muher let out a cry of pain. Tristan had no idea how the man had held back for so long, he was hanging limp from the shackles as Fuhrman shouted twenty. "Get him down from there."

The men released Muher and dragged him over and dropped him by Tristan and Thom. "I'kay," he muttered.

"This is the price for being loyal to the filth of Guild and the draft horses. This is what will happen if you help them. This is where you will be left until we drop you into space. Do you understand?" Fuhrman said to the crew.

"Sir, yes, sir," they caroled.

"Take them below while we prepare," he demanded. "And if you try something, Weaver, Barrett is next on the grating."

Tristan nodded silently and followed them back down to the cell. This time they were left with a small light, barely enough to breach the darkness, but after their eyes became accustomed to it, there was enough to see. He made his way over to where they had dropped the general—on his back of course—and gently managed to turn him over so the pressure was off the wounds the whip had left. Seeing the damage, Tristan swore under his breath.

"Chris?" he asked softly.

"Here," Muher groaned.

"Can we do anything for him?" Thom looked at Tristan. "There's water here, but I wouldn't trust it."

"I can help a little." Tristan closed his eyes and tried to remember the Healing spell for humans. As he spoke he felt the spell form and after a moment the general sighed. "I'm sorry, I can't do more than that. I'm not any good at the finer bits of healing." Tristan said, leaning back. "So was that for the crew's benefit or ours?"

"Both, I think," Thom said.

"What do?" the general muttered.

"What?" Thom asked. "Chris?"

"What are they doing? They need a Weaver to fly the ship, don't they?" Muher said.

"They do—maybe that's what's been in that sealed hold, a Rogue to fly the ship," Thom said. "They could have brought him on while we were docked."

"Then why not just kill me?" Tristan asked.

"My guess?" Muher said. "They want you to fly it for them to demoralize the Guild. If you refuse they will kill you and use their Rogue."

"I was thinking the same thing," Thom agreed.

"I won't do it," Tristan stated firmly. "I won't."

"We're not expecting you to, Tristan," Muher said. "And I'm prepared to pay whatever price that means. I am Dragon Corps, and those bastards murdered Lokey Fenfyr. I would like to peel their skin off for that."

"I refuse to believe Fenfyr is dead." Tristan shook his head. "Until I am sure, I... I can't."

"So, who is our Gunner? He is obviously not just a Naval officer," Thom mused. "Probably Intelligence—they are some of the most outspoken against the Guild and spend most of their time trying to scheme ways to reduce the Weavers' role. Although that is difficult when you need a Weaver to create the sails and fly the ship."

"They still need a Warrior," Tristan said.

"Yes, but there are a lot of Rogues, compared to the number of Sail Weavers. They could find someone, and a disgruntled Rogue would happily fly the ship for them." Thom met Tristan's eyes. "I've known a few, and they will do anything they can to help the fight *against* the Guild."

"But the sails need to be attuned, it's one thing when you have time, but they are planning on using this ship to stop the Vermin, there is no time to attune a Warrior to the sails," Tristan pointed out.

"Which is why you are still alive, I think," Muher said.

"And we are back to the 'I won't do it' portion of the discussion." Tristan leaned back, trying to get comfortable.

They were silent, each lost in their own thoughts. After several minutes Tristan became aware of the sound of movement. If he didn't know better, he would say it sounded like the masts were dropping down into the ship. That's when he noticed that the hum of the rigging had stopped, in fact there was no sound except for the clanking of tools and the hum of the mast motors. Something was happening.

He was getting ready to ask the others when the door opened and Rose Webber stepped in, her black medical bag in her hand. "Unshackle these men!" she snapped to the sailor with her. The man hesitated and Webber turned on him. "I said get those things off them, or do I need to…" She let the threat trail off, and from the way the man's face went from ruddy to white, Tristan guessed whatever it was, it was bad. The man came over and unlocked the shackles on Tristan, Thom and Muher. "Now, you, get out. I will buzz when I am ready to leave."

"Doctor, I was told…"

"And I am telling you. They are not going to attack me, and you can damn well get out of here. You really don't want to push me on this," Webber snarled. The man opened his mouth, closed it and stepped outside. Webber waited until the door closed before approaching them. She knelt down beside Muher. "Your back is a mess, Chris," she said, her voice light and teasing.

"I suspect it's just the beginning too," he replied. "Fuhrman said something about making me his servant."

"He'd better hope he never gets injured enough to fall under my knife. Hippocratic oath or not I will cut out his eyes." Her voice was mild, they might have been discussing the weather, except for the steel Tristan could see in her eyes and the set of her mouth. "I need to treat these wounds, Chris, some are deep and will get infected. I know what that creature uses on his scourge."

"Do what you need to, Rose." Muher put his head on his arms.

"This is going to sting." She pulled out an aerosol can and shook it up. "Topical anesthetic," she explained to Tristan and Thom. She sprayed Muher's back and waited for a moment. "Can you feel this?" She poked his back with her forefinger.

"Only pressure, no pain."

"Good, I'm going to get to work, then." She started cleaning his back, whatever she poured over his skin was bubbling bright orange. "That bastard," she said under her breath.

"What is it?" Tristan asked.

"The whip—it's not just a whip, it's full of poison, so each lash drives the poison in deeper. That's why the disinfectant is foaming orange. It's a chemical reaction to the poison. I guessed as much, which is why I demanded to see you. I have my rights as Chief of Medical, and they do not want to piss off the Med Corps. If we left their ships they would be out of luck."

Once it had stopped foaming, she swabbed Muher back. It was bleeding again, the blood flowing over his back and onto the floor. "I'm sorry," she said.

Tristan looked at her, she wasn't part of whatever the Navy had planned, she was only trying to do her job. "We understand."

"Let me check your cheek, Master Tristan," she said as she finished with Muher. As she daubed at the wound on his face, she bent close and said almost soundlessly. "There are many that support you and the Guild. We are waiting, you will need us."

"Thank you, doctor," Tristan said, meeting her purple eyes. "Your help is much appreciated."

She nodded and turned to Thom, checking him over, then moved back to Muher. She bent over and kissed his cheek. "Don't do anything stupid, Chris, please."

"I'll try, Rose," he said, laughing softly.

"Promise."

"I'll try. If I see a chance, though…" He trailed off, Tristan saw him look around the room his eyes briefly stopping on the camera in the corner. "I promise."

"Thank you," she whispered. "Mr. Aubrey will recover from his wounds, Mr. Barrett. I suspect he will be joining you in the brig by tomorrow. Ms. Avila was… She was injured a little worse. I am keeping her with me."

"Thank you, doctor." Thom stood, his eyes on the camera. "We appreciate the lack of shackles and I personally give my word that we will not try and escape from this cell." Tristan noticed the slight emphasis on "this cell" and hid his smile. "Please give Mr. Aubrey and Ms. Avila our best."

"I will," Webber said with a curt nod and then turned and buzzed the door. "I'm ready."

"At least we know that Patrick and Liz are okay," Thom said. "I was worried. He was covered in blood, but it might have been from someone else. When they moved to take they ship, a few crewmen protested." He sank back down to the floor.

"Whatever she put on my back is awesome," Muher said. "Can't feel a damn thing."

"Enjoy it, I doubt they'll let her back in," Thom said.

"No, as soon as I can walk, Fuhrman will have me leashed. Damn, I wish I knew who he was…"

"What do you mean?" Tristan asked.

"He knows me. I'm Dragon Corps, Tristan, and while the Weavers are used to seeing us, we don't mix with the rest of humankind. We serve the dragons and, indirectly, the Guild. The fact that he knows me leads me to believe we have crossed paths, but I never forget a face."

"He got a new one?" Thom suggested. "It doesn't even take that much to change a face, the shape of the nose, the thickness of the lips, then change the way you walk and a whole new person appears."

"You speak from experience?" Muher said, eyeing him suspiciously.

"I was taken by pirates when I was younger. I saw a lot of men become someone else," Thom said calmly, although his hands were clenched. "There are one or two I wished I still could recognize."

"It's a thought, but who?" Muher shifted into a sitting position. "Naval Intelligence, but who?" He stared into space for a long time. "Huh."

"Huh?" Tristan repeated.

"It can't be."

"Who?" Thom asked.

"I've always wondered what happened to Admiral Gerard Holton. He dropped off the face of the worlds. Right after the Stars Plot attack on the Guild. It was like he ceased to exist. I thought he might have been killed for botching the bombing, but maybe he was…" Muher cocked his head. "It might be him. Which would be bad, the man hates the Guild with a passion and believes that dragons are nothing more than… He said it, didn't he? It is him. Damn. I'm screwed."

"You mean he called dragons draft horses?" Tristan shifted so they could talk and keep their voices down low enough so they might not be picked up on the microphones.

"It's like the pirates that use Vermin ships—because of what they are made of. They think of the dragons as nothing more than building material for a ship," Muher said with disgust.

"I know, Chris, I heard a pirate say it, then realized later what he must have meant," Tristan said, swallowing hard, willing Fenfyr to be alive and not in the hands of the Vermin. He could feel exhaustion dragging on his body. "We should rest while we can."

"Agreed," the general said and closed his eyes.

Tristan slept fitfully. His body ached and the worry for Fenfyr was haunting his dreams. He was relieved when Thom shook him awake. "What is it?"

"Someone's outside, I heard the door code," Thom said.

A moment later, the door opened and Fuhrman and an armed crewman stood there. "Up, time to work." When they remained seated, Fuhrman sighed. "Get up, Weaver, or I will kill them. As much as I enjoy the idea of having Muher as my servant, killing him quickly would have a certain satisfaction as well."

Tristan stood. "We'll come." He walked out the door and into the passageway, trying to get an idea of how many of the other cells were occupied. He counted at least fifteen that had red lights on them, indicating they were in use. Some of the crew had stayed loyal and fought for it. Some, at least according to Webber, were loyal and free. It all depended on how many they could rally. They stepped into a lift and the doors opened on the quarterdeck.

"Now, Weaver, you can fly the ship."

Tristan glanced over to where the Elemental Interface had been, there was another in its place. "I don't understand."

"Raise the masts!" Fuhrman said, obviously relishing the moment.

The great mast began to rise above the decks and as they did so, Tristan felt a waved of nausea wash over him. It took everything he had to not vomit as he caught sight of the sails. He was shaking his head in denial, but there was no getting around the horror that filled the places of the once sparkling willowisps.

Tristan's sails were gone and in their place stretched Vermin sails, the skins of at least three dragons dangling from the masts. "No," he whispered.

"Oh, yes," Fuhrman laughed. "And now, you fly the ship."

XXIV

The dark shadows of the sails covered the deck and the death-scent filled the air around them as Tristan stared up at the masts. He couldn't believe the evidence before his eyes. Knowing pirates used Vermin ships was one thing, the Navy having these sails was something entirely different. It was then Fuhrman's words soaked into his head.

"What do you mean, fly them?" Tristan said in disgust. "I thought they flew themselves."

"Ah, yes," Fuhrman purred. "The dragon. We considered using the slaved dragon mind, like the Vermin do, but it is harder than we thought. We've come up with a hybrid solution. We can use these sails in the Winds without the disruption of the dragon's brain. It's also far easier to train someone to fly them."

"Then why do you need me?" Tristan looked at the man. "Oh, you don't really know if they'll fly this ship, do you?" He forced a laugh. "And you want someone who has skill to move them into the Winds the first time."

"Maybe, and the thought that it's a dragon lover like you makes it so much sweeter."

Tristan walked over to the Interface. It was ugly, bone and stone, the raw edges sharp and without the elegance he was used to. Pacing around it, he "felt" for the magic that had created it, and could sense nothing. It was just slammed together and rigged to the electronics that were there in the roughest way possible. It might have fit once, but after having the Elemental Interface he'd created in place, this new one would never sit correctly.

"No," he said, stopping in front of Fuhrman. He cast a glance over the man's shoulder to Stemmer and the others that supported this atrocity. "I will not fly this ship or touch those sails. By creating this, you are no better than the Vermin."

"We are!" Stemmer said, stepping forward. "That's been the problem all along. We need ships like theirs to fight, our Navy doesn't stand a chance with archaic sails and magic holding it together."

"I notice you haven't tossed the Air Weavers in the brig, I guess you still need that magic."

"Some is more useful," said Stemmer.

"I will not fly this ship." Tristan squared his shoulders.

"I'll kill you," Fuhrman said.

"I think we both know you are going to do that anyway," Tristan replied.

"I'll kill Barrett too!" Fuhrman snapped.

Tristan didn't want Thom to have to follow him to his death. It was his choice, not Thom's, that he was refusing to fly the ship. Tristan turned and met Thom's eyes. He saw Thom swallow, then nod. Thom knew this was coming and he was prepared. Tristan brushed some dust off his sleeve. "No."

"No what?" Fuhrman snapped.

"No, I will not fly your filth. I will not serve your kind. You are worse than the Vermin after all,"

Fuhrman began to turn red, it started in his neck and crept up his face until even the tips of his ears were beginning to turn purple. He took several slow breaths, and before Tristan could duck, backhanded him hard enough to knock him off his feet. Thom helped him up and they turned to face Fuhrman again. "Toss them overboard."

"Sir?" one of the midshipmen said.

"You heard me!" Fuhrman shouted, He grabbed Tristan by the collar and dragged him to the taffrail. "Bring the other!"

"Just me," Tristan said desperately. "Barrett's done nothing wrong." He looked over to where Sullivan and Sheea were standing. Sullivan moved his hands ever so slightly and Tristan could see the man's mouth moving as he whispered a silent spell. Hoping it was enough, Tristan stared at Fuhrman. "Not Barrett."

"Oh no, I've been waiting for a long time to get rid of him. You know, they actually intended that he *command* this ship? The Guild-chasing dragon lover! So, he gets to go swimming too, for as long as it lasts." Fuhrman waited until Stemmer hauled Thom beside them. "Open this spot!" he demanded. Sullivan stepped forward, speaking a spell and a small tear in the shield began to hiss.

Tristan closed his eyes, doing his best to remember the spell he would need. He started it as he felt the tug of the vacuum of space against his back. The Air Weavers were doing their best to give him a little extra room before he needed to create his own spell, but Tristan wasn't sure he could remember the words as the panic coursed through him. He'd had to learn them all to become Master Weaver, but this was one he'd never had the chance to try in an uncontrolled environment. Did the air come before the pressure or the other way around? He cast through his memory, trying to get it straight as he uttered the Latin.

"Praying won't help you now." Fuhrman laughed and shoved Tristan out the hole and into space.

He was caught in the drag of the vessel and held motionless at the taffrail. The spell was closing around him, so when Thom was tossed over the rail, Tristan was there to grab him, reaching out and immediately wrapping the spell around both of them. He could tell it was imperfect. There was a soft hiss at their feet, and the space itself was small, but they had air for the time being and were protected from the vacuum. How long he could keep the spell functioning was another question.

"The atmosphere of the ship extends too far! Fix that, Aether!" Tristan heard Fuhrman snap. As he spoke shot whizzed close by them, enough to catch Tristan's leg. He hissed in pain, but finished the last few lines of the spell.

"We need to get out of sight," he said as soon as he could. They didn't have much time, the Air Weavers could only keep them close to the ship for a few moments longer.

Thom nodded and pushed against the hull, before Tristan was

really sure what Thom intended, they were on the underside of the ship. "It's a blind spot on the sensors," Thom explained. "We can't stay here forever, they will figure it out.

"I'm trying to figure that out right now."

"Hey, we're not dead," Thom said with an odd laugh.

"I noticed," Tristan answered a smile. "Sullivan boosted the atmospherics long enough for me to get a spell started. He must have protected you as well."

"Yeah, or I would have popped."

"Lovely thought, Thom."

"They can't bring the guns to bear under the ship—it's the one weakness in her defenses."

"Nice to know they can't shoot us." Tristan tried to make the spell a little stronger, he could feel blood trickling down his leg, but he was desperate. He wasn't going to let Thom die because of him. Fenfyr was already gone, and now this. "I'm not sure how long I can keep this up. I'm not an Air Weaver."

"Any time is better than no time."

"I guess," Tristan said. "They are going to rendezvous with the pirates that use the Vermin ships. Are they going to take the ships or ask the pirates to fight with them?"

"Fighting fire with fire?" Thom asked. "I don't know. I know that even a lot of the Navy that dislikes the Guild will be horrified by this when it comes out."

"Unless they managed to stop the Vermin incursion. If they do, whether or not the sails actually made the difference, it will be because of those filthy sails."

"True." Thom looked around them. "I never realized how big it was when there was no ship around."

Tristan couldn't help it. He laughed. "It's a perfect day for swimming."

"I guess it could be worse," Thom said. "Although how, I'm not sure."

"I might not know the magic to keep us alive?"

"Yeah, that does help."

"And once we move away from the ship we're going to get caught in the Winds."

Thom frowned at him. "Can't you make a sail?"

"A sail? No, you have to gather the willowisps and…" Tristan trailed off, thinking.

"I hope Chris doesn't do something stupid," Thom said.

"He will, Thom, but I think Fuhrman won't kill him. He wants to torture him."

"I know."

The silence closed in around them, the huge mass of the *Winged Victory* above them. The ship was barely moving. They were right at the edge of the Winds and the sails had not been put to use yet. Tristan was turning Thom's idea about a sail over and over in his head. They had no mast, but maybe he could make something like the tiny sails spiders make. He could tell Thom was getting motion sickness, the other man was turning green. They weren't going to last long like this, maybe dying when they were first shoved overboard would have been better.

"Would you last longer without me?" Thom asked. "I drain the spell, don't I?"

"Not enough to justify you dying out here. We're getting out of this."

"You make it sound easy, what do you plan to do, Tristan? Sneak back onboard?"

"Eventually, but for now I think I am going to try something else. Give me a minute."

"Okay," Thom said quietly. Tristan knew the man was afraid. He could feel his own heart slamming against his ribs, panic kept just barely under control.

Taking a moment to focus, he closed his eyes and spoke the few words of the spell used to collect willowisps. At first nothing happened, but after several very long minutes, he could see light sparkling on his eyelids. He opened his eyes and saw that they were surrounded by willowisps. Seeing them gave him hope his plan might work. "I'm going to try and Weave us a sail, Thom. I can't guarantee it will do anything, as soon as it seems to be working, push us into the Winds, okay?"

"Okay," Thom said, placing his boots against the hull.

Tristan began the spell for the Weaving, carefully drawing the willowisps together. At first they seemed reluctant, and he was worried it wouldn't work. A second later he felt the spell "catch" and the sparks began Weaving together into a small sail. He shaped it carefully, using a tiny line of willowisps to reach into their bubble and then wrapping it around his belt, then Thom's. The belts would act as the ropes and the small sail looked more like a bubble than a sail. The last of the spell slipped from his lips and he felt the tug of the Winds on their small sail. Thom shoved them away from the ship and the Winds caught them immediately. Not having any control over where the Winds carried them, they were whipped back behind the ship and within seconds the huge mass of the *Winged Victory* was a tiny speck.

"It worked," he said, a little surprised.

"I noticed," Thom said with a laugh.

They rolled in the Winds, the sail catching each eddy, and soon they were tumbling. The movement was making them both ill. Worse, Tristan could sense the spell for the atmospherics starting to thin. The sail was strong, but soon it would be pulling nothing but a pair of belts through space. He had no idea how long it would last, his best guess was another two hours, and as soon as they were exposed to the vacuum of space, they would be dead in seconds.

"Thom," he said softly.

"I know, I can hear the hiss. How long?"

"I don't know. I was hoping we might get further, but I didn't know which way the Winds would blow us."

"It's okay, at least we didn't give those bastards the satisfaction of seeing us die."

"Yeah," Tristan agreed. "I will keep it as long as possible. If I shift a little from the air and more to the pressure we might last longer."

"Do what you need to do, Tristan. It was an honor serving with you."

"We're not dead yet."

"I know, I just wanted…"

A sudden gust caught them, and then they rammed into something very solid and warm. Tristan opened his eyes and saw red—the red feathers of a dragon. "Taminick?"

"I'm sorry it took so long to get here, I was tracking something else, then I smelled those sails. I came as quickly as I could," she said, catching them carefully in her foreclaws and cradling them against her as she opened her wings and swung into the full force of the Winds. "I will take you to the ship, and they can care for you while I track the other."

"Ship? What ship?" Tristan asked.

"The *Noble Lady,* they have been following you at a special request of the Dragon Guild. Fenfyr is there, recovering, and you can recover as well."

"Fen...He's alive?" Tristan whispered.

"Yes, no thanks to those Naval creatures."

"Alive," Tristan said again and smiled. "Thank you," he whispered to the willowisps and released the sail so the tiny sparkles could float through space freely again. He felt the bubble of air around them strengthen as Taminick closed her hand, he sighed and relaxed against the dragon's claws. They were safe.

It was nearly an hour before Taminick swept towards the graceful little frigate. As soon as the ship was in view, Tristan could see a dragon stretched out along the port side of the ship, his skin gleaming in the light of the sails. When Taminick canted her wings and dropped to the deck, Thom nearly collapsed and Tristan pulled free of her grasp and headed straight towards Fenfyr.

"Tris!" the dragon said, reaching out and pulling Tristan against him, his head tufts almost hugging him in his enthusiasm. "You're alive!" He wrapped a huge claw around Tristan.

"And you," Tristan said, leaning into the dragon's embrace. "I thought they'd killed you, I saw you..." He stopped when the tears broke free. "How did you escape?"

"I took one bite of the grapefruit and smelled the poison. It was enough to make me a little dizzy, they took advantage of that and grabbed me and threw me out an air lock. If I had known what they were planning, I would never have left you there, I would have struggled to get back no matter what, Tris, I'm so sorry."

"You're alive, that's all that matters, Fen. I thought..." He took a deep breath and turned to the rest of the ship. "Thank you all."

"You are very welcome, Master Tristan," Cook said. "We've been following the ship, waiting for orders from the Guild or the Dragons, since we happened to be going that way anyway. When Taminick brought Lokey Fenfyr to us, we knew there was trouble brewing."

"They do have Vermin technology, Fenfyr, you were right. The sails."

"Not the whole ship? They haven't slaved a dragon?"

"I think they tried," Thom said. "But the ship wouldn't fly for them. They must be lacking something the Vermin have to control the slaved ships."

"They don't understand the technology yet. They will, they just need to get to the pirates with Vermin vessels. They will be able to tell them how to override the dragon," Cook said.

"That's why they are headed there, then?" Thom asked.

"Whatever it is, we will stop them, Tommy Boy, but first you two need rest, medical attention and food, then we can have a small council of war."

"I need a secure line to the Guild, is that possible?" Tristan asked, still leaning against Fenfyr.

"I think we can manage that," Cook said. "This way."

Tristan followed the man through the ship to the communications room. Cook grabbed a first aid kit from a locker in the room and pressed a bandage against Tristan's leg. After establishing a secure line, he left Tristan alone.

"Tristan, what the hell is going on?" Brian demanded as he answered the line.

"I was thrown overboard."

"You were what?" the Guild Master's voice got louder on each word.

"There was a mutiny. Fuhrman and his monkey, Stemmer, had it planned all along. Brian, they have Vermin sails."

"What?"

"Vermin sails! They wanted me to fly the ship, but I refused. They are headed towards a gathering of pirates that use former Vermin vessels. I'm not sure if they intend to take the ships or if the ships are actually working for or with the Navy. Either way, the dragons need to know. They have to join the fight, and they won't with those sails on the *Victory*. I know a lot of the fleet will refuse to fly with the *Victory* now as well, and she is our last hope for that battle. She is the only one big enough to deal with the Vermin Ships of the Line."

"I know. I'll get Darius and we will find out where the Vermin are coming through. You stay out of trouble, Tristan."

"Sorry, Brian, I can't. I'm on a ship that's following the *Victory*. They still have Chris Muher and they poisoned Fenfyr, in addition to having Vermin sails and tossing me overboard. No, Brian, I am going after them with this ship. We have to have the *Victory*, and I'll be damned before I see them fight with that filth for sails."

"Tristan…"

"Demote me, transfer me, do whatever you want. I'm out here, and we don't have long."

"I know, but I get to worry, Tristan," Brian said softly.

"Yes, you do, and I'm worried too. I'll take as much care as I can."

"Dragon speed, Tristan."

"Get us help as soon as you can, Brian."

XXV

The high note of the Winds in the rigging woke Tristan. For a moment he thought he was in his cabin on the *Winged Victory*, then he realized the tone was different from his sails and their deeper song. Opening his eyes, he stared at the ceiling, disoriented. It took several moments for him to piece together what was going on. They'd been thrown overboard, and the dull ache in his leg had been caused by the graze of a weapon. Glancing over at the other side of the room, he noticed the other bunk was empty, the bed made with military precision. Thom was already up. Tristan swung his legs over the bed and carefully put weight on the injured one. It was still sore, but that was all. He decided to skip his morning yoga, and settled for pulling on his uniform and the clean, undamaged breeches that had been left for him.

Walking out of the cabin, he glanced around and spotted a lift in the corner. They must have been given a berth in officers' quarters. The large table in the center of the room and the doors leading to the officers' cabins had the same layout as the Gunroom on the *Victory*. He took the lift to the deck. Fenfyr was still stretched along the port side of the ship, his eyes closed as if he were sleeping. It made Tristan worry that the dragon was more seriously injured than he had been led to believe.

"Fenfyr?" he said, leaning against the dragon's side.

"Tristan! You're awake. I've been worried."

"Worried?"

"We all have," Thom said, walking up beside him. "You've been out for two days. Fenfyr was sure it was from the magic, but it didn't stop us worrying."

"Thom said you made a sail." Fenfyr moved so he could look at them.

"I did. It was only a small one, enough to get us away from the ship," Tristan pointed out.

"It was an amazing feat, or so our Weaver tells us," Cook said, joining them. "Not even Harkins claims to have seen anything like it, and if you know Harkins, he's seen everything."

"Even if he hasn't." Thom laughed. "I remember he had me believing this story about…" He stopped and turned bright red.

"Now, now, Tommy Boy, are you telling them about the Sirens of the Rim?" Harkins said, laughing as he walked over to them.

"I didn't believe long, and I was very young at the time."

"It was fun to see your face, though. Good to see you up, Master Weaver."

"Thank you." Tristan frowned. "Did you say something about following us?"

"Aye, we have been, Master Weaver, since you reported to the Guild and Dragons on Terra Octodecimus," Harkins said.

"Why?"

"Why?" Cook repeated. "There was obviously something going on, and they needed someone out here to check things out."

Tristan looked at them, then over at Thom. "I think I'm lost, I know you aren't pirates, exactly, but…?"

Thom grinned. "They are sometimes, but right now they have a letter of marque from the Guild and Dragons to hunt former Vermin vessels, gather intelligence…"

"And rescue swimmers," Harkins added with a snort. "Lucky for you, Taminick was that close. We've had to hang back in their shadow, so we would never have reached you in time."

"I know, she barely did," Tristan agreed. Fenfyr nudged him gently, without thinking about it he put his hand on the dragon's jaw. "So you've been tracking us."

"Yes, and the gathering of ships in sector nineteen. All Vermin vessels. It's been hard to keep Taminick and Fenfyr from diving in and tearing them apart."

"You promised we could as soon as you knew what was going on," Fenfyr said with a huff.

"Yes, and I meant it too," Cook said, smiling a feral smile. "Although I plan on taking a few myself. Filthy things. Thom said that the *Victory's* sails are…"

"Vermin bred," Tristan confirmed. "At least three." At this, Fenfyr let out a soft sighing sound. "They'll pay for it, Fenfyr."

"And for what they did to my ship!" Thom said. "So, it wasn't only a Rogue they had in the hold, but those sails."

"The sails had to have been placed onboard at Terra Octodesimus or I would have sensed them. After some time, the dirty magic would have built up to a point that they couldn't hide it any longer."

"What?" Harkins asked.

"He means that Vermin sails and Rogues stink," another voice said.

Tristan turned—and stared. "Alden?"

"In the flesh, what's left of it at least," the man said with a laugh. "It's good to see you, sir."

"So when you left you came out here?" Tristan asked.

"It was just like we discussed, with an additional thing or two. One of the Dragon Corps started a rumor that I blamed the Guild, then they smuggled me out of the Compound and onto the station with the letter of marque in my hands. The *Noble Lady* was waiting for me when I got there."

"We've worked for the Guild before, you see," Harkins said.

"So here I am, not quite Rogue." Alden laughed. "It's actually turned out rather well, they appreciate the Weaver on this ship, unlike some others." He glanced at Tristan with a grin. "They've never thrown me overboard at least. How did the Guild take that?"

"The Guild Master was very calm about it."

"Which means he is in a rage and all hell is about to break loose." Alden rubbed his hands together. "Good, we've been waiting for the fight."

Tristan was sitting on the bench by the bowsprit watching the stars rush by when Alden came and stood beside him. "Can I join you, sir?"

"Of course," Tristan replied. "The sails are well handled."

"Thank you!" Alden sat beside him. "I had to do some repairs, and then do the attuning myself. I have to admit, I respected you and your position a lot more when I finished. Weaving is exhausting! I nearly killed myself the first time, and it was just repairing a hole, which is part of what a Warrior is supposed to do."

"You hadn't figured out how to attune the sails yet?"

"How'd you guess?" Alden smiled. "It's still not like flying a ship that the Weaver attunes for me. I don't always feel completely in control. Luckily, you made these sails, and I have flown your sails many times. Once I managed to attune them a little, things were easier. Still it took almost too long for us to get out on a run. We stayed close to the station, waiting for you to show up. Word had gone around about a planned attack, and we wanted to be ready in case we were needed."

"Needed?"

"For evacuation, whatever we could do. This crew is made up of a lot of pirates—now former pirates, but they are all Guild loyal, and hate those that use the filth of a Vermin ship. They were hunting the Vermin pirates long before I handed them a letter of marque that makes it far more profitable. For every kill they can prove, the Weaver and Dragon Guilds pay them a hefty sum."

"I suspect the bounty is even better on the *Winged Victory*," Tristan said wryly.

"It's not quite the same. We need the *Victory*. She's our only hope. When I was first a Warrior, on my first ship, we were attacked by a Vermin scout." He swallowed. "We lost a lot of the crew, but worse, the dragon that flew with us was… he was taken." Alden shuddered in horror. "Never again. The *Winged Victory* is our best hope. She can stop their ships of the line, I've seen them fight, each ship fights as an individual, not as a fleet. With the *Victory* leading the big ships and frigates of the Navy in a massed attack, we could stop them."

"That's a lot to pin on one ship."

"Honestly, Tristan, there are only a few Vermin ships that are big enough to take her on at all. Think about it, each ship needs a dragon, how many dragons are the size of the *Victory*?"

"Darius, and a few others, not many," Tristan answered.

"The fact that the Navy has resorted to Vermin technology is not sitting well in a lot of the stations. I know it was something that was worrying the Guild, that people would do anything to win the war. That's not as true as we thought. I've heard gossip, you know? And they experimented with Vermin pirate vessels, they were talking about it in some of the less savory bars on station. Since I made it clear I hated the Guild for what happened, people talked to me."

"Until you shipped out with the *Noble Lady*?"

"Surprisingly, a lot of the pirates dislike their fellows that use the Vermin ships. Even if they are outside the law—or even disgruntled with the Guild—it doesn't mean they accept or approve of what the Vermin do to create a ship. What the Navy is doing now is, in some ways, even worse."

"What do you mean?" Tristan asked.

"Trying to make it palatable by only using the skins and not the slaved mind—as if that's better somehow. It's worse if you ask me. I'm happy I can help." He rubbed the back of his neck. "I know we never really saw eye-to-eye..."

Tristan burst out laughing. "Is that what you call it?"

"That's what I call it now," Alden answered, grinning at him. "I've learned a lot out here, and you know no matter what an ass I was, or am, I am loyal."

"I never doubted your loyalty, Alden, never once."

"Oh, good."

"In fact, I would have recommended you for the *Victory* if the Guild had chosen anyone else, and I was planning on giving her back to you after her maiden flight. You know I was surprised that they didn't make you Master Warrior after... after Master Miri's death."

"No one could replace her," Alden said softly. "I certainly couldn't. I belong out here, the Master Warrior needs far more patience than I'm capable of. I'm afraid I would bash the Navy rep over the head in a meeting, and that wouldn't do any good."

"They still haven't found a replacement," Tristan said. "You never know where we'll all end up after this."

"I know those bastards on the *Winged Victory* are going to end up keel-hauled at the very least," Alden growled.

The call to quarters suddenly rapped out over the ship-wide comm system "Ship sighted! Weaver to the sails, all hands to quarters!" Cook's voice boomed out. "It looks like a scout. We need to take her down. All hands to battle stations!"

Alden stood and ran towards the quarterdeck. Not knowing what else to do, Tristan followed him, hoping he could repair the sails if they were fired on, letting Alden concentrate on the battle. Thom was already there, his teeth clenched. Fenfyr was sailing over the ship, joined by Taminick. It took a moment for Tristan to spot the ship, but once he did, he could tell there was something different about it. There was no way to describe how he knew it was different. It looked like the former Vermin ship flown by pirates—but this was a Vermin ship piloted by the creatures themselves.

"I'll handle repairs, with your permission, Alden," Tristan said, stepping up beside the Warrior, and putting one hand on the Elemental Interface. It hummed as it recognized him.

"Thank you, Master Tristan," he said grimly. "Ready, captain!"

"Take us in!" Cook ordered.

The ship swung about and headed towards the incoming vessel. Before they were in weapons range, the Vermin ship started firing at them. The first few shots were torpedoes, massive metal monsters that headed straight for the *Noble Lady*. The crew was watching, and at the last moment, with a flurry of orders between the captain, Alden and the helmsman, the ship moved out of the way and the torpedoes continued on in a straight line past the ship and off into space.

As they reached the maximum distance of their guns, Tristan heard the order to fire and the *Noble Lady* sent a blazing broadside towards the Vermin vessel. Their ship wasn't fast enough to turn out of the way of the entire broadside, and he saw several explosions rock the vessel. The guns fired again, this time the Vermin answered and their shot screamed across the deck, tearing holes in the sails and ripping through the metal plating of the deck. Staring across the void, Tristan caught a glimpse of one of the Vermin crew in the bright flash of a gun. It was the first time he had seen one in the flesh, the dark reptilian creature was more horrifying than any description he had ever read.

Tristan immediately turned his attention to the sails. He'd recognized them when he saw them, and felt his mark on their initial

Weaving, so he began feeling the willowisps and tuning out everything that would distract him from keeping the sails whole. He had no sooner repaired the mainsail, than the mizzenmast was struck, some of the metal raining molten drops onto the deck. He was yanked aside, but stayed focused on his job. The sails were needed and he couldn't let anything break his concentration. As he repaired the tears, and idea struck him and he tightened the weave of all the sails, watching them change in color until they were sparkling with a fierceness he hadn't seen before. The next round from the Vermin ship only put a small hole through one of the upper sails. Tristan maintained the tighter Weave as he heard the *Noble Lady's* guns fire again and again. Finally, Thom clapped a hand on his shoulder, breaking his concentration.

"The dragons are going in," Thom said.

Tristan looked up in time to see Fenfyr and Taminick descend on the ship. They tore through the creatures on deck, tossing them into the vacuum ruthlessly. There was still scattered fire from the lower decks of the ship, but it was poorly aimed and whizzed past ineffectively. Finally, Fenfyr landed on the deck, close to where the Interface would be, and Tristan whispered the spell of release. He felt the dragon die as Fenfyr gently took its life. Once it was past pain, Taminick and Fenfyr tore the ship to shreds, leaving nothing bigger than a human hand.

"Thank you, Tristan," Alden said.

"You're welcome," Tristan replied, a little dazed by the magic he'd been using.

"Strengthening the sails like that was brilliant! How'd you manage?" Alden asked.

"I'm not sure." Tristan looked up, watching as the willowisps settled back to their usual configuration.

"It worked. One of those volleys should have taken down all the sails. I've seen it happen many times before," Cook said, walking over to them. "It's something you need to get back to the Guild, explain how you did it. You saved the ship, we were goners."

"We were?" Tristan asked, surprised.

"Yeah," Thom said softly. "We never stood a chance against them in a ship this size. They were bigger and once our sails were gone we would have been destroyed. I've never seen anything like it." He slapped Tristan on the back. "It really was something!"

"Finding that scout does let us know something," Harkins said.

"What's that?" Tristan looked around and noticed Fenfyr settling down on the deck. The dragon nodded that he was unharmed.

"The Incursion, they're coming through here. That's the third 'scout' we've seen."

"The third?"

"We were far enough out to cut and run with the last two, this time we were too close, it came out from behind a squall. Three scouts," Cook paused. "They're coming—and soon."

XXVI

The sound of hammers filled the ship as the crew of the *Noble Lady* repaired the damage from the battle. Tristan, Thom and the officers of the ship were seated around the table in the captain's quarters, a large map spread out in front of them. It had taken Tristan a moment to get his bearings, but now he was following the discussion about where the Vermin were expected to come in and the relative position of various stations and the fleet. He listened as they discussed their options, but he was worried about how to get back to the *Winged Victory* and take control again. Thom was staring at the wall, so Tristan assumed his friend was thinking about the same thing.

Someone knocked on the door. "Sir?"

"What is it?"

"We've got an odd distortion on the comm, sir, and I thought you should hear it."

"Pipe it in, Damian."

"Yes, sir."

The next moment a hiss of white noise surrounded them. It didn't take Tristan long to hear what the man had been talking about—under the steady hiss was a series of breaks in the sound. "What is that?"

"Shh," Thom said and grabbed a pen. He cocked his head and

started writing. "It's Riggan."

"Riggan?" Tristan asked.

"Shh." Thom was writing something down. Tristan leaned closer to read it. *...have Interface, still in hiding in lower hold. Sheea Aether here too. There is a small breach in hold. Riggan. I have Interface, still...* "It's a repeating message in Morse code."

"Morse code? How would Riggan learn that?"

"Marty Riggan?" Harkins asked.

"Yes," Tristan answered.

"He learned it with us. He wasn't always on a Naval vessel, and we use the old code to get around being overheard."

"He wasn't...?" Tristan looked at Harkins, a little confused.

"Riggan was taken too, Tristan, and served his time with the pirates. A lot of the able-bodied sailors have," Thom said, looking at him.

"He was going to be your servant, not Stemmer's," Tristan said with sudden realization. "You met him back then, it's why he reports to you, why he looks out for you."

"Yes." Thom grinned. "We've known each other a long time. He managed to escape before I did, but he's been on every ship I've served on since." Thom looked thoughtful for a moment. "I thought they'd plugged that hole. Hmm, I wonder what they've been up to?" It sounded almost like he was talking to himself. After a moment he looked up at Tristan. "How'd he get the Elemental Interface?"

"I gave it to him. Right before everything started, I went on deck and noticed someone had tried to pry it loose, so I unclipped it and gave it to him. As long as we stayed on course, and didn't need to raise or lower any sails, no one would notice, since the pedestal was still there."

"Good thinking," Cook said. "Would it have worked with the sails they have now?"

"No, it's attuned to my sails and created for them. If it had been destroyed, though, we couldn't use those sails again."

"We need to get you back onboard." Cook looked at Thom. "How many in the crew are loyal?"

"Far more than Stemmer thinks. The doctor let us know that much when she came to treat Chris after the flogging." Thom paused. "And there were at least fifteen cells in use in the brig. Each cell could hold as many as ten men."

"Sir, hail from the Guild," Damian said, knocking, then coming into the room.

"Thank you, pipe it in," Cook said.

"This is Rhoads," the Guild Master's voice boomed into the room.

"Darius," the dragon added.

"Admiral O'Brian," a third voice said.

Tristan raised his eyebrows as he met Thom's eyes. He knew O'Brian, the man was one of the moderates that sat on the Joint Council. "I'm here with Thom Barrett, and the Warrior and Officers of the *Noble Lady*. Lokey Fenfyr is listening in as well," Tristan said. "What's going on?"

"First, I would like to apologize for what happened to you, Master Weaver. The men behind this will pay for their crimes," the admiral said.

"I don't doubt that," Harkins muttered, then jumped when Thom kicked his shin.

"Thank you, Admiral, what's important now is getting the *Winged Victory* back and on her way to stop this Vermin Incursion."

"We agree," the admiral said. "We have diverted two frigates, but we're not sure they will be able to cut the *Victory* off before this rendezvous in sector nineteen that Darius and the Guild Master have briefed me on."

"I've been thinking about that, sir," Thom said.

"Is that you, Thom?" O'Brian asked, his voice warm.

"Yes, sir."

"Good to know you made it."

"Not many who've been thrown overboard can say they have. It was thanks to the Master Weaver that we survived, and that's what I've been thinking about."

"What?" Tristan said, frowning at Thom.

"What do you mean?" the Guild Master demanded.

"When we were tossed overboard, the Master Weaver created a small space for us to survive."

"Yes, yes, we know about that," Rhoads said.

"He also made a sail, just big enough for the two of us."

"You did what?!?!" Brian roared.

"It's true, Guild Master."

"That's impossible."

"I would have agreed with you several days ago, but it's the truth." Tristan shifted uncomfortably.

"How? You have to gather the willowisps, you need an Elemental Interface, you have to…"

"Brian! I did it, I made one just large enough to carry us away from the ship."

The Guild Master continued to sputter, but the calm voice of Darius blocked it out. "What was your plan, then, Thom Barrett?"

"If the *Noble Lady* could get us ahead of the *Victory,* staying in her blind spot, Tristan could make another small sail and we could head back to the ship that way. We've been informed there is a small hole in the ship. It's in the lower hold, so we would be off the sensors, and they purposefully have all internal surveillance on that deck off—it's where they were hiding the sails. We know at least some of the loyal crew is there, along with the Elemental Interface for the Master Weaver's sails. All we'd have to do is take the ship deck by deck. If there is enough loyal crew left, we should be able to manage."

Tristan—everyone in the room—was staring at Thom. "I'm not sure I can do it again, Thom."

"Of course you can," Thom said carelessly. "And with that new strength you can add to the sails, we stand a real fighting chance against the…"

"Excuse me?" Brian's voice was deceptively mild. "What was that about sails?"

"Master Tristan did something to the sails while we were fighting a Vermin scout. I was at the Interface, flying the ship during the battle," Alden said. "He volunteered to do the repairs, they were sails he created in the first place, so he was attuned. About halfway through the battle he did something, the willowisps changed and the shot started bouncing off the sails."

"And we were going to mention this when, Master Tristan?" the Guild Master asked.

"I don't know what I did, Brian. If I remembered the spell, I would have sent it back to you immediately, to see if anyone else could do it," Tristan answered. That was the thing he'd been thinking about since it had happened, not the spell so much, but how it had been accomplished. Would a Warrior be able to do it? Or would it take a Sail Weaver to accomplish the magic? If they needed both, there would be no time to get Sail Weavers to the fleet—more to the point, there weren't that many Sail Weavers. They ranked the rest of the Guild for a reason. They had to be far more adept, far more talented than any of the other branches of the Guild. "I'm not sure a Warrior can do it, I think it needs a Sail Weaver."

"Or maybe only you, Tristan Weaver," Darius said gently. "You always surprise us. As to the rest of the plan, we must gain control of the *Winged Victory* at all costs. The plan is a sound one, with two additions. You will need Fenfyr and Taminick to help disposing of the filth that is littering the ship."

"You couldn't keep us away," Fenfyr said.

"You need to get there before they reach sector nineteen," O'Brian said. "It's a well thought out plan, Thom, and you know we have frigates on the way. The whole fleet is heading towards the coordinates that Cook has sent, a small scout we sent into the area reports three more Vermin ships on the way in—they're still the little ones, but we know it's just the beginning. When you take *Victory*, if you can keep Stemmer and Fuhrman alive it will be helpful. The Joint Chiefs have met and we discussed what has happened aboard the *Victory*. Your rank has been restored, despite the howls of Davis and his supporters. As of now you are entered into the rolls as the Captain of the *Winged Victory*. Good luck, Captain Barrett," O'Brian said. "And, Thom? Be careful."

Thom blinked, cleared his throat and smiled. "Thank you, sir."

"I don't like this Tristan, not one bit," Brian said. "But I am out-voted, and I know you too well, you'd go even if I ordered you not to, so don't get yourself killed."

"I won't."

"Good luck, Tristan Weaver," Darius said. "We will meet on the battlefield."

The communications line clicked off. There was silence in the room as everyone absorbed what had been said. Tristan's heart was pounding. He wasn't sure he could gather the willowisps to make a tiny sail again, he might end up getting them killed this time.

"Well," Harkins said, breaking the silence. "At least it's not going to get boring."

Tristan was pacing the deck, cup of tea in his hands and Fenfyr watching as he paced. The dragon hadn't said anything, but Tristan could tell Fenfyr had reservations about the plan. Every time he walked past the dragon's head, he stopped and waited for a comment when none was forthcoming, he paced on.

"Tristan?" Thom asked hesitantly.

"What?" Tristan kept his back to the officer. He was upset that Thom hadn't bothered to ask him before he suggested the plan.

"About the…"

"The suicidal plan you got approved?" Tristan snapped.

"Look, it's not suicidal…"

"I don't know if I can make an atmosphere again, Thom, let alone the sail."

"You don't need the atmo, Tristan, we have suits. I was planning on that. I know you can do the sail again, you did it once."

"I was desperate, Thom, I'm not even sure I can remember the spell I used."

"Tris." Fenfyr spoke for the first time.

Tristan sighed, walked over to the dragon and leaned against him. "Sorry, Thom. I'm really not quite sure how I did it, and there's no way to control it, we'll be floating free like we were before."

"That's why we'll have something to hook onto the ship with. I've already alerted Riggan to be watching for us. Once we're onboard we can plan from there."

"You really think this plan is going to work?"

"Of course I do, what could possibly go wrong?" Thom asked, a grin of delight on his face. "All we need to do is get onboard, take the ship, get your sails back up and find the fleet. Easy peasy."

"I can't believe they gave command of the flagship of the fleet to a maniac," Tristan said, laughing. "I'll do my best, and at least with the suit, I can focus on the other magic."

"Like I said, easy peasy." Thom sighed. "We should be in position in a few hours if you want to get some sleep."

"I think I will, thanks." Tristan smiled and watched as Thom walked towards the lift to the lower decks. "This plan is insane, Fen."

"I know you can do it, Tris, you've already done it. Taminick and I have been talking and we will wait far enough out so they can't see us until it is too late."

"We'll need to arrange a signal," Tristan said, shifting so he was curled in the bend of the dragon's foreleg.

"I'm sure Thom already has a plan for that, too," the dragon snorted. "There'd better be some grapefruit left. Imagine ruining perfectly good grapefruit with brandy."

Tristan's heart gave a twist. "That's how they tried to poison you?"

"Yes, but they're numb noses and I'm not that greedy. I only ate one, and it was enough to know something was wrong. I was sick, but that's all."

"I'm glad," Tristan said fervently.

"And I of you," Fenfyr gently pulled him in close so he was partially covered by the dragon's feathers. Tristan relaxed against the warm body. "Sleep, Tris, I will watch until it's time for you to go."

The deck was alive with the bustle of activity as the crew got ready to launch Tristan and Thom. The *Noble Lady* had pulled ahead of the *Winged Victory* easily, Cook said he suspected that the larger ship was having trouble with the sails and was running with only the engines. That came as good news for Tristan, at least the ship wouldn't be going at a high Wind speed when they tried to slip by on his small sail. He'd spent the last hour trying to remember how it felt gathering the willowisps in deep space, and then Weaving them into the small sail. Every now and then he would check on Thom. Despite the man's easy assurances, Tristan could tell he was worried about what was going to happen and how many of the crew had remained loyal.

"The suits are ready," Harkins said, walking over to where Tristan was still leaning against Fenfyr.

"Thank you, Harkins," Tristan replied, then turned to Fenfyr. "I'll see you soon."

"Yes," the dragon said, gently touching him with his head tufts. "Be careful."

"You, too."

"Are you ready?" Thom asked.

"No."

"Comforting, let's go then."

Thom led the way to the quarterdeck where Harkins and Cook were waiting with two suits. Once they were in them, Cook showed Tristan how to control the air flow and use the suit-to-suit communicators. As they locked the last of the latches into place, Tristan had to fight an overwhelming feeling of claustrophobia. Somehow being out in the void with nothing but his hissing, half-strength bubble, seemed preferable to this. He sighed and gave the thumbs up. The plan was that the ship would slow and they would slip off the taffrail and into space. Then Tristan would call together the willowisps and make the sail while the *Noble Lady* was still in sight, just in case something went wrong. He took one last look around the ship then stepped onto the rail. At a signal from Alden, he and Thom stepped off and they were floating free. The suits were tethered together and Thom bobbed several yards from him.

Concentrating, Tristan focused on the spell to call the willowisps, the Latin echoed oddly in his helmet. He felt sure it wasn't going to work for them a second time when he noticed the small sparks starting to gather around them. They bounced between the two suits as if they were curious of what they were. Tristan ignored it and continued until he was sure he had enough to make their sail. Slowly he changed the spell, moving the words from the Gathering to the Weaving, watching as the sparkles began moving together, in and out and around until they had a small sail that looked more like a parachute than anything. With the final part of the Weaving spell, Tristan tied the willowisps to himself, using his body as a rough replacement for the Elemental Interface. Nodding at Thom to let him know it was time, he moved the sail out of the shadow of the ship and into the Winds.

Once in the Winds they were whipped along at breakneck speed. This time they didn't tumble, the sail was more stable than his first effort, and they pulled away from the *Noble Lady* faster than Tristan would have dreamed possible. He had no idea how long the suits would withstand the buffeting of the Winds, but no sooner had he thought that, than the huge mass of the *Winged Victory* appeared in front of them. Focusing on the sail again, he managed to maneuver them down and under the ship. He was working so hard to keep them stable that the *clang* of the hook catching the side of the ship surprised him. Speaking quickly, he released the willowisps with a soft thank you so they could continue on their way, and the next moment Thom was pulling him towards the hole in the side of the ship. It seemed only an instant and they were inside. Riggan helped them out of their suits as Sheea closed the hole in the atmosphere again.

"It's good to see you, sirs," Riggan said, grinning.

"And you, Riggan, I was sure you would have been found out by now," Thom said, slapping the man on the back.

"Who, me, sir? They couldn't find their asses…" He cleared his throat. "They never expected us to hide down here, and so they haven't come looking."

"I thought I ordered this hole closed," Thom said, gesturing to the side of the ship.

"Ah yes, and so you did. Mr. Shearer thought we might need a small hole, just in case, sir, and so he opened it. Now that you're here, I'm sure he will do his best to close it up."

"I'm sure he will," Thom grinned. "Now, let's figure out how to get my ship back."

XXVII

The massive lower hold was only partially lit, casting eerie shadows along the walls. In the distance, Tristan could see the gentle sparkle of willowisps. He ground his teeth together at the flash of anger that his sails had been dumped into the same space that had held the Vermin sails. *Not for long*, he promised them. Riggan had kept the Interface safe, hidden in the bag Tristan had given him. When he checked it, there was still a soft glow indicating it was connected to the sails. All they needed to do was drop it back into place and get the sails back onto the masts. The sound of a door swinging open made him hold his breath. A moment later, Shearer appeared.

"Riggan?" he called.

"Here, sir, we have visitors," Riggan answered.

"What?" The boatswain walked towards them, then stopped, a shocked look on his face as he recognized Thom and Tristan. "Mr. Barrett! I never thought I'd see you again!"

"Thank you, Shearer, it's good to be back," Thom said, shaking his hand. "How many loyal crew can we count on?"

"More than Fuhrman knows, that's for sure." Shearer laughed. "Even some of those that supported him at first are not so sure now. It's the death scent of those sails hanging above us. The Rogue can't get them to fly, and Stemmer told them to run under power to a rendezvous to get a, and I quote 'proper Interface for the sails' which, as I'm sure you know, can only mean one thing."

"A slaved dragon," Tristan said.

"Yes, and while there are those that still think that's the only way to win, there are others who are beginning to doubt it. They'll support you, Mr. Barrett."

"Captain," Tristan corrected him.

"What?" Riggan asked, delighted.

"Admiral O'Brian said that the Joint Chiefs had restored Captain Barrett's rank, and he is now rightful Master of the *Winged Victory*," Tristan explained, hiding a smile when Thom blushed.

"Good. Finally things are settling down the way they should." Shearer beamed. "We'll have to take the ship deck by deck."

"I figured as much," Thom said. "Once we get to the brig, we need to get everyone out without alerting the rest of the crew."

"You'll need a distraction to manage that."

"We'll figure one out. The quieter we can be at first, the more success we'll have when we reach the top decks. There are two frigates inbound to support us, I'm not sure that they'll be here in time."

"Fenfyr and Taminick are also waiting to join the fight at our signal," Tristan added.

"First things first," Thom said. "We need as many of the loyal crew who are off-watch to get down here so we can formulate a solid battle plan. And can you get us sidearms?"

"Yes, Captain!" Shearer snapped off a salute. "I'll be back as soon as possible."

"Thank you, Shearer." Thom waited until the man was gone before turning to Riggan and Sheea. "Report, Riggan."

"Well, sir, it's like Mr. Shearer was saying, some of the crew that supported Stemmer and Fuhrman are losing their courage in the face of those sails. Even their staunchest supporters are unsure about slaving a dragon on a Navy ship. Sure and there's a few who still think that the Vermin tech is the only way to beat the Vermin—fight fire with fire—but more think what's been done has put a stain on the ship. Some of the more superstitious are convinced that the dragons are haunting the ship, what with all the odd noises they're hearing on the crew decks." Riggan grinned. "Not that I know anything of that, of course."

"Of course not." Tristan smiled back.

"The Air Weavers are being held in officers' territory when not on deck. I managed to get Sheea away when they were taking her to the brig."

"The brig?" Thom asked.

"I refused to work with those sails on the ship," she said firmly. "I told them they could toss me overboard like they had the two of you, but I was not going to help them with that filth." She shuddered. "So they were taking me to the brig with the promise that I was to be a..." she swallowed unable to continue.

"You know what Fuhrman had in mind for her, Captain Barrett, sir," Riggan said. "His perversions are well known. So, on the way down to the brig, the ghost of the dragons struck and *poof* she disappeared right from the lift! Mr. Aubrey disappeared from the sickbay, and we've tried to get to General Muher, but they keep him chained in the Captain's cabin."

"We'll get him out of there, Riggan," Thom assured him.

"I know you will, sir. I never doubted that you and Master Tristan would be back. It's why we opened up the hole and have been waiting for your signal ever since. We knew you'd come, and that once you were here—well, sir, we knew you would be wanting the ship."

"I do, and more. The Vermin are coming and we have to be there to stop them. The fleet doesn't stand a chance without us, and I'll be damned before we miss that battle!"

"We'll be there sir, you haven't missed a battle yet," Riggan said.

"How hard will it be to get the sails up, Tristan?" Thom asked.

"It shouldn't be too hard, not if the men cooperate and the dragons help. Once the Vermin sails are gone, it should be only a matter of rehanging them. They were bonded to the ship, and they still recognize the Interface, so it *should* be simple."

"That would make things a lot easier." Thom paced. "We need to be quiet as we take the decks, so I think blades as much as possible if people won't join us. Riggan, is anyone in communications with us?"

"Officer Brown is, sir, and I believe this is her watch."

"Can you get word to her to lock down communications from the lower decks?" Thom asked.

"Consider it done," Riggan said and slipped away through the darkened hold.

"I have no idea how he gets around, but he appears and disappears all over ship," Sheea said. "Before they brought me down here, the rumors of the hauntings were already starting—odd clanks and other sounds would come through the walls. Several people disappeared on their way to various places and the Weaver's quarters have been sealed from the inside and, at least before I was taken, they were still unsure how to get in. There's a rigged charge on the door so they can't cut through."

"Riggan is a handy man to have on your side," Tristan said.

"Very," Thom agreed with a grin.

The sound of the lift and the door opening had them moving into the shadows. A large group walked out of the lift. Tristan guessed the lift had to have been over capacity to carry so many. Patrick Aubrey was with them. He stopped once they were out. "Captain?" he said to the dark.

"Aubrey," Thom said, stepping out so he could be seen. "It looks like you've gotten your promotion back as well."

"Thank you, sir," the man said, a feral glint in his eye. "I've been looking forward to the chance to explain to Fuhrman once and for all that I outrank his sorry ass."

Tristan was a little surprised. He'd taken Aubrey for a steady, older officer who was content with his position on the ship. Of course, now he realized that the Second Officer was probably originally the First Officer and Thom's second-in-command. A man didn't reach that rank without a few battles under his belt. Now that he had a chance to show his true colors, Aubrey's place as a fighting man seemed obvious. The sword at his side seemed natural.

"I know you have, Patrick, and I've been waiting to have the same discussion with Gary Stemmer." Thom grinned as Aubrey handed him a pistol and a sword. "We need a plan."

"I've been thinking about that for a long time," Aubrey said. "The next deck is nearly empty. Thanks to the hauntings, the crew has been avoiding the lower half of the ship. The few that remain are security on patrols, two patrols per deck, the size of the patrols vary.

They walk the deck, and their circuit takes about fifteen minutes from bow to stern. If one group takes the secondary lift and the other the primary, we should be able to take out both patrols simultaneously. We should be able to take the bottom four decks that way. Brown has communications blocked, even though everything is showing as green."

"Good start." Thom nodded.

"What about the other decks?" Tristan asked, accepting a sword and a pistol from one of the men.

"It might get tricky. I have no idea how many men are on those decks right now. More than the bottom few, less than usual. There is a twenty-four hour guard on the brig doors."

"Okay, we need to take those decks as quietly as possible, words by choice, blade if they fight, try to keep gunfire to a minimum. Once we're out of this hold, sound is going to carry," Thom said and the group nodded. "We will continue up until we can rendezvous on the brig deck. We'll come at them from both sides. If communications are down, the only problem we have is if someone gets away."

"No one is getting away, sir!" one of the men shouted. "If they are loyal they will fight with us, if they are Stemmer and Fuhrman's men, well, they can just go quietly into the brig or die like the Vermin filth they are."

A ragged cheer broke out at the man's words and Thom glanced over at Tristan. "The Master Weaver said that once we have the Vermin sails gone, our sails should go back up quickly. Once they are in place, we are heading off to meet the Vermin, they're coming in, men, and we're not going to miss this fight!"

"No, sir!" they chorused.

"Now, remember, quiet is the key, and we will rendezvous outside the brig. Once we've freed the others from there, we will decide how we want to take the upper decks. Understood?"

"Yes, Captain!" Aubrey said, and the others shouted agreement as well.

"Okay, let's go."

A small group formed behind Thom and Tristan. To his surprise, Tristan noticed that Riggan had rejoined them, sword in hand. Thom nodded to Aubrey and they set off, Thom's group headed towards the primary lift while the others moved through the hold to the secondary lift. Tristan stepped in beside Thom, aware of the weight of the weapons he was carrying. After the bombings, all the Masters had weapons training, but he didn't think the classes were intended for re-taking a warship. Still, he had no intention of being left behind. As the lift slowed, his stomach gave an odd twist.

Thom was out the door first, signaling the others to silence. In the quiet of the deck, all Tristan could hear was the breathing of their group and the hammering of his heart. After several seconds, Thom indicated they should follow him and he slipped silently down the corridor, holding up his hand when the sound of a door opening echoed through the hallway. Three men stepped into the corridor and stopped dead, staring at Thom and his group. One of them turned to run, but Riggan was on him faster than Tristan imagined, driving the man to the floor, his blade held against his throat.

"By act of the Joint Chiefs, I am legally Captain and commander of this ship, are you with me or against me?" Thom asked quietly. The men regarded him with round eyes.

"You're a Guild lover," the man on the floor said, spitting in Thom's direction. Before anyone could say anything else, Riggan slit the man's throat.

"I ask again, join me or fight me, your choice. He made his." Thom pointed to the corpse on the floor.

"With you, sir," one of the men said.

"Good." Thom looked at him. "Are there more?"

"Not with us, sir," the man said. "No one would patrol this deck."

"Okay," Thom said, turning back towards the lift. "You can keep up your patrol. I'm trusting in your word that you are with the crew. If I find out differently…" He let the threat hang in the air as he glanced at the body again before he gestured for the group to move out. "I need a volunteer to stay here and make sure this deck is secure."

"Here, sir." One of the men stepped out.

"Thank you, Ortiz, if you have any trouble, solve it simply."

"Yes, sir," Ortiz answered, grinning at the two security men. "Clean and simple is my favorite way."

Thom nodded and they piled back into the lift. The next two

floors went smoothly, the men surrendering even before Thom could open his mouth. Tristan was getting the feeling that they were being set up. Whether it was intentional or not, the vague sense of unease was answered on the next deck. There were seven security men waiting by the lift. Thom must have sensed something was wrong as they reached the deck—he shouted "Down!" to the group, shoving Tristan aside. As soon as the doors opened, the security patrol opened fire. Tristan heard one of their men shout in pain, and he was aware that Thom jumped out of the lift, blade drawn and, without hesitating, ran the front man through without a word.

The rest of their group was pouring out of the lift now, two of the patrol broke loose and started running up the corridor. Waving his sword, Riggan led a party of men after them. Tristan was pushing himself up when he sensed movement headed towards him. Instincts he didn't know he had kicked in and he was dodging the blow from the sword before it could connect with his head. He came up under the man's swing and kicked out towards the middle of the man's mass, the way he'd learned in his self-defense classes. It didn't do any damage, but it did serve to surprise the man long enough for Thom to step in and neatly disarm the man with a blow that removed his arm below the elbow.

"That was a little more difficult," Thom said, wiping sweat off his face. He turned, ready to fight again when pounding footsteps echoed through the passageway. He relaxed when Aubrey appeared. "Patrick?"

The man walked over, blood splattered his uniform. "They were waiting for us. I think we have a traitor in our midst. We should change our plan. They probably have half the crew waiting on the next deck," he said, his voice so quiet Tristan could barely make it out.

"I agree. Straight to the brig?"

"Yes, sir, but we let the men think we are still going deck by deck. There won't be time to warn anyone that we're headed to the brig."

"See you there!"

"Yes, sir!"

"We got them," Riggan said, walking up, his sword bloody. "Sorry it took so long."

"You made it in time, we're about to head up."

Riggan looked at Thom for a long moment, then over at Tristan. "Aye, sir. Understood."

Tristan had no idea how Riggan had guessed that the plans had changed, but he knew somehow. He could tell when Riggan stepped closer to him, blocking him from the men in the lift and from the door, so that if they were fired at again, he would be in the way of the shot. Tristan was opening his mouth to say something, when Thom shook his head. With a sigh, Tristan held his tongue.

Once they were in the lift, Thom shielded the buttons from the other men and punched the deck for the brig. The lift slid into motion and a few moments later the door was opening—not on the deck the men thought, but on the darkened corridor of the deck that held the brig. Some of the men muttered, but they all stepped out at the ready. Thom glanced over them, as if he could figure out which one had betrayed them. Of course, it could have been one of Aubrey's men as well. It was a full minute later when Aubrey and his group appeared. With a nod at Thom, they all set out for the end of the corridor, the men moving into the cover of the various openings and cargo, in case someone opened fire.

Tristan's hands were shaking and his throat was dry. This was the most exposed he'd been in the whole process and the walk from the lift to the brig seemed like miles. There was no guard on the door, he heard several men comment on that in quiet tones. In fact the entire deck was empty.

"They set the trap below us," Thom said. "We weren't supposed to jump over it."

Even so, they approached the door to the brig cautiously. The odd eerie quiet was all around them as Thom keyed the door open. It slid back to reveal two guards. Riggan and Aubrey were on them before they had time to draw their sidearms, and then Thom was hitting the button that opened all the cells. Rose Webber was one of the first to come out.

"Doctor? What are you doing in here?" Thom asked as she walked towards them.

"I disagreed with Fuhrman's treatment of his new... servant," she said, anger snapping in her eyes.

"Is he still alive?" Tristan asked.

"Oh, yes, I think that bastard plans on keeping him alive as long as possible. He's even made it impossible for Chris to kill himself." She frowned. "Are we retaking the ship then?"

"Yes, ma'am. Captain Barrett and the Master Weaver have come back to lead us to victory," Riggan said, sounding far too happy for the situation.

"You're enjoying yourself, Riggan," Tristan said.

"Yes, sir, I am, sir, and wait till we get to the upper deck." He laughed. "Just wait."

"We need to deal with the situation first," Thom said.

"Situation?" Webber asked.

"We have a traitor in our group, somehow they alerted security we were coming."

Riggan growled. "A traitor? I've had enough of traitors." He glanced over the group surrounding them. "You know," he said, his voice loud enough to carry over the crew. "I remember when I served with Captain Barrett before, we had a crewman who gave our position away to pirates. Vermin-lovers at that. You should have seen what he did to the man before we could stop him. I never knew you could actually tear a human apart, and then... *then* he gave him to the dragon to finish off."

Tristan was staring at Riggan, wondering what Thom would say, when one of the men towards the back of the group started edging away.

"Stop him!" Thom called. The man was dragged up before them. "You're lucky I'm in a good mood. I'm throwing you in the brig for now. We'll discuss the rest when the dragons join us."

"You're the traitor, Barrett. You know the only way we can win is to fight them on equal ground, just because you are a dragon lov..." He didn't finish. Riggan had grabbed him and thew him into one of the cells, hitting the close button on the door.

"So, sirs, shall we proceed to the top decks?"

"Are you all with me?" Thom asked the group.

A loud "Aye!" answered him.

"And now," Thom said, grinning at Tristan, "It's time to call in Fenfyr and Taminick as well."

XXVIII

The group gathered in the brig, looking expectantly at Thom. As they stood there, Tristan could see the change in his friend. Thom had always had an easy authority about him, but there was something more. He was in command, and it showed—his shoulders were square and even as they considered the seemingly impossible task of retaking the rest of the ship, he accepted it easily. It was his due, his ship and it was that simple. Thom motioned for Tristan, Aubrey, Webber and several of the freed officers to join him in the small space that separated the cells.

"We are going to need to take the main deck completely by surprise. We've locked up one traitor, but he was obviously talking to someone, so I suspect that they are going to start locking down the ship and hunting us sooner rather than later," Thom said quietly.

"If we can get onto the quarterdeck, we can swing the big guns around to the deck," Aubrey said. "I'm not sure I want to fire on our own men, but most of those on deck are handpicked by Fuhrman and Stemmer."

"So you don't mind a warning shot or two, Patrick?" one of the other officers said with a grin.

"Not at all, Jacob," Aubrey replied. "Although you don't get first shot at Fuhrman, you know."

"I was second gunner under him, I should, by rights," the man said.

"Enough!" Thom snapped. "If we can get control of the guns it will help, getting onto the quarterdeck will be the trick."

"Excuse me, sir," Riggan said quietly.

"What is it, Riggan?"

"If I may be so bold, sir, there is the private staircase from the Weaver's quarters onto the deck."

"He's right," Tristan said.

"I heard them saying the doors were all rigged with charges," Aubrey pointed out.

"Of course they are, sir. I would be a fool to let them into the Weaver's quarters, wouldn't I?" Riggan grinned.

"Wait." Thom turned to Riggan. "Does that mean you have a way to get in and out of there without using the lifts?"

"I have ways of getting around the ship without using any of the lifts or other public ways. How do you think the dragons have been haunting the place?" Riggan asked with a smirk. "I'll take you all up there, and disarm the charges on the door."

"That would be helpful. One group can head directly onto the quarterdeck, the other through the maintenance hatchway that services the officers' lift. It will put you onto the main deck, below the break for the quarterdeck. Can you get them there, Riggan?"

"I'll take them first, and be back for you in a few minutes, sir," Riggan said.

"Patrick?" Thom said softly. "This is a volunteer mission."

"Like I wouldn't volunteer. But don't shoot me, okay?" The man laughed and motioned to Riggan. "I need half of this group to come with me. Volunteers only," he said.

"I'm with you," the second gunner, Jacob, said. As soon as he spoke, a group gathered around Aubrey. With a quick salute towards Thom, they left the brig.

"Now, Dr. Webber, I want you to stay here until we give you an all clear from the deck. We're going to need med teams, and having you get shot up in the process won't be any help to us," Thom said, meeting her eyes.

"Understood. As much as I want to be there, I know my duty. I've served on the lines before and I know where I can do the most good. This is a good defensible position too, just in case."

"Good, I'm glad I didn't have to fight you over that." He turned to Tristan.

"No," Tristan said before Thom could speak. "I am going with you."

"If you get killed there is no one to fly the ship," Thom said.

"If I get killed, it means you and everyone is dead too, Captain, you know that. I might as well be there so we can get the sails up as quickly as possible."

"Master Weaver..." Thom began.

"Captain Barrett," Tristan answered, wondering if he would have to pull rank on his friend.

""Stay behind me."

"I will," Tristan assured him. He had no intention of running onto the deck first. He wished that there was a way he could prevent Thom from leading the attack, but he doubted there was anything he could say that would make a difference.

"Captain? Are you ready?" Riggan asked, appearing out of nowhere.

"I can see why the crew thinks the ship is haunted," Tristan said with a nervous laugh.

"We'll wait for your call, Captain," Webber said. "Try and..."

"We'll free him," Thom said quietly. "Don't worry about that. Riggan lead the way."

Riggan headed out of the brig and turned left, leading them away from the bow. "They've locked down all the lifts. The main work passages are closed up as well. They're expecting something," Riggan said as he moved further and further into the ship.

"I figured as much. Our traitor did a lot of damage before we caught him," Thom muttered.

"No worries, Captain, sir, I never used those ways. That would have gotten me caught on the first day."

"How have you been getting around?" Tristan asked quietly as they walked.

"Well, not that I looked, but there was a set of plans just sitting in your quarters, sir. I saw them there and it was a bit of a gift, they mark all the open spaces in the ship, and an old ship rat like me, well, it was easy to find my way around with a map in my hands."

Thom chuckled. "Very good, Riggan."

"Thank you, sir. Here we are."

It looked like all the other wall panels. Tristan could see the disbelief on the faces of the group as they stood in front of it. Riggan ignored them and pulled a small knife from his pocket. He slid the blade along the seal in the wall and suddenly the panel popped open. Pressing a finger to his lips, Riggan motioned them inside. Thom led the way, with Tristan right behind him. Once they were all in, Riggan sealed the panel behind them and turned on a small lamp. He stepped up beside Thom.

"We can't use much light, or they'll know," he said almost soundlessly. "And no talking at all."

"No talking," Thom said, and the order passed quietly down the group.

Once he was sure everyone was ready, Riggan set out. They were walking on a piece of grating that was no more than three feet wide. Tristan made the mistake of looking down once and nearly fell over as a wave of vertigo hit him. The grating ran along the inside wall, but he could see the sparkle of the willowisps on the sails many, many decks below. Suddenly the ledge seemed much smaller than it actually was. Knowing how far down it was didn't help the pounding of his heart at all. After what seemed like an eternity, Riggan stopped by a small ladder. He set the light down beside the first rung and started up. Thom followed, climbing easily. Tristan stepped onto the rung cautiously. His leg was still not as strong as it could be, there was the old wound from the bombing as well as the more recent graze when they were tossed overboard. He hoped that neither his hands nor his legs gave out on the climb.

It didn't take long before they were out of the small pool of light cast by Riggan's lamp and surrounded by a deep, impenetrable darkness. The lack of light seemed to suck away noise as well, and Tristan's world narrowed to the rungs that went on forever. One hand up, one foot, the other hand, the other foot, over and over. He was beginning to get tired, his leg aching and his back pulling along the old scar. Grinding his teeth, he kept going. It had been his idea to come along, and he was not going to let Thom and the rest of the crew down by falling to his death—and he knew that's what it would be. They were moving up the hull and there was nothing between him and the bottom deck but the men on the ladder below him.

Finally, a small star of light sparkled above them. In several more feet, Tristan could see it was another small lantern. Riggan stepped off the ladder and waited for Thom. They had to help Tristan over, much to his embarrassment, but his leg had reached the end of its endurance on the climb. Once he was safely on the small ledge, he took a deep breath and smiled that he was okay. He doubted Thom and Riggan believed him, but none of them had time to wait. Riggan picked up another that was sitting beside it the ladder. Turning it on, he set it back down and then started along the ledge, heading back towards the stern and Tristan's quarters.

They were nearly at the end of the walkway when Riggan stopped. He took his knife out again and pressed it against something on the wall. Tristan couldn't make out what. The panel moved aside and Tristan looked into his office in surprise. Riggan grinned at him as he stepped onto the carpet. Shaking his head, Tristan grinned back. Being in his cabin gave Tristan a much needed boost. It all seemed possible now that they were here. The group filed in silently as Tristan and Thom stepped into the main cabin.

Riggan was busy at the door to the quarterdeck stairs, disarming the charge. When he was done, he came back over to them. "I left the charges on the main door in place in case we need to retreat," he said. "It will only take a second to fix it, but…"

"Good idea," Thom said, pulling out his gun and holding it in his left hand, with his sword in his right.

"Just a moment, sir." Riggan disappeared back into the office for a moment, then was back. "Mr. Aubrey is about to make his appearance to give us a chance to get on the deck."

"I didn't approve that," Thom growled. "Okay, mercy when possible, but don't be fools. We need to take the deck as quickly as possible." Thom turned to Tristan. "Behind me."

"And me, sir, sorry," Riggan said, stepping in front of Tristan.

Thom eased the door open and the stench of the sails filled the cabin. With a nod to the group he slipped quickly up the stairs. Following him, Tristan was surprised when they stepped onto the deck. The officers on the quarterdeck were all focused on the fighting on the main deck below them. Stemmer and Fuhrman were standing by the helm, Chris Muher chained to the deck beside Fuhrman. Muher looked over as they reached the deck and grinned. Tristan breathed a sigh of relief that the man was still alive. Moving as silently as they could their group slipped onto the deck. Three men veered off towards the guns that sat at the taffrail facing outwards. Thom was nearly to Stemmer when they were spotted.

The deck exploded around them. Where they had been focused on the deck below a moment before, now the officers and men turned on Thom and his group. Tristan saw several men closing on Thom, before he himself was grabbed from behind. Desperately trying to break free, he tried to reach the blade at his belt, and when that failed he dragged his nails across the arm that was on his throat. The man holding him grunted in pain but didn't let go. Tristan's vision was starting to close down. He could hear muffled explosions, but his lungs were aching for air, the fight was going out of his limbs and he knew he was almost gone—when suddenly he was free.

"Sorry, sir, didn't mean to take so long, I got sidetracked," Riggan said, offering him a hand up. There was a large gash on Riggan's skull. "I brought the Interface, if you want to get it reseated. I'll watch your back."

Tristan nodded, his throat still aching, and stumbled towards the Interface that was in place. He eyed the thing with distaste and kicked it over. A black ooze ran across the deck from where he had broken the linkage. "I need to clean this before we can put mine back," he said to Riggan and then ran across the deck to his cabin, ignoring the fighting going on around him as he focused on what needed to get done. He grabbed his bag and ran back on deck. Glancing around, he could see things weren't going as well as they'd hoped. There were many men down on the lower deck—he recognized some of them. The three men that had headed towards the guns lay dead a few feet short of their goal, What stopped Tristan in his tracks was Fuhrman shoving a gun against Thom's head.

"Stop!" he shouted. "Or I'll kill him."

"They aren't going to stop," Thom snarled. "None of us are."

"Then I guess you get to die," Fuhrman said with satisfaction. The gun went off, but Thom was still standing and Fuhrman was on the ground, yanked off his feet by Muher. "I'll kill you for this!" Fuhrman shouted.

"Me first," Muher said, his voice weak.

"Thom!" Tristan shouted as he saw Stemmer pull his gun and

turn it on Thom. Tristan dropped his bag and pulled out his gun, firing carefully. The former captain dropped to the deck.

"Thanks!" Thom shouted.

"You can't win this," Fuhrman said. "There's too many loyal to the Navy and not dragon lovers like you."

"I think that's where you're wrong," Thom said with a grin. The big guns swiveled around to face the deck.

"You won't fire on your own men."

"Maybe, maybe not—but I am sure that *they* will happily eat any of your men, Fuhrman."

Tristan looked up; Fenfyr and Taminick were flying straight towards the ship at high speed. There was a slight hiss as the dragons came in, and as soon as they settled on deck—Taminick on the main deck and Fenfyr on the quarterdeck—the fighting paused.

Taminick looked around at the crew surrounding her. "I smell the stink of Vermin filth on some of you." She leaned down so her head was on a level with the men. "I don't like humans who smell of Vermin."

Weapons began to drop. One or two of the more foolish still tried to fight. Thom dispatched one of Fuhrman's men on the quarterdeck and Tristan saw three fall on the deck below. Taminick knocked another group down with one swipe of a massive foreclaw. One of the midshipmen tried to attack Tristan. Fenfyr laughed as he knocked the man down and put his foot on him.

"Can I crush him?" the dragon asked, sounding way too happy.

"That will make a mess, Master Fenfyr," Riggan said. "Perhaps we should throw him overboard like he did the Captain and Master Tristan."

"Hmm, or I could eat him…"

"No! Please, no! I'll confess, I'll sign anything, just please let me go!" the man shouted.

"Take him to the brig with the others," Thom said, walking over.

"Not even a little taste?" Fenfyr said sadly.

"Well, maybe a small one."

"No, please…" the man cried.

"I think he fainted," Thom said mildly. "It will make him easier to transport. Take the ones who still want to serve the former captain to the brig and lock them in!" He walked to the command area. "Med teams to the main deck."

"On our way," Rose Webber answered calmly.

"Where's the key to these chains?" Thom asked Fuhrman, pointing to Muher.

"I'm not giving it to you."

"Fenfyr, can you help?" Tristan asked. The dragon huffed and snapped the lock holding the chains in place.

"You're going to pay for this when Davis hears about it," Fuhrman said defiantly.

"This," Thom wave his hands, "Was sanctioned by Admiral O'Brian. I am Captain of the *Winged Victory* now."

"You're lying!" Fuhrman said. "I am here by a direct order, this is not going to sit lightly at headquarters. I'm going to report on your treason as soon as I can."

"It's going to take you a little time to do that, we have to rendezvous with the fleet. The Vermin are heading in, and we need to be there to meet them. Which reminds me. Fenfyr? Taminick? Would you be so kind as to remove those sails?"

"With pleasure," Fenfyr said, launching himself to the mizzenmast.

The two dragons made quick work of it, tearing the sails down, then shredding them so they could never be used again. Once the last piece was down, they dropped them overboard and let the Winds carry them away. Even though Tristan knew there was no dragon mind to mourn, he still whispered the spell of release as the last of the sails drifted away.

"Let's get our sails up," Thom said with a grin. He hit the ship-wide comm system. "This is Captain Barrett, we are going to raise the sails and head in to rendezvous with the fleet. The Vermin are coming! As you know, this ship was designed to be our best hope against a massed attack. It's time to put that to the test. The Master Weaver is seating the Elemental Interface and we should be ready to sail in three hours."

"You're going to kill us all," Fuhrman said, spitting at Thom.

"Well, then at least you'll die too," Thom said with a smile.

XXIX

The med team, led by Rose Webber, arrived on deck as Tristan was working to clean out the linkage for the Elemental Interface. She raced across the deck straight to where Chris Muher was, dropping to her knees beside him as she carefully inspected his wounds. Tristan couldn't hear what she was saying, but the smile on the general's face was gentle even though he was grimacing in pain. Thom was clearing the last of the mutineers off the deck and assigning security to escort them below. There were too many to fit in the brig, so he sent the officers, petty officers and other obvious leaders there and sent the rest to the second lowest deck to have them secured in one of the storage bays that quickly emptied of cargo.

Once they had been taken care of, Thom gave the order to stop the engines and lower the masts as far as they could so they could put the sails back on them. Tristan watched the masts going down, hoping that his assurances to Thom about the sails re-bonding with the ship were not misplaced. He had some doubts, the willowisps might sense the filth of the Vermin sails and refuse the crosstrees that had held them. He shoved those thoughts away and focused back on the Interface. The linkage was at last clean of the last vestiges of the "Interface" Fuhrman had tried to use. Tristan stood and gently picked up his Elemental Interface, placing it carefully over the linkage and softly intoned a cleansing spell that he hoped would help. He held his breath until he felt the thing seat itself. Looking down, he saw the lights slowly coming on. Smiling, he bent down and clipped it into place, ready for the sails as soon as the masts were raised.

He walked over to where Thom was standing watching the activity on deck. Webber was still kneeling beside Muher, which made Tristan worry about what the man had suffered at Fuhrman's hands. He knew that Thom would have preferred to kill the man, and Fenfyr had the same opinion, but he was one of the few that knew the details of the plan and who at Naval headquarters was involved. Stemmer knew, but the former captain had been whisked away by the med teams. Tristan was still dealing with how he felt about that. There was a very good chance that his shot would prove fatal, he'd never thought he'd take a human life, but Stemmer had thrown Thom overboard, taken the ship and possibly been involved in the bombing that had killed Miri. It was a lot to weigh, but guilt was not getting the upper hand.

"We're ready to drop the mainsail," Shearer called from the deck.

"Go ahead, Shearer," Thom said.

"Aye, Captain."

Tristan noticed that even though Thom was nervously tapping his fingers behind his back, he still smiled when he heard the boatswain call him captain. "It's make or break, Tristan."

"I know. Fenfyr's helping." Tristan muttered the same spell he had when they had first dropped the sails, hoping it would help them bond this time, too.

"Drop the sail!" Shearer shouted. Everything on deck stopped, it felt like everyone was holding their breath—maybe they were. "It caught!" The triumphant call echoed around the deck moments later.

Thom let out a long slow breath. "You were right."

"I'm glad," Tristan said with a relieved grin. "I was hoping."

"You didn't think it was going to work?"

"I had some doubts about the willowisps bonding where the Vermin sails had been." He watched as the men with the help of Taminick put the topgallants and royals in place on the mizzenmast. "Once they're all up, I will check them over carefully before we set out, there's still the question of whether they will fly."

"Sir, we have three ships on the long range sensor," the

communications officer, Brown, said. "They're hailing us."

"Pipe it through, please."

"Yes, sir."

"This is Captain Graham of the frigate *Surprise* in the company of the frigate *Leopard* and the privateer *Noble Lady*," the voice crackled over the system.

"You're late, Bill," Thom said with a laugh.

"Sorry, we ran into a little trouble on the way in, Captain Barrett. Permission to approach?"

"Of course, we're dropping the sails now and should be ready to sail in the next hour or two," Thom said.

"Good, we've heard reports that the fleet is already engaging advanced scouts, we need to get the *Winged Victory* there before the main taskforce arrives."

"We're working on it, Bill, I assure you," Thom answered.

The three ships came into view a few moments later. As the ships approached it really became apparent how big the *Winged Victory* truly was. He knew the *Surprise* well—he'd been the one to make her sails—and she'd seemed large the first time he saw her. The *Constellation* had been bigger than either of the frigates, but hadn't dwarfed them the way *Victory* did. Next to the *Victory* the frigates looked like toys bobbing alongside the massive ship.

"I didn't believe it," Graham's voice came over the comm line. "I knew she was big, but by all that's holy..."

"I am in complete agreement," a female voice said. "And I served on the *Constellation*."

"Mercy Allen? Is that you?" Thom asked.

"Yes, sir, Captain Barrett, I was promoted to the *Leopard*."

"Congratulations!" Thom said, grinning.

"And to you, too, sir, about time!" she replied.

"Thank you," Thom said. "What trouble did you run into on the way here?"

"Pirates with Vermin vessels," Graham said. "They were heading out of sector nineteen in this direction. We dissuaded them, thanks to the help from the *Noble Lady*."

"We intercepted some communications that indicated they were trying to find out where the fleet would be engaging the Vermin," Cook said, joining the conversation. "We're not sure if they were planning to head out that way or not. The dragons didn't leave enough for us to question. Not that they would answer anyway."

"We know that they were intending to take the *Winged Victory* into sector nineteen, but that was when she had the Vermin sails."

"We still can't believe that!" Allen said. "Vermin tech on our ships. No matter how you feel about the Guild, that's unacceptable."

"She's not a really a Guild sympathizer," Thom told Tristan quietly.

"Fun," Tristan said grimly. "I feel sorry for her Warrior."

"I do, too, but she's not as bad as some." Thom frowned. "Shearer, how goes it?"

"Mainmast is ready, we're just finishing up the mizzen and the fore, sir!"

"Good, the sooner we're out of here the better, I have a bad feeling about this spot for some reason," Thom said, keeping his voice low.

"I heard them talking about ships heading in to help them with their Interface problem," Muher said, limping up to them.

"I said you need to be in sickbay," Webber scolded.

"I told you, I'll go when I'm done making my report," he said, scowling at her. "Fuhrman said 'they', whoever 'they' are, would be reaching us soon. As I understand it, they were bringing a new Interface that would function with the sails."

"Did you hear that?" Thom asked the other captains.

"Yes, I'm pretty sure that's who we ran into," Cook said.

"Our sensors did show an abnormal blip on one of their ships," Graham said. "The dragons went after that ship first, and spent more time with it than the others. I did wonder about that at the time, but it's not like dragons talk to us to let us know, so who knows what they were thinking."

"Idiots," Muher muttered under his breath.

Thom glared at him before replying. "Thank you. We'll let you know as soon as we are ready to set sail. Set up a patrol until we're ready to move out."

"Yes, sir," Graham and Allen answered and broke the connection with a small snap.

"Do you need anyone over there?" Cook asked.

"Not right now, we have the mutineers in lockdown, but it's

good to know you're back there."

"We'll be behind the *Victory* all the way, Captain Barrett," Cook said.

"Can't let you have all the fun, Tommy Boy," Harkins added with a laugh. "Our Warrior would like a word with the Master Weaver."

"What is it, Alden?" Tristan asked, stepping closer to Thom and the communications board.

"I've been trying to duplicate what you did to the sails. I've managed to get the willowisps to move a little, but it's not enough. I'm not sure it's a Warrior's skill."

"I was wondering about that already," Tristan said.

"We don't have enough Weavers, and even if we did, we don't have the time to train them before this battle," Alden said desperately.

"I know." Tristan sighed, wishing there was something more he could do.

"On the upside," Alden added, "I am a lot faster at repairs now. It helped that, at least." He laughed. "That might come in handy."

"It might," Tristan agreed. The connection broke with a snap and he looked over at Thom. "It would have made a huge difference if he could manage the spell."

"It might, but…" Thom smiled at him. "You already did it once. If you can manage it with this ship, you could turn the tide of battle, Tristan."

"Sir, excuse me, you are not properly dressed." Riggan appeared with a jacket in his hands.

"What?" Thom frowned at him.

"I cleaned out the Captain's cabin and moved your things. I thought you should be wearing a proper uniform, though, sir," he said, holding out the jacket.

Thom looked at it, a soft smile playing on his lips. He reached out and touched the braid on the jacket, then nodded. "You're right, of course, Riggan." He discarded the coat he'd been wearing and put on the Captain's coat.

"That's better, sir. I'll just nip off and finish what I was doing," Riggan said, leaving the quarterdeck.

"He didn't waste any time," Muher said. "Good. The sooner the crew knows you are in command, the better." He swayed on his feet.

"Okay, you have made your report, you are going to sickbay *right now*," Webber said. "You can walk or I will sedate you and have you carried there, your choice."

"Yes, ma'am," he said with a chuckle. "I'll be back before the battle."

Tristan watched as Muher walked carefully across the deck. He knew that the doctor had already pumped a considerable amount of pain killers into the general before he even got up, Tristan could see it in the way the man's eyes hadn't quite focused. The fact that he was walking amazed him, Tristan had no doubt that Fuhrman had gone out of his way to make sure things were not easy for Muher. Once the general stepped into the lift, Tristan turned his attention back to the sails. They were sparkling softly on the exposed masts. Everything looked okay, but he wouldn't know for sure until they moved into the Winds.

Fenfyr slipped onto deck from the open panels leading to the mainmast. The dragon looked up at the masts, sizing them up, then leaped up towards the top of the mainmast. Tristan wondered what he was doing. A moment later he got his answer when a long pennant unfurled from the top of the mast. Fenfyr perched on the Dragon's Roost and looked down at the red pennant bearing the figure of a dragon. Tristan glanced at Thom, wondering what he would think about the addition to his ship.

"It looks good, and it makes it very clear whose side we're fighting on, doesn't it?" Thom said.

"It does."

"Masts are ready to raise!" Shearer called.

"Raise the masts!" Thom ordered.

Fenfyr hopped off the Dragon's Roost and settled on deck as the masts began to climb slowly out of the bowels of the ship. As each set of crosstrees cleared the deck, Tristan checked the sails. The willowisps all seemed okay, sparkling gently, waiting to be unfurled. The mizzenmast locked into place first, followed by the foremast, then with a huge *boom* the mainmast settled into place, soaring hundreds of feet over their heads. Tristan smiled, he never would get tired of seeing the sails on the ship. He was glad that Stemmer and Fuhrman hadn't destroyed them when they had replaced them with the Vermin sails.

"Prepare to sail!" Thom called.

"All stations prepare to get underway!" Shearer ordered.

"It will go well, Tris," Fenfyr said softly, then leaped up to soar over the ship.

Tristan stepped to the Elemental Interface and put his hand on it, feeling the hum as the sails and the ship connected. "Ready," he said.

"Loose the sails!" Thom's order stopped all activity on the ship as everyone looked up as the men on the crosstrees released the ropes and the sparkling sails rolled down, fluttering softly in the breezes.

"Sails are ready, ship to the Weaver!" Shearer said.

"Ship to the Weaver!" the cry was repeated on the quarterdeck.

"The ship is yours, Master Weaver," Thom said.

"Thank you, Captain Barrett." Tristan closed his eyes and started the spell, feeling the sails, making sure they weren't injured by their time in the hold. He fixed a few dark spots, shifting the Weaving and moving the dark out and away. He could feel the massive power of the ship again as the sails shivered in the first touch of the Winds. At first they seemed hesitant, unsure what was coming. He focused his spell, the Latin filling the silence on the quarterdeck. The sails started to catch the Winds, at first the topsails, then as Tristan spoke, he eased the mainsail into the path of the Winds. A moment later the immense sound that rattled through the ship surprised them all as the sails caught the Winds and the ship leaped forward, suddenly speeding away from where they had been. Tristan shifted the sails a little, moving the topgallants, unsure if they should have them out with the Winds this strong, but trusting Thom would know if they should bring them in. He looked up from the Elemental Interface and saw the pennant trailing over the ship, proudly proclaiming who they were.

He took his hands away from the Interface. The officers on deck were all smiling, looking up at the sails. Glancing back, Tristan could see the three smaller ships struggling to keep up, while the dragons. Fenfyr, Taminick and the two traveling with *Surprise* and the *Leopard* wheeled around the *Winged Victory* and playfully dashed back and forth between the ships.

"Sir! I have a report from the captain of the *Mercury*. They are under heavy fire, they've lost two ships and there is a larger group of Vermin ships on their sensors heading towards their position," the communications officer said.

"What's our ETA?" Thom asked.

"Two hours, sir."

"Tell them we're on our way—no wait, signal that *Surprise* and *Leopard* are on their way in. I have a funny feeling that not very many people knew about this ship, and the fewer that know now, the better. Understood?"

"Yes, sir!"

"Hopefully we can take them by surprise," Thom said. "It might give us the upper hand."

"Might?" Tristan asked.

"That's the idea at least. We need to get there in time. Will the sails hold in these Winds?"

"Yes."

"Then let's keep the sails set as they are, and make haste. Shearer, we will be leaving the sails set for the time being."

"Sir?"

"Be ready to pull them in if it gets stormy."

"Yes, sir."

"Now get us there, Tristan."

"I will, Thom," Tristan assured him. "I will."

XXX

The stars were speeding past as the ship raced towards the coordinates of the battle. There was a deep hum in the rigging, letting Tristan know that even though they were wheeled over and going far faster than they had ever gone before, things were still holding together on the masts. He was on deck for the third time in forty minutes, checking the sails and the Elemental Interface. The dragons were soaring along beside the ship, wings and feathers fully extended. Fenfyr had explained that they very rarely got the chance to "really stretch our wings" when flying with a ship, and they were taking full advantage of the *Winged Victory's* speed. The smaller ships were doing their best to keep up, but the best they could do was stay on the sensors, the huge sails of the *Victory* moving the massive ship through space faster than the smaller ships could hope to go.

Thom was pacing the quarterdeck—as far as Tristan could tell he hadn't left the deck since they set out. He was currently scowling at a group on the main deck as they worked to fit the ship for battle. Thom was doing all he could to strengthen the ship. The hole in the bottom hold that they had used to enter the ship had been sealed and double plated. Shearer made sure that the weaknesses showing on the plans were all dealt with as well as he could in deep space.

The gun decks were already swept clean of bulkheads and all

the guns were being carefully checked to make sure they hadn't been sabotaged. The fact that the second gunner Jacob Raiden, now promoted to Gunner Officer, had discovered that at least ten guns had been rigged to kill the men firing them had nearly pushed Thom over the edge. Tristan had watched the red creep over his friend's face, his hands clench tight, then the deep slow breath as he reined in his temper. More than once Thom had muttered that he wished he'd just killed Fuhrman when he had the chance.

"Do you want to come down for something to eat?" Tristan asked, catching Thom as he paced by.

"Um…"

"When did you last eat?"

"When you did," Thom answered.

"And I can't remember when that was, so I think it's time. Riggan has been sending notes." Tristan frowned at him. "Don't make me order you, Captain."

"Yes, sir," Thom said with a grin.

Tristan walked to his staircase off the quarterdeck and headed down into his cabin, making sure Thom followed. He loosened his cravat and jacket as he walked in, laughing as he noticed the table of food already waiting for them. He settled himself at the table and served himself, then passed the food to Thom.

"You know, I didn't think I was hungry," Thom said. "Turns out I am." He put a generous helping of food on his plate.

They ate in silence at first, the only sound the clink of silverware. Riggan appeared with a fresh pot of coffee and served them. He lingered for a moment, then started piling up the empty dishes, fussing at the end of the table.

"What is it?" Tristan finally asked, recognizing the look on the man's face.

"Well, sir, you know I'm not one to spread idle tales…"

"Riggan," Thom said warningly.

"I heard them talking down in the crew quarters, someone was listening in at the comm boards and said the fleet's been destroyed and all is lost."

"I'm sure we would have heard if the fleet was gone," Thom pointed out.

"I know and I told them that, but the rumor has gotten ahold of the crew and it's ruining morale."

"Damn all," Thom said. He pulled out his communicator and punched in a code.

"Yes, Captain?" Patrick Aubrey answered.

"Get down to communications and lock it down. The officer of the watch can go in, but no one other than you, myself and the Master Weaver, understood?"

"On it, Captain."

"Thank you, Riggan," Thom said. "That sort of thing can decide a battle before a shot is fired. I'm sure that the prisoners aren't helping. There have to be a few of their sympathizers left among the crew, even after the checking and rechecking we've done. After we're done eating, I think we need to go down there and listen in on the fleet-wide channel. We need to know what we're flying into. We're nearly there and we need to be prepared."

"The men know the *Victory* is special, sir, they trust you to do your best. It's that them that threw you overboard spread lies, and convinced them the only way to win was with those filthy sails hanging over their heads."

"We'll show them differently, Riggan."

"Aye, I know, Captain." He grinned. "I'll ready your formal uniforms for the battle, sirs, so you can get ready when you come back from the communications room."

Tristan sighed, fighting the ship in the strangling cravat of his formal uniform wasn't going to be fun, but like so many of their other rules and practices, they had returned to the tradition of the officers going into battle in formal dress. It had been common in the First Great Age of Sail and now in the Second Age, the old traditions were being followed. He'd heard arguments for and against it, but Thom had told him one night over backgammon that he'd known crews that had been vastly outnumbered fight all that much harder because they were in their formal uniforms reserved for battle and special occasions. Thom even admitted it helped him get ready for battle. "It's like putting on your armor before a battle, it lets you know you are going into a fight, Tristan," he'd said. Tristan believed him.

Thom finished his coffee and set his cup down. "Do you want to come?" he asked, looking at Tristan.

"Of course." Tristan stood.

The communications room was on the same deck as Tristan's quarters, set in the center of the ship in a small room next to where the mainmast rose through the ship. As they approached, a small group that was gathered outside the room dashed away. Thom grumbled under his breath, but let them go. When he reached the door, he didn't bother to announce himself, instead keying his private code into the door and letting it slide open. The comm officer on duty was the only one in the room.

"Captain!" he said in surprise.

"How much chatter has been getting out?" Thom snapped.

"None that I know of, I've had the earphones on the whole time, no one should be able to hear what's going on…" He paled.

"What is it?" Tristan asked.

"Unless someone hacked the line. I never thought of that!" The man's hands flew over the panel in front of him—as Tristan watched lights flickered on and off, turning red to green to yellow. "I've locked it down and scrambled it, sir."

"Thank you, Marble, can you open the fleet-wide channel?"

"Yes, sir."

"What about someone overhearing?" Tristan asked Thom.

"The secondary door closed behind us, the room is soundproof now. It's not a precaution we usually use, but I think in this case we need it."

"Channel is coming online, sir," Marble said.

"This is Marauder *we've taken heavy damage, we're pulling back.*

Get out of there, Mike! You don't stand a chance, we're sending in Lightning *to aid your retreat.*

Look out, Venture, *you've got a heavy cruiser bearing down in your six.*

We see it, we're braced for attack, they're trying to break the line here.

My god! Did you see that? We've lost Sirius, *repeat, we've lost* Sirius."

"*Sirius*? They're in trouble," Thom said.

"I made her sails, she was one of the few ships of the line left after the *Jupiter* Incursion," Tristan said. "They came to us for a complete re-Weaving while she was in dry dock."

"If the whole fleet is out, that means that *Sirius, Orion, Betelgeuse, Polaris, Rigel* and *Regulus* are holding the line. I'm not sure which frigates are out for sure, or if they are already there." Thom frowned. "We have *Surprise* and *Leopard* with us. Cook and Harkins contacted us and said that several of the letters of marque are heading into the battle."

Tristan nodded, half listening to Thom and half to the chatter of the battle. He didn't need to see the grim look on Thom's face to know that things were going badly for the fleet. As they listened, another ship called that they had to fall back, then came the most chilling communication yet.

"What the hell is that? God! They're hooking the dragons! Someone get in there and cut that damn line. Don't let them take the dragons. Odyssey *break off with five corvettes and break those lines. Don't let them take the dragons. Cut the lines—and if you can't do that you know the standing order from Darius."*

Tristan sucked in a breath. He couldn't imagine it was going that badly. The "standing order" was *"If a dragon is going to be taken by the Vermin and there is no way to free the dragon, the Navy has permission to kill the dragon to spare them the horror of what awaits them."* It had been there waiting, even during the *Jupiter* Incursion, but it had never been tested. If the Vermin were actively hunting the dragons, Tristan could see where they might not have a choice. "Thom..." he said, unable to hide the horror in his voice.

"I know, Tristan."

"We're on the outer edges of visual, sir," Marble said.

"Let's see." Thom looked gray.

The screen in front of them flickered to life. To Tristan it really made no sense. He could see bright sparks, and the softer glow of sails—at least he assumed that's what he was seeing. "What's happening?" he asked when he saw the look on Thom's face.

"The fleet's getting a pounding," Thom said grimly. He pointed to a line of glowing objects. "These are the big ships, the *Orion* and others in her class, these are the frigates," he said indicating a group of smaller objects. "And these," he ran a hand along the breath of the battle, "are the little ships, the corvettes and other small gunboats that serve to protect the bigger ships and go in and hit the Vermin hard and get out fast. They have fast engines in addition to the sails, so they can zip in and out of the lines."

"What's that?" Tristan pointed to a shadow across the stars.

"That's the Vermin fleet." Thom leaned closer to the screen. "There are a lot of them. They all seem to be circling around this area." His hand covered a huge black spot. "That would be their big ship or ships. It's hard to tell this far out, but those are the ones that took out the *Constellation.*"

Tristan watched the screen. As they got closer to the battle, he could make out the Vermin ships, dark sails over darker decks. He could also make out the dragons, diving between the ships, now and then settling on a Vermin vessel and tearing it to shreds. They were focusing on the smaller ships; the big ships in the center—it turned out to be three ships—were still untouched by navel fire and the dragons.

"We need to get ready," Thom said, straightening. "I'll change and meet you on deck." He punched a button on the comm. "We are fifteen minutes out from the fleet," he said over the ship-wide system. "All hands prepare for battle."

Tristan walked out and back to his room. His heart was pounding. Hearing the reports of the dragons being taken was unsettling and he worried about Fenfyr and Taminick. The grim look on Thom's face didn't help his nerves, the man looked like he was preparing for his death. For all his words of comfort and assurance, Thom wasn't sure they could win this battle.

Fenfyr was waiting for him when he opened the door. "Fen!" He walked quickly to the dragon and leaned against him as Fenfyr touched him gently with his head tufts and curled a claw around him.

"I thought we should speak before the battle," the dragon said softly. "We know things are not going well, Tris, and I'm worried about you."

"And I'm worried about you. We heard over the comm that the Vermin are hooking dragons and trying to drag them in."

"Yes, we were informed of this. The big ships in the center of the battle are the ones who are trying to take my kind. Darius is trying to decide the best way to deal with the situation."

"This ship, Fenfyr, we should help, this is what *Winged Victory* was designed to do."

"I know, and we have the other ships with us who are fresh to the battle. No one, not even the Navy, is expecting the *Victory,* so the element of surprise is on our side." The dragon sighed softly. "You will take care of yourself, Tris? Promise me."

"I have to fight the ship," Tristan said, leaning against the dragon.

"I know you do, and I have to fight, too, this is our first battle together. At least it's not like the bombing."

"What are you talking about?" Tristan turned enough so he could see Fenfyr.

"I was helpless to stop that—we had been talking half an hour before and I was at the Compound talking with Darius when one of the members of the Stars Plot contacted him. He said that he hoped we had wished the Guild Masters goodbye because it was over for them. No more than a minute later we heard the explosion. I flew as fast as I could," Fenfyr paused, sighing softly, the dragon equivalent of silent tears. "When I got there the council hall was gone, there was human blood everywhere. I was there before any of the rescue teams, Darius was right behind me, and we started moving the rubble. I found you."

"Fen…"

"This is easier, Tristan. I know we are walking into battle, it's not like that day when we were laughing together and then the world exploded." Fenfyr tapped him with his head tufts. "I am not saying it will be easy, but I know Thom is a fighter, I know you are a fighter and I know…"

"That I am not letting anything get through to you, sir," Riggan said, appearing out of nowhere as always. "I have your uniform ready."

"Thank you, Riggan." Tristan changed his shirt and coat in the main room so he could spend as much time before the battle with Fenfyr as he could. Once he had his formal uniform on, he leaned back into the dragon's embrace. "I'm not ready, Fen."

"Yes, you are, Tris, you are more ready than you know," the

dragon assured him. "You'll see."

The call to quarters rapped out over the ship-wide system followed by Shearer's voice. "All hands to battle stations."

"Be careful, Fenfyr." Tristan said, running his hand over the dragon's head.

"You too, Tris," Fenfyr said, gently nudging him with his nose. "Watch out for yourself and the Weaver, Riggan."

"Of course, Master Fenfyr, we will see you at the victory celebration."

"Yes," the dragon said and with one more small nudge, slipped out the stern gallery windows.

Tristan took a breath and tried to swallow around the lump in his throat. It was hard knowing what they were heading into, letting Fenfyr go. He knew the dragon had fought in battles before—in fact he'd been with Darius at the *Jupiter* Incursion—but somehow seeing it, experiencing it made it so much more real. He squared his shoulders and headed to the stairs and up onto the quarterdeck.

Thom was already there, waiting by the Elemental Interface. "I'm taking the helm personally, Tristan, I know this ship better than anyone, so together we should be able to manage it well."

Tristan nodded. "Good idea." He stepped up to the Interface, he realized that he could see the flash of fire and the sparkling glow of ships sails in the distance. He could see the crew and guns on the main deck, and the bright red of the Marines uniforms scattered throughout them all. On the quarterdeck the officers stood waiting while three gunner's mates manned the rear guns.

"Are you ready?" Thom asked.

"Yes," Tristan said firmly. He didn't have any other choice.

Before he could put his hands on the Interface, and before Thom stepped the three paces to the helm, the captain held out his hand. "If something goes wrong, Tristan, I just want you to know it's been a pleasure to serve with you."

"It's been a pleasure to serve with you, Thom. Don't get yourself killed."

"You either." The captain squeezed Tristan's hand again and stepped to the helm.

Tristan put his hands on the Elemental Interface and spoke the spell to ready the willowisps for the battle.

"Incoming vessel identify yourself!" a voice snapped over the comm.

"This is Captain Thom Barrett in the *Winged Victory*, we're coming straight in, can you keep the small stuff off us?"

"*Winged Victory?* I have no ship..." The communications broke off for a moment. "Yes, sir, *Victory.*"

"Well, Tristan," Thom looked over with a smile. "Here we go."

XXXI

The *Winged Victory* was drawing near the edge of the chaos of the battle when Thom requested the fleet-wide comm to be piped onto deck, so they could keep track of the action. The chatter continued for three minutes before a shocked *"My God, what the hell is that ship*?!?!" came over the system and all the noise fell silent.

"They weren't expecting us," Thom said with a grin.

"That's good." Tristan smiled back.

The *Victory* had reached the edge of the battle, and they backed off their speed, giving the Naval ships a chance to get out of their way as they drove in towards the front lines. A small frigate passed by, its sails tattered and hull broken. Tristan looked away, knowing he couldn't dwell on that now, or worry about helping them. The hospital ships were hanging at the back of the fleet and the smaller ship was limping towards them, he hoped they reached them in time.

The fleet-wide chatter started again. Tristan tried to guess where the ships were by watching the action in front of him. He quickly gave up. Space around them was full of ships and weapons' fire. Dark Vermin vessels were shadowing some of the smaller ships and then suddenly the ship would disappear in a flash of bright light. He swallowed and looked where they were heading to the massive dark shapes of the Vermin heavy cruisers. As he watched, something flashed out from one of the ships, heading towards a dragon fighting alongside Naval ship. A black line caught the dragon's wing and began reeling it in. Before he could say anything another Navy ship—he guessed it was the *Odyssey* and her back-up—headed straight for the dragon, then skimmed between the dragon and the Vermin ships—a moment later the dragon pulled free. Tristan swallowed hard, knowing Fenfyr would soon be close to those ships.

Something rocked the ship—a small Vermin gunboat had managed to work its way inside the fleet and was firing at every ship it passed. One of the Navy's small corvettes swooped in behind it and started firing. The *Victory* moved on, passing up the smaller battles for the main line of the war.

The fire got thicker as they got closer. The Naval boats were giving way as they moved through, but the Vermin were now targeting the *Victory*, trying to keep them from reaching the front line. Tristan heard a distant *thump* as shot pounded the lower decks. So far, Thom had not returned fire. Tristan wondered what he was up to, but trusted him and carefully kept the willowisps in line, knowing this sedate pace and seemingly simple cruise would not last for long.

He could see the big ships of the *Stellar* class, the largest ships the fleet had—before they built the *Winged Victory*. Smaller ships wove in and out between them, and Tristan could make out the debris of what had been the *Sirius*.

"This is Barrett of the *Winged Victory*," Thom said. Shot slammed against the ship.

"Welcome, Thom," Admiral O'Brian replied. "My flag is on *Polaris*. We've been waiting for you."

"We came as fast as we could, Admiral, thanks for leaving a few for us," Thom said confidently. Tristan saw the crew on deck grin.

"We couldn't have you cut your teeth on a few leftovers, could we?" O'Brian joked, but Tristan could hear the strain in his voice.

"Thank you, sir," Thom said.

"We'll do our best to keep them off your back. The big one in the center is the one taking the dragons. So far we've saved most of the dragons, though we're pretty sure they've hooked a few."

"Yes, sir!" Thom looked over at Tristan. The glance said volumes. The fleet was losing, the rumors had been right. If the heavy Vermin cruisers decided to move against the fleet, it wouldn't be a question of running, there wouldn't be anything or anyone left to run.

Thom thumbed on the ship-wide systems. "All hands prepare to engage." He put his hands on the helm. "We're heading in, Admiral."

"Dragon speed, Thom."

Tristan turned his attention back to the Elemental Interface, he slipped his hands into the battle straps and braced himself as the ship came up on the large Naval vessels. The Vermin shots aimed at *Victory* had stopped and that was worrying Tristan. Something flashed in his peripheral vision and he saw Fenfyr, Taminick and the huge mass of Darius beside them. There were two other dragons the size of Darius that Tristan had never seen before. They closed in formation with the others and plowed through the Navel line as *Victory* broke through.

As soon as the *Winged Victory* passed the *Polaris* the Vermin opened fire. The smaller ships—about the size of the Navy's frigates—opened up with full broadsides that slammed into the hull over and over. Then the fire changed, the shot heading up over their heads. Tristan sensed a hole in the sails and turned to repair it, focusing on the willowisps. Another round and more holes tore through them. The shot the Vermin were using seemed to be designed to destroy the sails. Over the screams on deck, Tristan found it hard to concentrate.

"Tristan, you need to strengthen the sails," Thom shouted. Tristan glanced over, blood was running over Thom's face.

"I don't know if I..." Tristan stopped when the Vermin ship in the center fired its hook again. The vile thing shot out and caught a dragon and began dragging it towards the ship. Tristan recognized Taminick's bright red against the dark sails. Before the ships could move in to help, another dragon was there, putting himself between the Vermin ship and Taminick. Another Vermin vessel approached, firing on them, and the dragon turned and attacked the small gunboat. Killing it, he left it floating as he turned his attention back to the red dragon struggling desperately to get free. The dragon flew back and snapped the black line between his teeth. As he did, another hook flew out and caught him, even as Taminick tried to pull away. The other dragon was being reeled in and when she tried to help him, he shoved her away. "No! Fenfyr!" Tristan screamed.

Tristan started to shift the sails to move the *Winged Victory* to where Fenfyr was being dragged helplessly through space. The sails responded, catching the Winds, and the ship started to turn. As it began a slow turn, Tristan caught sight of the embattled fleet, the *Rigel* currently under heavy fire. He knew he couldn't do what he was about to do and risk the entire fleet. With one last look at Fenfyr, he turned away and let the *Odyssey* and her companions do their job, trying not to think about Fenfyr being taken by the Vermin. Instead he focused that energy into the spell to strengthen the sails. He could feel the willowisps beginning to Weave themselves into a new configuration.

A huge *boom* shook the deck—the first of the heavy cruisers had opened fire. Tristan heard Thom swear, but he stayed focused on the sails. They had to be able to get to that big ship and stop them from taking the dragons, but before that they had to stop the other heavy cruisers before the Vermin finished destroying the remaining fleet. Another boom sounded followed by the rattle of hard shot across the deck. Tristan heard Riggan grunt in pain. The next shot had a weird whistling sound as it hit the ship high up on the masts. Tristan felt the blow through the sails, but knew it hadn't damaged them. The shot fell to the deck.

"They're glowing red!" Riggan whispered in awe. "I've never seen that."

Tristan risked a look up. The sails had changed from their soft golden sparkle, the willowisps were still moving and Weaving in and around each other, but they were stronger. He could feel that through the Interface and sense it in his spell. They were getting close to the first of the Vermin's big ships. As big as it was, though, the *Victory* was bigger. Constant fire was hitting them now. The small Navy ships behind them were returning fire, but Thom was still holding back.

"Bring her around for a broadside, Master Weaver," Thom said, his hands moving over the helm.

Tristan shifted the sails and felt the ship respond. It was almost like he was part of the ship, not just the Warrior fighting the sails. He was more aware of the ship than he had ever been before. He could feel the Winds tugging at the sails, and the willowisps wanting to race forward faster, deeper into the battle.

"Fire!" Thom ordered.

The next second, the *Winged Victory's* full broadside spoke. The sound made the decks shake and Tristan watched the shot as it crossed through space and tore open a huge hole in the Vermin ship.

""Fire!"

The second broadside opened the ship to space and Tristan could see into the dark hold of the Vermin vessel. The gun decks facing the *Victory* had been completely destroyed. The Vermin ship started to come about, but as it did, the three large dragons—Darius and the other two—dropped down on the ship. Tristan saw Darius reach down to where the Interface would be and gently kill the ship, then the three dragons launched themselves back into space.

"Finish it off!" Thom called over the fleet-comm. "We're going after the others." He looked over at Tristan. "That was too easy."

"Easy?" Tristan asked, looking at the blood on the deck, watching the med teams picking up the dead and wounded.

"Yes. I'm sorry about..." Thom trailed off.

Tristan swallowed, refusing to accept what that meant. The thought was horrifying, and it was as if he could sense the dragons' distress, it was echoing through his bones. He didn't know if it was real or a reaction to his own worry, but it was as if he could feel Fenfyr, trapped and helpless. "It's not too late."

Thom nodded, looking unconvinced. Tristan refused to look out and see if Fenfyr was flying free or had been reeled in. If he knew for sure, he wasn't sure he could go on. There was horror all around them, the wounded and dying and he couldn't tell if the blood on Thom was his, or from someone else. The quarterdeck was missing about a third of the people that had been there when they had crossed the line. And Tristan knew the battle was far from over.

"We're heading in to the lead ship, get ready!" Thom said over the ship's comm.

"I'd prepare for boarders," Muher said, walking onto the quarterdeck in his black formal uniform, sidearm and sword at his side. "They are going to try to get to the Weaver."

"Why?" Tristan asked.

"Have you seen your damn sails? Their shot is just dropping to the deck. They can't pierce our plating. They are going to come at us in a more personal fashion. Hall and the Marines are ready." He pointed to where two small Vermin ships were approaching them at high speed.

"Fire at will!" Thom ordered. The ship's guns started firing, the shots echoing around them. "Prepare to be boarded!" He turned to Tristan, Muher and Riggan. "We need to keep them off Tristan. We're still going after that big one."

"I'll be here," Muher said.

"Me too," Riggan assured them. He had a bloody bandage wrapped around his arm.

"Good." Thom turned back to the helm. "Take us in, Tristan."

Tristan focused back on the sails, turning them to catch the Winds, letting them race towards the huge ship in the center of the Vermin fleet. A *thunk* distracted him for a moment. He heard Muher swear, then small arms fire sounded from their deck. He looked up, a ship was pressing against theirs and dark figures were leaping from it onto the *Victory's* deck.

"Get rid of that filth!" Thom snapped out the order. Tristan was concentrating on the Interface and the sails, Weaving them even tighter for their attack on the huge ship. He saw a flash of red, then the Vermin ship was being torn away from the *Victory*. Tristan looked up, Taminick was dragging it away with the help of one of the big dragons. Fenfyr was nowhere to be seen. The two dragons pulled the ship out, Tristan saw Taminick flinch as a shot hit her in her already wounded wing. Still she dropped to the deck and killed the ship, and then the dragons tore it apart. Tristan focused back on the sails.

"Stop those things!" Muher called. Riggan stepped in front of Tristan as a wave of stench washed over the quarterdeck.

"Aubrey, look out!" Thom called.

Tristan looked up in time to see the creature crawl up onto the quarterdeck. It was in a suit made from bits of dragon skin. Swallowing the bile that rose in his throat, Tristan grabbed his pistol and set it on the Interface. Riggan and Muher were in front of him, blocking the creature from getting closer. The general attacked, shooting first, then drawing his sword as the Vermin kept coming. More of the creatures were crawling across the deck towards them, some had weapons, others were using their hands to grab the *Victory's* crew and tear into them. It was hard to stay focused as the screams rose in volume.

Turning his eyes from the deck, Tristan glanced out at the heavy cruiser they were heading towards. He ran his eyes over the ship, trying to gauge a weakness to bring the *Victory* in when he saw something that made his heart skip a beat. The dark sails had something covering them. In that moment, the helplessness and pain washed over him, he nearly collapsed but forced himself up.

"Thom!" Tristan shouted before the order to fire could be made. "The masts! Look at the masts! The dragons!" Tristan pointed to the Vermin masts and the graceful creatures tied to them. On the upper mainmast he could see black, silver and pearly white. "Fenfyr and the others, they're tied to the masts!"

"What?" All the color drained from Thom's face as he looked across the distance separating them from the ship. "We need to take down those masts!"

A sharp pain suddenly ripped through Tristan, he was caught by the arm and dragged away from the Interface before he could grab his gun. He kicked out at the creature, trying to look away from the horror of its face. The thing lifted his leg slowly up towards its gaping mouth and bit down. Tristan felt his ankle shatter as he struggled to get away. Another one was approaching when the one holding Tristan evaporated in a blast from the small cannon on the taffrail of the quarterdeck. Then Muher was there, hacking at the other one before it could get to him. Tristan started crawling back towards the Interface, Riggan helped him up and held him as he settled his hand on the controls again, blocking out the pain from his injured leg.

"Can you get us in close enough to target the masts, then get us out of there before they can hit us too hard?" Thom asked.

Tristan nodded. He would do anything he could to rescue the dragons held prisoner on the ship. He had no idea what would happen once the masts were free. "Chris!" he called to Muher. "Do we have a line to Darius?"

"Yes, channel four," the man replied as he shot another Vermin attempting to get onto the quarterdeck.

Punching the comm channel on the Interface, Tristan hoped the dragon would answer. "Darius, this is Tristan Weaver."

"I hear you," the dragon answered immediately.

"The dragons they are taking—they're tied to the masts on the big ship. We're going to try to break the masts free."

"We will come in and take care of our wounded, Tristan Weaver, you get them free."

"We will," Tristan said, breaking the connection. He glanced out—at the edge of the Navy line he could see a mass of dragons already gathering, waiting for the word to move. "I'm ready, Thom."

"Okay, we need to get as close as possible. Deck guns, load with chain, we are taking out those masts! We need them down in two rounds, do you understand?"

The men on deck shouted affirmatives even as they fought the Vermin trying to take the big guns away. Tristan watched as they loaded the guns with the special rounds designed to clear the decks of personnel and hopefully break the masts free.

"You take us in, I'll handle the thrusters." Thom said. "Ship to the Weaver!"

"Ship to the Weaver!" Shearer answered immediately.

Tristan focused, Weaving the sails as tightly as he could, strengthening them even more for what he knew was coming. Taking a slow breath in, he felt his way through the sails, then found the spot in the Winds he needed, the rigging started to hum with the deep baritone note he knew meant it was moving fast, on a perfect keel. They were heading towards the Vermin ship, the distance closing in seconds.

The Vermin started firing, the shot slamming into the sails and raining down on the deck. Several huge rounds hit the lower hull, shaking the ship. Tristan let it go and kept his focus on the sails. Something burned in his arm. He was yanked away from the Elemental Interface for a moment, a Vermin boarder suddenly dead in front of him. Pushing past the body, he got back to the Interface. They were almost on top of the Vermin ship. He backed off the sails as Thom used the thrusters to move the ship into position.

"Fire!" Thom called.

The first volley screamed across space, cutting down Vermin on the deck, but leaving the masts untouched. Thom swore. "Fire!" The second volley did little more than the first, the shot destroying the crew, but not damaging the masts. "What is going on down there? Raiden! Get those guns firing. Take out those masts!"

"Sir! I have an idea, permission to fire at will!" Jacob Raiden called.

"Permission granted!" Thom said, trying to keep the ship close enough to the Vermin vessel to make the shots count. Tristan could see his struggles and moved the willowisps in the sails so they were fluttering in place, holding the ship motionless. They were sparking red and orange as they hung above his head. He looked up, silently thanking them.

A volley from the guns pulled his attention from the sails. Shot flew through space and hit the masts right at the deck level, before the sound of the first shot had died out, a second one came, and a third. Tristan could see the masts now, a small fire burning at their base, the white of bone showing in the flames, slowly turning to char.

"Fire the chain!" Thom cried. The deck guns spoke and this time the masts started to break free. "Again!" Thom ordered and for a breathless moment it seemed like nothing was going to happen, then the masts all began to break away. As they did, the dragons moved in, flying in at high speed to pull the masts away from the ship. Tristan had a glimpse of Fenfyr still bound to the crosstrees of the mainmast, then the dragons were gone.

"That's it, let's break this thing!" Thom said. "Ship to the Weaver! Bring us around so we can hit her with our port guns."

Tristan shifted the sails, the ship wheeled around, and at Thom's command, the full broadside of the *Winged Victory* hit the Vermin ship. They reloaded quickly and hit them again. The other Vermin heavy cruiser had come up behind them, trying to hit them hard. Tristan was struggling to bring the ship around when two small vessels, their sails sparkling in the dark came up beside them. *Surprise* and the *Noble Lady* fired on the cruiser as they brought the *Victory's* guns to bear. Between the three of them, the ship was beaten down and the *Victory* turned back to the ship that had held the dragons. It was already moving away, heading into space.

"They aren't getting away!" Tristan growled, swinging the sails around, making the *Winged Victory* race after the huge ship.

It was easy to catch, without sails the Vermin ship it was moving under power and no match for the *Victory's* speed. By the time they were up beside it. Thom had the guns ready. Tristan whispered the spell of release as Thom ordered volley after volley emptied into the ship. Tristan knew the moment they managed to kill the enslaved dragon. It let go with a sigh of relief and thanks, and slipped away into death.

"Finish it!" Tristan said.

Thom nodded. "Fire!"

A huge fireball left the *Victory* and slammed into the Vermin ship, consuming it with white-hot flame, leaving nothing of the ship. In a way it was beautiful, the flames slowly moving up the length of the ship until it was a small shining sun in the center of the battle. Tristan held his breath as the flames reached the engines and the former ship blasted apart, the small bits sparkling for a moment like willowisps.

"It's gone!" Thom cried triumphantly.

Tristan smiled and shifted the sails, turning back towards the Naval fleet. He could still see the bright flash of guns in the distance, but the tide of the battle had changed. The Navy was pursuing the fleeing Vermin ships. Blinking, he tried to focus on what was happening. There were still Vermin on the deck, fighting hand to hand with the crew. The *Winged Victory* was heading back towards the fleet, as she approached, the last of the Vermin vessels—a small gunboat—poured on the speed and disappeared from the battle line.

It was over.

Tristan glanced up at Thom, the man was splattered in blood, one arm hanging limply at his side. Muher was finishing off the last of the Vermin on deck. He turned to look for Riggan and realized that world was wavering.

He thought he heard someone shout his name, but he fell into darkness.

XXXII

The darkness eased. There was heat, a confusion of sound and light, pain and voices screaming. Tristan tried to make sense of the maelstrom, but he couldn't. He knew that some of it was focused around him. There were dull *thumps* of explosions, and closer, the sharp crack of small arms fire. Someone was bending over him, urging him to hang on, a desperate male voice, a warm hand clasping his. Then, some moments—or hours—later a matter-of-fact female voice was there, snapping orders, and Tristan felt himself lifted. Then the darkness closed over him again.

The sharp scent of antiseptics crept into his awareness and Tristan opened his eyes on a small white room. There were the lines of IVs in his arms and the soft comfortable chirping of medical monitors. He was fuzzy from drugs, he could feel the sluggishness in his system and knew he wouldn't be able to stay awake for long. The only thing that had let him push this far into consciousness was his need to know about his friends—had they survived? Was Fenfyr...? Before the thought could form completely, he let the drugs pull him away, not ready to face that possibility yet.

When he fought his way through the haze again, it was because there was an argument going on outside his door. "You don't understand, Dr. Webber, he doesn't get to die. He saved the whole damn fleet, so you save him!" Thom's voice was angry and urgent.

Tristan wondered who they were talking about.

"We're doing everything we can. I've had the Healers in. Vermin bites are usually fatal."

"This one had better not be," Thom snapped. A moment later, Thom's voice was much closer, a warm weight fell on Tristan's arm. "Hear that? Not fatal." Thom sighed. "You hear me?"

Tristan struggled to answer, but the drugs wouldn't let him fight free. He could also sense the "lightness" that a Healing spell brought; he remembered it from the days right after the bombing when he'd hovered between life and death. Was that what was happening now? At least Thom was safe. He wanted to ask about Fenfyr, that pain was beating against his heart every time he was aware enough to think about it. Before he could find the strength to ask, the darkness caught him again.

"Sir, I don't mean to disturb you, mind you," Riggan was saying as Tristan floated towards the surface again. "And you know I don't spread idle gossip, sir, but I thought maybe no one had told you there is a guest waiting for you in your cabin. He is most distressed that they won't let him into sickbay. He is lying in the cabin, all drooping, refusing to even move."

Relief flooded Tristan's body in a rush of warmth. He heard a medical alarm go off, but it didn't matter. There was sudden activity and he heard people rushing in the room and Riggan's indignant voice defending himself. The words meant nothing. All that mattered at that moment was what had come before. Fenfyr was alive.

The soft chiming of the bells woke Tristan, it was seven bells, although he had no idea of what watch it was. He could hear the sounds of the medical monitors, and an IV was still pinching in one arm. Trying to get more comfortable, he sighed.

"Tristan?" Thom asked from somewhere beside him, his voice harsh with concern.

"What?" he answered automatically, opening his eyes, squinting in the bright light.

"Welcome back!" Thom was sitting in the chair beside the bed. He had dark circles under his eyes and a fresh scar along his hairline. His left arm was in a sling. Tristan wondered about that, slings weren't used very often, what with the various bone and dermal knitting devices. Thom followed his glance and smiled sheepishly. "I was doing too much with it, so the doctor insisted I wear this."

"Good job," Tristan said, surprised at how weak his voice sounded. There was a dull ache in his ankle and a throbbing that had been a wound in his shoulder. "How are we?"

"The ship is getting repaired, the fleet is slowly gathering itself together, the Vermin have headed back to their space for the time being," Thom said. "Our Master Weaver lived."

"That's comforting," Tristan said with a smile.

"Yeah," Thom agreed, his eyes bright.

"Did we lose many?"

"Not as many as we could have, thanks to you. That goes for the whole fleet, by the way, not only this ship, Tristan."

"I just fought the sails."

"Just, he says." Thom laughed.

"Thom, is Fenfyr…?" Tristan remembered Riggan's words, but he had to know.

"Currently sleeping in your cabin, making a nuisance of himself since the doctor wouldn't move you down there until you'd regained consciousness and the doctor doesn't think sickbay is a place for a dragon. He tried to sneak in." Thom stopped and grinned. "Fenfyr, a dragon the size of a shuttlecar, tried to *sneak* into sickbay. He managed to get his nose in, then realized that wouldn't work, so then tried to get his tail in, back to this room."

Tristan smiled. "She should have let him in."

"I know, Tristan, I did tell her."

"He's okay?"

"He was wounded, the dragons cared for him until the battle was over, but he was here as soon as he could fly on his own. He's been in your cabin since. Riggan has been spoiling him outrageously and telling him wild tales of his life as a pirate, of which a tenth are true. Riggan's also been here once an hour to make sure Fenfyr is kept abreast of your condition."

"Can I leave?" Tristan asked, sitting up.

"You just woke up, I'm not sure…" Thom stopped. "I'll see what I can do." He got up and disappeared.

Tristan closed his eyes, taking several deep breaths. He was surprised he was alive at all. His body hadn't had the chance to recover from the moment they left the *Noble Lady* until the end of the battle. So it wasn't really a shock that there was still actual pain in his body, even though he could feel the lingering effects of the Healing spells, the drugs and whatever surgery that had been performed. Without thinking about it, his mind ran over the words of the repair spell for the Weaving and strengthening of the sails. Oddly, he sensed the sails and felt a shift in his body.

"I don't like it," Rose Webber said, coming into the room.

"He can be monitored in his cabin, and you won't have to deal with dragons anymore," Thom said from behind her.

"Or Riggan or Chris. They've been driving me crazy with their questions, and I really want to avoid another call from the Weaver Guild Master and Guild Dragon Elder regarding the Master Weaver," she said, checking the monitors. She frowned and poked at one of them. "What did you do?"

"What?" Tristan asked.

"You did something. Your recovery is… Huh." She eyed him curiously. "I won't try and figure it out right now, but you can go to your cabin where you will *rest*. You *will not* under *any circumstances* repair the damage to the sails yet. There isn't much, it can wait. *Do you understand?*" She looked at him, her purple eyes snapping.

"Yes, ma'am," Tristan said meekly.

"If I catch you on deck, it's right back here to this room."

"Yes, Dr. Webber," Tristan said obediently. "May I please go now?"

"Yes, get out, and I don't want to see you back here for a long time!" she said, smiling at him.

"Thanks." He waited while she unhooked him from the machines and slid the IV out of his arm. Once she was gone, he sat all the way up and swung his legs off the bed. "I don't suppose there are any real clothes here?"

Thom opened a closet and handed Tristan a set of soft civilian trousers and a t-shirt. "Riggan brought these by yesterday."

"Good." Tristan dressed as quickly as he could. He was stiff from the time he'd been in bed and the injuries he'd sustained. He still didn't know how extensive they were—he wasn't sure he wanted to know. He could remember the voices at one point saying Vermin bites were fatal. He looked down at his ankle and saw a purple scar there. Cautiously putting his feet on the floor, he shifted weight onto that leg. It felt weak, but it held. He breathed a sigh of relief. Looking up at Thom's concerned face, he grinned. "At least it's on the leg I already limped on," he said with a laugh.

Thom smiled—a little wanly. "I guess that's a plus."

"Can we go?" Tristan took a step and felt the ankle give a little.

"Sure," Thom said, stepping beside him and pulling his arm over his shoulder. "If you fall down on the way out of sickbay, I doubt the doctor will let you leave."

"Good thinking," Tristan replied, grateful for Thom's support by the time they reached the officer's lift. He was sweating from the exertion and his leg was aching. "How bad are the sails?" he asked, trying to distract himself.

"Not bad, whatever you did to them kept them intact. We took one hit after you collapsed, from a Vermin ship that had been lurking behind some debris, and that was the one that did the damage. It's not much and it's only on the mainsail."

"I should be able to fix it in a day or two," Tristan assured him.

"Not until you are strong enough. I'm not risking losing you— we came too damn close this time," Thom snapped. "Sorry."

The lift doors slid open and they stepped out. The door to Tristan's cabin was partially open, he could see in, Fenfyr was lying in the middle of the cabin, his eyes trained on the door. Tristan walked as fast as he could, dragging Thom along with him and pushed it open.

"Tristan!" The dragon's voice was loud enough to shake the glassware on the sideboard.

"Fenfyr," Tristan said, pulling away from Thom and stumbling towards the dragon. His leg gave out as he reached him, but Fenfyr caught him and pulled him close, wrapping him in his feathers and a protective claw. Tristan couldn't swallow through the lump in his throat, and when the tears broke free and started down his cheeks he didn't care. He could hear the soft hitching of Fenfyr's tears as well. They stayed motionless for a long time, taking comfort in the fact that the other was actually okay and alive. Finally, Tristan pulled back. "How bad were you hurt?" he asked softly.

"Nothing that won't heal, and better now you're here," Fenfyr said. "And you?"

"I didn't even ask," Tristan admitted with a laugh.

"They wouldn't let me in, I tried to come, to let you know I was here," the dragon said, distressed. "It was bad enough I couldn't protect you during the battle, then they wouldn't let me see you."

"I know, Thom and Riggan told me."

"You need to sit, Tristan," Thom said, pushing a chair over.

"Thank you," Tristan replied, sitting in the chair.

"My watch starts in a few minutes, I'll be down to check on you in an hour, though. Sleep if you need to, I'm sure Riggan will be here...now," Thom said with a laugh as the man appeared. "Take good care of them, Riggan."

"I will, sir, I was just getting some grapefruit for Master Fenfyr. I guessed he'd be eating now that Master Tristan was back in the room."

Tristan digested that comment and reached out so his hand was resting on Fenfyr's head. Between the space of one breath and another he was asleep.

It was another two days before Tristan could do more than be up for an hour or so, eat a little and sleep again. He spent as much time as he could in the main cabin, finding he slept better in the presence of Fenfyr. When he was alone in his bedchamber, his dreams were filled with the memories of Fenfyr being hooked and the Vermin crawling over the deck of the *Winged Victory*. He still wasn't strong enough to fix the sails, but he did get up and wander into his office and open the communications to Guild headquarters.

"Tristan!" Brian Rhoads boomed the moment the connection was made. "By the First Spell, it's good to hear your voice! We thought we'd really lost you this time," he said, his voice soft with worry.

"I've heard that," Tristan replied with a laugh. "I still haven't asked exactly what they mean, I don't think I want to know."

"How are you doing now?"

"Better, Brian. I'm only waiting to get strong enough to repair a small hole in the sails so we can head back into the inner system."

"It will be good to see you, there's a lot we need to talk about! Chris Muher and Alden were both talking about what you did to the sails, and we need to see if that's something you can teach, or if it's only you."

"I'm sure anyone can learn it." Tristan felt the blush creep up his cheeks.

"We'll see about that, and Muher has some idea about training commandos that can use that small personal sail you created. You've caused quite a stir."

"It's true, Tristan Weaver," the deep voice of Darius added. "And your service to dragon kind will not be forgotten for many ages."

"I did nothing, it was Captain Barrett and the crew of the *Victory*, Darius."

The dragon snorted. "Yes, of course. It's a good thing I was there to see it. You saved ten dragons that would have become slaves to the Vermin, Tristan Weaver. We will not forget."

"Like I said, there is a lot to do when you get back," Brian said. "You should know there is a full enquiry into those sails that they put up on the *Victory*. Everyone is denying knowledge."

"And the dragons are not happy," Darius said. "It is a breach of the Treaty, the Edicts, and there is tension between our peoples."

"Well, between some of them," Brian said. "Not everyone is being painted with the same brush. The dragons acknowledge the ships that fought at the Battle of the Line. You should know there was an attack on the Weaver offices on Terra Decimus two days ago. The Stars Plot isn't dead, it seems. There are still sympathizers in the Navy and elsewhere. We discovered that when the ship carrying Fuhrman and the prisoners disappeared."

"Disappeared?"

"Supposedly taken by pirates. We obviously have doubts about that," Brian said grimly.

"I would, too."

"For now, we celebrate this victory, though," Darius broke in. "The Vermin are running, and they know we have something new they have to overcome. The *Winged Victory* stands between the Vermin and our space, and they will have to fight very hard to get through that line. She is a ship like no other—and that is in no small part thanks to you, never forget that, Tristan," the dragon chided gently. "I saw what you did to the sails with my own eyes. I saw how the ship flew. It is special. She is our hope and saved us all."

Tristan didn't know what to say to that, he thanked them both and promised a report as soon as possible, then broke the connection.

"They're right, you know," Thom said from where he was leaning on the door.

"Shouldn't you knock?"

"Fenfyr let me in." Thom stepped into the office. "I told you this ship was special when we first met."

"I knew she was the first time I saw her. I wanted to Weave her sails even before I was asked, even knowing that it might kill me. And, honestly, I was jealous that Alden was to fight her. I wanted to see her sails, see her in space."

"She is as much your ship as she is mine, Tristan. I'm not sure another Warrior could fight her," Thom said uncertainly.

"No, the sails—I can't explain it—but no, they won't accept another Weaver." He smiled. "I guess you're stuck with me. I'm not sure how that's going to work with the Guild."

"We'll figure it out. We can't be at the Rim all the time, that's what the frigates and privateers are for." Thom grinned. "Are you feeling up to a little formal company?"

"What do you mean?"

"Admiral O'Brian and *Polaris* are getting ready to head out, but before they go, there are a few medals they want to hand out. You'll have to wear your formal uniform."

"When?"

"Four bells in the first dog," Thom said with a grin. "On the *Winged Victory's* quarterdeck."

"Why are you grinning like that?"

Thom just laughed.

It was a few minutes before four bells when Tristan walked onto the quarterdeck. Fenfyr had left the cabin a few minutes before and Riggan had also disappeared shortly before the bells chimed. When he reached the deck he could see why. The officers of the *Winged Victory*, Chris Muher, Cook, Harkins and Alden from the *Noble Lady,* Taminick and Fenfyr as well as Riggan were all lined up, waiting. A man in an Admiral's uniform was pacing back and forth.

"There you are, Master Weaver!" the admiral said with a smile, walking over and shaking his hand. "Admiral O'Brian, it's a pleasure to meet you! Now that you are all here…"

A drum tapped out an unfamiliar call over the ship-wide comm. It sounded a little like the call to quarters, but Tristan hadn't heard it before. That was when he realized the deck was full of men and women in uniform, and space around them was full of ships. It hadn't been the ship-wide comm, but the fleet-wide one the call had gone out over.

"We are gathered here today to honor those who, by their service, led the fleet to victory during the Battle of the Line."

A cheer broke out on deck. The admiral waved at a man wearing a captain's uniform, and he walked over with a box in his hand. "The Silver Cluster is hereby awarded to Boatswain James Shearer, First Officer Patrick Aubrey, Gunner, now Second Officer, Jacob Raiden and Doctor Rose Webber of the *Winged Victory.* To the officers and Warrior of the *Noble Lady,* Commander R. Cook, Ship's Master Harkins and Alden Soldat, the Navy hereby awards you the Civilian Silver Cluster for service during the battle. Marty Riggan, for service above and beyond your station, you are awarded the Gold Star and promoted to the rank of chief petty officer, honorable."

Tristan grinned at Thom as the cheers on deck got louder.

"Finally…" the admiral said, and a hush fell over the deck. "The Medal of Honor, with the Constellation Cluster, is awarded to General Chris Muher, Captain Thom Barrett, Master Tristan Weaver, Lokey Fenfyr and Taminick of the Guild Dragons."

The admiral moved down the line, dropping the medals over each man's head, and hanging them from the dragons' foreclaws. Tristan stared at the admiral in shock as he stopped in front of him with the heavy medal hanging in his hand. Shaking his head in disbelief, Tristan bowed so the man could slip the medal over his head. He stared at the plating for a moment, waiting for the blush to recede. Tristan glanced up when a gasp ran through the assembled crew. Darius was dropping down towards the quarterdeck. The officers scrambled out of the way as the dragon landed.

Darius looked at them. "The Guild Dragons wish to acknowledge the crew of the *Winged Victory* for their aide in the Battle of the Line." The dragon waited as the cheering on deck quieted. "Thom Barrett and Tristan Weaver without your help, we would have lost many of our own. For this service, above and beyond the normal call of duty, we, the Guild Dragons, award you the Order of the Silver Wing." Darius held out a set of silver wings to Tristan and Thom. The dragon glanced over the crew again and leaped from the deck. Tristan stared at the Wings, as far as he knew, he and Thom were the first humans outside of the Dragon Corps ever awarded the honor.

The admiral smiled and stepped back, then raised his hand in a signal. The *Winged Victory,* along with the other ships gathered there fired off a salute. Tristan counted, his blush getting deeper and deeper as the count rose to twenty-one, an honor unheard of in more than a century.

"Thank you all for your service," O'Brian said again. "We will meet again!"

As the man walked off the quarterdeck and was piped into his barge, the cheering on deck increased. Tristan was still staring at the deck, not sure what he had done to deserve the highest honor the Worlds could offer.

"Well, look at us," Harkins said with a laugh. "We're heroes!"

At that, Tristan started laughing, and Thom took the opportunity to thump everyone soundly on the back. The dragons were fluffed out, holding their medals like they weren't sure what to do with them. The look on Fenfyr's face increased Tristan's laughter.

It was eight bells in the morning watch and the crew was on deck as Tristan and Thom walked up the steps from Tristan's cabin. Riggan was still fussing when they left. Even though he'd been promoted, he'd chosen to stay as Tristan's—and Thom's—servant and split his time between the two.

After a short argument, Tristan had convinced Thom he was not only well enough to repair the small hole in the mainsail, but that they could unfurl the sails and start towards home at a decent pace. It had taken nearly two pots of coffee and reassurances from Fenfyr and the threat of pulling rank, but Thom had finally acquiesced. They were both anxious to head back towards the inner system. There had been another attack on a Guild outpost, and someone had reported what might have been a Vermin ship on the other side of the Rim. Thom doubted the report, but they wanted to get in closer to get more information.

Tristan stopped by the Elemental Interface and set his hands on it. The willowisps recognized him immediately, happily moving back and forth as he gently began Weaving together the hole in the mainsail. The willowisps moved easily, flowing together into a whole with very little effort on his part. He barely had to utter the spell, it was more like they were connected and they understood what he wanted and did it.

"The sail is ready, Captain Barrett," he said.

"Loose the sails!" Thom called.

"Loose the sails!" Shearer repeated. "Sails loose, Captain!"

"Ship to the Weaver."

"Ship to the Weaver!" Shearer repeated.

"Ship to the Weaver!" Fenfyr bugled from the Dragon's Roost before launching off to fly beside the ship with Taminick.

"Weaver has the ship!" Thom said, smiling at Tristan. "The ship is yours. Take us out."

Tristan reached out and felt for the Winds, shifting the sails until he felt the first flutter of the Winds touch the royals. The ship shivered as she started to pick up speed as the sails slowly began to fill. Finally, with the now familiar *boom,* the mainsail snapped into place, full of the Winds, the ship wheeled over and headed into the stars.

ACKNOWLEDGEMENTS

There have been so many people who have helped, encouraged, held my hand and kept me writing during this project.

I would like to thank my editors, Anne Nielsen and Merisha Anderson, for their amazing work. Without their tireless efforts this book would not be what it is today.

I can't thank Gina Brooks enough for the artwork she has created for *The Sail Weaver*, not only the cover art, but the badges and banners. Her enthusiasm for this project has been wonderful and I can't thank her enough. I also would like to thank her for offering me the use of a name that led to a fabulous character.

I would also like to thank Mish, Anne, Ruth, Shannon Linton, Maria Mews, Rob Cook, Janice Grove, Sheila Gratsinger, and my friends and family for encouragement, kind words and hand holding throughout this project.

And thanks to Matt Youngmark who listened to me one night as the idea was first forming and asked why enough times to poke me in the right direction.

ABOUT THE AUTHOR

Muffy Morrigan began her writing career at the age of six, when after completing her first hand written novel she attempted to sell it to the neighbors for the lofty price of ten cents.

After myriad careers, including archaeological consultant, teacher, herbalist, shop keeper, news editor, reporter and columnist, she has settled in to her first love and passion—writing. She currently lives and works in the Pacific Northwest.

www.muffymorrigan.com
Twitter @muffymorrigan
Facebook: www.facebook.com/MuffyMorriganAuthor

The Sail Weaver on Facebook
www.facebook.com/TheSailWeaver

Made in the USA
Charleston, SC
14 August 2012